ALEXANDRA SELLERS
SEASON OF STORM

A SUPERROMANCE FROM

W🌐RLDWIDE

TORONTO · NEW YORK · LONDON · PARIS
AMSTERDAM · STOCKHOLM · HAMBURG
ATHENS · MILAN · TOKYO · SYDNEY

for
Mrs. Doreen Allen
who gave me
my Golden Year

Grateful acknowledgment is extended to the following:

Oxford University Press, Inc., for the quotations from
"No Worst There Is None" and "Pied Beauty" in
THE POEMS OF GERARD MANLEY HOPKINS, THIRD EDITION,
edited by W. H. Gardner. Copyright 1948 by Oxford University Press.
Used by permission.

McClelland and Stewart Limited, Toronto, for the quotation from
"As the Mist Leaves No Scar" in SELECTED POEMS 1956-1968
by Leonard Cohen. Copyright 1968 by Leonard Cohen. Used by permission.

Dorothy Poste for the lyrics "Wake Me Up to Say Goodbye."
Copyright 1983 by Dorothy Poste. Used by permission.

Published November 1983

First printing September 1983

ISBN 0-373-70087-3

PROLOGUE

THE WATCHER WAS STILL, WATCHING. A perfect, vital stillness held him, as though a statue pulsed with life. His skin was the color of golden new-cut trees—cedar or hemlock; and his high-bridged nose and wide prominent cheekbones gave his face a cast that men of other races would call noble. His eyes, like his hair, were black, and no emotion troubled their gaze as he watched what he watched.

The Watcher stood on a low promontory of rocks above an ocean, and what he watched was in the water, below and beyond him: a woman, struggling against the sea. She was naked, and her long wet hair was the color of foxes, or of fire.

Something flickered behind the Watcher's eyes: regret that the woman would die. Never had he seen hair of that color; and her skin was pale. He would be sorry to kill the woman.

It was evident that the waves would not kill her. The woman struggled valiantly to keep her head above the water, and although she was exhausted, the tide was with her. The gods, too, were with her: in all this rocky coast she was being carried toward the flat sandy stretch of shore below the promontory on which the Watcher stood. She would not be broken against rocks.

When the water was a little less than waist deep the woman found her feet and stood up out of the water. Her long hair fell dripping down her back and over one full breast; water droplets clung to her chilled skin.

She was exhausted but triumphant, and the Watcher felt a distant admiration for her, as he might for one of the Swimmers evading his trap, or the Bear his arrow. He wondered fleetingly if she were one of the Swimmers, taking human form. In that case perhaps he ought not to kill her....

The woman, nearly out of the water, paused for a moment, lifted her face to the heat of the sun and gasped deeply for air. Now that her goal was so close exhaustion gripped her more surely.

She moved forward again through the breaking waves, the water alternately pushing and pulling at her strong thighs. For all her exhaustion the motion of her naked hips was smooth, the glistening sway of her silky-wet breasts hypnotic.

She was beautiful. When she reached the sand above the water's reach her triumph was overcome by fatigue, and she dropped to the sand and lay gratefully drinking in the heat of the sun with her body. Her long hair was splayed out beneath her, and her body heaved as she gasped for breath.

Something stirred in the Watcher then: a fire that had not troubled him before lighted in him now. It flickered up behind his black eyes as he gazed at the heaving body on the sand. He would not kill her yet, he thought. Not yet.

The Watcher moved.

CHAPTER ONE

SOMETHING WOKE HER UP. Something frightening, so that her heart was beating as though she had just had a brush with death. Smith sat upright in the silent gloom, her ears straining for the repetition of a sound she did not want to hear.

The drapes and her window were open as they always were at night—she could feel the sea-scented breeze stroke her forehead as she motionlessly listened, but the noise hadn't come from outside the protective shell of the house. It had come from within.

It came again, after a long moment when she hardly breathed; and with the sharp grace of a cat Shulamith turned her face toward the noise, as though drinking in its location as much through her wide eyes, sightless still in the dark, as through her ears. The sound was muffled, certainly not as sharp as the one that had awakened her, but still unmistakably threatening: a noise of quiet scuffle and a single low-voiced command.

"Daddy!" she called wildly into the night. Her voice came out as a whisper, a cat's frightened hiss, but there was no point in calling again—she mustn't waste time. Shulamith ripped back the light blanket covering her legs and was running as soon as her feet hit the soft thick carpet.

A gleam of light showed around the door to her father's room, she saw when she reached the doorway, and the sight quickened her breathing and her pace, because the door should have been open, not firmly shut. She sped silently around the wide balcony that overlooked the large front hall, terror snapping at her heels, clutching her throat. *He should have listened to me, he should have hired a nurse,* she thought, and then, *I should have argued more, I should have insisted.*

She had got him to promise to sleep with his door open, and that was all.

But the door was closed now, the fine thread of light around its well-cut seams proof, at this hour in the morning, that the noise that had caused her to start up out of a sound sleep, heart pounding, had been no nightmare. Smith bit her lip. Why was it closed? She realized she had already begun a prayer in her head. Prayers were so simple, after all. *Please. God, please don't let him be dying, please....*

She was almost crying the last words aloud as she fought for a clumsy second with the door handle, and then the door flew open under her determined, desperate hand. And then she screamed.

It was a pipeline of sound from the deepest reaches of terror within her, an icicle of comprehending-uncomprehending horror that destroyed the close hot silence of her father's room at a stroke. The scream lasted only a moment before abruptly dying, and in its frozen aftermath Smith felt her body begin to shake, felt her muscles quiver, and then a chill sweat exuded from every pore.

Around her father's bed four darkly clad men wearing black wool balaclava helmets stared at her in mute surprise. On the bed lay her father, his pajama top drenched with perspiration, or water, or both; his face grayly, sickly pale and beaded with the same icy perspiration that was forming on Smith's own forehead. His breathing was shallow and fast. For one second there was no motion, no sound in the room. Then, some movement on the periphery of her vision released Smith from immobility, and she whirled to see that a fifth man, his eyes fixed on her, was replacing the phone receiver in its cradle.

Ever after she would be amazed at the speed with which her mind suddenly functioned in that terrified moment. In a strange, half-consecutive, half-simultaneous burst of understanding she realized that if the man was using the phone, then the lines had not been cut; that there was a phone in her father's bathroom and a dead bolt on the door; that if she tried to run away from these men down the stairs they would certainly catch her but that if she ran *into* the room she might make it to the bathroom before they understood her intent. Her thoughts were superimposed one on the other in a fascinating ripple, like the individual colors of a landscape painted on separate squares of glass that together form the image. Her brain was so clear that she did not have to make even the smallest glance toward the bathroom. Some instinct told her, with a combined sensation of darkness and space, that across the room the bathroom door was wide open.

By the time the receiver in the fifth man's dark hand clicked in the cradle Smith was in midflight across the room. She wasted no energy on imagining pursuit, on listening for a stifled shout or a footfall behind her. She thought of nothing but running, of moving the mass of her body through as much space in as little time as possible; she thought of getting into her father's bathroom and ramming the bolt before those evil animals behind her—animals dangerous with the cunning of men—got their unimaginable hands on her. She thought of the phone with three outside lines, one of which she would surely be able to dial O on before they blocked the lines or kicked down the door.

Then she was through the doorway into the cologne-scented darkness, reaching unerringly for the door with one and then two outstretched hands; she was turning, with a coordination so perfect it felt like slow motion, to ram the door shut. She saw with an unsurprised satisfaction that the fifth man—the quickest of all, since he had been the farthest from the bathroom—was still only halfway across the room. The other four were in various postures of surprise, consternation and motion, but too far away to be of any threat.

The door, half shut, stopped moving under her weight. Smith's gasp of horror ripped out of her throat as she felt the door run aground, but she cut the sound off instantly. There was no time to waste on fear. Her eyes dropped down from the threateningly advancing fifth man to find what was blocking the door. . . .

Her father's bath towel, draped on the handle of the door, had caught on the carpet and been ground underneath until the door could no longer move. In one sharp motion Smith pulled the door back off the obstructing towel and plucked the material from the knob.

But the fifth man was too close; she had lost the

precious advantage that surprise had given her. In a last, wild effort she flung the giant blue towel—still damp from her father's shower last night—at the man's head and turned into the familiar darkness to grope for the phone that rested on the broad stretch of marble by the sink.

By the time they had moved into this house, Shulamith had been far too old to sit on the edge of the tub watching her father shave, and it had been many years before that since he had encouraged it. So she had never seen the phenomenon of her father shaving and discussing business on the phone at the same time. In those long-ago days of laughing, sun-filled Paris mornings there had been no business to discuss in the morning, no phone anywhere in the flat, let alone the bathroom, but there had been sun on the dusty roofs and pouring through the tiny bathroom window, and the aroma of breakfast mixed with that other constant scent of oil paint and turpentine.

But still she could reach for the phone unerringly in the dark now, for she had polished the marble countless times and placed the plain black phone back in position. This blind knowledge of the room gave her a momentary advantage again, and she pushed a plastic button and dialed O seconds before a lean bronzed hand, darker in the gloom, reached out from behind her to push down the hook and extinguish the tiny orange glow that for a second in time had been a light of hope to her.

Shulamith St. John, who had committed very little violence in the course of her life, threw the receiver at the man's masked head with a force that surprised her.

Not waiting to see it connect, she dodged around him to run back into her father's bedroom.

Two of the masked men were close enough to make any more running futile. She drew up short, suddenly aware that she was breathing in tortured, shuddering gasps.

"He's got a bad heart!" she choked out as the fifth man came up behind her. Her voice broke oddly on the silence. For the first time she became fully aware of herself, of her flimsy cotton-and-lace nightgown, of her total vulnerability. But that way lay insanity, and she pushed the awareness away and concentrated on the gray face of her father who lay in her line of vision between the two men facing her. No one moved.

"He'll have a heart attack! He'll die!" she shrieked, suddenly angry at the blank, insensate balaclava masks they wore, each of them knitted with a contrasting color around the eyes and mouth.

"He'll die!" she repeated. "Call the hospital!"

The red- and turquoise-trimmed masks in front of her blinked back, but White Trim, behind her—the tall, fast-moving, fifth man—said quietly, his voice resonating strangely in the room after her high, tense shrieking, "An ambulance has already been called. Your father may have had a heart attack. If you...."

"His pills!" she choked desperately, wishing her voice were not this terror-stricken cry that gave her away so obviously. She pushed between Red Mask and Turquoise Mask, who seemed unsure of what to do and might have let her pass. But the tall man behind her, obviously more in control of the situation, restrained her with the firm hand that closed on her arm above her elbow.

"He has been given the pills he required," he said. "You can do nothing more for him at the moment. If you will...."

She turned on him, almost spitting. She had never in her life felt such a blinding burst of anger, hatred, helplessness and violence as the one that flamed through her now, a supernova exploding simultaneously in her brain and her stomach, sending its fires through every cell of her being.

"Get your hands off me!" she commanded, in something between a hiss and a deep primal growl. "I want to go to my father!"

Two of the men, in yellow- and green-trimmed masks, were still bending over her father in a kind of helpless anxiety; suddenly the three surrounding Smith took on a little of the same confusion, as though she, too, were deathly ill. The grip of White Mask's hand on her arm relaxed, and the two men by the bed straightened.

With an imperious motion that dared them to stop her, Smith crossed to the bed and placed her hand on her father's damp forehead. She drew in a shaking breath: she knew almost nothing about heart attacks. Was he unconscious or asleep? Why, oh, why, hadn't he let her hire a nurse?

There was a whispered colloquy going on among the five men. White Mask crossed to her as the other four started uncertainly toward the door.

"The ambulance is on its way," said White Mask quietly. "Will you...."

For some reason their uncertainty made her triumphantly strong. And stupid. In that momentary rush of unthinking elated anger, she rounded on them.

"You mean you're not going to kidnap my father after all? You're afraid no one would pay money for a dead man?" she burst out, her voice contemptuous. "You stupid bloody fools, don't you do any research at all? Don't you know that my father has made it impossible for the company or me to pay a ransom for him?" Her breath was coming in gasps of love and rage and fear. "But he still couldn't stop a bunch of cretins trying, could he?" She pointed to the bed beside her. "That's his second attack in a few weeks. You've probably killed him, damn you! Damn all of you and your damned mindless greed! You...."

White Mask lifted his hand to touch her shoulder. Through the mists of her rage the gentle gesture seemed unbearable from such a menacingly powerful man. She was suddenly reminded of how strong her father had seemed as a child, and how gentle he had always been in that long-ago past, before.... Smith's throat tightened, and she shrugged off the comforting hand with an animal violence.

"Don't *touch* me!" she shrieked. "You're all cheap cowards, afraid even to show your faces! Why don't you at least have the courage of your convictions? Why don't you stand up and show yourselves as men who get what they want by violence and murder?"

The short burst of a distant siren broke sharply on the air. Four of the men started toward the door again, while the fifth, White Mask, stayed looking down at her.

Then Shulamith St. John was very stupid indeed.

"Who are you?" she demanded suddenly. "I want to know who you are!" And without any thought of the consequences she reached up and tore the white-trimmed mask from his head. Only when she saw his face did she understand what she had done.

"Oh, my God!" she exclaimed in whispered dismay Now the silence of the room, threaded through with the nightmarish ululation of the oncoming siren, was electrified with danger.

The man was dark, the skin of his hawklike face bronzed and firm, his black eyes hooded. His hair was black, too, wavy and thick, falling to his ears in two wings from a central parting. He had a high-bridged nose, and his wide mouth was grim as, his eyes boring into hers, he called something to his four masked accomplices. Then he reached for her.

Smith jumped back from him too late. His lean, black-clothed frame had already moved, imprisoning her against a muscled chest between arms like fine steel.

She reacted like a wildcat, spitting, clawing, cursing, but she was slim and light and he had the advantage of height and strength. She fought anyway—twisting and clawing desperately till her long red hair was tangled around his head and her own, and his black sweater was torn open at two places—fought with all her strength, and then some.

It was not enough. The hawk-faced man overpowered her at last, pressing her head into his shoulder with a hand held over her face so that she could neither breathe nor scream. Then he carried her swiftly and noiselessly through the house, and, as the ambulance men burst through the front door with a clattering stretcher in tow, he moved out a back patio door into the damp, sea-scented air.

Her heart was laboring from lack of oxygen, and Shulamith stopped her frantic backward kicks at her abductor's legs and tried with her free hand to pull those large strong fingers away from her nose.

Abruptly his voice said very softly in her ear, "I will let you breathe if you do not fight me. Otherwise I will force you into unconsciousness." Not waiting for her agreement, he eased his hand down away from her nose, still maintaining his sure grip over her mouth.

Shulamith breathed deeply, her heartbeats slowing. With an effort of will she calmed her thoughts, resolutely pushing away anger, hatred and most of all fear, and concentrated on her situation.

Her abductor was tall and strong. Her head was being pressed firmly into the hollow of his shoulder with one arm and hand while his other arm, wrapped tightly across her midriff, held her left arm immobile against her own body. Her toes just barely reached the ground. It would be foolish to kick, especially if he was to deprive her of air again.

The man's attention was not entirely on her, she sensed suddenly, though his grip did not relax. She felt an extraordinary stillness about him, as though even his blood had ceased to flow; his breathing had become almost imperceptible.

He was listening. He had not closed the door behind them, and now he listened to the noises coming from the house as though his hearing allowed him to see what was happening inside. Fascinated, Shulamith listened, too, hearing almost nothing until, after what seemed an age, there was the unmistakable sound of two people and a stretcher coming down the stairs and moving out the front door. Then ambulance doors slammed, and the sound of an engine roared away down the curving drive. There was no sound of the siren, and Shulamith sucked in a shuddering breath. He was dead. Her father was dead, or they would be using the siren. . . .

"There's no traffic in these streets," said that deep voice softly in her ear, and Shulamith was surprised by her response to the understanding tone: she wanted to cry. "They'll use the siren when they reach the main streets."

She listened intently for a long moment, not knowing whether to believe or not. Then, far down the mountain, a short burst of the siren's shriek made her sag against his body with relief. Her father was alive.

He moved then, back through the patio door and across the thickly carpeted room to the large, brightly lighted front hall and then out into the night. At the top of the stone steps he whistled softly and waited, his hold on her not relaxing even enough to shift his grip or ease his muscles.

Below them, behind the black shadows of fir trees, the lights of the city center sparkled in the black surround of the ocean, and out on the water the glint of oceangoing vessels beckoned to her, as always, with the promise of distant shores. The scene before her was so familiar that she could scarcely believe all this was really happening. Shulamith closed her eyes tightly: either the familiar beauty of Vancouver at night or her attacker would disappear, she was certain. This was a dream.

But the man's grip on her body remained real, and when she opened her eyes, so did the city.

After a moment her ears picked up the quiet sound of an engine, and through the trees along the drive a small van crept, without benefit of lights, and stopped beside them just as her abductor, moving down the broad steps, reached the ground.

Panic filled her with a renewed force, and, tasting it, Shulamith realized that she had lain quiescent in the stranger's hold for long minutes, as though his silent strength had somehow stilled her wild fear against her will. She cursed herself for a fool. If she had had little chance against one man in the past few minutes, she now had no chance at all against the additional four who were certainly in the van. As the driver's door opened she twisted and kicked with all her might, clawing behind her with her free hand for any vulnerable area within reach.

The man swore, dropping his hand from her mouth to grasp her twisting body, her flailing arm. Immediately she screamed, a short sharp scream because she had little breath, and stopped to draw breath for more.

"Get her mouth!" the dark man ordered the other, still masked, who had climbed out of the driver's side and was now running around the front of the van to them.

Shulamith let fly the hardest kick she had delivered since her days on the high-school girls' rugby team, and the second man grunted and went down like a hewn tree. She waited in terror for the man holding her to take revenge somehow, but he was not cruel as he caught her free arm in against her body and put his hand back over her mouth.

The man she had kicked was cursing steadily and painfully. Slowly he got up off the ground. It was Turquoise Mask.

"Rope," suggested the man who held her, and Turquoise Mask moved to the back of the van, opened the doors, and, the soft stream of his curses mingling oddly with the scraping noises in the night air, rummaged for a few moments, then stepped back with a small bundle of binder twine in his hand.

It looked wispy, like angel hair, but its roughness cut her skin, and Turquoise Mask tied her wrists tightly and cruelly, so that the twine bit into her flesh.

Every new assault took her terror one notch higher. Being tied filled her with such a panic-stricken dread she felt as though she were hanging on to reason by a tiny thread. The dark man placed her in the front seat then, and she saw by the scarf the masked man held that they meant to gag her, too. Her eyes widened in horror above the bronzed hand still clasped tightly over her mouth, and she moaned pleadingly and tried to shake her head.

The dark hawk face, which she saw again for the first time since that moment in her father's room—it seemed an hour ago, though it could have been only minutes—looked consideringly at her for a moment, and then he regretfully shook his head.

"Sorry," he said, as though he meant it. "Even if you gave me your word not to scream, you are too much of a fighter to keep it."

She moaned again behind his palm, her eyes pleading and promising. A white smile lighted the shadowed planes of his strong, bronzed face; strangely, it was a smile of admiration.

"Not even for your solemn oath," he said, his eyes glinting at her. "Even if you meant to keep your word, you would not do so. That is the way of fighters. Now, if you breathe deeply and slowly and calm your panic, this will not be so bad."

She was thrown into confusion by his kindness. It must be a ploy calculated to put her off her guard, she decided. If so, it was not going to work. Shulamith took the deep calming breath, but stared stonily at the man while efficiently he gagged her.

He spoke a few quiet words to Turquoise Mask then, and turned back up the steps and into the house. After a moment he returned, flicking off lights as he came and locking the door.

He had an animal grace that gave her a curious pleasure to watch, a leanness of hip that was strangely compelling. Shulamith watched the man, whose face had a grave nobility in the moonlight, until he moved out of sight behind the van. She heard his low voice in conversation with his still-masked accomplice.

With a shock of remembrance, Shulamith realized that there was no sign of the other three men. Had they another vehicle, or were they waiting farther down the drive? Shulamith repressed a shudder. She wished she had not remembered them.

"You will have to ride in the back of the van," the dark man was saying at the door beside her, and she came to with a start to realize that Turquoise Mask was sitting beside her now in the driver's seat.

Wordlessly she stood up—clumsily, since she hadn't

the full use of her hands—and stumbled between the two bucket seats to the carpeted dark interior of the van. To her surprise and dismay the hawk-eyed man did not sit in the passenger seat but followed her to the interior of the van.

"I am not going to hurt you," he reassured her quietly. "Merely keep an eye on you. Please sit down."

He helped her down, so that she was sitting with her back against the side of the van behind the driver, then dropped lightly beside her.

"All right," he said, and the driver, his face turned away from her, pulled off his turquoise-trimmed balaclava, started the van's engine and let out the clutch.

Smith couldn't see where they were going. All she saw of the passing landscape were the tops of trees or street lamps, and after a very few minutes she gave up the attempt in despair.

He was watching her closely, and she caught his gaze over the uncomfortable gag. After a moment, as Smith wiggled uncomfortably in an effort to free the ends of her hair she was sitting on, he reached out a hand and lifted a lock of it from where it lay over her arm.

"Your hair is very long," he said, in the tone of wondering admiration she was used to. Not many women could sit on their own hair these days; it often aroused comment. "Her hair was the color of foxes," said the man softly to himself, "or of fire." It sounded as though he was quoting something. Smith shivered.

The gag was making her claustrophobic, and the intent look in the man's hooded eyes, which were in light and shadow, light and shadow as the van rhythmically progressed past street lamps, made her think of an animal or a bird of prey. Behind the gag, which smelled, surprisingly, of after-shave, she tasted the bitter taste of fear. She raised her bound hands to try to loosen the cloth, though she had already learned it would not loosen. The dark man lifted a hand to forestall her.

"Close your eyes," he said, "and breathe slowly and deeply."

As she obeyed, Smith wondered distantly how many kidnap victims he had calmed with just these words. She was amazed that someone she feared so much could simultaneously exert such a calming influence on her. Like a lamb going to the slaughter, she thought, and a small self-deprecatory snort escaped her.

It was hard for her to judge time as they drove; the wild emotions that she had experienced did not seem to be measurable in any recognizable time frame. The van needed new shock absorbers, but if she swayed with its motion she found a kind of rhythm.

She gave in to her own sense of helplessness, not fighting the gag or the rope any longer, but somehow adjusting to them, allowing them to become part of her. She discovered that the bonds were not impossible to bear and gave herself over to examining her captor.

He was at least part North American Indian, she realized. That was a little like saying someone was part European, but Smith was not familiar even with the various West Coast bands. The bone structure of his face was strong and sharply planed, and his eyes, with a faint but exotic slant, were hooded. He reminded her of a painting of some nameless Mongol invader she had seen somewhere, and Smith wondered suddenly whether his long-distant ancestors had come across the Bering

Strait from the Steppes. She laughed a little, deep in her throat, and the man looked at her. *I was just wondering if you were distantly related to Genghis Khan,* she told him silently, *because if so, you're a chip off the old block.*

Slightly more civilized, of course, she thought grimly. *No looting and burning, just carrying off the women for ransom. . . .*

But of course they hadn't meant to carry off the woman in this case, they had meant to kidnap her father. They had taken her as a last resort, unwilling to let their plan fail entirely. It would have been too much of a risk to kidnap a man who was prone to heart attack.

They wouldn't have known that before, of course. No one had known that Cord St. John had a bad heart until a few weeks ago, when he'd had his first attack. Smith remembered her shock and disbelief on the day her father's executive secretary had phoned her at a client's office in Brussels to tell her that her father was in the cardiac ward of the Royal Columbia Hospital. Cordwainer St. John was young; he was still in his early fifties. He was a strong, healthy-looking man with hair graying attractively at the temples—a solidly built handsome man who exuded power. He was not a man who could be felled by the most determined business rival, and no one would have thought that his health was going to give him trouble for another twenty-five years. Certainly not his daughter.

For sixteen years, her father had been the most energetic, hardest working person she knew. For sixteen years he had been devoted to work—devoted to building his company and to making money.

Sixteen years ago, at the age of thirty-six, late for such an abrupt career change, Cord St. John had bought up a small "gypo" operation, which he had immediately renamed St. John Logging. If at first the name had seemed more impressive than the company, it had not remained so for long. Cordwainer St. John had been tough and ruthless in what was already a pretty ruthless industry. Three years later he was making enough profit from his logging operation to buy up a medium-sized sawmill. He had modernized it overnight with a computer sawing system that had made more than two-thirds of the workers redundant and paid for itself in less than a year. After St. John Lumber had followed St. John Pulp and Paper, St. John Trucking and many others. Together, these companies were now known as St. John Forest Products. Within the trade it was nicknamed "St. John's Wood," though not with affection.

"Oh, is there a St. John's Wood in British Columbia?" a visiting English businessman had asked once, thinking of the area of London known by that name, and had caused an entire table of lumbermen to burst into laughter. "You've got it wrong," one of them told him. "What you mean is, is there a British Columbia in St. John's Wood?"

Now, after the small warning heart attack, Cord St. John had been told in plain, almost brutal terms that he must slow down. A long holiday and then a four-day, instead of seven-day work week, his doctor advised, not without sarcasm.

"Paris!" Smith had said immediately. "You haven't been to Paris for years." In fact, it was sixteen years since Cord St. John had seen Paris. "Visit Paris daddy. Or take a long cruise. I could go with you... '

He had let her plan. But as soon as he'd regained his strength, he had gone back to work, six or seven days a week; ten, sometimes twelve hours a day.... She had begged, had reasoned, had argued, but her father had gone on working, like a man driven or a man courting death.

Smith's gaze focused again on the darkly intelligent face of her abductor, the would-be abductor of her father. When Cord St. John had made it legally impossible, a few years ago, for his company or his daughter to pay any ransom if he was kidnapped, the fact had been well publicized. Naturally, since it was meant to act as a deterrent to any potential kidnappers. All executives of St. John Forest Products had been informed that in the case of their kidnapping, too, no ransom would be paid. Out of curiosity once Smith had asked her father if that ban extended to her. She was not exactly an executive yet. But her father had never answered her.

Well, no doubt she would find out soon enough. Smith closed her eyes against a brief spasm of pain. If her father had been kidnapped tonight in accordance with this dark man's plans, she would have moved heaven and earth to circumvent that ruling and pay the ransom. If there was only the smallest chance of his coming back alive. No matter how angry it would have made him.

She opened her eyes and eyed the dark man specula

tively. Would her father pay him money for the promise of her life? He looked like a man who usually got what he wanted, but then so did her father. And her father would not want to pay a ransom demand. Of that she was suddenly certain. A mirthless laugh rose in her throat then, and if she could have spoken she would have told her dark abductor, *you miscalculated when you took me in place of my father. My father wouldn't pay a counterfeit nickel to have me returned alive. My father couldn't care less if I was alive or dead.*

CHAPTER TWO

IN THE GRAYING DARKNESS of early dawn a full moon
hung distant and cool above the ocean in the western
sky. In the east, behind the city and the mountains, the
pink and golden clouds catching the first of the sun's
rays seemed almost to be part of another sky, another
world. A sky in which night and day were perfectly
balanced, each with its own territory, Smith thought,
and wondered dryly if there was significance in the fact
that she had her back to the sun and was walking into
night.

No one noticed the casually strolling couple that
made their way along the dock past the schooners,
catamarans, sloops and launches berthed on the edge of
English Bay. Perhaps there was no one to notice, at this
hour. In the long walk from the van she hadn't seen
anyone, had heard nothing except the gentle slap-slap of
water against the hull; the intermittent comforting
squeak of wood against a protective rubber tire; the
familiar, ever present, overhead cry of gulls.

Anyone who saw the two would have had to look very
closely to catch anything amiss, in any case. A barefoot
woman in a long cotton skirt might be thought a little
foolhardy at this hour, but would cause nothing more
serious than a raised eyebrow. Especially as she was

wrapped up so warmly in her boyfriend's thick jersey. From a distance no one would see that her arms were not in the sleeves of the sweater, nor that the casually loving arm her boyfriend had flung around her was in fact a grip of steel. Nor would they notice, except at very close quarters against the backlighting of the sunrise, that the woman's magnificent, tangled red hair disguised a cloth gag that was going to drive her insane if it was not soon removed.

Nevertheless, Smith prayed as fervently as she had ever done in her life that someone—preferably large and burly, but anyone would do—would step out of one of the moored boats as they passed and hear the choked moan that was the only cry she could make behind the gag.

No one came. Not a soul breathed; not one human noise fell on her ears. She was surrounded by examples of God's most incredible handiwork—ocean, mountains, moonset and sunrise—and yet her prayers could not conjure up one insignificant human being in a city of one million!

Perhaps behind them. Perhaps someone had been slow to respond to the inexplicable urge to begin the day early and had come too late to his afterdeck and was now gazing incuriously after the two figures moving along the wooden dock between the rows of boats. Smith did not turn her head to see: she was too filled with despair even to hope.

She felt sick—sick with pain and fright and useless anger at herself. Why had she pulled off the man's mask? From now until doomsday she would be able to identify him, and he knew it. Even if her father or the company paid a ransom for her, how could he let her go? The few kidnap victims who did survive never saw their captors' faces, she knew that. It was only common sense. Kidnappers got the money whether the victim lived or died.

Would no one really come? There was not one light in any of the boats around her—hadn't *anyone* slept aboard last night?

Smith let out a strangled moan that threatened to become a sob and her dark companion bent his head with concern. Whether it was concern that she might be weeping or concern lest she be trying to make a cry for help she couldn't tell, but she calmed instantly under the searching gaze and willed her stinging eyes to dry. He might kill her, but he would not make her cry. She was damned if he would see her cry!

She was not sure whether he meant to drown her immediately off the end of the dock or whether he would take her on a boat. If he was going to drown her she hoped he would take the gag off so that she could beg him to knock her unconscious first. Smith closed her eyes. The thought of drowning terrified her: fighting for air while something pulled you down and down. . . .

When she was a child her nightmares of death were always of quicksand and drowning. She had never seen quicksand so far as she knew, but she had been haunted by it ever since she had read of it in a cowboy comic book. The day the Cisco Kid had been thrown into quicksand had been a bad day for Shulamith. The whole idea of it had terrified her eight-year-old mind. With horrifying immediacy she had envisioned the foul smell, the slime, the horrid sucking noises as the innocent-looking sand pulled you slowly under until you choked. . . .

One day at breakfast, watching her father read what she was sure must be less mail than usual, she had asked him what a person should do if she fell into quicksand.

That was in the early days, in the first year after they had moved to Vancouver. Shulamith hadn't yet fully absorbed the enormous, terrible change that had taken place in her father: he was the man who for eight years had been her protector, her utter security, someone whose love was unquestionable. Sometimes she did not remember, or would not, that now he had no time for her. . . .

No doubt she had been hoping he would say there was no such thing as quicksand or that it only existed in the state of Nevada (so far away!), and she need never go there. Or he might have said that if she fell into quicksand he would be there to pull her out, and the nightmare would have lost its power.

Her father had not had time or patience for her question that morning, however. Shulamith did not remember now what he had said, but afterward she had read up on the ways to save yourself if you fell into quicksand, because that day she had known she was on her own. Her father would not be there to save her if she fell into quicksand. She could never count on her father again.

She had also read about how to save yourself from drowning, she remembered. The first rule had been to learn to swim. Shulamith could swim now; she swam like a dolphin, but she doubted if that would save her if she was thrown into deep water bound and gagged. . . .

"Here we are," the deeply resonant voice said in her ear, and when she opened her eyes she was looking not into the blue depths at the end of the dock, but at a large white sailboat of sleek, powerful lines whose name, navy on white, was *Outcast II*.

Were it not for the gag, Smith would have laughed aloud. The sudden relief was overwhelming. If he was going to put her aboard this, he must intend at least to keep her alive. In this he could sail around the islands indefinitely until the ransom money was paid, without fear of discovery. Smith's heart soared.

And then sank. Where on earth did her captor get a boat like this? Where did anyone who was kidnapping someone for ransom get such a boat? She looked at the dark man in a new and frightening confusion. She didn't understand anything at all.

SMITH FELT the engines start up only a minute or two after the stateroom door had closed on the tall figure of her abductor. The powerful engines were close; their throbbing pulsed through her body where she lay on the bunk, making her head throb, too. He had tied her bound hands to a small handgrip at the head of the bed. She could not move, except to sit up or lie down. Her jaw ached unbearably. The gag that held her mouth firmly open was still tightly bound behind her neck. Smith would have given a million dollars at that moment for the privilege of being able to close her jaw.

Her eyes had pleaded with him again, as he tied her to the bunk, to remove the gag, silently promising utter docility if he gave in, but the dark man had shaken his head and said again, "You think you wouldn't, but you would. As soon as I was out that door you'd be screaming the place down."

She wondered if he was speaking from experience gained on previous kidnappings or from an estimate of her character. When she thought of it, of course she would have to be a fool not to try to attract some attention while they were still near human habitation. No doubt he was right. A promise given to a kidnapper would not have bound her. She would have screamed if he had removed the gag.

She would scream right now before they moved too far out to sea, if only she could get the gag off by herself. She could see by the moving lights through the porthole that they had already begun to move.

Abruptly the noise of the engines died, and silence settled around her. They were under sail. Shulamith fought her way awkwardly to a sitting position on the bunk and lifted up her bound hands.

He had given her a little leeway: the rope tying her to the small handgrip was about eighteen inches long. She could lie down without having to stretch her arms over her head, and she could move her hands from her lap to about shoulder level when she sat up. But she could not reach the knot of the gag with both hands at once, and she could not, even with a great deal of pain, pull the gag down over her lower jaw. What she might be able to do, she discovered, was slide the gag around, so that eventually the knot would be within reach.

It burned her skin and hurt her mouth, but worst of all was that fact that the gag, tied against her neck under her long hair, had somehow also incorporated a chunk of hair. Which would have to be pulled out by the roots if she was going to get the knot within reach of her fingers.

It was more achingly painful than she could have dreamed of in a hundred nightmares. And a short, sudden jerk was impossible: she had to settle for a sustained pressure, a slow tearing that made her head ache and a tortured scream rise like bile in her throat.

The stateroom door opened suddenly, and her pain and tear-filled eyes swept up and locked with the piercing gaze of her black-clad abductor. He took in everything with a look, and then with a muttered curse he stepped to where she half sat, half lay along the bunk bed.

For the second time in that awful night Smith was suddenly aware of the thinness of the nightdress that covered her body. Her firm breasts were voluptuously outlined by the twisted bodice now, and in her struggle with the gag the green cotton of the skirt had ridden up around her thighs, revealing all the length of her slim pale legs.

She shrank away from him as he approached, his gaze hooded. Then he stood for a moment looking down at the red wrists that had strained against the bonds, at the twisted gag wet with her saliva, at the damp strands of red hair on her forehead and cheeks.

"Damn," he said apologetically, and not without admiration. "What were you going to do? Climb out of the hatch and swim home? And I nearly took that gag off, even against my better judgment." He paused. "Maybe it would have been better all round if you *had* escaped," he said reflectively.

She couldn't make sense of that and didn't try. He took a small knife out of his pocket, and that drove every other thought out of her head, because surely, surely he was going to cut her free?

He cut her hands free first, put the knife away in a pocket and lifted her heavy hair to find the knot of the gag. Involuntarily Smith winced as the motion pulled against the lock of hair knotted tightly into the scarf.

The dark man opened his eyes in surprise, but in the next instant they were angry slits as he caught sight of the lock of hair, and the telltale angry red of her scalp and neck under it.

He swore violently, so that she jumped. But he bit back further comment, and with a gentleness that startled her in a man so tensely powerful, he bent to undo the knot. But it was stubborn, and for Smith these last few minutes of near freedom were the worst, impatience on top of everything else driving her closer than she had yet been to the edge of madness.

"Almost there," he said in a deeply soothing voice, and she was reminded of the way people talk to wild animals, calming them with speech. "Almost there," he said again, his deep voice drawing out the vowels almost musically, and she caught her breath in a tiny sob, feeling as though a gentle knowing hand stroked her nerves.

The voice continued as he sank onto the bunk beside her, but she no longer heard the words. She was hearing only the deep resonance of a voice that touched her deepest self, that spoke without language to a part of her that understood without language, that had never needed language.

When the gag was finally unknotted he removed it gently from her face, and then his hands soothingly massaged her aching jaw, and the dark eyes smiled down at her.

In the most extraordinary, unbelievable way she suddenly wanted him to kiss her. Her breath caught, and her sore lips parted under the thumbs that stroked her cheeks, her neck; and her eyes locked with his, and she needed his lips on her.

"God!" he whispered as he saw the look, and she felt the shock of comprehension—and something else—jolt through his body to the hands still upon her throat.

She was someone else, she was not herself. She had neither volition nor conscious thought, only need and the memory of his voice in the pit of her stomach. Hypnotized, she lifted her face to him and did not know her name.

She saw that he wanted to resist the compulsion that was now between them like a physical thing, and dimly she wondered why. She saw him battle against it and lose. Then his dark head bent, and his lips covered hers.

She gave herself up to solace with a long sigh, relaxing against his body like a wild animal that has learned to trust implicitly. Never in her life could she remember such comfort. The strong hands at her throat slid into her hair and encircled her head, so that she felt weightless, as though she need do nothing, not think, not breathe, ever again. . . .

Afterward she would try to believe that she came to her senses herself, that it was her own reason and not the fact that he lifted his lips and drew his head away that caused her brain to kick into action, caused her suddenly to push and struggle and jerk so violently away from the dark man's kiss that she cracked her skull against the bulkhead.

She stared at him, her breath coming in shallow gasps as though she were about to have a hysterical fit.

"Don't touch me!" she commanded in a catlike hiss. She could not control her voice. "Don't ever touch me again!"

He stood up, looking at her for a long, considering moment, his own breathing unsteady. Then he turned and left the room without a word.

Her first thought was of escape, and Smith scrambled up and looked out the porthole. A glance showed her that there was nothing to see except water and sky, the winking skyline of Vancouver, and higher up, Grouse Mountain silhouetted against a pink sunrise. She was an excellent swimmer, but she knew from long experience that the water in the strait between Vancouver Island and the mainland was very cold. In her present condition she wouldn't be able to swim any distance in that water.

Smith sighed, turned exhaustedly away from the view and slid off the bunk. Then she stopped abruptly, staring, as she caught sight of her reflection in the full-length mirror that hung on a door.

Her face was filthy, grimed with tears and sweat. On one of her cheekbones a long graze was lightly crusted with blood. Her turquoise eyes were dark with a wild, haunted look that reminded her of pictures of herself at the unhappy age of nine, and they were red and bloodshot. On both sides of her mouth a raw redness that the gag had caused stained her skin, and across her finely tapered chin was a black smear of grease. Her hair clung in damp tendrils to her forehead, ears, cheeks and neck, and fell over her shoulders and down her back past her waist in thick rat's-tail tangles. The white eyelet lace of her bodice was torn revealingly over the milky fullness of her breasts, and the soft green cotton of the skirt was stained and dirty.

She looked awful, and her mirrored image was a sharp and brutal reminder of what had happened to her and of what might yet happen to her. A hollow sob rose from deep within her, and Smith pressed a fist against her teeth to hold it back.

He had kissed her. After doing *this* to her, he had kissed her! She wanted to be sick or scream. She wanted to claw his eyes out, to beat him with her fists, to pour out her suddenly overwhelming anger and hatred on his head. Whirling with a force that made the cloth of her nightdress whip around her legs, Smith ran out the door and up the companionway to the cockpit.

He was between the hatchway and the wheel, his right hand on the wheel, his left stretching out to adjust the genoa sheet. Above her the mainsail and the genoa billowed out on two sides like wings: the wind was blowing from astern. The man turned his head toward the noise she made, his dark eyes narrowed, but she was on him like a wildcat before he could move.

"What the...?" he exploded in surprise, while Smith, half on his chest, half on his left arm, clutched at his hair and clawed at him. Immediately he loosed the wheel and grabbed at her.

She saw her chance. Reaching out with her free hand she jerked the wheel hard to starboard. She heard the moaning *thwack* of the boom sweeping over in instant response to its changing angle to the wind, while under her the dark man lost his balance.

They fell together with an awkward force that nearly threw her overboard, but Smith was an experienced sailor, and she caught herself on the deck ropes. Hoping her abductor was unconscious, but not wasting time to find out, she scrambled over his prone body to the wheel.

He was not unconscious. Catching her ankle with an agile twist he brought her down on the deck and flung himself full length on her

"You bloody little fool!" he shouted in her ear. "This is a busy shipping lane! Do you want to get yourself killed?" His body was heavy on her, and she was winded by her fall; she didn't answer. In another moment the dark man was on his feet and jerking her up after him. With a grip so strong his muscles were quivering he held her against him, one arm behind her back, and grasped the wheel.

The sails were luffing badly, and maliciously she hoped they would rip. But with another shuddering whack the mainsail moved to catch the wind again, and the big boat was no longer at the mercy of the battering waves but running before the wind.

His angry eyes were on her as he took his arm away from her body, but he kept the merciless grip on her wrist behind her back.

"Get below," he said through his teeth. "Any more tricks like this one and I'll tie you to the goddamned mast."

The genny was still luffing, and he eyed it impatiently. "Get below," he repeated sharply.

Suddenly Smith knew, as clearly as if he had told her, that the situation was not at all to this man's liking. Whatever his plans had been, *she* was not part of them. She looked at him over her shoulder as he held her arm, an idea taking shape in her brain.

"You're stuck with me," she said slowly, "you don't want me. You wanted my father, and you're sorry you took me instead."

The dark man said nothing. He was watching the genny, not able to adjust it as long as he held her wrist. Smith bit her lip, eyeing him. "If you take me back no one will know. I'll jump over half a mile out. I could swim half a mile, I'm a good swimmer. You don't have to worry about me." Her voice was softly persuasive, as persuasive as she knew how to make it. "You could tell the others I got away from you."

She waited, but his grip did not slacken.

Smith took a breath. All her anger was gone. Now she was only afraid. "I'll. . . I have money of my own," she said tentatively. "Not a lot, but. . . my father won't pay a ransom for me, you know. That's the truth," she said urgently, unaware that the sound of pain in her voice had already testified to the truth of what she said. "Not for me as his daughter, and not for me as an executive of the company. But if you let me go now, I'll pay you. I'll find a way to get the money to you, I promise. And I won't ask questions, I. . . ."

"No," he said, his voice harsh with a suppressed anger that surprised her.

"Please," Shulamith whispered, finally and utterly at the end of her tether. *"Please."*

The dark man stared up at the sails, his jaw tight. He made a minute course alteration that seemed to require all his attention.

"Get below," he repeated, his voice resigned. "There's coffee in the galley if you want a cup. Then I suggest that you get cleaned up."

Shulamith raised a self-conscious hand to her lace bodice, suddenly remembering that it was torn. Suddenly remembering what an utter mess she must look al together. To her amazement, she felt a blush staining her cheeks.

She hadn't blushed for years, since before she'd entered college: in logging camps and sawmills and sales meetings it was better for the boss's daughter if she did not blush. The knowledge that she was blushing now confused her and made her want to escape.

The man did not smile at her, however, nor were his dark eyes mocking. If anything they grew more somber, and his jaw tightened almost imperceptibly.

She stared helplessly over her shoulder into his dark eyes, and it was a sensation like drowning. She felt oddly shaken. Her lips were dry. Nervously she licked them.

The dark man looked away to the water ahead. He breathed once and let go of her wrist.

"Please go below," he said evenly, and Shulamith scrambled down the companionway as though she had been standing on the brink of an abyss.

HE WASN'T GOING to sail around waiting for her to be ransomed, Smith discovered when her captor docked at a small island some time later. She came up on deck barefoot and wearing a pair of too-large jeans and a sweat shirt she had found below in a locker. Her long hair was finger-combed and tied back, and she had taken a shower. The silence of the place fell on her ears as she watched him bring down the sails in the light of early morning, and Shulamith breathed deeply in unconscious release from the intolerable tension that had

gripped her ever since she had entered her father's bedroom. She heard a few waking birds lazily querying each
other's existence, sensed the water's quiet lapping
around the hull beneath her feet and wondered be-
musedly why these sounds of nature should only empha-
size the perfect stillness.

She watched him silently as he worked, taking an
immediate pleasure in the sight of the play of his
muscles, the efficient motion and interplay of arms,
hands and feet.

He was tall and large, but not the giant that she had
imagined when he held her and his hand was suffocating
her. When at last the boat was ready and he came to
stand beside her on the dock, his weary sigh was very
human. But he was certainly strong enough to carry her,
and she realized that was his intention as he bent to pick
her up in his arms.

"The path is rough. You would cut your feet," he explained tersely, then set off with her along the dock and
up the hillside. He had one arm under her knees, one
supporting her back; Smith felt the warmth of his hand
against her ribs, his thumb just pressing the fullness of
her breast. After a moment she felt the thumb move
away.

He carried her up the steep path in long easy strides,
as though her hundred-ten-pound weight was not much
of an encumbrance on him. He did not look down at
her; his eyes, hooded, were on the path ahead. It was
long, steep and overgrown, meandering through the
dank green rain forest. The hush of nature was over
them—Smith felt they could be anywhere, in any time.
Nothing had meaning except that particular, soothing

calm. She heard a birdcall she did not recognize, but she felt sure that the man carrying her could identify it. He walked so quietly, so surefootedly.

"Where are you taking me?" she asked. Her voice was almost a whisper; she was mentally exhausted and no longer cared what was going to happen to her. She couldn't fight anymore.

"You'll see," he said.

She felt an odd intimacy settle on them, a feeling of closeness that might exist between brother and sister, she thought, or between lovers who have known each other long and well. Shulamith had had neither brother nor a lover she had known long and well, and it was years since she had learned how little her father loved her. She had experienced a certain amount of cama- raderie with the men she had worked with and later supervised in her father's logging camps and sawmills, but what she felt now was very different. It took her a moment to sort it out, and it was with an odd little jerk that she realized that what she was feeling was a sense of comfort and security she hadn't known since early childhood.

Even more oddly, the feeling brought a lump to her throat.

There was no clearing to give advance warning of a human habitation; merely, the forest stopped and the house began. Her captor paused beside a tree, and when he set her down, her feet touched the cool rough stone of a step carved into rock.

Shulamith looked up. She saw an incredible, unique house that ran on level after level up the steep hill away from her. It was made of glass and weathered cedar and was hung with vines and green plants. On one side of the house water fell gently over the levels of the hillside to end in a large reflecting pool by the rock-hewn steps. The glass, when it was touched by the sun, seemed lightly golden, and on all sides trees grew close to the house, so that she felt like someone coming upon an Aztec ruin in an overgrown jungle

Shulamith breathed through open lips. "What a beautiful house," she said softly.

The dark head was inclined. "Thank you," the man said, with a slightly ironic emphasis.

She gazed avidly around as they mounted the rock steps toward the door.

"Is it yours?" she asked at last.

He spared her a glance from hooded eyes. His profile was as strong and roughly hewn as the rest of him. It occurred to her suddenly that he was extremely good-looking.

"Of course," he said.

There was no "of course" about it, that she could see. A man who owned a house like this—and, presumably, a boat like the *Outcast II*—was not your normal run-of-the-mill kidnapper of lumber barons. Or their daughters. Shulamith wrinkled her brow.

"It's a Winterhawk design, isn't it?" she said, for something to say.

"What?" he asked, stopping on the top step and turning sharply to look at her.

"The house," she said. "It looks as though it was designed by Johnny Winterhawk. Wasn't it? I've seen a few of the private residences he's done, and—" She broke off and looked at her abductor. He was rigidly immobile, looking at her with the oddest expression in his eyes.

"What's the matter?" she said impatiently. "Don't you know who designed your house?" Johnny Winterhawk wasn't exactly a household name, but she would have expected at least a spark of recognition. Winterhawk had very original ideas about awkward locations and natural sites, and he had already designed a number of public buildings in Vancouver and a university in the States that they were still talking about. "He's very good, isn't he?" Her glance wandered to the house again. "I wanted a Winterhawk house when we moved into the house we're in now," she remembered wistfully. "But daddy...."

As the realization crystalized in her brain Smith's voice died, and her lips parted on a soft gasp. Slowly, slowly she turned her head to look at her dark, hatchet-faced abductor. He was staring at her, his eyes filled with mingled amazement and disbelief. He looked thunderstruck.

No more thunderstruck than she.

"You can't be. You *can't* be!" she said slowly, her voice a whisper, her turquoise eyes mirroring the dark man's amazement. "But you are! *You're* Johnny Winterhawk!"

"Damn it! Damn it to hell! You mean to say you didn't *know*?" Johnny Winterhawk thundered, looking as though he wanted to hit something.

CHAPTER THREE

SMITH STARED UP into those dark incredulous eyes in amazement. Of course she recognized him now— Johnny Winterhawk had designed enough public buildings in Vancouver for her to have seen his photo in the newspaper several times, but she wouldn't have thought he courted publicity. She shrugged.

"No, I didn't recognize you before," she said. "Why?"

"You must have!" he thundered, ignoring the question. "Right when you pulled off my mask."

"This is an odd time to be concerned about fame, I must say," Smith said dryly. "I'm a kidnap victim, not a prospective client, believe me!"

"You didn't recognize me?" he asked, an odd emphasis in his voice. He was standing one step above her, and he was six or eight inches taller than she was to begin with; if they stayed here much longer she was going to get a crick in her neck. "But you...."

"All right," she capitulated lightly, shrugging. "I did recognize you. You're my favorite architect. Is that what you want?"

He looked coldly at her, his mouth a grim line. Sighing, Smith resigned herself to staring uncomfortably up at him.

"You may stop laughing when you hear what I have to say," Johnny Winterhawk said in a clipped voice. "When you ripped off my mask I got the distinct impression that you recognized me. That, Miss St. John, is the only reason you're here right now."

It took a minute to sink in. *"What?"* she demanded.

It was his turn to look sardonic. He said, his jaw tight, "Did you really not recognize me?"

"Look, I wouldn't have recognized King Kong if he'd bitten me!" Smith returned. "I still don't see—"

He interrupted. "What was the suddenly enlightened look that crossed your face?"

Smith thought back to that terror-filled moment of bravado when she had ripped off the white-trimmed mask. "I—I suddenly realized how stupid it was to have got myself a look at your face," she remembered. "That's the only thing I can think of."

Johnny Winterhawk made an exasperated noise. "Yes, it was," he said. "Very damn stupid. So was I, obviously, but it was a tense moment, and you're here now."

Ever since she'd recognized him, Smith's fear had been slowly leaving her, and when he had admitted he hadn't wanted to kidnap her she had felt as though the world was returning to normal. But that "you're here now" had a finality about it that jerked her back to apprehension.

"What do you mean?" she demanded, leaping up the last step and grabbing at Johnny Winterhawk's arm as he turned to open the door.

He looked at her without speaking and stood back for her to enter the house. Smith looked into the beautiful, inviting interior past his shoulder and felt a sudden inexplicable dread. It was as though once she entered this house her life would never be the same again. She wanted to plead with Johnny Winterhawk, but she didn't know for what, and his silence suddenly seemed implacable. Smith took a quick deep breath, straightened her back and walked past Johnny Winterhawk into his extraordinary house.

It was rough-hewn inside, not at all like the interiors of the elegant homes he had designed for some of Vancouver's wealthy, which Smith had visited or seen in magazine photo spreads. In his own house the interior was an extension of the exterior, all green plants and golden cedar and hewn rock. Entire walls were made of glass, so that it seemed almost as though the forest were an integral part of the house.

In other houses Johnny Winterhawk had designed Smith had seen soft white carpeting and drapes and painted plaster walls, but here in his own house there were no such refinements. On the varnished cedar floors were scattered bright woven Indian rugs, and on the cedar walls hung a collection of antique and modern masks and carvings and paintings that even her inexperienced eye could tell comprised a variety of contributions from different native tribes of Canada. Works of Haida and Chopa and Kwakiutl artists she picked out without difficulty, but there were many that she did not recognize.

The house was like a staircase up the steep hillside; Johnny led her up through a few rooms and several levels and opened a door onto a bedroom that looked out on a soft waterfall and a small reflecting pool surrounded by lush forest growth. Smith felt the peace of the house enveloping her like a physical thing. She sighed deeply.

Johnny Winterhawk stood in the doorway, looking very dark in his black jersey and trousers, and half smiled down at her.

"If there's a way out of this," he said, "I'm too tired to think of it right now." He paused uncertainly and rubbed his hand over his head. "There's no way off the island except by the boat, and I've got the keys. Can I trust you to try to get some sleep yourself, or do I have to stay with you to prevent you from trying to burn down the house for a signal fire?" As Smith blinked protestingly up at him he smiled. "And don't tell me you wouldn't consider it," he said.

He seemed to think she was very resourceful and ruthless. Burn down the house for a signal fire! As if she would do any such thing! Still, it was a thought.... Her eyes dropped from his, and she gazed into the distance. Well, why not? A kidnapper deserved whatever he got. And a victim had the right to escape by any method she could.

Johnny Winterhawk laughed shortly, watching the thoughts play across her face. "All right," he said. "I won't put temptation in your way." And stepping into the room behind her he closed the door.

Smith stood stiffly against the alarm that ran up her spine. "What are you going to do?" she asked levelly.

Johnny Winterhawk regarded her curiously. "Are you always so cool under fire?" he asked, as though somehow she had piqued his interest.

"Am I under fire?" she countered, in the same level tone.

"You do let yourself get angry, though," he mused. "Is that the only emotion you ever show, or do you allow yourself others?"

She compressed her lips and stared at him, measuring his size against her own agility, weighing her chances.

"If you rape me the emotion you can expect is murderous rage," Smith said tightly. "And I do mean murderous."

Johnny Winterhawk looked back at her in annoyed disbelief. "If I *rape* you?" he repeated incredulously. "What the hell are you talking about? Of course I'm not going to rape you."

She wanted to believe him; she wanted to be able to trust him. "You closed the door," she pointed out, "and then you asked me about showing emotions."

"Look," he said reasonably, "I want some sleep. I've been up for about fifty hours straight and I'm seeing double, and kidnapping you wasn't exactly easy." He smiled briefly. "I'm not leaving you alone while I sleep. That's all."

He crossed to the bed and as she watched began to pull it across the room. Before she was quite aware of his intention the big double bed, covered with a large woven Indian blanket as a bedspread, was solidly jammed against the door. Johnny Winterhawk stood gazing at her across its width.

"Through that door," he said, pointing across the room, "is a bathroom. There may be a book or two in that closet." Another door was indicated. "I am going to sleep—on this side of the bed. If you want to lie on the other side you can be sure that I will not touch you. However, if you try to break the windows or move the bed from the door I will wake up.'' He smiled at her with his eyes. ''If you get bored while I'm sleeping remind yourself that you could have promised not to try to burn the house down.''

With that he dropped down on the bed, stretched out and fell asleep.

SHE AWOKE with an unfamiliar slow ease to find her head resting on a black-clad shoulder. For one exhilarating moment of looking into the face of this dark, sleeping stranger, Shulamith couldn't remember who she was. Then she jerked away from the warmth of his nearness back to her own side of the bed: it was she who had moved in sleep, not he.

She felt a sudden sense of loss, as though she had dreamed that they belonged together. She gazed in wonder at the dark face on the pillow. It was an effort not to roll back into the comfort of his body.

At that moment Johnny Winterhawk opened his eyes and looked across the bed at her, directly into her soul.

Smith sat up and swung her legs over the edge of the bed, turning her back on him. After a moment her breathing and her emotions were back to normal. ''Sorry, did I wake you?'' she asked coolly, then stood and turned to glance down at him, proving—to herself? to him?—that there had never been a moment when she was afraid to look at Johnny Winterhawk.

''I don't know what woke me,'' he said. He rolled onto his back, watching her as she crossed to gaze out the window. ''Did you sleep or pace the cage?''

Smith turned away from the view out the window and looked back at him in some irritation, hands in the pockets of the overlarge jeans she was wearing.

"I'm not a wild animal, you know," she observed. Johnny Winterhawk swung his feet to the floor and sat up on the edge of the bed.

"Except when you're cornered," he answered with a grin. He rubbed his hands lazily in his shining black hair. "I haven't forgotten how you tried to pitch me overboard or the way you threw the phone at my head."

"I hope it connected," Smith said with relish. "You were lucky. If that towel—" She broke off and turned back to the window, remembering the engulfing terror of the early morning with a shudder. It was hard to believe that only a few hours ago she had been safe in her bed and in her life.

A noise made her turn around: Johnny Winterhawk was dragging the bed away from the door back to its original position. He thumped it into place with his leg, then crossed to open the door. He held it open and waited for her.

"Yes, I was lucky," he agreed. "You're a quick thinker and a tough fighter. If I was in a tight corner I'd rather have you on my side than against me."

Smith could think of nothing to say in answer to this, so she said nothing, passing out of the room in front of him uneasily, wondering where he might be taking her now.

He led her back down through the house, then onto a cantilevered, square, open balcony that had several trees growing right up through the floor of it.

"I always thought a site had to be completely cleared

before a house could be built!'' she exclaimed, thinking of the rather lovely lot that had been ravaged when her father had had the new house built.

"That's a myth perpetrated by lazy architects,'' Johnny Winterhawk replied, "and accepted by tradition-bound clients. Even if a site does have to be dismantled during construction, it can be restored afterward. There's absolutely no need for importing shrubs and lawn by the yard on a site like this.''

Smith sighed, thinking of the terraced expanse of green surrounding her father's house, so unnatural amid the natural flora of Hollyburn Mountain.

The large balcony looked west, overhanging a rugged gorge where, many feet below, a narrow arm of the sea pounded magnificently against the rocks. Beyond was the ocean, sprinkled in the distance with the dark mossy mounds of neighboring islands. The view was breathtaking. Smith crossed over to the railing and stared down at the hypnotic motion of the waves running in and out and breaking whitely over the rocky shore.

While she slept her long red hair had lost the string she had tied it back with on the boat, and it was blowing wildly around her face and body in the wind that rushed up the gorge. Oddly, she felt suddenly free. It had been an age since she had last let her hair loose. It seemed to her that this past year in Europe had been unremittingly formal and constrained. There had been a great deal to learn, many people to please. The marketing end of a large lumber concern was no small operation, as her father's European manager had soon shown her.

Smith laughed into the wind and turned to meet Johnny Winterhawk's eyes. "This is indescribably beautiful,'' she said, and smiled at him in real admiration as they left.

The kitchen had a large window—most of one wall, in fact—facing on the same view, slightly below the balcony. The opposite wall was also largely window, looking out over the path they had arrived by that morning and the rock stairs.

Johnny Winterhawk made the best scrambled eggs she could remember eating since her favorite cook had quit at the St. John logging camp in Dog's Ear four or five years ago.

"Are you an aficionado of scrambled eggs?" he asked her when she told him this.

"I was hooked on them that summer," Smith remembered with a smile. "Big Ben was a fantastic cook, and scrambled eggs were his forte. He used to put tarragon or something in them." She sighed, scooping up the last mouthful of the breakfast Johnny Winterhawk had just cooked, relishing the taste. "He quit in the middle of that summer. After working for my father for *years*, he quit the only summer I was at Dog's Ear. The cook who came after Big Ben left was terrible," Shulamith wrinkled her nose. "Just my luck," she laughed.

"Are you unlucky?" he asked with a smile of disbelief. "You seem to lead a pretty good life. Are you being groomed to take over your father's business?"

Fleetingly she wondered if he had any reason other than conversational interest in the answer to that. Was he trying to judge her value to her father and St. John's Wood?

"I went to my first logging camp the summer I was sixteen," Smith recalled. "That was sort of a test: I had one more year of high school and had to decide whether I wanted to go on to study forestry in university. That first summer I was just a worker, a lumberjill, but after that the grooming started. I worked in a different logging camp or sawmill or pulp-and-paper mill every year while I was taking my forestry degree. I was always in some position in charge—foreman or supervisor. My father believes in the deep-end theory.''

Johnny Winterhawk bit into a piece of warm buttered toast and looked inquiring.

"You know—throw them in at the deep end," Smith laughed. "I think I've done half the jobs there are in the forestry industry—some of them only for a week or two, of course, just long enough to learn the work. And I've been in charge of a minimum of fifty men ever since I was eighteen." She laughed shortly. "And if you think the boss's son has trouble with the employees, you should try being the boss's daughter."

Johnny nodded slowly as he poured two cups of coffee. "I would imagine you have to prove yourself constantly."

That was exactly what she had to do, but not many people understood that. Most people she talked to imagined that her biggest problem in such a male-dominated industry was sexual harassment. But in fact the opposite was true. Now and then one of her father's employees would ask her to go out with him, but not one had ever had the temerity to make a pass at her. Smith was no ordinary woman trying to break into male-dominated ranks: she was the boss's daughter. There had never been the least question in Cord St. John's company that that would be a very quick way to get fired. If they wanted her to prove herself to be as tough and as smart as any of them, well, Cord St. John had started in the camps himself. He understood that. But as to "proving" anything else. . . .

That first summer—the summer she was sixteen—there had been a young man. A student like herself, but he had been in university, working his way through, and in a strange and sometimes hostile environment Shulamith had found him a comforting symbol of the kind of life and people she was used to.

They had been drawn to each other. He was a big shy boy who played the guitar, and in the evenings they had sat out under the stars, and he had taught her to play it.

It had been as sweet and simple as childhood friendships, though of course, given time, Smith realized now, it might have developed into something else. But they hadn't been given time.

Someone in the camp hadn't thought the friendship innocent, though she'd never known who. And late one afternoon, while Shulamith and the boy had been lying lazily in the grass away from the camp and talking—of all things—of her options for university and whether she should go on in forestry and go into her father's business or whether she should study English and literature and go on to be a poet and songwriter. . . her father had marched through the grass up to them, and without asking a question or allowing the least word of explanation he had called down the shy boy in the most violent, abusive terms imaginable.

The boy had blushed. Shulamith had blushed, too, and afterward wept, and later, as the boy had been dragged off ignominiously to his tent to pack up his

things and had been flown out of the camp with her
father in the helicopter that had brought him, she had
become remote and withdrawn, pretending she did not
notice the looks the men gave her. The boy had never
worked for St. John Forest Products again, and Shulamith had never seen him again. Now she couldn't
remember his name.

Smith abruptly became aware that she had been talking too openly, telling the man who was, after all, her
abductor, far too much about her father and herself.
She shifted uncomfortably in her chair. "Now that
we've finished eating," she said hardly, "could we get
down to business?" She was uneasily aware that his
questions had made her forget more important things.

"Such as?" he caught her eye while he leaned across
the table to refill their coffee cups. They were sitting at a
table by the window looking out over the inlet, and her
eyes slid away from Johnny Winterhawk's to the scene
outside.

"Such as the fact that my father, if he lives, is not going to pay one cent to ransom me," Smith said, in a
voice made brittle by her effort to sound matter-of-fact.
She returned her gaze to his face. "You're looking at
the only person who would pay you money in exchange
for my freedom or my life. Me," she finished for emphasis. "No one but me."

His dark brows flattened and moved together over the
bridge of his nose. "No one else?" he asked in surprise.

"No one else," she reiterated in a light high voice, as
though she hadn't a care in the world. "And I'm afraid
my personal fortune will not suit your expectations of
what this little enterprise might have netted you if you'd

taken my father. The fact is, Mr. Winterhawk, I won't be able to drum up even a half million, and most of it will be in St. John Forest Products stock. Which of course given time will appreciate—unless your last night's idea of fun has killed my father."

Her voice was beginning to shake, and Smith stopped speaking and looked at him. But Johnny Winterhawk said nothing.

"Well?" she prompted aggressively.

"Well, what?" he asked, taking a sip of his coffee and setting the cup on the table with a little thud.

She breathed deeply, dismayed by how ragged the breath was. Even after sleep and a good meal, she could not seem to keep her emotions under control. She closed her eyes for a moment.

"Will you let me go free for that amount of money?" she asked slowly and precisely, fighting her anger at his deliberate refusal to understand.

"Half a million dollars?" he asked, his carved face expressionless.

"No, not quite—more like four...say four twenty-five," Smith said, unconsciously slipping into the attitude of someone used to bargaining in large figures. She looked at Johnny Winterhawk guardedly. It was every penny she could raise and then some. But she had plenty of experience in making deals, and she knew Johnny Winterhawk was no fool. He probably knew what she was worth better than she did. But in any case she was not going to haggle over the price of her life. He would take her offer or leave it.

"Well, will you?" she repeated edgily when he said nothing. Her dark abductor stared at her consideringly.

"No, I won't," Johnny Winterhawk said at last.

She set her coffee cup down so violently she heard it crack, but she ignored it; and standing up she cried, "What do you want from me? What do you *want*? I don't understand you, I don't understand anything that's happening! Why are you doing this? What are you after?"

Her voice climbed to the edge of panic, and Johnny Winterhawk stood up and gripped her wrist over the table. "All right," he said, his deep voice breaking into the confusion of her thoughts. "All right, sit down."

She sat because there was nothing else to do. Her turquoise eyes looked up at him as she fought for control. Johnny Winterhawk sat, too, and watched her for a long moment over the rim of his coffee cup.

"What do you know about Cat Bite Valley, Miss St. John?" he asked at last.

CHAPTER FOUR

"CAT BITE VALLEY?" she repeated in stupid surprise. It was a change of topic so abrupt he might have been talking about a sea of the moon. Smith thought she might have misheard him, but he nodded briefly and watched her.

"Well, it's a tract of provincially owned land up by Jeremiah Bay," she said bewilderedly, wondering how this could possibly be relevant. "My father has the timber rights on it," she added.

Johnny Winterhawk's black eyes bored into hers in sudden anger. "That's all?" he demanded.

She shrugged. "That's all I can remember about it. Why?"

His angry eyes became tinged with contempt as he gazed at her. "Where the devil have you been this past year?" he demanded scornfully.

"In Europe," she replied in surprise, for surely he knew, but her answer seemed to take him aback.

"What?"

"I've been in Europe for a year, studying the markets," she said. "I came home when my father had his heart attack." She looked at him. "As if you didn't know," she finished coldly.

His firm lips pursed and he raised an eyebrow in curious inquiry.

"You must surely have done some research on my father before you decided to kidnap him. Don't tell me you only made your plans yesterday," she explained with sarcastic condescension.

"Mmm," he grunted, and stood up. "Come with me," he said shortly.

She followed him out of the kitchen, along corridors and steps and through rooms, moving up the hillside as though the house were itself a flight of stairs. When they were near the top he opened a door onto a room that was obviously a study and ushered Smith inside.

In front of a wall of living rock that seemed to be a part of the actual cliff face a huge desk dominated the room. Johnny Winterhawk crossed to the desk in a few long strides and in a moment was unfolding a large map across its top.

"Look at this," he commanded her, as, head bent over, he stood smoothing out the map with his broad bronzed hand. Fascinated, she crossed to his side, aware as she did so of the tension that filled his body, making his movements surer, more economical, a tension that crackled in the air like electricity.

She looked down at a large-scale map of a section of the coast between the northern tip of Vancouver Island and the city of Prince Rupert. Johnny Winterhawk's broad finger pinpointed one blue inlet and ran along its length inland to the tip and to the winding blue line that joined it.

"Cat Bite River," Johnny Winterhawk said, and stopped. After a moment Smith looked up to find his gaze on her, waiting to be met. "Jeremiah Bay and Cat Bite River have been the fishing grounds of the Chopa

nation since long before the advent of the white man."
His tone was dry, succinct, like the voice of a university
lecturer. He dropped his eyes, and the brown finger
moved along the line of the river, encircling it. "Cat
Bite Valley is the traditional hunting ground of the
Chopas. This is Stony Water—" his finger stopped a
short distance north of the river, then moved to the
south of it "—and this is Eagle's Nest. They are Chopa
reserves. From Jeremiah Bay in the west—" the strong
forefinger followed the track of his words "—to
Feather Mountain in the east, and from Hackle Ridge
and Salmontail Lake in the north to the Chopit Range in
the south is the Chopa land-claim area."

Johnny Winterhawk raised his head to shake the two
curving wings of his black hair out of his eyes. He
looked at her again. "Do you know what that means?"
he asked.

"It means land that the Indians claim belongs to them
and should be returned to their use and control," Smith
said, irritated by his implication.

Johnny Winterhawk nodded briefly. "This land
claim was registered with the federal and provincial
governments in 1968," he said. "In 1976 the timber
rights for the land from Cat Bite River north to Hackle
Ridge, including Cat Bite Valley, were sold to St. John
Forest Products by the provincial forestry ministry,
although lumbering operations never began. Ever since
then, the Chopas have been trying to have all timber
rights on the land-claim area—which includes the traditional hunting and fishing grounds—revoked."

"It's a lot of land, the land-claim territory," Smith
said dubiously, eyeing the map. How could the Chopa

people hope to get control of this amount of land?

He looked at her for a moment. "It is less than one-quarter of the original territory of the Chopa," he said quietly. "But then the population of the Chopa nation is less than one-half of what it was three hundred years ago, so no doubt we can get along on less land."

He spoke so calmly that for a moment she did not believe she had heard him correctly. Then, looking into his eyes, she understood that she had.

"What?" she demanded incredulously.

"Does that surprise you, Miss St. John?"

The cynical mockery in his eyes disturbed her. "Surprise me?" she repeated. "I don't believe you! How could—"

"Of course you don't," he agreed. "No one does. It's easier to ignore facts that make you uncomfortable."

There was contempt in his gaze now, and she couldn't help reacting to it. "All right," she said. "Then tell me why. What happened?"

He laughed outright. "What happened to reduce the population of the Chopa nation by one-half while the population of Canada increased by nearly six hundred percent?" he asked dryly. "The white man happened, Miss St. John. The white man, with his hatred and his diseases and his greed for land. And his broken promises. Our infant mortality rate is four times the national average, Miss St. John. Our life expectancy is ten years shorter than the white man's. Does that surprise you?"

Smith drew in a slow breath. Everybody knew that the native population had suffered dreadful losses in the early years of European settlement in Canada, but she was sure that in more enlightened times the population had at least returned to its original numbers.

"What's this got to do with my father?" she asked, after a moment.

"About a year ago your father announced that cutting operations would begin in the Cat Bite Valley and Hackle Ridge areas. The Chopa band mounted a protest with the Environment ministry of the provincial government and with federal Department of Indian Affairs and others—all of them useless bodies, but the publicity was good. It attracted church groups and wildlife foundations, as such causes do, but it had no overt effect on your father. However, last year's strike of the forestry workers had a crucial timing as far as we were concerned. In August, St. John Forest Products announced that continuing manpower and technical problems had delayed the start of operations in Cat Bite Valley and that it would be impossible to go ahead until this year." He paused, leaning over the desk, his hands on either side of the map. "No one knows exactly why your father did this. If he hoped that the protest would die down over time, he was wrong. From a business point of view he'd have been smarter just to get in there and start chopping as soon as the strike was over, and it might have been just one more battle lost for the Indians. What he did surprised us."

It surprised Smith, too. Her father hadn't got where he was by backing away from a battle, or by refusing to step on the toes of innocent people. "Don't talk to me about goddamn Indian rights," was what he would have said. "Just get in there and start sawing." With a start Shulamith realized that her mental imitation of her father's phrasing repeated Johnny Winterhawk's own phrasing almost word for word. She looked into the dark eyes beside her and wondered if Johnny Winterhawk was as ruthless a man as her father.

"We didn't know, of course, that he was having heart trouble. Maybe he's slowing down because of his health," the dark man said.

Not if the past few weeks were anything to judge by, Smith thought, remembering her futile efforts to get her father to do just that.

"What happened then?" she asked.

"People began to perceive us as having achieved a moral victory," Johnny Winterhawk said dryly. "They forgot about the strike and all the legitimate business reasons there might have been for putting off new operations and insisted on seeing your father as having backed down; and the number of groups that wanted to be in on that was legion. Everybody, it seemed, needed one good rousing victory over business or capitalism or the establishment or male supremacy or polluters or wildlife destroyers—you name the cliché, we had the group on our bandwagon. We had, and still have, women's liberation groups, organic-farm groups, Marxist-Leninist groups, dedicated young lawyers—anyone and everyone who was looking for the back of a good cause to climb on." The cynicism in his tone was almost cruel.

"Is that how you look at it?" she asked in disapproving surprise.

"That's how it is, Miss St. John," he said coolly. "There are fast-buck artists in the moral-conscience business, too. Whether they realize it or not."

"And you would know, of course," she put in sarcastically.

The dark eyes considered her. "Why do you think so?" he asked.

"Why were you going to kidnap my father?" Smith countered.

"Ah, of course. We'll get to that," he said calmly. "Here, sit down." He indicated the leather chair behind the desk. When she had sunk into it, Johnny Winterhawk pushed the map to one side, hiked one leg up onto the desk and sat looking down at her.

"Both the federal and provincial governments ignore native land-claim rights in this country every day," he began. "Our only real hope lay in the fact that lumbering in the area would destroy the salmon spawning grounds of Cat Bite River, which is my people's traditional fishing ground, as well as damage the wildlife habitat of Cat Bite Valley, which is our traditional hunting ground. This is an argument that is harder for government to ignore. Eventually, the provincial government announced the setting up of a commission of inquiry."

That was an achievement, she knew; commissions weren't set up every day. She wondered why her father hadn't mentioned it to her.

"What did the commission decide?" she asked, although it was a foregone conclusion: if they were kidnapping her father, the decision had gone against them.

With a sudden clarity she understood why Johnny Winterhawk had refused her offer of money: the ransom he was seeking was worth a lot more to him than a few hundred thousand, or even a few million dollars.

"The inquiry is still in progress," he said surprisingly. "The commission is holding public hearings that begin tomorrow."

Smith wrinkled her brow as a faint memory jogged. "Is my father scheduled to appear at that hearing?"

"Yes, he is," said Johnny Winterhawk. "So am I."

"I don't understand this," Smith said. "What exactly were you hoping to achieve by kidnapping my father now?"

Johnny Winterhawk sighed. "We weren't kidnapping him. We were hoping to frighten him."

"Frighten him?" Smith sat up with such a violent start the chair slapped forward and almost threw her across Johnny Winterhawk's black-trousered lap in front of her. But she sat back with an equally violent jerk before he had time to do more than touch her shoulders in a brief firm clasp. "Frighten him?" she repeated, outraged.

"Or reason with him. We weren't sure what kind of man he was."

She was too angry to remain still. Shaken, she got to her feet. Her eyes were now almost on a level with his, but her anger was so violent she couldn't look at him.

"What did you hope to gain?" she demanded fiercely, her eyes on the map, on the desk, on the floor—anywhere but on him, because she was afraid of the force of her own fury. Her hands were tense, her fingers extended like upturned raven's claws. "You got your inquiry, you got your time, what else did you want? *Frighten* him? You nearly *killed* him! For all we know, you did kill him!"

When she looked at him he was watching her, his hooded eyes grave. "Why?" she demanded. "Why did you do that to my father?"

Johnny Winterhawk breathed once and stood up,

moving around the other side of the desk away from her. The late-morning sun slanted through greenery and glowed on the warm wood of the floor, and on his black-clad thighs and chest and the sleek black wings of his hair as he crossed the room. He stopped and stared out the window, his hands in his pockets.

He said, "We knew that your father was going to move an outfit into the northern part of Cat Bite Valley, up by Salmontail Lake, as quietly as possible, and begin logging operations as early as next week. We were hoping to convince him last night that he should wait until the inquiry had issued its report before he did any logging in the area."

Shulamith stared across the room at him. "What on earth do you mean?" she asked, amazed. "Surely you first got a temporary injunction against St. John's to prevent any lumbering in the area during the inquiry?" If they hadn't done that, she didn't think much of their organization.

Johnny Winterhawk shook his head. "The supreme Court of British Columbia refused to grant us an injunction," he said matter-of-factly. "The appeals court heard the appeal this week, but it's reserved its decision. If the appeals court upholds the earlier decision then the Chopa are in limbo and legally your father can do anything he damn pleases."

In some perhaps naive way, Smith had faith in the justice system. She was not blind to its faults and errors, but she believed in the country's urge to justice. What she was hearing from Johnny Winterhawk now shook her.

"The Supreme Court refused to grant a temporary injunction even though the government had appointed a commission of inquiry?'' she repeated. Some basic sense of security began to crumble; she felt as though the world had shifted a little under her feet. ''But that's impossible!''

''Is it?'' Johnny Winterhawk asked quietly. Hands in his pockets, he was gazing down over the inlet and the sea. Below them on the cliffside she could just catch a glimpse of the cedar wall of the kitchen; at a different angle, far below through the trees, she could see a small sandy beach.

''But...'' she stammered, trying to remember the arguments of environmentalists and native groups that she had heard in the past. ''But if logging operations are even begun in the area, the salmon spawning grounds will be destroyed,'' she managed. ''Won't they?''

''Of course.''

''So then, whatever the commission recommended after that would be pointless. The decision will have been made...by my father, really.'' It was impossible, and yet looking at him, she had to believe what he had told her.

Johnny Winterhawk said nothing. And suddenly in the silence she believed it.

''Doesn't it make you angry?'' she asked, a frown settling on her brow as a distant outrage flickered into life in her.

He laughed, throwing his head back and showing his teeth. The wings of his hair fell back and then forward over his forehead as he turned from the window to look at her. His dark gaze was frank and steady.

''Yes, I'm angry,'' he said. ''But it's futile to get

angry over the predictable or the inevitable, and what happened in the courts was both.''

"Was it?'' Smith wondered suddenly if she'd been living in a cloister all her life. Between learning the ropes at St. John Forest Products and doing her father's business entertaining she had had little time for getting involved in social issues. She had somehow assumed that other people were looking after social progress, slowly, perhaps, but surely. And yet this man thought that rank injustice was inevitable from the courts of the country, and he was the sort of man whose word, in other circumstances, she would have accepted at face value. Well, that just showed how wrong her judgment of people could be.

She said dryly, "And after all this you want me to believe that you weren't planning on kidnapping my father?'' And had taken her as second best, it was obvious. On the spur of the moment he had decided to use her to blackmail her father and force him to stop the logging in Cat Bite Valley. She wondered what her father would do. He was a man who didn't like to be challenged. "Kidnap and be damned,'' might well be his reaction. "He doesn't love me, you know,'' she said, not knowing why she said it.

"He's a fool, then,'' commented Johnny Winterhawk, looking at her as though he understood more than she had said aloud. "You're a daughter any man should be proud of.''

Smith blinked and swallowed and dropped her eyes. She couldn't understand where the well of emotion that engulfed her had come from.

"I kidnapped you,'' Johnny Winterhawk continued,

"for the reason I told you earlier. Because I thought you recognized me when you pulled my mask off, and the last thing I need when I'm due to testify before the Cartier Commission is a charge of breaking and entering or attempted kidnapping and extortion being laid against me. Firstly because we would lose credibility, and secondly because it would be difficult for me to testify before the commission from a cell in Okala prison."

Smith looked at him. He must think she was very naive. "There is such a thing as bail," she told him. "And I'm sure a man like you would get bail."

Johnny Winterhawk laughed again. "Would I?"

What did that mean? "You're a well-known architect," she said. "And you seem to own enough property."

"I'm an Indian, too," he said.

"No," she said levelly, "please don't tell me the statistics about how Indians are treated before the courts. I do not believe that the system is that bad. Anyway, you're very different from the general run—" She broke off, appalled by what she had been going to say.

"Of drunken Indian?" Winterhawk finished for her.

She was silent.

"That's different, of course," he went on, a dreadful sarcasm in his voice. "Of course, the fact that Indians are all drunkards means it's justice that Indians make up sixty-two percent of the prison population in areas where we make up only twenty percent of the general population, doesn't it? And it's only fair that the suicide rate among my people is six times the national average. After all, what can you expect of drunken—"

"All right!" she shouted, to drown out that scathing

voice. "All right, I'm sorry! I'm an unconscious racist and you've found me out!" She drew in a shaky breath. "I'm also tired and I've been kidnapped and I've been through enough in a day to last anyone a lifetime and if I have to listen to any more I'll go crazy!" She was trying to keep her voice calm, but she heard it climbing to a panicky squeak. She stopped and took a deep breath. "Please, when are you going to let me go?"

He wasn't going to let her go at all. Smith could see it in his eyes, which were simultaneously apologetic and determined.

"Please," she begged, "my father is ill—maybe terribly ill. Please don't keep me here."

There was a pause while they looked at each other across the sun-filled room. Then Johnny Winterhawk spoke.

"I'm damned sorry you're here at all," he said flatly. "But there's a lot more than your father's health riding on this. My people are fighting a battle for their way of life and for their lives. It's a losing battle before it even begins." His voice and his face showed he was implacable. "Your temporary peace of mind is not important in the stream of things, Miss St. John. Nor is my comfort. I don't want you here, either, but here you are going to stay until this thing is over."

CHAPTER FIVE

"LUMBER BARON Cordwainer St. John is in stable condition today after being admitted to the Royal Columbia Hospital in the early hours of the morning. He is suffering from his second heart attack in a few weeks. He is the president of St. John Forest Products."

It was the next-to-last item on the afternoon news, and when the newscast was over, Smith flicked off the radio, leaned back and gazed at Johnny Winterhawk in silence. The item hadn't changed since the noon newscast.

"They keep saying the same thing," she said irritably to Johnny Winterhawk. "What in hell does 'stable condition' mean?"

"It means he isn't better and he isn't worse," Johnny Winterhawk replied calmly, and Smith looked sardonic.

"Isn't better and isn't worse than what?" she demanded in annoyed exasperation. "We haven't had any real news out of that thing all day."

At six o'clock that changed. Johnny Winterhawk had made her stay with him all day, spending most of his time working in his study while she tried to concentrate on a book. But they were in the kitchen making dinner when the six o'clock evening news came on.

"Police were called to the bedside of heart-attack victim Cordwainer St. John at the Royal Columbia Hospital late this afternoon,'' was the first thing they heard, and Smith dropped her knife and rushed to bend over the radio. Johnny Winterhawk followed.

"The president of St. John Forest Products, who suffered a heart attack this morning,'' the announcer said, "has informed a sergeant of the Royal Canadian Mounted Police that he was awakened in the early hours of the morning to find himself surrounded by five masked men, when he suffered the heart attack and briefly lost consciousness. He reawakened as he was being put into an ambulance, but could not remember anything of the few minutes immediately prior to his attack until late in the day, when he called the police. His daughter, Shulamith St. John, an executive of St. John Forest Products, is apparently missing. An RCMP spokesman said that they are looking into the possibility that she may have been kidnapped. No ransom demand has so far been received.''

As a slow-talking RCMP officer made a brief statement Smith and Johnny Winterhawk stared at each other over the radio. Winterhawk cursed briefly under his breath, and she reached out and gripped his arm tightly.

"Let me go,'' she pleaded in a low, intense voice. "Let me go now and I'll lie, I won't tell them anything, I promise. I'll say I was away—"

"No,'' he interrupted firmly. He broke her grasp on his arm and turned away.

"Can't you see you're just making it worse?'' she begged, following him back to the counter where he calmly picked up his knife and continued to chop an onion. "I could tell them I went out, that I wasn't there when it happened. They would never find you."

"Unless you told them how," Winterhawk said dryly, looking sideways at her.

"But I wouldn't! That's what I'm telling you, that I wouldn't! And you—"

"Why not?"

The abrupt question startled her. "What?" she asked.

"Why not?" he repeated in a reasonable tone. He turned to face her. "If I let you go I have no hold over you. What's to prevent your telling the police the truth as soon as you're free?"

Smith paused only momentarily. "I would give you my word," she said.

He laughed. "What loyalty do you owe me that would make you inclined to keep your word?"

"Well, I . . . ."

In the silence that fell after her voice trailed away Johnny Winterhawk turned back to the counter and resumed chopping.

He was right. There would be no reason for her not to tell the police the truth. Involuntarily or not, he was a kidnapper. He couldn't let her go now. But then. . . .

Smith drew in a small frightened breath as she saw the truth. "But when *can* you let me go?" she asked huskily. "When can you ever let me go?"

Johnny Winterhawk crossed to the very modern stove console and scraped the chopped onion into a frying pan. It sizzled and spat into the silence, and Shulamith's voice climbed a notch toward panic.

"Kidnapping is a criminal offense." She pursued the

thought to its relentless conclusion, her turquoise eyes darkening in fear. "No matter when you let me go my testimony could put you in prison. So if you don't trust my word, you can't ever let me go. You have to keep me here forever—or kill me." His back to her, Johnny Winterhawk stirred the onions in silence. "Have you thought of that?" she demanded shrilly.

"Yes," he said brusquely, "I've thought of it."

"What are you going to do?" Her high voice was painful even to her own ears. "Have you decided what you're going to do?"

He did not answer, and with a strange, unfamiliar little snap her panic turned to rage. For the second time she flung herself bodily at him, her anger driving her beyond reason.

"Answer me!" she demanded.

Johnny Winterhawk whirled to reach for her, and with a loud crash the frying pan sailed to the floor, spilling a mess of onions and melted butter as it went. Ignoring it, he caught her by one wrist and reached for the other, but for once his strength did not outweigh her angry litheness. She dragged and twisted against his firm grasp, trying to pull him off balance, and aimed for his head with her flailing free hand.

Like a practiced boxer, Johnny Winterhawk swung his upper body easily backward, allowing her to move across the floor, but not letting go her wrist.

"Stop it," he said in a gentle, low-voiced command, and even when he moved his head to dodge her swinging blows, his dark eyes never left hers.

"Damn you, damn you!" she cried. "You're going to kill me, and you haven't got the guts to admit it."

Her bare foot came in contact with a thick patch of butter and onion, and her feet shot out from under her so suddenly that she was flat on the floor before she knew it, and Johnny Winterhawk was coming down on top of her.

He managed to break his fall a little, letting go her wrist to land with a hand at each side of her head, but still his body was full-length along hers, and suddenly Smith was breathless with panic. She said huskily, "Get away from me!"

"Stop it," Johnny Winterhawk answered her, in the same low voice as before. She tried to twist away from him, then stopped on a hiss of pain.

Her long hair was tangled all around her, and fanned out on the floor under his hands; she could not move her head without tearing it. She gritted her teeth.

"Will you please get off me?" she demanded with a forced calm she wasn't feeling. "You're pulling my hair."

Johnny Winterhawk raised a hand to straighten her hair, lifting the long silky amber strands away from her eyes and face. His strong fingers were gentle and soothing along her cheeks and forehead, and across her just-parted lips. His dark eyes looked deep into hers as her breath shuddered in her throat.

Then it was not his fingers but his thumb that was against her lips, and his touch was no longer gentle. Shulamith's pulse began to pound in her temples. She swallowed convulsively, then her lips parted again, and she heard her own breath enter between them. She waited, watching him, hypnotized by the dark flame in his eyes, as certain as if it were written in letters of fire that Johnny Winterhawk wanted to fight the compelling magnetism that was alive between them, that he was trying to force himself to let her go. But he could not.

"Dammit," Johnny Winterhawk breathed hoarsely, and his mouth came down and covered hers.

Smith closed her eyes to reeling darkness, and her small competent hand closed convulsively against his chest into the thick warmth of his sweater. Suddenly the kiss was all she had ever wanted out of life, and the small involuntary moan of need she heard came from her own throat.

The sound of it seemed to ignite something in him. Johnny Winterhawk's body leaped against hers, and he gathered her to him, his arm sliding under her head and his hand clenching tightly around her upper arm.

His fingers burned the side of her breast, and suddenly every inch of her skin was electrically alive. She wrapped her arm up around his neck and clung to him as his tongue pushed deeper and deeper into the soft warmth of her mouth.

When he lifted his lips at last her head fell back over his supporting arm, as, like an animal, she bared her neck to him in instinctive surrender. She felt his breath against the soft hollow of her throat, and her body leaped in response in a small, expectant spasm.

Johnny Winterhawk groaned as his lips pressed against her; and then suddenly and without warning he let her go, rolling away from her and sitting up. Smith shivered with the sudden cold that enveloped her.

"Are you a witch?" He was shaking his head as if to clear it, his arms on his drawn-up knees, his breathing deep and unsteady. "What the hell are you doing to me?"

Fear washed over her. Smith frantically scrambled to sit and then to stand up. She had forgotten who she was, where she was, she had forgotten everything. She looked down at Johnny Winterhawk's dark form in sheer terror. She had never reacted to a man like that in her life.

She wanted to run, but her feet were coated with butter. So were the clothes she was wearing, and so were Johnny Winterhawk's. On the tile floor she could hardly move.

"All right, don't panic," said Johnny Winterhawk in a deep, flat voice. He stood up, and Smith gazed at him accusingly, unable to speak.

"It won't happen again," he said in answer to the look. "I am not going to seduce you, and I am not going to rape you." He heaved a breath and ran a hand through one thick black wing of hair. His carved lips widened in a half smile, and Smith sighed as she involuntarily relaxed. But she did not return the smile. She had not forgotten, if he had, that *she* had not been the one to pull back from what was happening. She had never felt so threatened in her life.

CHAPTER SIX

"WHAT WOULD YOU have done today, ordinarily?" Smith asked as they finished their meal. It was evident that Johnny Winterhawk could cook more than scrambled eggs. Each mouthful of salmon she had eaten had seemed to melt into nectar on her tongue, and the spiced sauce he had served with it went to her blood like wine.

Smith's long hair was still wet from her shower, and she was wearing a Chinese robe in deep blue silk that was decorated with the most exquisite embroidery she had ever seen, in the shape of a glittering turquoise, green and purple dragon who breathed marvelous fire. Winterhawk had brought the robe, obviously a woman's, to her bedroom an hour ago, and ever since Shulamith had been wondering about the woman who had left it here. He had also given her a pair of corduroy trousers and a couple of shirts that just as obviously were his own, and she was wondering why he hadn't given her more of his friend's clothing instead. Judging by the robe, her clothes would fit Smith better than his did.

Winterhawk pushed his plate away and leaned back. "If you weren't here?" he asked with a faint smile that lit his dark eyes. Smith nodded and then winced as the elastic she had used to hold up the heavy twist of her wet hair pulled uncomfortably on her scalp.

"Because of the commission hearings I would probably have worked most of the day anyway. But ordinarily on the weekends I go canoeing or fishing or oyster digging with Wilfred Tall Tree."

Smith smiled at the name. "Who is Wilfred Tall Tree?" she asked.

"My only neighbor on the island," Winterhawk said. "He's an artist—a woodcarver—and he also keeps us supplied with fish and oysters. He's a very old man, a Chopa. He teaches me the old ways. You'll meet Wilf tomorrow, if he gets back. He took the canoe over to Oyster Island for a few days."

"Are there only the two of you living on the whole island?" She picked up the pot and poured two cups of coffee.

"It's not a very big island," he said.

"Canoeing," Smith repeated reflectively. "Does he prefer a canoe to an ordinary motorboat?"

Winterhawk took a sip of coffee and slowly replaced the cup in the saucer, regarding her steadily. "Have you ever handled a canoe?" he asked.

"No," she said quickly. She hadn't been subtle enough, and she thought it would be better now if Johnny Winterhawk didn't know about the time she had spent at summer camp. She wasn't sure how much she remembered of what she had learned about canoeing, but perhaps it would be enough.

He said, "Canoeing can be dangerous, especially in these waters. If you take Wilfred Tall Tree's canoe and try to make a run for it you can expect to end up drowned—unless you are very expert indeed."

Smith looked indignant. "I wasn't—"

He interrupted her. "Yes, you were," he said. He gave vent to a little laugh. "If ever I saw anyone who didn't know when to quit, you're it." His tone was exasperated but admiring, and Smith felt like a child being praised. She could not help a little delighted laugh escaping her.

"Well, why should I make life easy for you?" she pointed out.

"Why indeed?" He was so reasonable it was impossible to hate him. "But don't take Wilf's canoe. You couldn't handle it on your own in these waters."

Later that night in her room, she felt the silence of the place descend around her, and realized how impossibly alone and helpless she was. Johnny Winterhawk could do anything he wanted to her here, and no one would ever know. Lying in the dark, with moonlight streaming in through the large window, she was suddenly assailed with fear again. Somehow tonight, in his presence, fear had left her. But alone now, she felt the weight of her situation fall on her.

She slept fitfully, her sleep troubled with dark dreams in which Johnny Winterhawk was sometimes her enemy, sometimes her friend. By the time dawn had turned the sky blue, she knew she wouldn't sleep anymore.

Smith got up quietly and dressed in the clothes he had given her last night, rolling up the pant legs and shirt sleeves, and feeling like an undersized orphan as she did so. The wooden floor was cool on her bare feet, and if Johnny Winterhawk expected her to stay here for very long, he was going to have to come up with a proper wardrobe for her. She needed shoes.

The house was completely silent when she opened the bedroom door, and when a thin dark figure rose unexpectedly at her feet Shulamith screamed.

"Well, she can scream, anyway," said a dry, crackly voice to no one in particular, and Smith immediately calmed.

"Wilfred Tall Tree," she guessed aloud.

He was short and wiry, his bones and his long thin muscles very evident under the aging brown skin. His white hair was thick and hung down his back, and his dark, deep eyes sparkled with amusement as he looked at her.

"She knows things, too!" he remarked appreciatively, and his eyebrows went comically up and down in the brown lined forehead.

Smith felt a little off balance, not sure whether she was in the presence of a saint or a fool. "Do you always speak in the third person?" she asked, half amused, half irritated.

The old man looked behind him over both shoulders, and then shrugged in broadly drawn mystification. "Third person?" he asked stupidly, but she knew suddenly that he was not at all stupid, and that he was poking fun at her. She decided to try a little sauce for the gander.

"He thinks he's very funny," she said to the air, and was rewarded by the sound of Wilfred Tall Tree's delighted cackle.

"Is he?" he asked, his bright bird's eyes fixing her.

"Doesn't he know?" she countered, leaning against the doorframe and crossing her arms.

"When I laugh at my own jokes I'm not sure," he

confessed in a throaty confidential whisper. "If someone else laughed at me I'd probably think I was a pretty funny man."

She couldn't somehow pinpoint his character; he seemed to be in a constant state of change. She looked down at the sleeping mat across her doorway. "Are you my watchdog?" she asked.

"A *dog*! Am I a dog?" he repeated, again with a look of arrested interest on his face, as though she had asked a question of profound philosophical import. "Well, sometimes I'm a dog; I've been called a dog." He looked down at himself in surprise, holding out his arms and, one after the other, his feet for a better view. "I didn't think I was a dog right now. But maybe I am." His eyebrows were going up and down again as he looked at her, and again Smith was sure that he was making fun of her, that he wasn't in the least crazy.

"Am I allowed to go to the kitchen and make myself a cup of coffee?" she asked, pointedly ignoring his last remarks.

"She's asking a dog for permission!" the old man marveled. "I must be a very dangerous-looking dog. Usually I'm a friendly mongrel, but today perhaps I'm a Doberman pinscher!"

He was having the oddest effect on her: she began to feel as though *she* was the foolish one and he was making perfect sense. With a small exasperated exclamation she stepped across the sleeping mat at her feet and started off in the direction of the kitchen.

Wilfred Tall Tree followed her, his bare feet as silent as her own on the wooden flooring. He was dressed neatly and casually in a pair of denim trousers and a long-sleeved cotton shirt; she realized with a start that except for the long mane of white hair, the old man was absolutely unremarkable. Until you looked into his eyes.

She deliberately went by way of the large open balcony, although she had yesterday been shown that there was also a closed passageway leading to the kitchen, and when she got into the fresh morning air she paused. The sky was a clear, cloudless blue, and the only sounds were birdsong, the water breaking on rock far below and intermittently, if she listened closely, the wind in the trees.

Smith breathed deeply and stretched in the pleasure of the cool morning, aware that Wilfred Tall Tree had stopped beside her.

"Why *do* you speak in the third person?" she asked, and he winked at her conspiratorially.

"That's the way to get to talk to a wild animal," he said. "Never talk directly to a wild animal until he's talked to you first: they're very snobby, especially squirrels. Birds, too, sometimes. Some of them, like deer, are just shy. They get embarrassed if they think you're looking at them. So what you do, you find yourself a nice interesting rock, or maybe a tree, someone who knows how to keep up his end of a conversation, and you talk to him. It's very hard for an animal to resist eavesdropping when someone is talking about him. Then of course once he's interested it's only good manners for him to come and sit down and join in the conversation."

Smith remembered the way she had calmed down earlier when he spoke, and she looked at the old man in curious annoyance. She could almost imagine him deep in conversation with a rock, with wild animals all around. After a moment she continued on to the kitchen, wondering if he had told her the truth or had merely been laughing at her again.

"Would you like coffee, Mr. Tall Tree?" she asked as she filled the small coffee maker. Behind her the hoarse chuckle sounded again.

"Mr. Tall Tree!" he repeated in respectful admiration. "Good, that's *very* good. You don't like someone, you talk politely and offer him coffee, eh? That's pretty smart."

There was no mockery evident in his voice this time, but she knew it was there. When she turned to face him his look was all open interest. Smith set two cups down on the counter and took an infuriated breath.

"Well, what would you like me to call you?" she demanded. He had hit close enough to the truth to make her angry: she realized that she had unconsciously hoped to disarm him with her polite conventionalities.

The black, black eyes opened wide, and the eyebrows went up and then down. "This is very confusing for a crazy old man who's also a dog," he reproached her. "First when you're angry you smile and get very polite, and now suddenly when you're angry you bash the cups around and your voice gets very sharp. How can I learn the rules of good social behavior if you keep changing them?"

Smith had never in her life felt so close to losing all control. She was completely off balance. She wanted to scream. She glared at the old man, who had sat in a chair by the table and was watching her. Perhaps he was crazy after all.

"My friends call me Wilf," he said with a broad smile, "but since you don't feel very friendly toward me you can call me Wilfred. That's formal enough for a watchdog, eh?" He laughed loudly and slapped his thigh. "Even a Doberman pinscher!" His raspy, cackling laugh deepened till his whole body shook with it.

"Good morning," Johnny Winterhawk said close behind her, making her jump. "Morning, Wilf." He was wearing a gray suit and a white shirt, but no tie. He looked very different from the tousled, tired abductor of the day before. "Is there enough coffee in there for three?" he asked her, eyeing the dark liquid trickling through the filter.

The old man, wiping his eyes, finally stopped laughing. "Good morning, Johnny!" he caroled; a last little hiccup of laughter escaped him.

Automatically Smith reached into the cupboard for another cup. She was nervous around Johnny Winterhawk this morning; she could vividly remember his voice saying, "Dammit," and the way he had kissed her.

"Have you two introduced yourselves?" Johnny asked, pulling out a tray and setting the sugar bowl on it. He moved to the refrigerator. He seemed to have no special awareness of her now.

"She introduced *me*," said Wilfred Tall Tree, "I'm Wilfred Tall Tree, a dog. But I didn't introduce her yet."

Johnny Winterhawk smiled slowly and glanced to Smith with a speculative look.

Smith gritted her teeth. "He was sleeping across my doorway!" she explained sharply. "I asked him if he was my watchdog! And he's been laughing about it ever since!"

Wilfred Tall Tree slapped his thigh again. "That's right, Johnny!" he called.

"And you told me the way you talked to me was the way to talk to wild animals," she reminded him with a flashing look, "so I think as far as insults go we can call ourselves even."

Johnny Winterhawk was laughing, his square, white teeth flashing against his dusky skin, and it was like a sudden breath of normalcy blowing across the odd confusion of her mind. Smith shook her head and laughed, too. Was it something about the old man that had made her so strangely irritable, or was it just the pressure of the whole situation?

Curiously, she eyed the old man, who was laughing with them more uproariously than ever.

"Wilf, allow me to introduce Miss St. John, whose first name I don't know. This, as you've guessed, Miss St. John, is Wilf Tall Tree."

"We've met," she said dryly, and all three of them laughed. "Everybody calls me Smith," she said. "My real name is Shulamith, but nobody calls me that."

Picking up the tray with the coffee things on it, Winterhawk crossed to the table where Wilf was sitting against a backdrop of sky and trees and the breathtaking rocky gorge. Smith followed.

"Shulamith," Winterhawk repeated slowly. "That's an interesting name. Where does it come from?" His forehead was wrinkled as though he were trying to catch an elusive memory.

"From the Bible, the *Song of Songs*," Smith said. "The quote is, '*Come back, come back, O Shulamite.*' Some people think it means 'maid of Shunam', but my mother believed it came from the Hebrew word for peace."

"Peaceable Woman," Wilfred Tall Tree said suddenly, and then something that sounded like *nalohka'am gah*.

"What did you say?" asked Smith.

He repeated the words, but this time it sounded like *nalohga'am kah*.

"What does it mean?"

"Young woman of peace," said Wilfred Tall Tree. "That is how we would translate your name into the Chopit language."

Stirring her coffee, Smith tried to repeat the name, but she couldn't get her tongue around the sound that sometimes seemed to be *k* and sometimes *g*. Suppressing the suspicion that Wilfred was laughing at her again, she gave up the attempt with a smile.

"I think I'll stick with Smith," she said. "It's easier to pronounce."

Johnny Winterhawk finished his coffee and stood up. "I'm going into the city," he told Smith. "I've asked Wilf to keep an eye on you."

"I suppose that means he won't let me out of his sight all day." Smith turned to Wilfred Tall Tree in renewed irritation.

He looked at her from twinkling dark eyes. "Maybe," he said. "But maybe you won't notice me all the time."

"I hate the idea of being watched," she said flatly, "and I'll hate it no matter how quietly you creep around after me."

The old man winked and said nothing.

"I'll be back by six," said Johnny Winterhawk. "Try not to come to blows with Wilf, will you, Peaceable Woman?"

"Are you going to Vancouver?" Smith asked abruptly.

He looked at her. "Yes," he said, after a pause.

Smith extended a slim bare foot from under a rolled-up cuff. "I need a pair of shoes," she said. "Size six and a half. Preferably sneakers."

"I'll see what I can do," said Johnny Winterhawk.

"In the meantime," Smith persisted, "do you have anything that would fit me for today?"

Winterhawk smiled. "Do I look as though I have a pair of shoes that would fit you?"

Smith looked at him from under lowered lashes. "I thought the lady of the dragon robe might have left something more behind," she said.

Johnny Winterhawk didn't rise to the bait. "Did you now?" he said dryly. "Well, I'm afraid not. But perhaps if you behave Wilf will show you how to make yourself a pair of moccasins."

Smith glared. "No, thanks," she said, not sure why she was angry suddenly. "I've no intention of chewing hide for a week before I take a walk!"

There was a momentary pause while she realized how unforgivably rude that was.

"Oh, I think the leather is already cured, isn't it, Wilf?" Johnny Winterhawk said, his voice deceptively soft. "And now that I think of it, it might do you good to perform a primitive labor to fulfill your own needs. If you want shoes, make them. It'll be a lesson in basic economics."

Smith sputtered.

"Not to mention diplomacy. For example, I advise you to be polite to Wilf, if you want the benefit of his expertise."

"Go to hell!" snapped Smith, finding her voice.

The air was crackling with their suppressed anger as turquoise eyes stared into black ones. Smith could not understand what had made her so angry so quickly.

"Not me," he said.

Wilfred Tall Tree was watching them from shining dark eyes, saying nothing.

"There's one good thing about this," Smith said coldly. "When I finally do get away from you—and believe me, I'll get away—when I finally get you in a courtroom, they'll be sentencing you for torture as well as kidnapping. I bet that'll get you a nice long sentence."

"Of course," Johnny Winterhawk agreed. "But then, you could get me a nice long sentence by telling the judge I'd spit on the sidewalk. I could rape you every day for a year or take you home tomorrow, and I'd still get the same nice long sentence." He looked down at her. "I still haven't decided which course to take, so be a good girl and make a pretty pair of moccasins with Wilf."

He turned and was gone. A minute later they saw him from the other window, running lightly down the rock steps. Smith watched without moving until he had disappeared into the trees. She was trembling with a rage so strong that the coffee was making waves in her cup. She stood up.

"I want a pair of shoes," she declared flatly to Wilfred Tall Tree. His steady gaze disconcerted her, but she forced herself to stare back at him. "If you're going to be tailing me, you might as well start now." She strode across the wide kitchen, not waiting to see if Wilfred Tall Tree followed her.

Johnny Winterhawk's bedroom was at the top of both house and cliff, on the highest point of the island. It was as much like a watchtower as she could imagine: from here he looked out over his whole domain. A broad central panel in each wall was cedar; the rest was glass. The bed abutted on one panel; two others appeared to be closets; the one in the fourth wall held the door she had come in by.

She had virtually an unrestricted view of the island, and she gazed around in startled wonder. The flat roofs of the other rooms fell away from her like terraces down the cliffside, swallowed up at the bottom by the various greens of the rain forest. From the opposite wall through the trees, she could see the length of the island, ship-shaped, stretching more than half a mile out into the sea. The small promontory of land on which this room sat had been partially cleared to form a small shady area that was more inviting than any place Smith had ever seen. With a sense of fighting against hypnosis Smith closed her eyes and turned away. She crossed at random to one of the two closets in the side walls and opened it to the wafting scent of cedar and the sight of an array of masculine clothes.

Under Wilfred Tall Tree's bemused eyes she pulled out a pair of white canvas sneakers and slid a bare foot easily into one. She grimaced. Even with several pairs of socks the shoes would be too big. Smith looked helplessly at the other shoes on the floor of the closet. Nothing here would do.

"Oh, *damn*!" she exploded. A feeling of utter helplessness swamped her, one which she had been holding at bay ever since she had been awakened by the noises from her father's bedroom. Bursting into tears, Smith sank down to her knees on the floor in the closet doorway. She buried her face in her hands, unable to control the loud sobs that escaped her.

Wilfred Tall Tree walked slowly across the room and stopped near her. "She's angry," he explained, apparently to the closet door. "The world isn't exactly the way she wants it."

CHAPTER SEVEN

"In Vancouver today, the British Columbia Court of Appeal upheld a provincial Supreme Court decision not to grant a temporary injunction against St. John Forest Products to prevent logging operations in the Cat Bite Valley area."

It was the top story on the one o'clock news, and Smith dropped the soft golden deerskin she was working on with a little start and turned her eyes to the radio. Across the room she sensed rather than saw Wilfred Tall Tree stiffen into a like attentiveness.

"Madam Justice Jennifer MacFarlane read the majority decision at noon today to a courtroom packed with members of the Chopa band, who brought the appeal, and representatives of wildlife foundations and other groups who support the band. Chief Joseph Three Elk spoke to reporters outside the courtroom."

A startlingly deep and gravelly voice said, "No, we are not surprised. The native peoples of Canada are no longer surprised by the justice of the white man's court. It is not we Indians but white men who are naive about white man's justice. You, for example, are here to report on news. Your unquestioning acceptance of Canadian justice has blinded you to the fact that this is not news. This is the same old story. It would have been *news* if the courts had given the Chopa people true justice.''

So, St. John Forest Products was still legally entitled to begin cutting operations in Cat Bite Valley. Johnny Winterhawk was right. Smith was surprised to feel anger burning in the pit of her stomach. Chief Joseph Three Elk was right, too. She was naive about her country's dispensation of justice: she had expected the injunction to be granted. She glanced over at Wilfred Tall Tree, who had returned to the carving of the elaborate mask on his worktable.

''I suppose the chain saws went in at five minutes after noon,'' she said bitterly, just as if she herself were not a part of St. John Forest Products.

''Meanwhile—'' the announcer's voice called back her attention ''—the Cartier Commission on the Chopa land claim opened public hearings today in Vancouver....''

Smith shook her head unbelievingly. ''It's like a game,'' she said. ''They're all pretending.'' She hadn't wanted to believe it when Johnny had told her. But she had to believe this. ''My father is no fool. He'll have had the logging crews standing by since last night. They'd have been radioed to go in as soon as....'' She paused, staring at Wilfred Tall Tree, her eyes widening in surprise.

''But my father's in the hospital!'' she remembered suddenly. ''And they might be afraid to make a decision like that without him.... That would have to be Rolly's decision.'' Rolly was her father's vice-president of operations. He had what her father called ''a business-school mentality.'' By that he meant someone without his own high degree of decisive ruthlessness. With a sudden certainty Smith knew it would take Rolly at least a day to issue any order to send chain saws into Cat Bite, and then he would congratulate himself on the speed of his response. Or he might even wait to talk to her father, and if Cord St. John was too weak for visitors....

She had the power to set things right. In her father's absence she had the right to give the orders. *She* could see justice done.

Smith waited till the weather and sports reports were over and music had begun to play again, waited in an agony of tension that she fought to disguise while she threaded the soft leather lace through the tiny holes in the toe of one half-finished moccasin. Then casually she laid it aside and stood up.

"I'm hungry," she said to Wilf. "All right if I go up to the house and make lunch?"

In the end, the prospect of not having anything to do had made Smith give in and ask to make a pair of moccasins. She could not bear the thought of being cooped up in the house for even a day. She wanted to explore the island, to find a means of escape. And she was too used to hard work to enjoy enforced idleness.

Wilfred Tall Tree had brought her down to the studio workshop that was attached to his cabin, where he spent much of his time carving ritual masks. The examples of his work that hung on the walls were almost unbelievably beautiful, and Smith had looked at Wilfred Tall Tree with a new respect.

Now he raised his head and fixed her with a deep, luminous gaze.

"Sure," he said. She could not be certain whether or

not he suspected her reason for wanting to go to the
house alone.

The cabin was out of sight of the house, and vice
versa, situated as it was down on the eastern shore of the
island. The path was rough and hard and in places nonexistent, but by going slowly Smith had negotiated it
without damage to her feet. Now she wanted to run, but
a stubbed toe and a few sharp pebbles convinced her
that was impossible.

The door to Johnny Winterhawk's study was locked.
Smith thumped experimentally against it with her hip:
she would not be able to break it down. She could not
avoid stepping on a board that creaked just in front of
the door; and she wondered if it had been put there
deliberately. She ran to the kitchen, keeping an eye out
for Wilfred Tall Tree through the windows. From the
cutlery drawer she extracted the largest knife she could
find and ran like the wind back along hall and staircase
and balcony to the study once more.

The door was locked because there was a telephone in
Johnny Winterhawk's study. With all her strength
Smith jammed the huge knife between door and jamb
and tried to force the lock.

On the third try it gave, and the door swung back
around to the wall with a crash like thunder. With a
guilty start she looked out the hall window toward the
path to Wilf's cabin. Through the trees she spied movement.

Wings on her feet, she pushed the lock catch, pulled
the study door shut, snatched up the knife from the
floor where it had fallen and dashed back to the kitchen
with a speed that made her dizzy. When Wilfred Tall

Tree entered the kitchen, Smith was busily slicing a tomato for a salad.

She could not get away from him all afternoon. If he had slipped once, in letting her come up to the house alone, he did not intend to slip again. Eventually she was forced—by sheer boredom—to go back down to his cabin after lunch and finish her moccasins.

Now she worked harder and faster than she had before. Having something on her feet would give her far greater mobility if Wilfred Tall Tree were ever to let her out of his sight again.

Shortly after five o'clock she looked at the pair of golden deerskin moccasins with more pride than she would have imagined possible in her handiwork. As a child she had always enjoyed handicrafts, she remembered. At summer camp each year her work had taken prizes. She had dutifully written to her father about them, and he had usually praised her, but he had never come to see for himself on parents' day. He had always been too busy.

"Finished!" she announced matter-of-factly to Wilfred Tall Tree, hiding her odd little burst of pride at having made something as pretty as the delicate moccasins she was holding up for his approval.

He smiled at her, his dark eyes piercing hers, and nodded his head. "Very good," he said softly. "You work well with your hands."

It was as though he had recognized that small pride she hid, and uncomfortably Smith looked away. "I hope they fit!" she muttered self-deprecatingly and bent to slip them on her bare feet. She lifted one moccasin-clad foot with a casual air. "Perfect!" she said to Wilf with a smile. "And just in time to go and make dinner."

A few minutes later she was at the house, breathless and panting, having run all the way. Almost sobbing with exertion, she ran up through the house to Johnny Winterhawk's study, slammed the door behind her and ran to pick up the radio-telephone.

It took an age to raise the operator, but at last her number was ringing. Smith glanced at her wrist out of habit: her watch was on her dressing table at home. She bounced impatiently. Did Rolly leave the office at five or five-thirty?

It wasn't easy to talk on a radio-telephone, but at last the switchboard operator at St. John Forest Products connected her to Rolly's office. A male voice answered the phone.

"Rolly?" she said in a high urgent tone that wasn't at all like her normal voice. "Rolly, is that you? This—"

And then, as though she were in a recurring nightmare, she saw a dark lean hand reach from behind her to cut the connection.

Smith gasped and whirled to face the hard angry stare of Johnny Winterhawk. Without a word, he took the receiver from her hand and replaced it on the hook, his body uncomfortably and threateningly near. Then he lifted his hand and grasped Smith's arm above the elbow.

"Come on," said Johnny Winterhawk shortly. "You're going home."

NEVER IN HER LIFE had she sensed such tightly controlled haste in another person. Johnny Winterhawk walked quickly beside her down the rock staircase and the path, his hand on her wrist, shortening his steps to match hers. But there was a boiling urgency just under the surface, an awful tension that made her feel like a cripple being led away from disaster by a healthy person.

He wanted to run. He wanted to be exerting the utmost effort, as though in the face of the greatest danger. His urgency filled Smith and turned to fear and then to nameless dread inside her.

She broke into a half run, and beside her, without comment, Johnny Winterhawk lengthened his stride to match.

"What is it?" she asked breathlessly. "Johnny, what's wrong?" The feeling of being united in danger let her use his first name without either of them noticing.

"Not now," he returned briefly.

They were both running by the time they reached the dock, where *Outcast II*, engines idling, was tied to the dock only by the painter.

"Get aboard!" Johnny shouted, running to untie the rope, and Smith leaned out to grasp the chrome-plated rail and pulled the *Outcast II* back close enough to the wooden dock to allow her to jump in.

Johnny Winterhawk followed her immediately and ran to the wheel. He reversed till they cleared the dock, then rammed the engines into forward and swung the big boat around to the east.

Smith sank onto a seat and looked at him, her heart beating more with trepidation than exertion. When he had cleared the eastern shore of his island and adjusted his course to northeast, she said, "It's my father, isn't it? My father is dying."

"No," he said.

"Or dead," she prompted, feeling the tears press up in her throat and the back of her eyes.

"No," he repeated shortly, then turned his dark gaze onto her stricken face. "As far as I know," he added, "your father is still recovering."

"Then why are you taking me home? What's changed?" she asked, not sure whether to believe him or not.

Johnny looked at her with an oddly speculative look, then returned his gaze to the dark water ahead. He bent to look at the speedometer, then pushed the throttle, wanting more speed, but it was already as far forward as it could go.

Fear crept from its hiding place in her mind and settled in her stomach, a horrid deadweight that made her ill.

"You. . .you are taking me home, aren't you?" she stammered. The water in the strait between Vancouver Island and the mainland was cold and deep. She looked down at the golden moccasin on one foot, soft and bright in its newness, and pictured it washed up on a pebbly beach somewhere, sodden and gray.

If she had read about it in the safety of her bed at night it would have been hard for her to believe that someone like Johnny Winterhawk would kill anyone, especially someone he had talked to and laughed with. . .and kissed passionately the day before. He seemed so sane and warm and real, and in spite of what was happening she had instinctively trusted him. If she had been reading all this, she would not have believed that trust could so easily turn to growing fear and mistrust.

But what did she really know about him? Nothing. Nothing. . . except that her presence was a threat to him. Except that she would have virtually the power of life and death over him if he set her free. There was no capital punishment in Canada, but the sentence for kidnapping would be a long one. And she could imagine that for a man like Johnny Winterhawk—for anyone— life behind those cold stone walls would be death in life. Worse, much worse. Her imagination could not compass it.

It was the deep, unconscious realization that she herself would do nearly anything rather than go to a life like that was the root now of her fear of Johnny Winterhawk.

"Yes, I'm taking you home," Johnny Winterhawk replied, and his jaw tightened. "I've done some stupid things in my time, but nothing I've done compares with the monumentally self-destructive idiocy of kidnapping you in the first place." He looked at her. "Well, I'll have a long time to think about it, no doubt."

Smith swallowed against the hope that was flowering up inside her. "I promise I won't say anything," she said softly, standing up and crossing to where he stood at the wheel. She laid a tentative hand on his arm. "Truly, I promise," she repeated. "You haven't hurt me, Johnny. I—I couldn't send you to prison."

His glance found hers and locked with it. He bent and brushed her lips lightly with his own, and a soft, melting warmth flowed through her. "Thank you," he said. "Your father is a strong, ruthless man even in a hospital bed, and he might inspire the police to be very tough with you. If you do decide to press charges against me,

Peaceable Woman, I'll deny everything.'' His dark eyes gazed into hers. "I'll be calling you a liar. There'll be no evidence to corroborate your testimony. I'll do my best to make you look like a woman with rape fantasies.'' He smiled apologetically at her. She knew he was warning her, trying to prepare her for the ugliness that he foresaw. Smith blinked against the unexpected tears that burned her eyelids. His eyes were full of concern for her, and it had caught her off guard. She swallowed and stared helplessly into the depths of those eyes.

Without warning the odd, compelling force was between them again, making her muscles weak till she felt that her whole being burned into his through her wide eyes. Johnny Winterhawk muttered a curse and turned away, as, with a barely perceptible unsteadiness, his hand moved out to the switch of the portable radio on the seat behind him. The voice of the news announcer filled the air of the cockpit.

"...police, who were at his hospital bedside when the call came. Shulamith St. John has been missing since early yesterday morning. Police refused to comment on whether the ransom demand would be met.''

Smith stood at shocked attention, gazing at the radio. "*Ransom demand!*" she repeated. "Who...but....''

"Find another station!" Johnny Winterhawk commanded, and with fumbling obedience her fingers spun the dial to CBC.

The national newscast, unlike the local one, had led with a political story, which was just finishing. Then, "In Vancouver this evening, a startling development has apparently confirmed that Shulamith St. John, who had been missing since the early hours of Sunday morning, has been kidnapped; and has linked the kidnapping with the battle being waged by the Chopa Indian band against Cordwainer St. John, her lumber-baron father. Mr. St. John, who suffered a heart attack early Sunday at the time of his daughter's disappearance, received a phone call at his bed in the Royal Columbia Hospital today, demanding that he call off plans to begin lumbering operations in Cat Bite Valley and the surrounding area, as the price of his daughter's safe return.

"The Chopa band's court appeal for a temporary injunction against lumbering in the area, which is considered their traditional hunting and fishing grounds and which is the subject of an inquiry by the federal government, was turned down by the British Columbia Court of Appeal earlier today. Two officers of the Royal Canadian Mounted Police were at his bedside when the kidnapper phoned St. John.

"Mr. St. John was unavailable for comment."

Johnny Winterhawk cursed softly and steadily, his low voice pulled tight against violent anger. Smith stared at him. "How—" she began, but he cut her off.

"Too late," he said, and swore again.

Smith sat motionless, gazing at him. Behind his head, in the distance, the skyline of Vancouver was silhouetted against Grouse Mountain. As she gazed, Johnny Winterhawk turned back to the wheel, and the city, dead ahead of them, slipped slowly around the starboard bow, and then, slowly, to the stern. Vancouver was behind them in a moment, and with the late-afternoon sun in her eyes, Smith knew they were facing back in the direction of Johnny Winterhawk's island.

With a protesting cry she jerked her head around and

saw the city beginning to recede in the distance. Her hands tightened into fists, and she squeezed her eyes shut, then opened them and ran to Johnny Winter-hawk's gray-clad figure at the wheel.

"What are you doing?" she asked, though somewhere in her being she understood that the radio broadcast had changed her life. "Where are you taking me? We were nearly there!"

His eyes were haunted. He looked at her as though she were someone in his nightmare. "I'm sorry," said Johnny hoarsely. "I wasn't quick enough. I should have hired a helicopter, but I didn't think they'd act so fast."

"But why.... Take me home, Johnny! Take me home now and.... Why is it so important? I'll say it isn't true!"

The wheel did not move under his fingers, and the big boat slapped steadily through the waves toward the southwest. Johnny Winterhawk said nothing, just stood and watched the waves, his brow furrowed, his dark eyes squinting against the sun.

"Please, Johnny, I—" she was beginning, when he interrupted her in a flat, calculating tone.

"When I found you in my study you were phoning someone. Who?"

"Oh!" Funny, she had forgotten. And now it seemed as though an age had passed since then. She gave an incredulous little laugh. "I was calling Rolly Middleton, my father's vice-president of operations. It's a stupid title, really, because my father still runs everything. And Rolly—"

"Did you get through?" he interrupted.

"Only for a second. Then you—"

"What did you tell him?"

"I didn't tell him anything! You were there before I had a—" Smith broke off, biting her lip. What a fool she was. She should have said she'd told Rolly everything.

"Did you tell him who was calling?"

"I. . .no." Hadn't he heard anything of what she was saying before he cut her off?

"Would he have recognized your voice?"

Oh, God, what was the right thing to say? If he thought Rolly had recognized her voice, would he keep her safe, or kill her? Could the phone call be traced?

"Yes," she said breathlessly at last, with a certainty she did not feel. "Yes, I'm sure he would have recognized my—"

Johnny Winterhawk interrupted again. "Is he your lover?"

Smith choked. "Is he *what*?"

"Your lover," Johnny repeated, his voice unaccountably rough. "You called him when you could have called the police, and you're sure he recognized your voice." He looked at her from hooded hawklike eyes. "And he has a sinecure in your father's business."

It was no sinecure; her father was not the man to suffer fools for any reason. Rolly was simply very, very different from her father and therefore sometimes despised by him. He was also forty-three years old, and his wife had just had twins.

"No," Smith replied after a moment. Her mind was a jumble of thoughts. Johnny Winterhawk was right: she could more easily have called the police than Rolly. She was aghast now, to think that she had broken into his office, not to call for rescue, but to try to save Cat Bite Valley from her father's chain saws! What on earth had possessed her? What had she been thinking of?

"No," she repeated slowly, "he isn't my lover. I was calling him because with my father in the hospital, it would be his decision to send a logging team into Cat Bite. I was calling to... to tell him not to."

Johnny Winterhawk went suddenly still, as though his whole body were listening for some distant sound. He turned to look at her with eyes that riveted her.

"Why?" he asked after a long moment during which she forgot to breathe.

"We heard on the news that they wouldn't grant you an injunction, and I—I thought I could try to delay cutting until the commission reports." She took a deep breath, still feeling threatened by her own foolishness. "Rolly doesn't like making decisions—not that kind. I knew he'd be grateful if someone took the responsibility."

Johnny Winterhawk wasn't saying anything, he was just looking at her. "My father won't give in to that demand," she whispered urgently, indicating the radio with a hand. "He hates anything like that—blackmail or ransom. He hates anyone telling him what to do. He'll tell you to kill me and be damned."

Johnny Winterhawk's gaze was steady, his voice firm. "I doubt that," he said.

"You don't know him," she persisted. "Please don't take me back to your island. What difference does this ransom demand make? I can stop the cutting more easily if you let me go, I swear."

"I'm sorry, Peaceable Woman," Johnny Winterhawk said, as, away in the distance, she saw the small dark shape that was the island. "But an hour ago there was no evidence to corroborate your story if you told it. It would have been only your word against mine. Now the hotheads who decided on this course of action have given you all the corroboration you could want."

"I would deny it all," she said with emphasis. "Why can't you believe that? My father couldn't browbeat me."

He smiled and shook his head. "You're an innocent," he said. "You have no idea of what they would do to you to get that information. Believe me, this is not the time for me to let you go."

"When will it be the time?" she demanded harshly.

"I don't know," said Johnny Winterhawk. "But I'll find a time and a way to let you go, Peaceable Woman. You've got my word."

Smith snorted. "Your word!" she snapped. "What good is your word when you obviously can't even keep your cohorts in line? You knew they were going to pull this today, and all you could do was try to forestall them! You couldn't *stop* them, could you? That's obvious. What good is your word going to do me when my father starts cutting down trees in Cat Bite Valley? And he will, as sure as you're standing there, Mr. Winterhawk, because, I told you before, my father doesn't care about me! He will certainly care one hell of a lot less about my life than he will about giving in to terrorism! That's a principle, you see!" Her voice was growling with emotion and sounded deep and unnatural. "What good is your *word* going to do me when your friends decide to deep-six me in revenge for their lost hunting grounds?"

His hand closed around her wrist, and he snapped her close to him so that her breast was pressed against the muscle of his upper arm and her thigh brushed his. When she looked up at his profile, his jaw muscles were tensed.

"My friends are fools, but they are not murderers," he said quietly, watching the water. "No one is going to 'deep-six' you, no matter how many spy novels tell you otherwise. Please try not to panic, Miss St. John. I'll take you home as soon as possible, whether you think my word is good or not."

His calm voice and the touch of his body were soothing the frightened animal in her; involuntarily Smith heaved a sigh and her breathing calmed. She was conscious of a strong desire to bury her face against his chest and howl out all the pain she had ever known.

"Anyway," he said softly, "you're judging your father too harshly. Unless he's an absolute madman he will not start cutting down trees yet. At the very least he will bargain for time."

"He hates me," Smith said flatly, and felt the smart of tears. "He's hated me ever since my mother died."

"Even so," said Johnny.

"You think he'd worry about public opinion," she said, somehow wanting to prove her point. "But you're wrong. There's only one way to stop the cutting in that valley of yours, and that's to let me go."

But the *Outcast II* did not alter course.

THE SHADOW OF THE ISLAND fell over them then, and now that she knew where to look she could pick out Wilfred Tall Tree's cabin down at the shore, and above, through the trees, the flash of sun on glass. Smith stared fixedly up, blinking and swallowing against the tears that threatened, glad of the wind that blew her long hair across her face. She didn't know where the tears were coming from, but she wished they would stop.

Johnny Winterhawk's firm fingers left her wrist and fastened gently under her chin. He turned her face toward him and looked down into her eyes; and Smith's heart leaped painfully against her ribs, and she gulped on a sob.

He smiled at her. "Come on," he said coaxingly. "Let yourself cry. You're a brave, strong woman, but the past couple of days have been pretty rough on you. Come on now."

She tensed her jaw and swallowed and blinked back the tears. "I'm all right," said Smith forcefully.

"Ah, Peaceable Woman," he said. "There can't be another woman in the world like you. I salute you."

Johnny Winterhawk bent his head, and his mouth met her full, trembling lips with a sweetness that spread through her soul like honey. Her arms crept up to his shoulders, and she clung to him with a helpless need that shook her to the roots.

When he lifted his head she drew back and looked at him.

"I love you," said a voice that Smith recognized as her own.

She clapped her hand instantly over her mouth and jerked out of Johnny Winterhawk's light hold as though his touch burned her. "I can't imagine why I said that!" she said in a horrified tone. "It isn't true in the least!"

She glared at him as though she expected him to contradict her.

Winterhawk was concentrating on turning *Outcast II* in toward the dock, and for a moment he didn't answer. Then he glanced at her. "Of course you didn't mean it," he remarked calmly, and turned his attention back to the boat.

They were silent while he docked the big sleek racing sailer, and Smith helped to tie her up. Afterward she stood on the dock and watched as he padlocked the main hatch. Against her, of course. After all, there was a ship's radio inside.

Smith couldn't forget what she had said to him, though Johnny Winterhawk seemed to. She felt the heat rise in her cheeks every time she thought of it. She couldn't imagine what had made her say it. In that moment she had felt as though someone else were speaking, not herself at all.

"Why, Peaceable Woman." Johnny Winterhawk's deep, caressing voice broke in on her thoughts, and she looked up to find him beside her on the dock, gazing at her feet. "You made yourself a pair of moccasins!"

Smith grinned up at him, and suddenly it was easy to forget what an idiot she had just made of herself.

"I had to," she confessed. "Yours were too big for me to fill."

Johnny Winterhawk lifted his head and laughed, and the late sun glinted on the wings of his black hair and on his thick eyelashes. She watched him, laughing, too, while pain like a small fist closed on her heart: he was beautiful, she thought, the way a work of art was beautiful, like a statue in glowing dark marble; and he moved her the way art sometimes moved her. It was as though the sight of him matched some image that resided in the deepest recesses of her being. She could not have drawn the image or described it; she would not even have known it existed. But Johnny Winterhawk stepped into the shape and brought it to life, and the little fist tightened its hold on her heart.

A river of knowledge ran in her too deep for her to touch, and its incomprehensible murmur filled her ears like a mysterious oracle.

He should have let me go home, she thought. But some small, silent part of her looked up at the forest and was glad he had not.

THE MOON was just past the full, and its light shone brightly into her room and across her bed, patterning the floor and the bed with shadow leaves that moved with every breath of wind.

Shulamith had known she would not sleep long before she had undressed and crawled into bed, the sheets cool on her naked skin. She hadn't tossed and turned. She had lain quietly through the hours, watching the moonlight make its progress across the room, listening to the noises of nature that seemed like silence.

Finally, with a sigh, she took her arms from under her head, swept back the bedcovers and got up. She slipped on the dragon robe and buttoned it tightly up to the high mandarin neck, then opened the door as silently as she could.

She had expected to see the sleeping form of Wilfred Tall Tree, but the sleeping mat across her doorway was empty. With a glance up and down, Shulamith closed the door behind her and moved silently along the hallway.

As she stepped out of the house onto the balcony, she was enveloped by beauty. Moonlight bathed the world: the sea, the gorge, the balcony; and the sounds of the breaking waves and the rustling of the leaves were startlingly loud in the night air.

Johnny Winterhawk was sitting in one of the deep, low chairs, shirtless, his knees angled up in front of him, his hands folded across his bare stomach. His face seemed full of angles in the moonlight; his eyes were dark unreadable hollows as he looked up at her. Smith crossed to the railing, looking out and down over the magnificent gorge. The breeze tangled in her loose hair and turned the silky cloth of her robe cool against her skin. She shivered a little.

"There is a story in my family," Johnny Winterhawk's low-pitched voice said behind her, and Smith turned to him, leaning her hips against the wooden railing, "that generations ago one of my ancestors saw a woman come up out of the sea, in the place where Cat Bite River meets the ocean. She was not like anyone he had ever seen, it is said, for she had pale skin and hair like fire.

"My ancestor's name was Iniishewa, or Tree By Itself. Iniishewa felt his soul fly out of him to the woman when he looked at her, and he wanted to make her his wife.

"In the Chopa nation, strangers were not welcome. Usually they were killed or sold as slaves. But the people might be asked to accept a stranger as one of them."

His quiet voice was hypnotic in the moonlight. Shulamith stood watching him, watching the play of muscle under the skin of his face as he spoke, watching the breeze touch the black wings of his hair.

"Iniishewa took the fire-haired woman to the women of the tribe and asked them to accept her into the tribe so that he could marry her. The women discussed the matter for four days, and in the end they voted against her. The fire-haired woman was put to death.

"Iniishewa left the tribe then, abandoning the family he already had, and went to live in the forest. He spent the rest of his life alone, waiting for the fire-haired woman to take another form and come to him to give him back his soul that he had lost to her."

Johnny Winterhawk pulled himself up out of the chair and came to stand beside her at the railing, looking out over the gorge. Smith remained where she was, her back to the sea, unable to move. She felt as though waves of electricity flowed between their bodies. She gazed at the house behind them, unreal and magical in the moonlight that poured over it, and wondered whether if she closed her eyes it would disappear, and she would be standing in a forest above a rocky gorge with a man who would demand that she return his soul. . . .

When the silence became terrifying she asked, "Did he find her again?" and Johnny Winterhawk turned and took her in his arms.

His kiss was more pain than pleasure, because she was too desperate for it. She was like a child that has never been held, her yearning for his touch so deep that the fulfillment created an even deeper ache of remembered emptiness. She felt as though whenever he touched her, her blood rushed to meet his hand so eagerly that she bruised.

She would not have believed that such need could exist in a human being. She had stepped into a trickling stream, and now she was drowning in a rushing river that had no bounds.

Shulamith began to tremble in his strong hold, and in answer Johnny Winterhawk's arms tightened around her, and his kiss grew fierce. Her palms were against the heat of his naked chest, and she felt the motion of muscles under his skin as his hands moved convulsively in her hair.

Every ache that had never been healed with love rose to his kiss with an urgency that shook her. She could not remember her name, because she had no name. She had no personality. She was only a small, nameless, wounded soul that wanted the aching peace of his mouth on hers.

He tore his mouth away and buried his face in her neck, crushing her body to him. In a hoarse urgent voice he whispered, "God!" Then he drew back and looked down at her, still in his embrace. He raised his hand to her cheek, and she could feel the barely controlled tremor in his hand and arm. "You are unbelievably beautiful," he said huskily.

He had lifted his head into the moonlight, and now its cool glow bathed the harsh features of his face, and that swamping desperate emotion left her with a cold rush, and fear took its place.

Smith jerked her palms away from his chest and strained back against the terrifying pressure of his arms. For a moment it seemed as though he would not let her go, and then his hands fell to his sides. He watched fixedly as she dropped her face in her hands and tried to control her erratic breathing.

Never in her life had Smith felt so profoundly stirred. She felt all at sea, and it was a frightening uncomfortable feeling. She hated it. She hated Johnny Winterhawk.

"You hypnotized me!" she accused, before she could stop herself. That was insane, of course. She hadn't meant to say that.

Johnny Winterhawk laughed. "Funny," he said, "I was going to say that to you."

Her stomach was churning; Smith wanted to scream and scream. She glanced out over the balcony and imagined she heard her scream rushing down the gorge and out over the ocean into the night. She jerked her gaze back to the harsh dark face above her.

"You have to leave me alone," she said, her voice low and quiet on the night air. "Don't touch me anymore, Mr. Winterhawk. I don't like it."

There was a long pause. A sudden wind gusted noisily through the trees and over her face. Smith shivered.

Johnny Winterhawk stared at her. "I will teach you to like it," he said flatly.

Smith closed her eyes as panic fluttered in her stomach. The thought of being taught to like that disturbing confusion of emotion, desire and need she had just experienced left her shaken. Yet she knew that what he implied was true. The instinctive knowledge frightened her.

"You can't," she whispered.

He reached out and pulled her against him again, and the heat of his skin burned her through the robe. His hand circled her throat as he bent her head back and stared into her eyes.

"Then teach yourself," he said, his voice raw, "teach yourself. Because I'm as close to taking a woman by force as I've ever been in my life!"

CHAPTER EIGHT

SHE THOUGHT the sun would never come up. She lay for hours in the glow of the treacherous moonlight, waiting for the sky to lighten into day.

The robe lay where she had flung it over a chair, and she stared at it blindly in the cool white moonlight, as though the intricate exotic design by engaging her eyes might allow her mind to rest.

It was pricelessly beautiful, the robe. She had never seen anything quite like it. On midnight-blue silk the dragon, richly scaled in lush greens and turquoises, arched his thick neck up the back of the robe and breathed red and orange fire across the shoulder and down the sleeve. On the other side his finely veined wings in shades of purple stretched to the front of the robe. The green lashing tail ran everywhere in intricate coils. There was a wide border on the square sleeves and the hem, and small flowers covered the background. The embroidery work was amazingly delicate, and the glittering thread on the rippling yards of silk made the dragon seem alive.

Smith realized with a small absentminded start that it was very odd that Johnny Winterhawk's nameless woman friend should have left just this and no other piece of clothing in the house, as though she had forgotten it. *If I owned a robe like that,* Smith thought, *I would be about as likely to forget it as my own hair. I wonder if Johnny bought it for her.* For some reason that thought irritated her, made her restless. It must have cost a lot of money.

Her father had taught her always to get a good idea of the income of anyone she had to negotiate with—and if you couldn't get the information directly you sized a man up and made an estimate, she had learned. The sailboat was in keeping with the estimate she had made of Johnny Winterhawk, but his ownership of this house had thrown out her calculations.

Still, whatever its price, the robe was something he would only have bought for someone special, someone he loved very deeply. Shulamith moved restlessly in the bed and remembered how Johnny Winterhawk had slept beside her there the morning after that awful night and how she had moved against him in her sleep. . . .

Deliberately she looked at the robe. *I'll ask him where it comes from,* she thought, *and buy one like it when I go home. . . .*

If she was ever allowed to go home. Panic quickened Smith's heartbeat, as it did every time her mind slid back down into awareness.

"I will teach you. . . teach you. . . teach you. . . ." She heard Johnny Winterhawk's voice like a whisper under the sound of her heartbeat, a whisper that pulsed with her blood along her veins.

She had pulled away from him, and he had let her go without a word. Only his eyes had followed her across the balcony—his eyes and the panic that his kiss and his words had unleashed in her. . . .

She fell asleep at last at dawn, when the sky had lightened and moonshadows no longer tormented her. She dreamed about being led down and down in a huge cavern whose walls were embroidered in rich, moving colors like the robe. The colors were vibrantly beautiful, like nothing she had ever seen before, but Smith was terrified. She knew that at the bottom of the cavern the dragon was waiting for her, the dragon of the robe, come to life.

SMITH WAS DOWN in the kitchen early, wide awake in spite of having had so little sleep. She made coffee, thinking about the story Johnny Winterhawk had told her last night, of his long-ago ancestor and the fire-haired woman.... Shulamith shuddered. How awful that she had been put to death....

It was as though there had been a compulsion between them last night, pulling Johnny as much as it pulled her. It was no wonder he had remembered that story, because last night she really had felt almost possessed. If she hadn't suddenly seen Johnny Winterhawk's harsh features in the moonlight and remembered who and where she was, she might have let him make love to her out on the moonlit balcony.

But it had only been the effect of moonlight, and in future she would be careful to stay well away from Johnny Winterhawk on moonlit nights....

The kitchen door opened behind her, and Shulamith turned her head and looked at Johnny Winterhawk across the room. She opened her mouth to speak, and then she closed it again, because suddenly she was choking, suddenly she had to swallow.

It was there between them again, as palpable as thick smoke, and she felt its twisting fingers reach deep into her being, clutching her and drawing her to him.

"Good morning," said Johnny Winterhawk calmly, and even though she could hear the effort this casualness cost him, she felt a loosening in the clutch of those smoky fingers inside her.

"Good morning," she responded lightly, in a tone that matched his, but how long had they stared at each other before he spoke? "Is Wilf coming down to breakfast?" she asked, as though she had been doing this for a dozen years, making Johnny Winterhawk's breakfast in the morning.

Their speech had released him, too, and he moved away from the door and crossed to the refrigerator. She hadn't made breakfast, only coffee, but Johnny Winterhawk was taking only the milk from the refrigerator, so it looked as though he wasn't interested in eating.

"Wilf's down at his cabin," he remarked. "He'll be up in a while. He probably thought you'd sleep later than this."

But Smith was used to early mornings and hard work. Even though there was nothing to get up for she wouldn't have been able to sleep in.

"I wish there was something for me to do," she said, pouring coffee into the cups he had set. Yesterday she had made moccasins, but that certainly didn't occupy the brain.

"I could give you some reading matter. You could fill some of the gaps in your social education."

"No, thanks," Smith said coldly. "The last thing I

need is to be cooped up with a lot of propaganda designed to brainwash me.''

"Or enlighten you?" he asked without heat. "Or shake up your comfortable, narrow view of the world?"

Smith flinched. "My mother was a Jew," she said evenly. "She died in the Six Day War. Her parents emigrated to Israel in 1930. If they hadn't, I wouldn't be here. They both lost their entire families in Europe, in the war. So my world view probably isn't quite as narrow as you are so fondly imagining, Mr. Winterhawk. There are other people besides your own who have suffered at the hands of the ruling class.''

It was his turn to look chastened. "Right," he said. "Sorry."

The silence that settled over them then was almost companionable, as they drank the last of their coffee. Then Smith said, "Is there anything I could do? I hate forced inactivity, I'll be—"

"Don't think of it as forced inactivity," he said. "Consider it a holiday. After your year in Europe you probably need one."

Smith gave him a half smile. They had somehow conquered that earlier compulsion, but now her wry smile seemed to catch him unawares, and she saw his response leap behind his eyes.

"I haven't had a vacation since I was sixteen," she said quickly, fighting not to let the look affect her. "I wouldn't know what to do with one."

Winterhawk was calm again. "What's something you've never had time for but always wanted to do?" he asked.

Love you. The words were there in her brain, quietly,

unsurprisingly, like a primary, a given, an axiom placed there before time began but only now discovered. She felt the glow from it as from a rich dark gemstone deep in the mine of her being, and then she started in surprise. What an extraordinary thing to be thinking!

"Oh, well," she said, for something to say, something to hide that strange, deep response, "I guess I used to want to write poetry." That was true enough, though she hadn't thought about it for years. Funny it should come up like this, as though she really meant it.

"Ah," said Winterhawk, nodding as though he was remembering something, and she realized he was—he was remembering what she had told him about the boy at Paper Creek. The boy had set one of her poems to music, but she doubted if she could recall a trace of either words or music at this distance in time.

"There's lots of paper and pencils in my study," Johnny Winterhawk was offering. "Shall I get you some before I leave?"

Smith shook her head, as much to clear it as to say no. "No, but thank you," she answered with a small smile. "I think if I had any great talent it would have surfaced before this."

"Do you only allow yourself to do things at which you'll be brilliant?" he asked curiously, and she didn't see what was so surprising in that.

She shrugged. "What's the point in doing something if you don't do it well?"

"Is that the opinion of the great Cordwainer St. John?" asked Winterhawk, and it was—she had heard her father say it hundreds of times, but that didn't mean it wasn't true.

"You don't have to sneer!" she said hotly, suddenly feeling that she loved her father very much. "What's the point in doing something badly?"

Johnny Winterhawk grinned. "The point is that quite often practice makes perfect. If everyone followed your father's rule the human race would have died out long ago."

She blushed, though he had probably not meant anything sexual by it, he was probably talking about raising children. But she blushed because that had suddenly made her think how inexpert she was at making love, and how willing she must have seemed to try. . . .

Johnny Winterhawk was pushing back his chair and standing up. "Maybe Wilf could give you lessons in wood carving," he suggested. "Or there are lots of books around the house that do not address the issue of native rights." He grinned. "Don't speak to any strange men while I'm gone."

"When will you be ho—back?" she asked almost wistfully, almost as though she might miss him while he was away.

"I'm usually back by six," he said. "Take it easy on Wilf, won't you? Remember he's an old man."

"*Me* take it easy on *him*?" Smith sputtered. This struck her as rankly unfair. "Why don't you tell *him* to take it easy on *me*?"

He looked down at her, and the laughter went out of his eyes. He ought to be kissing her goodbye, and she knew they both felt it.

"So long," said Johnny Winterhawk, and left her.

THE ONLY FAULT Smith had to find in the design of the house was in the location of the laundry room: it should have been next to the kitchen, but instead it was halfway up the house near the bedrooms. A lot of distance to cover for someone who might be trying to prepare a meal and do the laundry at the same time, she thought. If it were her house she might turn the laundry room into a storage closet and move the washer and dryer down into the kitchen.

The problem was that she felt cut off, Smith realized. The laundry room was small, and its window looked onto a tiny plant-filled space against the cliff. Part of the roof also was glass, so there was plenty of light, but she could not see out over the island or the ocean in any direction. She felt uncomfortable: she wanted to be in the kitchen, where she could see the approaches to the island and the path to the house; she wanted to be in touch with what was going on.

She wanted to be able to watch for Johnny Winterhawk coming home.

Smith jumped away from the thought as though it had burned her. Anyway, the idea was ridiculous—it was hardly noon, and he wouldn't be back for hours yet. Smith leaned against the dryer, feeling the soothing warmth of the metal against her body. She felt oddly desolate and aimless, oddly alone.

But she had been alone many times in her life without feeling like this. This past year in Europe she had spent many, many hours alone in foreign hotel rooms without being assailed by this nameless longing.

Was it loneliness? Was that what the feeling was? How extraordinary to be suddenly aware of it like this.

Of course she had felt it, many times. She had felt it almost constantly after her mother died, when her father. . . . It was a horrible, hopeless feeling, and she would have felt it in those European hotel rooms, too, if she had let herself. . . .

Odd, how a feeling could really *hurt*. Loneliness hurt. And somewhere back in time Shulamith St. John had decided not to feel lonely.

If she felt lonely again suddenly now, it must be because her desperate situation, the terrible fear of losing her father to death, was breaking down her defenses. It was nothing to do with Johnny Winterhawk. She was thinking of Johnny because she could have told him about it. She could probably tell Johnny Winterhawk anything. Already she had told him things she had never told anyone before—even how her father had humiliated her up at Paper Creek.

A buzzer went off to signal that the dryer's cycle was finished, breaking into her train of thought. Smith bent to pull out the clothes she had borrowed on the boat and her torn nightdress. The hem was permanently stained with grease or engine oil, and at home she would have discarded it. But here she didn't have that luxury. She would borrow jeans and shirts from Johnny Winterhawk because she must, but she was damned if she was going to ask to borrow a pair of his pajamas. And so long as she was in this house she had no intention of sleeping in the raw again.

As she left the laundry room, Smith glanced up the hallway to the door of Johnny Winterhawk's study and then on impulse walked back to it over the creaking floorboard and tried the handle.

The door opened. With a swift, surprised intake of breath Smith stepped inside the room and silently closed the door. Her heart thudded in her ears as she crossed to the bookcase, but before she reached it she was brought up short in dismay: the phone was gone.

Well, she might have guessed. But a small setback like that wouldn't stop her. Smith set her little armload of clean clothes down on the beautiful woven Indian rug that graced the center of the shining wood floor and began a systematic search of the room.

She paused for a long moment in front of the wall that was living rock. The house had somehow been pushed right into the side of the cliff, and the rock wall dominated the room. It was dry and cool to the touch, and unadorned save for the green plants that hung and stood nearby.

The phone was not in the room, unless it had been locked away in one of the filing cabinets that stood against the wall. She had picked locks before, and though these looked rather more solid than usual she knew that if you pushed a filing cabinet over on its side you could often release the lock. Now was not the time to try it, of course, not with Wilfred Tall Tree in the house. Smith picked up the pile of clothing and, with a quick eye out for Wilfred, let herself out of the study and ran down to her bedroom.

"OH, DAMN," Shulamith said abruptly, as she sat in the kitchen watching Wilfred Tall Tree put the finishing touches to lunch. "We've missed the news." Not even in Europe, in countries where she couldn't understand the language and had sometimes had to depend on two-day-old English newspapers, had she felt so isolated from what was happening.

Wilfred was serving an interesting-looking vegetable concoction onto their plates. "Are you afraid a war will start if you aren't keeping track?" he asked her, comically waggling his eyebrows.

"Of course not," she responded shortly, confused once again by how swiftly this harmless old man could ruffle her. Wilfred laughed, dropping the wooden spoon into the saucepan he held. He leaned forward and tapped her forehead with a finger.

"Or maybe if things get too quiet on the outside the war will start in there?"

Well, what on earth did he mean by that? "It just so happens," Smith told him irritably, "that my father is dangerously ill in the hospital, and that my life has been threatened if he doesn't accede to your people's ransom demand. So I'm kind of curious about whether the two of us are going to live or die."

"No, this isn't true. You know you are going to die," said Wilfred, placing a plate of thickly sliced brown bread on the table and sitting down opposite her. Smith stared at him, her eyes wide, her heart pounding crazily. "Everyone knows he is going to die. What you want to know is *when*. Because you think that if you did know, you could control events."

Smith breathed out on an outraged sigh. Her heart was still thumping in fear. "I thought you were telling me that they were going to kill me," she said, and then after a moment, "Are they?"

Wilfred stopped chewing. "I don't know," he said. "The world is very crazy. Things are crazy. Maybe there are some Chopa people who have been listening to the news too much.''

"I'd be more interested to know if there are Chopa people who have been to one of the PLO's terrorist training camps,'' Smith said. The words came out as the thought formed, and the moment she heard them, a fear unlike anything she had felt before overtook her. She remembered her first vision of those five balaclava-masked figures around her father's bed, and suddenly anything seemed possible—except that she would get out of this alive.

For the first time the thought that if her father didn't give in to the ransom demand she really might be killed sank deep into her mind.

He must, she thought desperately. *He has to love me enough for that, he has to give in. If I could only make him understand how much I want to live....*

"Where's the phone?'' she demanded suddenly. "Johnny's hidden the phone, and I want it.''

Wilfred Tall Tree looked at her from gentle wise eyes and said nothing.

"I want it! I want to phone my father!'' she demanded hoarsely, her voice beginning to crack. "I can tell him, I can make him understand, Wilf, if you'll let me call him. He'll listen to me—'' Smith broke off as the sobs welled up from within, choking her. She felt a terrible sense of urgency, as though somehow she had lived her life all wrong up to this moment, that if she died now her twenty-four years on the earth would have been a waste. She wanted to live, she had to live so that she could change things, so that her life would not have been wasted....

Gradually Smith became aware of the regular click of fork against her plate, and she lifted her head embarrassedly. Across the table from her Wilfred Tall Tree was calmly eating the meal he had prepared. Smith wiped her eyes with her hands and sniffed. Then she reached for the paper napkin beside her fork like a guilty child. She didn't even know *how* to cry, she thought suddenly. Women were probably supposed to cry delicately into a handkerchief, not howl like a bull and then blow a reddened nose with a sound like a trumpet.

But there hadn't been much training in femininity since her mother had died. And lumber camps and sawmills weren't the best places to succumb to tears. Not for the boss's daughter.

Smith blinked her tear-spangled lashes at Wilfred Tall Tree as she forced her breathing to calm. Then she scooped up a forkful of the vegetable concoction and tasted it. It was a delicate mixture of flavors, almost like a Japanese dish.

Her eyes were dark with suspicion. "I'm always crying when I'm around you," she said. "I never cry."

Wilf chewed thoughtfully. "Why not?" he asked.

She hiccuped into laughter. "I don't know. I really don't know." She paused and rubbed a damp cheek again. "It's really not so bad, is it?"

THE TELEPHONE would very probably not be in the filing cabinet, Smith had realized. The idea had been a product of her angry determination. Chances were it was in Wilf's cabin, because it would be almost criminally negligent for Johnny Winterhawk to lock away their only means of communicating with the mainland.

Still, Smith stood inside the doorway of Johnny's study, looking around—there was always the chance, and she couldn't afford to pass up any chances.

Sometime later she sank down into the chair behind the desk and gave up. She wasn't going to get into those filing cabinets. She had searched the room high and low for a key. Cursing, and remembering how easily she had picked the lock of one of the filing cabinets at St. John's Wood once when it was necessary, she had spent a long fruitless hour trying to conquer Johnny Winterhawk's. At St. John's everyone had been so appalled by the ease with which she had jimmied the lock that the cabinets had immediately been changed for stronger ones that promised to be more secure. Even in her frustrated anger Shulamith was hoping that the cabinets now housing St. John's company secrets were as difficult to break into as Johnny Winterhawk's and was making a mental note of the manufacturer's name in case they were not.

She had tried to pull the cabinets over on one side in the way she had heard about, but all but one of the four high cabinets were so heavy she could not even move them. She might have been able to tip them forward on their faces and let them smash to the ground, but unless they broke open on impact, which she doubted, what would have been the advantage in that? The noise would bring Wilfred Tall Tree, and that would be that.

There was one cabinet at the end, which she could move, and she had laid it on its side, but nothing magical had happened to the lock and it was too heavy for her to lift back. Now it lay on Johnny Winterhawk's polished oak floor, mute testimony of her activities.

Smith sighed. Oh, well, she supposed she would be

confined to her room after this. What difference did it make? She looked down to the nonexistent watch on her wrist, a habit she couldn't seem to break. She wondered how long it would be before Johnny Winterhawk came home.

She wandered to the bookcase that ran the length of the wall that faced his desk. He was right: there were lots of books here that looked as though they might fill the gaps in her social education as far as native rights were concerned.

Bury My Heart at Wounded Knee. She had heard of that one. *The Unjust Society, I Heard the Owl Call My Name.* He had shelves full. Conscious of a sense of reluctance, Smith put out her hand and pulled one off the shelf. *The Unjust Society* by Harold Cardinal. The title didn't bode well for her feeling that someone had been looking after social wrongs while she was concerned with other things.

"Chapter One. The Buckskin Curtain. The Indian-Problem Problem," she read. "The history of Canada's Indians is a shameful chronicle of the white man's disinterest, his deliberate trampling of Indian rights...."

Smith closed the book with a snap and put it back on the shelf. "No, thank you," she said aloud. "Anyway, it's not my fault." Restlessly, she moved to his desk and sat. She flicked an eye over the things on his desk top and then pulled open a drawer she had searched earlier.

It was full of paper and writing pads and notebooks, and at length, resignedly, she pulled out a lined notebook and picked up a pencil.

I could always keep a diary of this, she thought dryly. *Someone might publish it for its curiosity value, espe-*

cially if I'm killed in the end. Kidnapped people pro-
bably go through some interesting mental processes....
Dear Diary, she thought wryly, *this morning I did the*
laundry and read a book but didn't go outside even
though it's a beautiful hot day; and after lunch I tried to
get into Johnny Winterhawk's filing system. I was hop-
ing to find the phone. Last night....

Smith bit her lip. She didn't want to think about last
night, because last night she had been crazy. Last night
she hadn't been herself at all, and what had happened
was the scariest thing that had ever happened to her,
even if she hadn't realized it till later.

Shulamith rubbed her thumb along the length of her
pencil and looked at the faint blue lines of the empty
page. She could hear the soft sound of the waterfall outside the broad span of glass, and all the greenery was
glistening and rich. She suddenly felt almost feverish in
her need for some sort of activity.

"Something you've always wanted to do but never
had time for," Johnny had said, and she was thinking,
right now it feels as though I've always wanted to escape
from you.

Each moment, blazing eyes and myriad faces
You watch me. You are a nomad, your throat is dry.
Do you see, on this desert horizon, the traces
Of a mythical, murmurous paradise of oases?

It is only the reflection of your desire in the burning
sky.
I am not an oasis, not water for your parched
mouth.

The roar in my ears is the fire of my own thirsty
cry.
Your kiss scorches my body. My throat also is dry.

Shulamith sat back, torn between dissatisfaction and
discovery. She had forgotten what hard work poetry
was. Over the past few years she had been tending to remember that brief year or two of writing as being filled
with a stream of flowing creativity, but the hour of hard
labor she had just put in to produce only a pale hint of
what she wanted had reminded her, forcefully, of how
dedicated to her art she had once had to be. The process
was familiar to her, but after eight years it was a distant,
difficult familiarity.

She had wanted to convey a sense of that nameless
longing that she felt from time to time, that was somehow stirred into a heaviness of need in Johnny Winterhawk's presence, but whatever this attempt at a poem
was conveying, it wasn't that.

Slowly, Shulamith stood up. There was a languor in
her limbs, as though whatever had produced the poem
had been somehow erotic. She clenched her jaw briefly.
Perhaps it wasn't the subject matter but the creative
process itself that was erotic. Smith took comfort in
that. Of course there was something almost sexual in the
act of pulling out your own deep responses and submit-
ting them to the light of day....

She didn't think much of this one as poetry, though,
however disturbing the process had been to her. *Call it
psychic exercise,* Smith thought with an inward smile. *A
few days or weeks of hard slog, and I might start producing something.*

With an unregretful last glance she dropped the poem into Johnny Winterhawk's deep wastebasket and, clearing the desk top, did the same with the half-dozen scratched-on sheets of his paper she had used.

But the languor remained in her limbs and her brain as she moved restlessly through the rooms and corridors of Johnny Winterhawk's house to, finally, the balcony outside the kitchen.

It was a hot day. Too hot. The house, protected by trees, was cool without benefit of air conditioning, and the heat that beat on her now as she stood in the sun-drenched square of the balcony surprised her. Vancouver must be in for a heat wave.

Still restless, she moved from the railing toward the chair that he had been sitting in last night, telling her that story of terrible beauty. As Smith put out a hand to the smooth wood of the chair back her stomach knotted, as though Johnny Winterhawk had left some trace of his desire behind to reach for her now with invisible hands.

"I will teach you to like it," she whispered, and felt the sun burning on her hair, her breasts, her thighs. It was too hot for her; it was making her faint.

Below her, the Pacific sucked and pounded in the rocky gorge, and suddenly Smith was running, through the house and down the steps as though someone chased her, to follow the winding narrow trail that led deep into the forest cool, down and down toward the sea.

"There's a piece of beach down that way," Wilfred Tall Tree had explained when she had caught faint sight of the trail from the kitchen window. "It's a good place to beach a canoe, but there's no canoe there now." He had laughed, and she had known he was laughing at her. "But still, it's a nice place to swim."

It would be the beach she had seen from Johnny's study, Smith knew, but when she emerged from the forest to find herself nearly at the water's edge she had lost her sense of direction. To her left the rocks looked too rough to be easily passable, especially for feet unprotected by anything thicker than moccasins. Smith turned right, climbed up over a promontory of rock that dropped abruptly to the sea on one side, and, on the other, she saw as she reached the crest, to the small, sandy beach.

The sand was dry and hot above the water's reach, and before long Smith was kicking off Johnny Winterhawk's heavy jeans and lying back to let her pale legs bake a little in the sun. It was so hot, and who would disturb her here? The island was totally private. Wilfred, if he did catch sight of her, would leave her alone, and Johnny... Johnny Winterhawk would be away for hours....

STAYING IN THE WATER for long was going to be impossible: it was so cold it took her breath away. But the contrast of the icy water and the burning sun on her skin was a strong sensuous pleasure, and Smith rolled and stretched in the waves, floating on her back to offer her naked body up to the sun's heat with a luxurious abandonment that was slowly washing away the memories and confinements of the past horrid year in Europe.

Her long hair floated around her body as the water tugged each strand loose, and she felt its freedom in her scalp and closed her eyes on the sensation with as much pleasure as if she had spent the past year in prison.

When the cold began to reach her bones Smith swam close in to shore and stood up amid the froth of the breakers and felt the sun like a sacrament on her chilled, invigorated body, a holy wine warming body and soul together.

Smith moved forward through the breaking waves, the water alternately pushing and pulling at her slim thighs with a force that staggered her until, after a few steps, she found firmer footing.

Oh, this was glorious. This was the most perfect moment she had experienced in all her life. Even the weight of her hair pulling sleekly back from her scalp and hanging long down her back was a new, sensuous excitement, as were the insistent motion of the water against her legs and the texture of pebble and sand underfoot.

When she reached the beach she dropped to the sand and lay just out of reach of all but the strongest waves, so that every now and then she was startled by a silken touch of water sliding up the warm sand under her legs and hips.

Bending one knee a little, she dug her toes and foot into the wet sand and closed her eyes and smiled. . . .

When the shadow fell across her she knew there could be no cloud in the blue clear sky. Her eyes flew open and with a tiny gasp she met the fierce gaze of the dark man standing over her. Shulamith froze where she lay.

He was naked except for the blue jeans that covered his hips and legs. His muscled chest was smooth and his arms hung easily, almost helplessly at his sides. All his energy was in his dark look, black flames licking out over her skin to scorch her into awareness.

"Johnny," she whispered, half pleading, half inviting, all aware.

He looked at her as though he did not hear her voice, but only saw the movement of her lips, as though the sight of that stirred him unmercifully. She felt a whole series of tiny sparks against her skin then, running upward from her feet to her shoulders; her fingers clenched in the thick gritty sand at her sides, and she felt water run down over her knuckles. *Water,* she realized in erotic amazement. The look in his eyes had made the touch of water an electric shock on her skin. She looked at his strong hands then and wondered distantly if his caress would scorch her to death.

She felt a shiver in her breasts as under his gaze her nipples suddenly contracted, hardened; and Johnny Winterhawk watched with a look of pleasure that was nearly pain.

"Johnny," she choked again, and then, because she had somehow begun to fear, "No." But his hands had already dropped to the waist of his jeans, and she knew the fear had come too late. She watched the smooth line of his hip and thigh as he stripped off the thick, worn denim; then her breath caught in her throat as he stood straight and dropped the jeans, already forgotten, at his side. He was watching her watch him, and when her tongue flicked involuntarily between her parted lips she heard the intake of his breath.

He dropped to the sand beside her, not taking his eyes from hers, not allowing her to look away, to evade the intent in his eyes that she knew was answered in her own.

Johnny Winterhawk's hungry mouth came down on

her lips, which were parted in need, and her small stifled breath of response was abruptly transformed in her throat into a growl of deep, erotic, animal need that destroyed Johnny Winterhawk's restraint at a stroke. His hands on her upper arm and in her wet hair closed convulsively in a grip of such naked need that she tore her mouth away from his to cry out her passionate response to it.

A wave rustled up the beach under their bodies then, frothing around their legs and hips and up under Smith's back to set her hair afloat all around her as she arched her head back into sand and foam, and Johnny kissed the throbbing pulse of the throat she offered up to him.

She was trembling profoundly, almost shuddering, as though he already possessed her. Nothing in all her life had ever affected her like this. His hands and his mouth were fire on her skin, and she was beginning to sob with need.

Suddenly and overwhelmingly, panic took possession of her brain. What was she doing, what was happening to her? She felt drugged or mad or both. This was a violent man, a kidnapper. *Her* kidnapper! She didn't even know him!

The small hands that a moment before had caressed and pulled and urged him on were suddenly pushing against him.

"Stop," she said hoarsely. "Stop."

The black wings of Johnny Winterhawk's hair were flung off his forehead as he jerked his head to look into her face.

"What?" he rasped, as though it was hard for him to

follow or form speech. His hand did not stop its heated caress of her.

"Stop," she repeated, but the groan of her response to what he did gave the lie to the word. Johnny Winterhawk looked at her.

"No," he said deliberately. He bent his head to her breast and ran his tongue roughly over the hard bead of her nipple.

She could hardly lift her arm against the torrent of sensation that rushed from her breast down to her fingertips, but she pushed his mouth away.

"I don't like it," she whispered, and Johnny Winterhawk showed his teeth in a soft laugh.

"I will make you like it," he promised.

She made a sudden frantic push to get away, turning and scrambling onto hands and knees, and immediately he was on her, pulling her back, holding her face for his thrusting kiss. Shulamith gasped. Her body was on fire, hungry and melting. Violently she pushed his shoulders, clawed at his restraining hands, tore her mouth away to let out a high desperate cry, whether of need or of fright she no longer knew. But he would not let her go.

They struggled and rolled together in sand and water, the silence broken only by his rasping breath or her small animal cries, until at last he held her immobile, his legs restraining hers, his large hand implacably gripping her wrists above her head.

Then they were still, looking into each other's eyes, and deliberately Johnny Winterhawk lifted his free hand and stroked it over her breast and down over the curve of waist and hip. . . .

"You see," he said, almost angrily, as her body

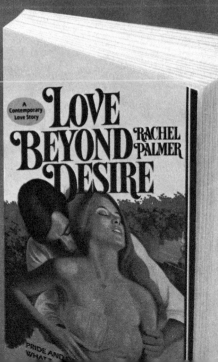

A SUPERROMANCE™
the great new romantic novel she never wanted to end. And it can be yours

FREE!

She never wanted it to end. And neither will you. From the moment you begin... *Love Beyond Desire,* your **FREE** introduction to the newest series of bestseller romance novels, **SUPERROMANCES**.

You'll be enthralled by this powerful love story... from the moment Robin meets the dark, handsome Carlos and finds herself involved in the jealousies, bitterness and secret passions of the Lopez family. Where her own forbidden love threatens to shatter her life.

Your FREE *Love Beyond Desire* is only the beginning. A subscription to **SUPERROMANCES** lets you look forward to a long love affair. Month after month, you'll receive four love stories of heroic dimension. Novels that will involve you in spellbinding intrigue, forbidden love and fiery passions.

You'll begin this series of sensuous, exciting contemporary novels... written by some of the top romance novelists of the day... with four each month.

And this big value... each novel, almost 400 pages of compelling reading... is yours for only $2.50 a book. Hours of entertainment for so little. Far less than a first-run movie or Pay-TV. Newly published novels, with beautifully illustrated covers, filled with page after page of delicious escape into a world of romantic love... delivered right to your home.

A compelling love story of mystery and intrigue... conflicts and jealousies... and a forbidden love that threatens to shatter the lives of all involved with the aristocratic Lopez family.

← Mail this card today for your FREE gifts.

**EXTRA BONUS
MAIL YOUR ORDER
TODAY AND GET A
FREE TOTE BAG
FROM SUPERROMANCE.**

☛ Mail this card today for your FREE gifts.

Canada Post
Postes
Canada
021

quivered and shuddered in response. She kicked futilely against his restraining legs, protesting the response of her body to him. Fear and desire were a confused jumble in her brain. She was going mad.

"Leave me alone," she whispered, and his eyes were black with the impossibility of it. His hand's knowing caress of her continued as he watched her face, watched her lips part and her eyes grow heavy with what he did to her. When her body arched with strain, seeking, seeking, she no longer struggled. She pushed up against him, all her energies devoted to finding the answer to the deep need he had created in her.

When her body heaved and trembled with the warm pleasure that suddenly radiated through her he bent and kissed her and drank in her moan of gratitude through his lips. It was all over.

He looked into her eyes when he lifted his head and noted her sleepy satisfaction with one dark raised eyebrow.

"Yes?" he queried softly, and somewhere behind his eyes the angry intensity was still there.

"Yes," Smith acknowledged.

"Good," said Johnny Winterhawk flatly, and the muscles of his jaw clenched as deliberately, easily, he slid over her body and parted her legs with his own. Then she knew that it was far from over. He had only just begun.

CHAPTER NINE

SHULAMITH LAY CURLED in a heap on the sand, her back to Johnny Winterhawk, her hair half dry, half wet, caked with salt and sand.

She felt devastated, utterly drained. He had destroyed her with passion, had reduced her to the most basic element of her soul, had shown her, through her terrifyingly passionate response to the invasions of his body on hers, all the shape and texture of her own animal nature. Under his hands she had lost her personality, had lost the human veneer. She had cried out when he told her to cry out, begged when he demanded that.

He had not often demanded that she beg. Mostly he had given her much more than she wanted, and it was only as she felt what he meant her to feel that she had understood how desperately she had needed it. Once, to escape the racking pleasure that was destroying her soul, she had tried to crawl away from him up the beach, but he had pulled her back to the stormy nest of their passion, and made her grateful that he did.

When, at long last, his passion had burned itself out, she had no more strength than to curl up on the sand at his side, and now the sun dried the sand and salt on her body and a faint breeze stirred the wild tangle of her hair.

And then a hand. Johnny Winterhawk raised himself on one elbow and stroked the hair from her face and forehead with a tender featherlight touch that distantly surprised her.

"Come," he whispered, gently turning her, and then, in spite of everything, she was rolling over and curling up against his body; instinctively, unaccountably, seeking and finding comfort in the warmth of his body and arms.

Hot tears surprised her eyelids, and then she was crying, sobbing wildly against Johnny Winterhawk's chest in some nameless release she could not understand.

Wordlessly he held her and undemandingly stroked her as the sobs shook her frame. And when it was over and he wiped her cheeks and mouth with a firm, loving hand Smith knew that there was nothing she need ever hide from this man, nothing that need ever shame her in his presence. She felt the gentlest of kisses on her cheek. Johnny's arms tightened around her, so strong, so protective; then he raised himself on an elbow and looked down at her. Suddenly he blinked and shook his head. "Good God!" he exclaimed, and it was as though he had just wakened out of a dream, "We've got to get the hell out of here!"

They leaped to their feet simultaneously, he purposeful, she in a state of shock.

"What?" she babbled, shivering as the late-afternoon breeze touched her. She had been so overheated that now she felt chilled. "What?" she demanded again, looking around nervously as though a platoon of cavalry might come out of the woods at any moment.

Johnny thrust long legs into sand-dusted jeans. "Get

dressed," he said. "They want you. We've got to get off the island before they come."

His words drove icicles of terror to the root of her being. In instinctive animal reaction Smith's arms closed over her breasts and her naked, unprotected body jerked into a crouch.

"Who. . . who?" she stammered.

"Call them the new 'provisional wing' of the Chopit Brotherhood," he said bitterly as he fastened his jeans. Then, catching sight of Shulamith, he crossed to hold her. "Sorry," he said, "sorry. Don't be frightened." He stroked her flank gently, but did not try to hide his tension from her. "No one's going to hurt you."

He moved to the huddle of her shirt and jeans lying a short distance away and brought them to her. Was there an unspoken "not while I'm around" in his voice, or did he really mean they did not intend to hurt her? As she took her jeans from him and stepped into them, Smith unconsciously straightened her back. Whatever trouble was coming, she wasn't going to be hiding behind anyone's back when it arrived, not even Johnny Winterhawk's. She buttoned her shirt with an almost angry determination and then looked up to be surprised by Johnny's glinting smile.

"What's the matter?" she demanded. She might have thought it was all a joke, except that the tension was still in him.

"You *are* Shulamith St. John, the poor little rich girl?" he asked. "I haven't made a mistake and kidnapped a small street ruffian?"

Smith's brows snapped together in a frown. "What are you talking about?"

He laughed. "Your chin is pushed forward about a mile, and your fists are clenched. You look as though you're about to take on the town bully."

He was right. Smiling, Shulamith forced her body to relax as she slid her feet into her small golden moccasins.

"Ready," she said, turning.

"I can see you are." Johnny Winterhawk gave her a smiling, admiring nod. He was mightily pleased about something.

THE MAINSAIL bellied out in the wind as Johnny moved lightly around the deck, tightening and stowing away. They were steering west southwest, directly into the setting sun, but as the dark shape of a large island loomed ahead of them Johnny told her to shift to a more southerly direction and finally came and sat beside her behind the wheel.

"Where are we going?" Smith asked, relinquishing the wheel. The sun blinded her when she looked at him, and she tried to shade her eyes so she could see his face.

"Around in circles till I can think of something," Johnny said ruefully. "First we have to get somewhere where we can take on gas."

They had taken as much as they could of the nonperishable food and supplies in the kitchen, and filled the boat's small fridge to bursting. Smith had assumed from this that Johnny was intending that they stay on the boat, but it had not occurred to her that he had nowhere to dock!

"You mean we're going to sail around all night?" she demanded, surprised and dismayed.

"Maybe," he said briefly. "I have to think."

"Well, before you do that," she said dryly, "do you think you could tell me what's going on? What on earth is the provisional wing of the Chopit Brotherhood and why do they want me?"

He looked grim. "A few young hotheads have decided that they should really be holding you for ransom. They're beginning to get visions of mailing your baby finger or your ear to your father to press our demands," he said baldly, for there could be no way to dress it up.

Smith shuddered, and her eyes searched his face. "I'm very attached to both," she said, with a small smile. This time her fists did not clench. She felt deeply frightened and was unspeakably hurt, as if she had just learned that everyone in the world hated her. She looked down at her hands. These people didn't know her, they didn't know her at all, and yet they wanted to mutilate her....

Johnny's large bronzed hand covered hers. "They're young hotheads," he said gently. "They're drunk with this sudden power they think they have. My people are not a violent people, Shulamith. Joseph Three Elk has forbidden them to do it. He said there was no room for a provisional wing of the Chopit people."

"Is that really what they call themselves?" Smith asked in angry wonder.

"No. It was Joseph Three Elk being sarcastic."

"I heard him talking on the news yesterday," she said quietly. The Chopit chief had sounded to her like an intelligent and humane, if angry, man. "Will they listen to him, the hotheads?"

Johnny Winterhawk adjusted his course minutely before answering.

"Possibly not," he said reluctantly, but she was already expecting the answer, for why else was she here on the boat? "They privately demanded that I hand you over to them, and when I refused they threatened to come and get you."

"Did they know I was on the island?"

"I'm sorry, yes."

Shulamith jumped to her feet, suddenly angry. "Well, this is just great!" she fumed. "First I was prisoner on an island, and now I'm on a damned *boat*! And there's still no solution in sight! How the hell am I ever going to get home? You don't even know where we're going to drop anchor tonight, so how are you planning on getting out of this? The police are after you, and now the entire Chopit nation is after me, so just what the hell are we going to do about it?"

"Not the entire Chopit nation," he corrected her softly, but Smith was in too great a rage to care.

"Oh, fine!" she exploded. "That's fine! I appreciate the distinction! *Not* the entire Chopit nation is after me, but sadly it doesn't *take* an entire people to cut off an ear! Not the entire nation, but you'll forgive me if I consider them a significant minority!" She looked balefully at him. "Over whom you don't seem to have much control!"

"No," he agreed, and she caught the sound of pain in his voice.

"Why not?" she demanded suddenly, for Johnny Winterhawk seemed to her the sort of man who would command respect anywhere. "Why can't you control them?"

He was checking his course again, looking up at the

sails while the sun glinted off the raven black of his hair and bathed his saddened face in a golden glow.

His voice was quiet against the wind. "I left the reserve," said Johnny Winterhawk, and he was no longer seeing the sail in front of him, but looking into the past. "I was taken from the reserve as a child and put into the white man's world. And I wanted to make it in the white man's world. I crossed over. When I saw my mistake it was too late to go back. I am tolerated by my people because sometimes I am useful to their cause, but I am not an Indian. I am not one of them."

Shulamith gasped. There was an anguish in his voice that it hurt her to listen to. She stood looking at him, almost afraid to move.

"Why?" she whispered on a long, horrified, unhappy note.

"Because that is the way of the world," said Johnny Winterhawk bitterly. "You have to lie in the bed you've made for yourself."

"I'm sorry," she whispered, desperate to take away his unhappiness, knowing she could not. "I'm so *sorry*."

Johnny Winterhawk did not reply, and there was a painful, unbreakable silence.

"I'm going to run into Sidney," he informed her a few minutes later. "We'll take on fuel and water there."

"Wait a minute," Smith said, as an idea struck her. "Sidney! Rolly's got a place not too far from Sidney. We could probably drop anchor there."

He looked at her in dry amusement. "And you can finish the conversation you started with Rolly yesterday," he suggested lightly.

"No. That's just it. Nobody'll be there. Valerie's just had twins; she's not there now. Valerie's his wife," she said impatiently as Johnny continued to gaze impassively at her. "We can moor there for ages without being bothered."

He shook his head. "I don't think so."

"Why not?" she demanded.

"Do you really think his neighbors would take no interest in a strange boat moored at his dock?"

"Oh." He was right. "But then what are we going to do? We can't sail around all night. It's ridiculous to think we can!"

"I don't think it."

"Well, then what are we going to do?"

Johnny Winterhawk sighed as though she was being tedious. "I guess we'll go to a provincial marine park and hope like hell no one recognizes you," he said flatly, as though it was a last-ditch choice, and he made it reluctantly.

FIVE HOURS LATER the big engines churned in the darkness to bring the *Outcast II* close in beside a small mooring buoy. There were no lights except those on the boat, and when they were docked and Johnny switched off the engines and the running lights the night fell black and silent around them.

"My God, I'm exhausted," Smith said gratefully, breathing in air that smelled faintly of their gas fumes. The journey to this small, out-of-the-way provincial marine park had been hell. Navigating after dark she always found a nightmare, eyes and ears on the alert both for the expected and for the unexpected.

There had been an additional strain this time: the never-ending sense of being hunted that was more exhausting, she felt, than any physical effort could ever be. Smith had told herself over and over again that no one could find them at night on the water, but each time they had seen the lights of another boat her heart had pounded and her stomach churned until the strange boat passed. Even now, in this tiny fairly remote cove, she could not feel safe.

Johnny Winterhawk made the boat fast for the night while Smith stood stupidly on deck, hands clenched deep in her pockets, unable to relax.

When he was finished Johnny leaped into the cockpit and stood for a moment gazing down at her in the softly welcoming glow that spilled from the light window. In a convulsive little movement Smith turned to him.

"Will they find us here?" she asked worriedly.

A small smile moved to one corner of his mouth. "My hunters or yours?"

But of course the police might already be on his trail! She had forgotten that. If one of the men who had been in the house that night had been arrested....

"Let's get below," Johnny said matter-of-factly. "If they do find us it won't help to be standing around on deck worrying." He shepherded her down the companionway to a seat in the lounge, then moved into the galley. "Coffee and food, in that order," he said, filling a kettle and lighting the gas under the hotplate. "We need it."

A responsive growl in her stomach reminded Shulamith that she hadn't eaten since lunch—about ten hours ago. "You said it! Johnny, I'm starved," she exclaimed, and his name was easy on her lips.

It had been easy on her lips all that day, she realized, glancing across the room at him with an imperceptible gasp of awareness as he caught her eye. Suddenly her head was filled with the burning memory of the afternoon and the erotic devastation she had experienced at his hands.

As he turned back to his task, she watched the play of shoulder and arm muscles under the blue cotton shirt with a new, uncomfortable pleasure that she scarcely understood.

There was a bed in the aft cabin, she was thinking. That was where he had put her the night he had kidnapped her. He had kissed her on that bed.

What would he do to her there tonight? Smith leaned back against the plush sofa cushions and spread her arms deliberately along the back, quelling the rising disturbance she felt. The fabric of the navy cushion covers was strong and rough under her fingers, like a light denim. Smith stroked it appreciatively, gazing around at the brass fittings and varnished teak.

"It's a beautiful boat," she said softly, groping for a subject of conversation. She had seen in his movements on deck that Johnny Winterhawk loved the *Outcast II*. It was no wonder, she thought. She was not so experienced a sailor as he was, but she had enough of a feeling for it to know that the *Outcast II*, as well as being beautiful, handled superbly.

"Yes," he agreed, moving toward her with cups and plates. Smith sat forward to lift one flap of the dropleaf dining table where he obviously intended to place the crockery.

"How long have you had her?" she asked, hiding her face under the long sweep of her hair as she bent down.

The *Outcast II* was a big boat, but it somehow seemed claustrophobic with Johnny Winterhawk inside.

"About eight months," he said, as the table leaf snapped into place. As Johnny set down the dishes she looked at him to find his dark eyes on her, watchful and determined. She erupted into nervous speech.

"Daddy likes motorboats. He's got a big one," she babbled. "But I have a small sail—just a twenty-nine footer—a C & C. This isn't a C & C, is it? It looks custom-built. But of course I haven't sailed her lately. She's been out of the water for a year...." Johnny was gazing at her, saying nothing, not helping her at all. "Her name is *Sweet Cherry Yacht*, because when I was a kid I thought that's what the song was about. You know, Swing Low, Sweet Cherry Yacht?" she laughed lightly, but the sound was tinged with hysteria. "I used to—"

"Shulamith," Johnny Winterhawk interrupted firmly, and his deep voice had a quality that instantly stilled her. She was silent, not looking at him.

"They aren't going to find us tonight," he said. "Relax. If they're going to sail around every marina between Vancouver and the States they've got more than one long night's work ahead of them."

Smith looked up. "They don't have to sail, though, do they?" she countered, the fact that he had mistaken the reason for her nerves relaxing her. "You had to register the boat to get this mooring, didn't you?" She shuddered at the memory, because he had bound and gagged her briefly during the time he was ashore. "All they have to do is call around."

"Which will be easier for the police than anyone

else,'' Johnny pointed out, and there was a little silence.

Her eyes searched his. "Are you frightened?" she asked. If the police found them now, she would be safe, but Johnny. . . Johnny would never be safe again.

He raised his eyebrows in a gesture that reminded her of Wilf. "Any non-WASP in this country who isn't afraid of a confrontation with the police needs his head examined," he said bluntly. "Of course I'm afraid. Not only have I abducted a white woman, but also I have already given her grounds for a charge of rape. And it's still all I can do to keep my damned hands off her."

The sudden high whistling of the kettle drowned out Smith's shocked gasp. Reaction twisted her stomach with a force that made her feel faint. With wide eyes she watched Johnny Winterhawk walk back to the galley and lift the kettle from the fire. She watched every movement of his hands as he turned off the stove, collected a can of condensed milk and went back to the table to pour water on the instant coffee in the two plastic mugs he had placed there. When he had returned the kettle to the stove, he flung himself onto the sofa opposite her.

The sudden aroma of coffee hitting her nostrils was a sensuous assault on Smith's overcharged system, and the hand that she lifted to the tin of milk then obviously trembled. Johnny Winterhawk's hand reached it at the same time, and both of them jerked away from the brush of skin on skin.

"Damn," he muttered under his breath, and irresistibly his black gaze found hers as he poured the milk into first her cup and then his own. "Drink," he ordered, as though it was imperative they both find something to do with their hands. Obediently Smith clutched the smooth plastic with both hands and lifted the liquid to her lips.

"Listen," said Johnny Winterhawk suddenly, his voice growling in his throat. Smith looked at him. "I don't know what this is between us, Peaceable Woman, but I damned well want it to stop."

Smith took an outraged breath. "I hope you don't—"

"It doesn't look as though it's stopping on its own," he went on inexorably, "so we are going to have to stop it."

Smith set her cup down with a little snap. "I expect you have more experience with this kind of thing than I have," she said with studied sweetness. "Perhaps you'll tell me how?"

His jaw tightened; she could feel the invisible tension humming in his body. "You might start by not swimming nude anymore," he said in sudden harshness.

Smith laughed a high mocking laugh. "Oh, *really*?" she said sarcastically. "That was *my* fault, was it? I suppose you think *you* were dressed with decorum!"

"I. . ." he began.

"And who asked you to watch me?"

"Look," replied Johnny Winterhawk, striving for calm, "all I'm saying is, whatever this is, I want it to stop."

"Well, then, don't start it!" Smith was utterly incensed. How dared he blame her? "I didn't know you were coming home early!" She had picked up her coffee cup, but now she banged it down again. "Why the hell did you come down to the beach if you didn't want it to happen? Why didn't you stay away when you saw I was naked?"

"Because I damned well didn't want to stay away!" he snapped. "Especially not after reading the erotic literature you so kindly left lying around my study!"

Smith's jaw fell open. "Erotic literature? What are you talking about? I never—" She broke off in amazement and jumped to her feet. "Do you mean my *poem*?" she demanded shrilly. How dared he! How dared he! She was sounding like a fishwife, but she didn't care. "Are you telling me you think—"

"That's what I mean," interrupted Johnny Winterhawk. "Are you telling me it wasn't deliberate?"

"In your *wastebasket*!" She was almost incoherent with rage. "I threw it in your wastebasket! It was garbage!"

Johnny was lying back against the cushions in a negligent posture, but his mood was anything but negligent. At any moment she half expected that the crackling tension in him would leap out and strike her.

"And it never occurred to you that the sight of my filing cabinet lying on its side on the floor would cause me to have a close look around my study?" he demanded, as if they both already knew the answer.

"Ahoy, *Outcast*! Ahoy, *Outcast*!"

Neither of them heard it. "Anyway," she shrilled, "if you thought that poem was an invitation, you don't read very well! I distinctly remember it said—"

"Ahoy, *Outcast*!"

"It said that my kiss scorches your body. And I'd—"

"And you call that an invitation? *Scorch*? That means burn, in case you—"

"You see, Harvey, it isn't the *Outcast*, it's *Outcast II*! I told you so!"

Johnny Winterhawk was standing over her now. "I know what it means," he said hoarsely; and pulling her into his arms, he set his mouth on hers.

"All right, all right, Vicky, I heard you! Ahoy, *Outcast II*! Ahoy, *Outcast II*!"

At last, in the silence, they heard it. Jerking apart, Smith and Johnny stared at each other in horror, listening in frozen silence to the noise of an engine and the muted thump and clatter as a boat bumped lightly against the *Outcast II*, both of them filled with the certainty that it must be the police. Without a word Johnny Winterhawk turned toward the companionway.

She caught up with him at the foot of the ladder and clung to hold him back. Desperately she whispered, "Tell them we've been sailing! Tell them we haven't heard the news! Don't admit anything, Johnny!"

"Hi, there! Anybody home?" This time it was a female voice, bright and giggly, and with a deep sigh they both relaxed. Johnny shook his head and grinned at her.

"Stay below!" he whispered, and went lightly up on deck and closed the hatch behind him.

She stayed where she was, listening to the voices and laughter overhead, not distinguishing anything except the vital fact that their visitors were not threatening.

There was a small shriek of delighted chatter from the woman, and then, after a minute, the engine roared away, and a few moments later the man's voice, from a distance, shouted, "Now don't fight with the little lady! You just give her whatever she wants, you hear?" There was heavy innuendo in the voice, and Smith wrinkled her brow in puzzlement as Johnny came down the companionway with a bottle of red wine in his hand.

"Who were they?" she demanded.

"Our neighbors across the cove," he said. He was looking at her oddly. "Why didn't you come up?"

"Well, you. . . you told me to stay below."

"And you obeyed me." He moved to set the bottle of wine on the table, then turned to face her. "Those people would have helped you escape. Didn't you think of that? All you had to do was come on deck and tell them who you were."

Smith looked at him, thunderstruck.

"Why didn't you?" Johnny persisted.

She was breathing through her open mouth, staring at his face.

Because it had been them against the world—that was why she hadn't called out. Because in that moment she had forgotten that Johnny Winterhawk was her kidnapper and enemy. He had been the one she loved most in all the world, the one she felt ready to die for.

Shulamith swallowed. "I—I'm going mad," she whispered, then whirled and rushed to the companionway.

He caught her on the first step and lifted her bodily away from the ladder. "No," he said calmly as she clawed and kicked against the restraint.

"Let me go!" she wailed on a high, hoarse cry, and dragging her down to the settee he clamped a hand over her mouth.

"When they're out of earshot," he said grimly, holding her tightly.

They were both silent then, listening to the small

friendly noise of their neighbors' engine recede across the cove. An ugly hopelessness washed over Smith, as thorough and devastating as what she had felt the first night of her abduction.

When finally he released her she slumped against the corner of the sofa and dropped her head back.

"I'm not myself," she said despairingly. She lifted her head and looked into Johnny Winterhawk's dark eyes. "I don't know what's happening to me, but I feel as though I'm going out of my mind." A sudden thought struck her.

"Have you drugged me?" she demanded harshly.

"No."

Her head fell back again. "You wouldn't tell me anyway, would you?" she said flatly. She raised a hand to her forehead, pushing her hair out of her face. "I'm losing my volition, losing my brain. It isn't like me, you know, not to have taken advantage of that."

"I know," he said.

"I should have gone out the forward hatch and over the side before you knew what I was doing, then called to them from out in the middle of the cove."

"Yes," he agreed softly.

She opened her eyes again and sighed. "I don't suppose I'll get another chance, will I?" she asked, a light humor returning to her. "Did you tell them we had the black plague aboard?"

Johnny Winterhawk grinned. "No," he said. "I told them. . . . Never mind what I told them."

"Why. . .but. . . ." She glanced at him, surprised by the tone in his voice, and found that in spite of his grin, his steady gaze was pensive on her. She jumped. "What on earth could you have told them to make you look like that?'' Smith demanded. She let out a sudden enlightened laugh. ''If I had jumped in the water I suppose they'd have thought it was just a lover's spat?''

Johnny's eyes lost the brooding look, and he grinned in amusement. ''That's exactly what they did think,'' he informed her. ''They could hear us shouting halfway across the cove, but they were determined to be neighborly.''

Smith looked at him. ''I don't believe you,'' she said. ''Halfway across the bay? What were we arguing about anyway?'' Then immediately she blushed.

''We were arguing,'' said Johnny wryly, ''about which of us had done more to tempt the other.''

Smith jumped up and crossed to the table. ''Mmmm!'' she said casually, picking up the bottle. ''A Beaujolais! Not bad. Who were they, anyway?''

Johnny Winterhawk walked into the galley and opened a drawer. ''Vicky and Harvey Mehan, from San Diego, California,'' he said. Picking a padlock out of the drawer he moved to the companionway, reached overhead and closed the hatch more firmly. As Shulamith breathlessly watched, he fitted the padlock. ''They've sailed up the coast in a fifty-foot motor yacht called the *White Dolphin*. They're a bit desperate for new faces.'' The lock snapped shut. ''Tomorrow they're continuing north. They want to go all the way up to Prince Rupert and the tip of the Panhandle.''

''You're locking us in,'' Smith choked.

Johnny turned. ''We have a problem, Peaceable Woman,'' he said softly.

Unblinking, she gazed at him.

"Both the forward and the aft cabins have hatches that open from the inside." His voice was measured, he was citing facts. "That means we sleep in the same cabin."

"*No!*" she shouted.

He was silent.

"No!" she said again. "Let me sleep out here, on the sofa." Her voice grew desperate. "You've *locked* the hatch here."

Johnny took a deep breath. "I don't like this any better than you do," he pointed out. "But there's no way to lock the door to the forward cabin. We sleep together."

She was burning up with the memory of the scene on the beach, of how desperate and helpless his touch had made her. If he did that to her again....

"Anyway," she said wildly, "the aft cabin hatch is too small for anyone to get through!"

"Desperate people do desperate things," Johnny Winterhawk said. "For someone as small as you I wouldn't bet on that."

"Then stay up and keep guard if you're so worried!" she snapped.

He lifted an eyebrow. "That would mean tying you up for five or six hours tomorrow while I slept."

He sounded as though he would prefer that, as though he would rather sit up all night than sleep beside her. But Smith knew the choice was hers.

"Oh, *God!*" she wailed. "I couldn't stand that again, Johnny, I *couldn't!*"

"Then I take it we are sharing a bunk," he said. And he looked at her with the eyes of a man who knows he is digging his own grave.

STARLIGHT GLIMMERED through the hatch to relieve the gloom of the cabin. Smith moved a hand slowly to the edge of her sleeping bag, listening intently to the deep breathing beside her.

It didn't change. Slowly, slowly, biting her lip lest in the black she bang against the bulkhead or the storage locker, she slid to a sitting position beside the sleeping shape of Johnny Winterhawk. A small pale reflection of starlight showed her that he was sleeping on his side, facing her.

He had thrown two sleeping bags on the aft stateroom bed, and had made her go to bed before him. When, after half an hour, her forced deep, slow breathing had convinced him she was asleep, Smith had heard him slip gently into the cabin and quietly undress and get into the sleeping bag beside her.

Then had begun a waiting game that nearly drove her mad. For the next hour or more she had had to continue her own deep breathing, fighting sleep, while she listened for those same slow sounds that would tell her Johnny Winterhawk had fallen asleep.

He had been tense and restless so long she wanted to scream, but at last, at last, he had fallen asleep. Then Smith had forced herself to wait another half hour before making a move.

As she pushed the bag down around her waist the rope that he had tied from her right wrist to the hand-grip at the head of the bed caught against something with a small brushing noise that made her freeze.

Johnny didn't stir. Gingerly, Smith felt in the depths of the sleeping bag with her toes to find the small paring knife she had hidden there.

She had known he would have to tie her up somehow. He couldn't be certain of waking up when she tried to escape unless she was hampered in some way.

"I'm giving you a long rope so you can be comfortable," he had said; and she had been reasonably so—the rope was more than three feet long. "Please don't hang yourself with it." Shulamith had smiled at the joke, trying not to laugh aloud at the comforting feel of the knife under her toes and the knowledge that she had thoroughly second-guessed him.

Her foot found the cool metal again now, and slowly, slowly, pulled the knife up to within reach of her outstretched hand. It came up point first, and she gasped as a too eager move made her prick her finger.

She breathed deeply to calm herself as she pressed the sharp edge against the thick rope and, wincing at each sound, carefully sawed it back and forth.

A few minutes later, though it seemed much longer, she was standing in the forward cabin, the length of the boat between herself and Johnny Winterhawk. With purposeful motions now, Smith lifted the towel she had picked up in the head and held it up to each of the hatch fasteners in turn, muffling the sound as she snapped them open.

Speed was essential. With light grace Smith climbed onto the edge of the bunk and eased the hatch lid wide open with hardly any sound. Then, catching up the full skirt of her nightgown, and getting purchase with her foot on the locker, she clambered up onto the deck and closed the hatch without a sound.

The world was at peace, dark and silent. Smith took in a deep breath and tried to get her bearings in the starlight. It cost her a few precious moments to find the dark shape of the *White Dolphin*, and then she was at the ropes on the starboard bow.

The water looked icy cold and probably was. Still, the nightgown had to go, she knew. It wouldn't warm her, and it would hamper her swimming. Smith sighed and slipped the lacy green gown, which she had painstakingly mended only yesterday, up over her head and dropped it at her feet. She hoped Vicky Mehan was a lighter sleeper than her husband.

"Very beautiful," said Johnny Winterhawk's deep voice, and the forward hatch cover lightly banged the deck behind her.

Smith, her toes curling the gunwales preparatory to a dive, involuntarily clutched the deck rope behind her and froze, looking over her shoulder at the dark shape looming out of the hatch behind her. Just then the full moon sailed triumphantly out from behind the large cloud that had been obscuring it, and painted all the tensed curves of her body silvery white under his unmoving gaze.

The moonlight slid across the deck behind her as she watched and illuminated that dark watchful face in all its angry tension.

Shulamith broke free of the spell first, in one smooth motion letting go the ropes and arching into a soaring dive that cut the water almost silently.

It wasn't as paralyzingly cold as she had anticipated; the cove must be protected, she thought in one corner of her mind as panic numbed the rest. She broke surface in a powerful racing stroke, facedown, her light arms cleaving the silky surface of the swell with every ounce of her strength.

All her nerve endings were on the alert for the impact of his body entering the water behind her, but what she heard instead was the muted roar of the *Outcast II*'s powerful engines. Smith's heart sank. She hadn't expected that. If he had tried to outrace her in the water she would have felt some hope, because he was an unknown quantity, and she was an excellent swimmer. But she couldn't hope to outdistance a boat—unless she could get close enough to shore or to the *White Dolphin* before he reached her that Johnny would be running the risk of an accident.

But the closest shore was a smooth cliff face that bespoke deep water beneath, and the *White Dolphin*.... Smith glanced over her shoulder to see the gleaming hull of the *Outcast II* bearing down on her.

Gasping a deep breath, she dived and had the satisfaction of hearing the engines stop. Johnny could only chase her as long as he could see her. It would be criminal negligence to risk running over her while she was underwater. Smith smiled in the tingling cold water. She would have to surface to get her bearings and for air, but that wouldn't give him enough time to catch up before she went under again. She would win after all. All she had to do was calm her panic and take her time, and she would get to the *White Dolphin*.

A few yards behind her she heard the unmistakable sound of a diver plummeting into the water. Surprised panic robbed her of all her oxygen, and Smith fought for the surface and air.

As she surfaced she took in her surroundings with a glance: the *White Dolphin* was still far away across the cove, the *Outcast II* was much closer, behind her, and

Johnny Winterhawk still somewhere under the waves.

The obvious course would be to try to outswim him to the big motor yacht, hoping that they never broke surface at the same time so that he could never be sure where she was. The less obvious course....

Smith dragged in a painfully deep breath and sank silently under the water, then changed course, breaking right in a wide semicircle that would bring her up behind the *Outcast II*, so that it would be between her and the *White Dolphin*. Then everything would depend on whether Johnny had left the keys in the engine. It was a calculated risk: he had had to react so swiftly that it wasn't likely he had taken time to hide the keys from her before diving in.

Smith surfaced as silently as she could, not looking in the direction of the *White Dolphin*, for the moonlight glinting off her white face would be far more easily seen than the back of her head. She was parallel now with the silent gray shape of the *Outcast II*, and one more breath would get her there.

A minute later Smith surfaced in the moonshadow of the sleek white yacht, where all its forty-foot length shielded her from the *White Dolphin*. The swim ladder was fixed on the stern, however, which was bright in moonlight. She couldn't risk clambering up it until the stern had moved into shadow.

With a little help from her. As the *Outcast II* lightly rode the swell Smith tried to ease the stern toward her. But her efforts were nearly useless, and when the yacht had moved halfway around to where she wanted it, inexorably it moved back again to its original position.

Smith decided to risk going up the ladder half in

shadow, half in moonlight. On the next swell she grasped the chrome rungs with slippery hands and as quickly as she could scaled the ladder. At the top she crouched and went over the rails and down into the cockpit.

"Welcome aboard," said a male voice, and Johnny Winterhawk's hand closed like a vise on her wrist.

CHAPTER TEN

As HER MOUTH OPENED to gasp in air he pulled her against him and stifled the scream behind his palm. Angrily Smith fought him, but he moved behind her, holding her hand behind her back, and as on the night he had kidnapped her, kept the other glued relentlessly to her mouth.

This time he did not lift her. "Quick, march!" he whispered angrily in her ear, and forced her up onto the cockpit seat, along the deck and down through the open hatch over the forward-stateroom bed. When she was standing on the bed he forced her down with a light push and let go of her, then braced his arms against the sides of the hatch to jump through.

Underneath, in his dark moonshadow, Smith scrambled to the tiny area of floor at the bunkhead and wrenched open the small teak door. As she rushed out into the lounge she heard him land on the teak flooring behind her and snap the hatch cover shut.

Near the navigation table she stopped running: there was nowhere to run. The main hatch was still securely locked and in spite of what Johnny had said about desperation, she did not think she could squeeze out of the small aft cabin hatches without fighting her way through.

She was tired of fighting, tired of a losing battle. She had been helpless against Johnny Winterhawk from the start. She turned to face him as he strode toward her, her hair dripping wet down her back, her naked erect body still beaded with seawater.

Johnny Winterhawk jerked on the cabin lights as he moved, and the lounge was filled with a warm glow that shut out the rest of the world and made the boat seem safe and homelike. Its small comfortable proportions reminded her suddenly of the long-ago flat in Paris, the only place in her life that had really felt like home.

Johnny's hair, too, was thick with seawater, and his body was wet. He wore a snug pair of navy briefs or swim trunks—she wasn't sure which—that clung to him wetly.

He stopped two feet away from her, and his dark eyes flashed.

"By God," he bit out, "next time I'll truss you like a rodeo steer!" and he was angrier than she had ever seen him.

The injustice of his anger annoyed her—what did he expect her to do? And suddenly Shulamith wasn't too tired to fight anymore.

"Fine!" she snapped loudly. "Truss me any way you like! Do you think I'm going to give in to this gracefully? You kidnapped me, remember? Don't expect me to apologize over your lost sleep! My father is ill, I'm being held hostage for a band of lunatics who want to mutilate me, and if you expect me not to try to escape, you're...." She began to shiver. "I am not going to stop! I am going to get away from you if it's the last thing I do!"

With one stride he closed the gap between them and pulled her shivering body into his. "You'll never get away from me," he growled hoarsely, like a man possessed, and covered her mouth fiercely with his own.

She tired to recoil, but his mouth followed her, so that she was bent over his arm, her body arched into the commanding curve of his. His hand moved to cup her head, and she felt the cold wet press of her hair against her scalp. His other arm wrapped her tightly, so that her breasts pressed against him, and his water-beaded flesh slid erotically against hers. Smith could feel the strength in his arms and hands and body, a strength it would be futile to fight against, and the beat of panic at the base of her throat abruptly took on the rhythm of desire.

When at last he lifted his head and looked down into her eyes she swallowed convulsively and gasped in a shaky breath. "Wait," she begged softly, lifting a small hand to cup the curve of his shoulder. That touch of flesh fitting flesh was so sensual it shook her, and she closed her eyes and swallowed again. "Wait," she breathed, like a woman fighting for breath in a burning building.

In answer he kissed her throat, her neck, her shoulder, as though the taste of her were all the sustenance he needed. "Don't make me wait," he whispered hoarsely, desperate. "For God's sake, don't make me wait!" And his mouth moved over her skin with a keen stinging so intense she could not tell if it was fire or ice.

Her breath escaped in a moan, and as panic and desire together beat higher in her she pushed against his chest, struggling against the unfamiliar heat that threatened to close over her.

"Wait...stop, I can't..." she gasped, unable some-how to get the oxygen she needed.

He raised his head and looked into her face again, and his eyes were changed. They were black now and hungry and determined, and the look in them poured gasoline on the desire that flamed in the pit of her stom-ach; and it whooshed up and burned like hot honey along every nerve. Her hands went still against him then, and her breath began to shudder between her part-ed lips as helplessly she felt him move to clasp her wrists in one firm hand behind her back. The grip hurt her shoulders, and her head fell back to relieve the stretched muscles. Then, suddenly, her back was arching so that her breasts were offered up to his mouth, and she was impatient for him to taste her needy flesh, for the hot wetness of his lips to enclose her beaded nipple.

But still that black gaze stared into her eyes, electrify-ing every corner of her mind, and she knew that this was the lover she had waited for every day of her life without knowing it. His free hand stroked the taut muscles of her arched stomach, and she quivered with desire and pressed her body to him. She was being stripped down to essentials, as she had been in the afternoon on the beach, but now it was without interest that she felt the human veneer fall away. Now she was Cinderella, throwing off her rags for the ball gown, her whole atten-tion turned on the glittering fury that enwrapped her.

"Wait?" he queried her hoarsely, as his hand stopped its hypnotic stroking and waited; and it was only a min-ute ago that she had asked him to stop.

"I...what?"

"You asked me to stop," Johnny said, and his deep

voice stroked her nerves like animal fur. "Stop me now if that's what you want. Don't expect to be able to stop me later. More than anything on God's earth I want to see you tremble. Once I start, there'll be no stopping."

Shulamith smiled in sensuous, slow understanding of everything he said and did not say. She wondered fleetingly what would happen if she told him to stop, because Johnny Winterhawk was lying to himself. His possessive rage was only stilled because she lay quiescent in his arms. If she fought to get away. . . .

But she did not want to fight to get away. She was dressed in the flames of a fire that licked and flickered unmercifully at her flesh, and it must consume them both. She felt the curve of her own flesh under the hard shape of his palm, as though through him her femaleness was defined. Some new understanding hovered on the periphery of her mind, and again she smiled. The confidence of womanhood through millennia flooded her.

"You will tremble, too," she promised, and his arms tightened almost savagely on her, and she was drowning in a sea of flame.

He lifted her body up against him, cradling her hips on his, and covered her mouth with a fierce kiss, pressing her body against his aroused hardness, and his tongue between her lips, in a double assault that overwhelmed her senses. Fingers in his hair, she held his head and tore her mouth away.

"Johnny," she whispered, her voice husky with passion and a kind of animal panic, "Johnny, I'm frightened."

He had moved through the door into the darkened aft

stateroom. When she spoke he set her on the bed and leaned over her, protectively, so that she could not escape. "So am I," he said, touching her face with a hand that trembled. "I've never been closer to insanity in my life."

She had thought that he at least was experienced in this all-consuming need that had her in its grip as surely as a drug. Smith felt terror finger her throat as she watched Johnny's trembling hands struggle to remove the wet fabric that hugged his hips and realized what she had understood before only partially: this was taking him unawares, too. Johnny Winterhawk was out of control.

He threw one sleeping bag to the floor and flung the other one, open, over them both as he slid onto the bed beside her.

One half of her mind was frankly terrified, but it was the other half that ran her body. She moved against him with a convulsive need that she could not hold at bay and held her mouth up for his kiss with an urgency that the other part of her could only watch in mute terror.

"Shulamith," he whispered against her lips. "You belong to me, you're part of me. Do you know it?"

"Yes," she cried softly. "Yes, Johnny, please, please."

He kissed her breast, circling the tightly hardened nipple with his tongue, and the warmth radiated through her body from his mouth. But it was no longer what she wanted, no longer enough.

"Please," she gasped, curling desperately into him, touching the blazing heat of his center with a moan of mingled pleasure, discovery and anticipation that palpably shook him as he heard it.

He lifted his lips from her skin then, and, as though in spite of his intentions, he lifted his body to draw her under his sheltering warmth. Then, in a pleasure so profound it was almost torment, he sank down into her.

She cried out her sense of completion, of oneness with him, and saw in his dark, half-lidded eyes that this was the cry he needed to hear from her—this, and more.

He needed every response that his body drew from her, every moan, every whimper, every convulsive press of her fingers against the pillow or against his flesh. He drew them from her steadily, unrelentingly, and drank them in with a look of such possessive need she had to shut her eyes against it. Johnny did not shut his eyes, however, not till the very end. But when the wild climb of passion that gripped her exploded in her body and throat she cried out with an intensity that was too much for him to bear, and he closed his eyes as his body surged against her, and shuddering and trembling, he cried out his release and her name together.

SHE AWOKE in the early hours, long before dawn. The moon was gone; only starlight flickered into the darkness of the unfamiliar stateroom. But Shulamith knew instantly where she was and curled against Johnny's warm frame without a flicker of surprise that he should be here in her bed, her lover.

When his hand moved to stroke her hair she felt that, too, without surprise. Never again would she be alone in those terrible small hours between midnight and dawn.

"Awake?" breathed Johnny above her head, and she nodded against his shoulders.

"Mmm," she agreed.

"Shulamith, let's get married," he said, his voice softly urgent. "I love you. I can't live without you. Will you marry me?"

His arm gripped her protectively, and she snuggled sleepily into his embrace and gave a satisfied sigh.

"Yes, Johnny," she said.

"GOOD LUCK!" the young woman shrieked delightedly, trying to be heard over the drone of the *White Dolphin*'s powerful engine as she sailed past. She and her husband, grinning ear to ear, waved boisterously. "Have a happy honeymoon!" they bellowed in unison.

Smith's wave faltered. She had been standing halfway up the companionway ladder, her elbows resting on deck, but at this she nearly fell down. Clutching the hatchway for support, she blinked up at Johnny. "How on earth. . .?" she began, assailed by a host of sudden doubts.

The *White Dolphin* was already at the mouth of the tiny cove, and Johnny turned to the hatchway. As she retreated before him down the ladder he grinned at her. "Don't worry, we will have," he said, following her nimbly down the companionway—she backward, he frontward.

But that wasn't the worry that had sprung to her mind. Smith walked backward to the lounge in her bare feet, pulling at the hem of Johnny's baggy old gray sweat shirt, which was the only garment she was wearing. It covered to nearly halfway down her thighs, and she had pushed the baggy sleeves up above her elbows to give her freedom of movement. She had been comfortable in it—till now. Now she felt naked and vulnerable and afraid.

As though he had suddenly become aware that something was wrong, Johnny's dark heavy brows snapped together. "What is it?" he demanded.

Smith stood straight by the aluminum mast that ran through the boat to the keel. "Who were those people?" she demanded.

It took him aback. "What people? On the *Dolphin*?"

Shulamith looked at him steadily in answer, and he shrugged. "I told you as much as I know last night. Vicky and Henry Mehan, from the States."

"Harvey," she corrected in a rigidly emotionless tone, her wide eyes riveted to his face. "Last night you said Harvey."

"Harvey," he agreed with a nod. "Why? Do you know them?" His look was suddenly intent. "Do they know you?"

She brushed that aside. "You only saw them once, last night when they came over?"

"What the hell is the matter?" he demanded, moving to her side and grasping her arm above the elbow. "Are you telling me those people are going to go and report seeing you to the police?"

She eyed him stonily. "You're good, you know, but this is all wasted on me!" she snapped. "What a pity your friends aren't so word perfect in their parts! What a pity they've given the game away! What a pity—" But the stony control that served her so well in business meetings and sawmills deserted her suddenly. A forlorn ache gripped her throat, and she choked on something that threatened to be tears.

Johnny caught her in his arms. "Love, what is it?" His voice was thick with concern, but she pushed him

violently away and stood straight and alone as she had
always been, as she would always be.

"Let go of me!" she ordered hotly. "Leave me
alone!" But Johnny Winterhawk's eyes crackled with
anger, and roughly he pulled her against him again.

"I told you not to try to get away from me," he
growled, holding her tight into his chest. "Now will you
please tell me what the damn hell is going on?"

"Will you please tell me," she countered, feeling safe
and warm in his embrace in spite of everything, "what
the damn hell Vicky and Harvey Mehan are doing wishing us a happy honeymoon when you only proposed to
me at three o'clock this morning?"

"Oh, Peaceable Woman," he breathed, and she felt
relieved laughter shake his frame. Threading his hand
into the matted tangle of her hair he drew her head back,
and she looked into his eyes and knew suddenly that
everything was all right. She was safe with Johnny. . . .

He said, "Last night, the Mehans were looking for a
nice friendly party. I didn't want to be rude or attract
the wrong attention, but I had to make them go."

There was a pulse beating at the base of his throat,
and she was filled with the need to kiss him there.

"Yes," she said. "I asked you last night what you'd
told them. You said never mind."

"I told them—" Johnny swallowed "—I told them it
was our wedding night, Peaceable Woman." She
gasped, and laughed a breathless laugh. "That's why
they left us the wine, which we forgot to drink." Gently
he lifted a hand to stroke her cheek.

"Why didn't you tell me when I asked?"

He bent and kissed her. "I was about to tell you," he

said, "and then I looked at you, and suddenly I was wishing more than I've ever wished anything that it was true. I wanted you to be my wife. I wanted to be able to pick you up and carry you to bed and...." His mouth covered hers with a desperate urgency that melted her being. "Marry me, Shulamith," he whispered against her lips. "I need you so much."

As long as she was in his arms, she was home. "Yes, Johnny," she said, and clung to him in the sudden certain knowledge that without him she would die.

"From CBC Radio News, World Report with...." Smith stirred gently in Johnny's hold, uncertain how long they had stood wrapped in each other's arms, oblivious to everything until that intrusive voice broke in on them. "In this morning's headlines...."

Johnny's arms loosened on her, and he looked down at her. "We'd better listen," he said, and she nodded and flung herself on the sofa while Johnny moved restlessly to the nav station and fiddled with the radio dial.

The headline stories were all political or international, with no mention of kidnapping or St. John's Wood, and Shulamith picked up the small comb, which was the only one on board and nearly useless for her hair, and resumed her earlier attempts to straighten out the million tangles that last night had caused.

Nothing. Not a peep, not a mention of her father or herself. They listened right to the end, looking at each other in the abstracted way of people whose attention is focused on their hearing, Johnny with one eyebrow raised and his full mouth relaxed.

When the sports report began he reached out a slow hand and flicked the knob to silence.

"Interesting," he said.

On last night's news there had at least been a mention of her case, if no real news, and to Smith this was not so much interesting as disturbing.

"Johnny, what do you think it means?" She grimaced as a particularly nasty tangle met the comb she was absentmindedly pulling through her hair.

"It means we don't know what the hell is going on, doesn't it? It means we're not getting any clues about whether they've taken anyone in for questioning yet."

"Who would they have taken in?"

"They probably have a pretty good idea who of the band might be behind a stunt like this." He was leaning back casually in the nav-station bench, but his fingers were restlessly flicking the edges of the charts on the table. "The question is, have my four cohorts in crime kept their mouths shut, or does the entire band know who's behind this?"

Smith looked at him. "Why would they have a pretty good idea? Has someone done something like this before?"

"No," Johnny said shortly. He was deep in thought over something.

Slowly she asked, "Well, then, how would the police know anybody's name? How would they know who is a Chopa and who isn't? They can't just arrest every—"

Johnny's brow unfurrowed as he focused on her. "Don't be naive," he said flatly.

"What do you mean?" she demanded, beginning to get angry. "If no one has a criminal record how are the police—"

She stopped because he was laughing. "Come on,

Peaceable Woman, where have you been all your life? You know as well as I do that the Mounties have a file on just about anybody that moves in this country. Particularly if they move against the stream.''

Smith set down the comb. Of course he was right. One of the things that the McDonald Commission into RCMP wrongdoing had disclosed was that the RCMP maintained hundreds of thousands of files on law-abiding citizens who were deemed to be "potential" threats because of their political or sexual leanings. But somehow that had all seemed so far away....

"I...do you think they've got one on you?"

"I don't think about it," said Johnny. "It makes me too damned mad."

Which must mean he thought they did. "And your... friends? The new provos?"

He laughed as though he understood her question better than she did. "It strikes closer to home than that, Peaceable Woman," he said flatly. "I'd be very surprised if they don't have one on you."

She jumped as though he had burned her. "On *me!*" she protested in a squeak. "What would they want...?"

"You've just spent a year in Europe, Peaceable Woman," he said, his dark eyes watching her levelly. "Visit any Communist countries?"

"No...well, only Yugoslavia...."

"Bingo," said Johnny softly.

She felt her breathing stop. Beyond the silence of their little cove there was a distant roar of a motorboat going past.

Smith swallowed. "But I...that's ridiculous! I was on business! Why would they...." She faltered to a stop, feeling the world shake under her feet, as it had done when she had stood in his study and he had told her about justice and his people.

She stood up without grace and walked over to the open hatch to stand in the sunlight and the clean seabreeze. She felt more threatened than she had ever felt in her life, even when she was being kidnapped.

"Nothing's safe, is it?" she whispered. "Nothing in the world." And Johnny stood and moved behind her and took her in his arms.

"I used to think that nothing was safe," he said softly, but a strong emotion was threading his voice. "But that isn't true. Love is safe, if you can find it. I found that out the first time I looked at you." He turned her to face him. "Love is safe, if you can be sure of it before they take it away from you. Let me be sure of you, Shulamith, before they take it away from us. You'll be safe with me. I love you. I'll always love you. Marry me now, before they take you away from me."

JOHNNY DROPPED LIGHTLY through the hatch and moved past Smith in the galley to fling himself down on the sofa in the lounge.

"Where were you baptized?" he asked abruptly, and she goggled at him.

"Where was I *what*?"

"Baptized."

"I was afraid you said that. What for? Anyway, I wasn't."

"To get a marriage license," said Johnny, gratefully taking the cup of coffee she passed him. "Weren't what?"

"Baptized. At least I don't think I was. Is that the only thing we can use?"

Outcast II was sitting in the marina dock where Johnny had taken on gas and water and then gone to phone for information.

"Or passport or birth certificate. I thought the baptismal would be easiest. Why weren't you baptized?"

She sat down opposite him, sipping her coffee. "My father's an atheist, and my mother was Israeli. I don't think they thought of it."

"Birth certificate, then," Johnny said purposefully.

She looked at him. "You mean apply for one?"

"Mm-hmm." He nodded.

"It would take weeks. I was born in Paris."

There was a pause. "France," he said flatly, making it a statement.

"There's another one?"

As though he could not keep still, Johnny pulled himself to his feet and walked the length of the teak flooring to the companionway. "There's a Paris, Ontario," he said, turning to lean his shoulders against the ladder. "You sure you weren't—"

She interrupted with a laugh, "Sorry, no can do." And Johnny smiled at her, but their humor was a lie. The lounge was filled with a powerful sense of urgency, of a battle against overwhelming odds.

"That leaves passport," said Johnny, in a matter-of-fact determination.

"I can't apply for a passport," she protested. "I've already got a valid one. It's against the law to have two."

"Where's your passport now?" he asked, following

some trail behind his dark eyes that she couldn't fathom.

"At home."

"Where at home?"

"I don't know. In my bedroom, I suppose; so's my birth certificate. Probably I didn't take them out of my handbag after I got ba—why?" she demanded suddenly.

He was silent.

"You aren't thinking of going *back* there?"

Her shrillness broke through his reverie. "Why not?" he asked.

"Because you—what if they caught you? What if they've got someone staying at the house?"

He shrugged. "Do you keep an emergency key outside?"

"Yes...well, I put one there ages ago, but I don't—I mean, it's never been used. I don't know if it's still there." She was sitting bolt upright, staring at him. "Johnny, they'll arrest you! It's not worth it."

"If I've got a key, what are they going to arrest me for?" He spoke as though there was no danger, no possibility anything could go wrong. "Where's the key, and where's your handbag?"

"Johnny, please! Can't we go somewhere else and get married? Can't we go to another province, fly down to the States somewhere? Maryland or Delaware or somewhere. Isn't it supposed to be easier there?"

"Mmm," he said. "There are nine other provinces, two territories, and fifty states. How are we going to find the one that will marry us without identification?"

"There must—"

"And how the hell are you going to get into the States, anyway, without identification?"

"I...oh."

"So where is—"

"That still leaves us nine provinces and two territories," she interrupted. "Let's try it, Johnny, please."

"All right," he said. "If I can't find your passport. Where's the key, and where's your handbag?"

In her heart she could not really believe that one could get married anywhere in Canada without some sort of identification. And she wanted to marry him; before they found her and dragged her back to the world she wanted to be assured of always belonging to Johnny Winterhawk.

She was not aware that she thought of it in terms of being dragged back to the world, nor was she aware of how limited her scope was. The logic seemed irrefutable: she loved Johnny, she must marry him immediately before the outside world could interfere.

And she told him.

SMITH SAT TERRIFIED in the ship's lounge, without light, without movement, biting her lip each time a boat sailed near, each time she heard a footfall on the dock.

When the footsteps stopped beside the stern, and she heard someone jump aboard she leaped nervously to her feet, then thought better of making any noise that would inform an intruder that she was there. Caught between the need to hide and the necessity for silence, she stood stupidly immobile, staring at the slowly opening hatch.

"It's you!" she croaked thankfully, running to the

companionway to touch him, to hold him, to be sure he was there safe. "You've been gone *hours*! What happened?"

Johnny smiled at her and shook his head. "Nothing happened," he said. He handed her a plastic shopping bag from a grocery chain. "Here's your handbag. Your passport's in it."

She closed her eyes. "My God, you got it!" she exclaimed, feeling suddenly light-headed. "How did you do it?"

But she knew how he had done it, just as they had planned: he had rented a car, a big Cadillac that would not seem out of place at her father's house; he had waited till dark, then driven to the front door, found the key and gone in, as though he owned the place. He had turned on the hall light, and then he had gone quickly upstairs and into her bedroom and come back down and into the car before anyone could come to investigate.

"Just as planned?" she asked, and he nodded.

"I didn't realize it would be so long!" she chattered in relief. "I was afraid you weren't coming back!"

Johnny stroked her hair and smiled. "That's fair," he said. "I was afraid you weren't waiting for me."

She had wanted to go with him, but he had said the risk would be far greater if she did. He had left her unguarded on the *Outcast II* at a public dock by a restaurant. He hadn't tried to lock her in. She could have left at any time. She hadn't wanted to. The world was as much her enemy as Johnny's now....

They applied for the license at noon the next day, in the Robson Square court buildings. Smith had wanted to sail to a small town up the coast, but Johnny's arguments had convinced her that no town was cut off from radio and television, and as strangers they would be more noticeable in a small town than in the crowded lunch-hour traffic of Robson Square, where a marriage license was probably issued every five minutes.

"You see?" Johnny said as, nervously entering the marriage-license office at twenty past twelve, they saw a number of people filling out forms and standing at the desk to pay.

"We aren't out of the woods yet," Smith said, feeling extraordinarily conspicuous in her borrowed clothes and handmade moccasins and, to hide her striking hair, a navy sports cap Johnny had had on the boat. As Johnny led her to a seat by the wall she giggled nervously. "Aren't you afraid they'll ask you why you're marrying a lumberjack?"

"That's good," Johnny smiled approvingly. "You look as though you've got bridal jitters already. Keep it up."

The mission was accomplished without mishap; the woman behind the desk scarcely reading their names, simply smiling in kindly but impersonal congratulation as she took their money and handed them the license.

As they moved through the doors they passed another couple coming in: a young girl of no more than sixteen, who was heavily pregnant, and a boy not much older, petulantly angry about something.

"Geez, Middy, I *told* you I wanted..." they heard, before his voice was lost in the general babble, and the door shut behind them. Shulamith shivered.

"I guess you have to be a real optimist for a job like that," she said in a quiet voice.

Johnny understood what she meant.

"Yes," he said. "When I look at you I'm an optimist." And the moment of fear was drowned in the smile in his dark eyes.

After that, she insisted on going shopping for some clothes. "Do you realize you've never seen me in anything but your baggy old clothes?" she declared. "I want to look nice for a change."

"I've seen you naked in my bed," said Johnny softly. "Nothing and no one could be more beautiful than that."

Her cheeks burned faintly. "You're trying to put me off," she laughed. "But I want some clothes!"

She wasn't spendthrift, but she was used to buying what she needed, and Smith needed the lot. After a preliminary stop in lingerie and then shoes to get some things so she could be decent while trying on clothes, she moved into the women's-wear department of a store she rarely patronized and within an hour had clothes for nearly any eventuality, including a wedding outfit.

As they walked to the cash register behind an overburdened saleswoman, Smith, rooting in her handbag for her wallet, felt some of her old self return to her. The clothes she had chosen, though cheaper than she usually wore because she was afraid of shopping at her regular haunts, had made her look smart again and reminded her of who she was—and who she was not.

Just being able to hold her handbag seemed to bolster her, to give her a sense of herself. She was not a penniless, helpless nonentity, after all. She was Shulamith St. John.

She had paid for the shoes and underwear with cash, but now the bill was nearly a thousand dollars, and she began to proffer a credit card. But suddenly Johnny covered her hand and held it back, reaching for his wallet with his other hand.

"Let me," he said, and she was suddenly bridling at the tone in his voice. She had been earning an excellent salary for years and she was used to paying her own way. She had paid her own way all over Europe for a year without masculine help.

"No, Johnny," she said evenly, twisting her hand in his grasp. "I want to pay."

"I'll pay for it," he said flatly. His grip tightened, and his dark eyes flashed a warning at her.

Smith began to burn. "They're my clothes," she said, "and I'll—"

"They're your wedding trousseau," he said, with an arrogance that made her gasp, "and I'll pay for my bride."

Her credit card dropped to the floor, and Johnny slipped his foot over it, then casually bent and picked it up, passing his own to the curious saleswoman.

"Johnny, will you—" Smith began, and then broke off, her eyes following his thumb as he stroked it over her name raised in plastic: SHULAMITH ST. JOHN.

"Oh, my God!" she said quietly, and took back her card and slipped it into her wallet.

"Sorry," she said later, her arm through his as they left the store laden with packages. "I should have known you weren't a male chauvinist."

He said, "What the hell difference does it make who pays for what? We might have—"

"Well, we didn't," Smith said. "and you know it makes a difference! I earn my money, and I want to spend it. I don't need a husband to buy me *clothes*, that's for sure!"

But it had been a dangerous moment, and Johnny was still seething with reaction. "Well, congratulations! What *do* you need a husband for? I want to be sure of getting it right on my application!"

A woman passed them, her mouth twitching with repressed amusement, and Smith realized with a start that for all the extraordinary circumstances surrounding them, here they were having a most ordinary lovers' spat. Suddenly the argument seemed foolishly unimportant. She stopped in the street, pulling Johnny to a halt beside her, then reached up on her toes to mutter in his ear.

"Sex," she said softly. "That's what I need a husband for. And you got it right on your application."

Johnny Winterhawk choked and dropped a parcel, and Smith went into a fit of laughter. She had never felt so free. In all her life she hadn't flirted like this with a man; she had never had the confidence. Somehow Johnny had given her the confidence. Looking into his heavily message-laden eyes she understood, but only dimly, that there was a huge and qualitative difference between the confidence she felt being reunited with her handbag and credit cards, and what she felt now, with Johnny. Smith puzzled over the discovery for a vague moment and then let it wash away in the slipstream of Johnny's meaningful smile.

"Wait till I get you home," he was saying, and her heart skipped an anticipatory beat.

THE MANDATORY TWO DAYS of waiting between the time of getting the license and being able to get married passed in a golden glow of loving. They sailed back to their secluded cove and swam and lazed in the sun and ate milk and honey, and at night in the small aft cabin they reached a rapture of passion that answered every yearning and shook Shulamith to the roots of her soul.

On Saturday night she stood in the tiny washroom attached to the aft stateroom and showered and made up, then went next door to dress, with a surprising intensity of solemn excitement in the pit of her stomach.

I am committing myself to you for life, she thought, in soft wonder that the idea could give so much pleasure.

Her lacy underthings were new, as was the beautiful, silky cream-colored dress and full-sleeved jacket she had chosen. Gold thread shot through the material and on the left jacket cuff formed a tiny horseshoe.

"For good luck," she smiled, pointing it out to Johnny. "I have to remember to hold my arm down so the luck won't run out."

For "blue" and "old," she had a neckerchief of Johnny's that she would tuck into her stocking. She had planned to make that do for "borrowed" as well, but then she found something in her handbag she had forgotten—a gold bracelet she had bought for Valerie Middleton in Zurich and hadn't given to her yet. It made everything seem more right, somehow, that her "borrowed" should be from a good woman friend.

Johnny, very dark in a black suit, smiled at her satisfaction. "Where would we be without ritual?" he asked.

"Marriage is a ritual," Shulamith pointed out softly, and he looked momentarily shaken.

"Yes," he said, "you're right." And she wondered if his own atavistic need to engage in society's ritual of mutual commitment had somehow escaped his notice.

They were married in a small chapel, maintained by a marriage service, at eight o'clock on a balmy Saturday night. Never having had a religion, she chose the only service she knew, that began "Dearly beloved"; and as the ritual words flowed out into the tiny chapel and bound her irrevocably to Johnny, as they bound so many thousands—millions—of people before them, Shulamith was filled with a deep, comforting certainty that she had never experienced before. *I believe in God,* she thought with distant surprise, as though she had always believed, but had never known it before. She looked into Johnny's stern face as he repeated his vows and felt the blur of inexplicable tears. *I have to believe in God,* she was thinking, *because love like this is only possible if God exists. Because science can never explain what I know in every pore—that what I feel for you is a reflection of the face of God.*

A tear rolled softly, secretly down her cheek, and she turned to the warm bright gaze of their minister.

"I, Shulamith," she repeated softly, "take thee, John..." and each word was a perfect crystalization of what she wanted to say.

"YOU'VE GOT A FAMOUS NAME," said the man who was signing as her witness, but he spoke lightly, carelessly, to pass the time as he signed his name, and her inner serenity was not disturbed. Her father's given names were Lucas Cordwainer, and she had written only Lucas in the space provided.

"No relation," she said, smiling as easily and mock-ruefully as if it were true, as if she would like to be that rich, and the moment passed.

She wondered if they would find out one day, the professional marrying man and the professional witnesses. Would they read it in a paper or hear it on a radio and remember? Or was it all just a meaningless blur to them, another job done—this moment that was of such crystal clarity to her?

Johnny's face as he signed was as stern, as tightly drawn as when he had made his vows, but she could not read what emotion pulled him. Not until he took her arm to lead her out of the chapel did she sense in him the barely controlled pride of possession and the need to get her away from their three smiling well-wishers—alone.

In the taxi she sat back in his hold and felt his lips brush her brow. "Wife," he whispered possessively, and she turned and gripped his black lapel and raised her face almost desperately for his kiss.

"And in Vancouver," said the taxi's radio, snapping them both to awareness, "a lumber giant gives in to an unusual ransom demand. That story first." They stared at each other, listening. "St. John Forest Products has apparently acceded to an Indian rights group's unusual ransom demand. Roland Middleton, a senior vice-president at St. John Forest Products, Limited, this evening denied rumors that timbering operations in Cat Bite Valley and the surrounding areas were scheduled to begin as early as next week. He said no firm schedule had ever been drawn up for cutting in the area, and that such a decision would be delayed indefinitely until company president Cordwainer St. John is released from hospital and fully recovered.

"Mr. St. John suffered a heart attack a week ago, apparently when terrorists kidnapped his daughter, Shulamith. Later, at his hospital bed, he received a telephone call demanding, as the price of his daughter's safe return, that he delay timbering operations in Cat Bite Valley, seen as the traditional hunting and fishing grounds of the Chopa Indian tribe, and the subject of a provincially appointed commission of inquiry, which began Monday in Vancouver.

"Mr. Middleton said, however, that no decision had been made regarding the kidnappers' threat and that the announcement was being made merely to clarify the issue regarding Cat Bite Valley.

"Meanwhile, Mr. St. John was unable to talk to reporters. A hospital spokesman said his condition is listed as 'serious.'"

Neither said a word until they stood on the deserted dock by *Outcast II* and the taxi's lights had gone winking off into the distance. Then Smith let go the excitement that bubbled in her, and laughed a tinkling, triumphant laugh.

"We've won!" she said softly, delightedly, suppressing a need to shout in case people on neighboring boats should overhear. "I don't believe it, we've won!" She put a delicately shod foot on the gunwale and lightly leaped aboard. "The old phony!" she laughed. Johnny was grimly quiet as he unlocked and opened the hatch, but she didn't notice. "He must love me after all!"

"Rolly?" asked Johnny dryly, as they moved down the companionway and turned on the soft lights that made this boat home to her.

Laughter bubbled over again. "That wasn't Rolly. That was my father's brain dreaming that one up!" she told him. She nodded, agreeing with herself. "It's daddy all over. He does not, repeat not, give in to ransom demands. He loves me, you see, but not enough to admit it publicly. Or would you call that *liking*? I wonder what he'd have done if they'd asked for money?" She felt oddly near tears for a moment.

"He'd have paid it," said Johnny softly. "Can't you s—"

"*Sure* he would," she said lightly, unconvinced. "The old coward. Hiding behind his 'condition' and making poor Rolly do the dirty work."

"You think he's not really worse?" Johnny asked curiously.

She smiled and shook her head. "Of course he's not worse. My father isn't the sort to—anyway, it's obvious what he's doing—it's a ploy! Isn't it obvious?"

"Not glaringly."

"Can I phone the hospital?"

"What?"

"I'd pretend to be someone else—his secretary. Or Valerie. I just want a report on how he's really doing."

"If you're right about it, you won't get a report. They'll repeat what they told reporters."

"I could say I was—"

"No."

Smith gave him a quizzical smile. "Is this my kidnapper talking or my husband?"

"Your kidnapper. I still haven't figured a way out of this."

"Yes, you have. We'll go back and say we were on our honeymoon and daddy forgot because of his heart attack."

"Very shrewd," he said. "Very cunning. And what will we say when daddy starts squawking that it isn't true?"

"He won't. I'll tell him not to."

Johnny laughed. "Either you haven't been telling the truth about your powers over the man, or else you're underestimating him badly."

"It's not a question of power," she said. "Daddy doesn't like to look a fool. If I say I've been on my honeymoon and he keeps on saying I was kidnapped, you know what they'll start saying?"

"No."

"Well, daddy will. They'll start saying he opposed the marriage, and I had to run away with you to make it stick. And all the wives will nod and say he's a closet racist—not that he'll care a hoot about that: he'll say he doesn't discriminate, that he hates everybody—but he won't like being talked about. Imagine if they started saying he'd had his heart attack because I'd married against his wishes! How *weak* he'd look!"

There was an edge to her voice, and Johnny smiled at her gravely.

"For a woman who loves her father you're sounding pretty bitchy," he remarked.

True enough. "Well, he's a bastard," she said calmly, although it was the first time she had ever expressed such a thought even to herself. "And he's been an absolute bastard to me for years. Ever since mother died he's made me feel I was a burden. For years I felt guilty, as though it was my fault mother died.'' She looked up at him. ''I still feel it, a little, even though it's ridiculous. Mother died in the Six Day War. She went home for her brother's funeral—just in time to get killed herself. He didn't want her to go. I remember that. But somehow I got the feeling it was all my fault, and I've been trying to make it up to my father ever since, trying to make him love me. But no more. If he doesn't love me for what I am, I'll do without.''

She looked into Johnny's eyes, feeling the bond that was always between them as though she were attached to him with vibrating wire, so that everything they did hummed with a deeper significance.

''I've changed,'' she whispered, looking into the eyes of the man whose love she needed more than oxygen, and inside her a voice whispered, *you've changed your father for Johnny Winterhawk.*

She shivered suddenly without knowing why and turned to him and willed his kiss to drown her memories.

THEY SAILED BACK to moor in the little cove and poured the deep red wine that the Mehans had given them in congratulation and drank looking deep into each other's eyes.

''Wife,'' he said again.

And she smiled and said, ''Husband.''

Then he took her into the little room that would always remind her of their passion and undressed her with a slow exactitude that was like worship.

"Johnny, do you believe in God?" she asked softly.

"When I look at you," he breathed, "I believe anything." He laid aside the beautiful cream jacket and dress and put his dark hands at her waist to lift her to sit on the bed. He bent to slip off her shoes and stockings and discovered his blue hankie tucked into her stocking and bent and kissed the skin under it.

She gasped as though his touch scalded her, and his fingers began to tremble, and his touch lost its precision as he stripped off her stockings and her lacy underwear.

Then his mouth was on hers, his hand on her breast, and the darkness reeled around her as his body pressed her down and down....

SHE AWOKE to the distant drumming of rain on the hull, filled with inexplicable dread, as though from an unremembered dream; and when she turned her head on her pillow the dark sleeping face beside her was the face of a stranger.

Suddenly and completely she was filled with panic. Who was he, this man she had married? She knew nothing whatever about him. Nothing, except the fact that he was her husband.

I must have been mad, she thought, a desperate cold fear taking hold of her and hanging on. *I must have been temporarily insane.*

She tried to calm the panic before it choked her, before she died of the suffocation of fear. *It'll be all right when he opens his eyes,* she thought desperately. *He won't look like such a stranger then.* But somewhere inside a voice that spoke too late told her that before she had been mad, and now she was sane, that nothing would be all right for a long time to come.

She was torn between willing him to open his eyes and calm her terror and wanting to jump up and escape before he could wake; and before she could decide to move he stirred.

She froze, watching him, mute terror clutching her from every angle.

He did not grunt or moan or roll over. Merely he was asleep, and then he was awake, his eyes open, gazing full into hers.

She opened her mouth on a soundless gasp, and then an unbelievable, indescribable look passed over his face, shocking her to rigid silence; and his voice when he spoke was deep with horror.

"My God," said Johnny Winterhawk. "My God, what have I done?" And the brightest dream of her life shattered into sawdust.

CHAPTER ELEVEN

THEY STARED at each other for a long, appalled moment, each taking stock of the mute dismay and shock in the other's eyes. "My God," he said again, as though he could not believe what had happened to him.

Then he angled himself up and around to a sitting position at the head of the bed beside her, and she knew that suddenly, after all that had passed between them, he felt awkward being naked in front of her, as he would with a complete stranger. Immediately she was ashamed of the delicate, sweet-sexy negligee she was wearing, that she had put on for him, teasing, wanton, during the long hours that they had not slept. She made a half motion to cover herself with the sheet and stopped while Johnny pulled open a drawer of the teak cupboard that was fitted against the hull on her side of the bed's head and stuck his long legs into an old pair of Levi's.

She felt in a state of shock, as though someone else had been inhabiting her body, and she had indeed awakened to find herself married to a stranger.

She said, "I...are we crazy? Did we go crazy?"

"Seems like it," said Johnny Winterhawk, fastening his jeans. He sounded so coolly matter-of-fact, as though nothing he remembered of the past few days touched him.

"But...but how? Jo...I..." she stammered. It no longer seemed right to call him by his first name. "How could it happen?"

"People go crazy every day, don't they?" He shrugged. "Call it temporary insanity, mob hysteria... or—" He stopped. "Or now that I come to think of it, call it Stockholm Syndrome. Ever hear of Stockholm Syndrome?" And he threw back his head and laughed in angry self-mockery.

She had heard of Stockholm Syndrome, of course, but she was unsure what it meant. "I remember hearing about that," she began slowly, sitting up with a frown as she tried to remember. "There was a case in a prison a couple of years ago, during a—" She broke off to swallow convulsively. *Oh, please God, no. Don't let this be true.* "During a hostage-taking crisis. One of...one of the prison employees—" she swallowed again, aware of Johnny's eyes hard on her like flints, forcing her to remember, to understand "—one of the...the hostages was a woman...." Oh, how difficult it was, as though something inside her did not want to remember! "She and one of the hostage-takers—one of the prisoners were...were—" she was staring at Johnny Winterhawk, her eyes wide, and felt long chilly hands finger her brain, her heart, her stomach "—they fell in love," she whispered hoarsely, and the icy hands clenched, and she knew they would never let go.

Johnny Winterhawk nodded once and turned and walked out into the lounge.

Smith dressed shakily, remembering other cases that had been labeled Stockholm Syndrome and what its symptoms were. Sometimes the hostage-taker and the hostage fell in love. A woman hostage would then willingly engage in sexual activity with her captor. And the hallmark of Stockholm Syndrome, she remembered with sudden anguish, was that the hostage embraced the cause of the captor.... Patty Hearst, as Tanya, willingly robbing a bank.... Some of the American hostages in Iran reading the Koran and getting lessons in religion and history from their "kind" Iranian captors.... The young classifications officer so in love with her criminal captor that she was shot dead, perhaps because she refused to leave his side when his refuge was stormed....

Smith's hands stopped in the process of getting dressed, as though unable to work on automatic pilot while so much of her brain's energy was needed for thinking. She jerked back into motion, concentrating on the simple actions, button after button, as though she had never performed them before....

There was a tall, dark stranger in the galley when she came out, making coffee in two mugs. His name was Johnny Winterhawk, and she knew nothing about him.

"I guess we're a classic case," she said, with a faint attempt at humor.

"And then some," said Johnny. He carried two cups to the table in the lounge, and Smith looked around and wondered how she had ever felt at home in this boat or imagined it held peace for her. It was her prison; it always had been.

"I doubt very much," he was saying, "if anyone else has ever got married while under the influence of Stockholm Syndrome."

"God," she breathed. *That's right, we're married,* she thought. Perhaps that was what had snapped them out of it. She felt as though her submerged self, which had several times in the past few days tried to come to her rescue and been pushed back, had panicked after last night and become strong enough to overcome all her stupid, Stockholm Syndrome illusions.

Married. That chilled the blood, that really did. She asked, "Can we get it annulled?"

He was sitting opposite her, on the other bench, the table separating them. They had sat like this before, late at night, talking, but now there was no closeness—no artificial, insanity-produced closeness—to bridge the distance and make her feel cozily cocooned with him. Now the air was cold and clear and she felt as though she were at a board meeting.

"I don't know," said Winterhawk, gingerly sipping his hot coffee. "That may depend on whether we're willing to lie about consummation."

She pressed back her panic at the memory his words called up. *Consummation*. That was the word for it, all right. They had been consumed by it and by each other. Yet she could look at him now and feel nothing but a dry cold fear. She might have convinced herself it was all a dream, except for the languor of her muscles and a lingering sensitivity in her thighs.

"Would that be perjury?" she wondered aloud, and Winterhawk shrugged.

"How would anyone prove it?"

"We'd always have a hold over each other," she said. "We'd never be free."

"A lot freer than being married," he said, and there was so much self-loathing in his voice she was startled into pain.

"There's something more, isn't there?" she said. "More than just...." She waved her hand all-encompassingly and looked off, and he finished his coffee and stood up.

"Marrying a white woman," he said jerkily, "has just about put paid to any hope I had of...." He faded off, staring out the port at the soft gray rain.

Of being accepted by your people, she finished for him mentally. *Of being one of them again.*

She said, "Are your people so opposed to mixed marriage?" and realized she did not know how her own father would have felt about it.

"I have already embraced too much of the white man's world. I renounced my Indian status when I was eighteen, and that is irrevocable. My wife cannot become an Indian. My children can never be Indian unless the law is changed."

His voice was hoarse with anguish. She gazed at his back, the muscles taut with the effort of controlling his emotions. Suddenly, irrelevantly, she was thinking, *I'm glad we're not really in love. I'm glad I don't have to fight against that. That will always be the most important thing in your life, and I'd hate that. If I loved you I wouldn't want to take second place to anything. I'd want you to love me, only me—the way you did when we thought we were made for each other.*

SHE JUMPED SHIP an hour later, when they went to the marina for gas and supplies. She waited till Johnny was out of sight, then slipped through the hatch, with two plastic shopping bags and her handbag, and into the tiny marina store. She left her wedding ring on the table and her dress with its tiny golden horseshoe on the state-room settee where Johnny had thrown it. She could not bear to touch it.

Johnny saw her sitting there when he went in to pay for the gas. He looked at her the way he had looked at her once before, as though he had dug his own grave. Then he smiled faintly.

"So long," he said, and she felt herself stiffen inside to ward off any regret she might feel. She raised a hand and a smile.

"So long," she agreed, and he turned and went through the door, and she watched him move across the dock toward the proudly beautiful shape of *Outcast II*.

"I'M SORRY, MISS," the nurse said coolly. "Dr. Collier isn't in the hospital today."

Smith sighed. "Well, who is?" she asked. She felt weary and irritable, and there was something in the nurse's attitude that was making her grit her teeth.

"Well, what patient would it be for?" she asked, with the air of one talking to a cretin.

Smith took a deep breath. "Cordwainer St. John," she said levelly. "Isn't there a doctor covering the whole—"

"I'm sorry, miss!" the nurse said, as though Smith had breached all the rules of etiquette at once, "Mr. St. John isn't allowed any visitors."

"Who is the doctor on his case?" Smith enunciated slowly.

"His doctor is with another patient, miss," the nurse said, as though this was a triumph. "I don't know how long—"

"Who's the head nurse on this floor?"

"I am." Another triumph.

"All right, head nurse," said Smith, her anger coming out like little bullets, with a soft, deadly accuracy, "listen carefully, because I am not going to repeat myself. I am Shulamith St. John. I am here to see my father. My father thinks that I have been kidnapped by terrorists. He is not expecting me. Now—" she glanced at her wrist, where there was still no watch, then coldly up at the clock above the woman's head and back to her goggling eyes "—you have five minutes to go in there and prepare my father for the shock of seeing me. Because in five minutes I am going in to see him."

The woman looked paralyzed with astonishment. Not only her father, of course, thought she had been kidnapped by terrorists, Smith remembered belatedly.

"Oh! Ah!" the nurse gasped as Smith spoke, and then "Oh!" again. Now she said, "Wait here, please, just wait here!" and, signaling madly to the other nurse sitting in the station, dashed off down the corridor. She returned in record time with a man in a white coat who introduced himself politely as Dr. Ramasingh.

"Your father will be delighted to see you, of course, Miss St. John," he said. "When the initial shock has worn off I am confident it will do him enormous good."

"Not that he's doing so badly, in spite of the radio reports?" she asked dryly, and then bit her lip as she saw her error. If her story was going to stick she would have to stop talking as though she had followed her father's progress on the radio.

Dr. Ramasingh didn't seem to notice anything odd,

however. Outside the door of a private room he motioned her to silence. "Wait here," he said.

She had caught a ride from the marina with a rowdy group of teenagers who had dropped her at a neighboring island, much larger, that enjoyed ferry service. The ferry brought her to Sawwassen, Vancouver's ferry port, and she had to take a bus to Vancouver. Checking her shopping bags in a locker at the bus terminal, Smith had taken a taxi straight to the hospital.

Rolly Middleton was in the room when she went in, so she must have guessed right about her father's condition.

"Hello, daddy," she said with a grin. "How are you?"

The man in the bed looked as brown and robust as ever; the only signs of illness were the white band around his wrist and a slight bruising around his eyes. If to her he seemed shrunken, it was not because of his illness.

"Shulamith!" he croaked, but the croak was caused by emotion, not illness. "They've let you go already? Who was it? Where have you been?"

She crossed to the side of his bed and kissed him. "How are you Rolly?" she asked the business-suited figure by the window. "I wasn't kidnapped, daddy," she said. "I was on a boat with friends, and we never turned on the radio. How *are* you?"

He blinked and looked at her from under lowered brows. "I'm fine!" he growled. "What the devil are you talking about?"

She said slowly, looking at him, "I left Saturday night for a trip on a friend's boat. That must have slipped your mind later, in all the trauma."

"It did, eh? All right, Rolly, that's all," he nodded shortly. "See you tomorrow."

Rolly lounged away from the window. "Right," he said. "Good to see you back, Smith. You had us all worried. Give Valerie a call, won't you?"

When the door had closed behind him her father punched a pillow and sat up straighter. "What happened?" he demanded, his eyes searching her face.

"I was on a boat with friends," she repeated doggedly. "You—"

"Now you listen to me, girl." The tone of his voice brought her up short, as always. She cast him a glance: her father's head was lowered, like a bulldog's, and his eyes riveted her. "Did those filthy bastards rape you?" She was mute with astonishment. "You don't have to tell the world, Shulamith. You don't even have to tell the police. Nobody has to know the details of what you went through. Believe me, I can make that stick." He paused, but she was speechless. "But you have to tell me, Shulamith. I promise you. I give you my word that those bastards will be hunted down and made to pay. No goddamn terrorist is going to hurt my daughter and get away with it." He held up his hand to stop her speech. "And you don't have to tell me that the law is no damn good at getting rapists. I'm not talking about the law. A man who leaves his daughter's rapist to the *law*—" he said the word with disgust "—was born a fool. Now you just tell me here privately...."

She was aghast, shaken to the core. This had never occurred to her, however clearly Johnny Winterhawk had seen it. "Daddy, I...." She swallowed. "Truly I wasn't kidnapped. I was on a boat with a...with friends."

"What the hell are you playing at, girl?"

"Daddy, I'm not playing at anything! I—"

"Listen," he said. "I've seen more liars than you've had hot suppers, and I'm telling you, girl, you're lying, and you won't stick it. They're going to be onto you, and they're going to be onto you hard. The man doesn't exist who's going to swallow that story of yours. They're going to think you're protecting someone, and they're going to want to know why."

"Then I advise you to make sure they leave me alone." Her voice was cold and hard, like perfect slivers of ice. She had never spoken to her father in that tone before, but he appeared not to notice. He merely looked at her, assessing the information coming from her as he would that from a ticker tape or computer.

The head nurse bustled in then, all coy smiles, talking about "enough excitement" and "happy news" and "supposed to rest." The woman got to within ten feet of her father's bed.

"Get out of here," he said flatly, as though she were an inferior species of life, and without a word the head nurse turned and went.

The bully outbullied, Smith thought, finding it in herself to feel faintly sorry for the head nurse. Her father took a breath.

"I can't buy every goddamned cop and newspaper in the province," he told her. "Even if I wanted to. So you better get your story sewn up tight—because no matter what you've promised those bastards, I am not going to let them get away with this. Nobody is going to do this to my daughter and get away with it!"

SHE WAS HALFWAY ACROSS THE LOBBY downstairs when they came to meet her, mikes waving and cameras flashing. "Miss St. John!" one began. "How does it feel—" "Where were you held, Miss St. John?" "What did your captors—" In an instant the hospital lobby was bedlam. Smith was amazed and appalled by their numbers. Had they been staking out the hospital, or had Head Nurse taken her revenge by tipping them off?

Just then the main doors opened and a television camera and crew came self-importantly in. *The little bitch,* thought Smith wildly, *has she called everybody in town?*

She picked her position near the door, then waited while all the mikes and cameras jockeyed for position.

"I was not kidnapped," she said clearly. "I was away on a week's sailing holiday with friends. I did not hear any news reports and did not know my father was ill until this morning. I returned as soon as possible. Thank you."

With an agility that surprised them all she turned and was out the front door while they were still asking questions.

There was a taxi just outside the door, and she jumped in. "Drive!" she shouted to the driver. He moved his head slowly around and looked at her, chewing ponderously. His hands were full of money. He had been counting.

"I'm waiting on a fare, lady," he said. "Din't you see I ain't got my light on?" He gestured lazily at the roof with one wad of notes.

They were coming out the door behind her. She wanted to kill him. "How about around the block for a hundred dollars? Now!'' she insisted, slamming the lock on her door as what looked like half the hospital erupted onto the pavement, the television cameraman in the lead.

The driver's head jerked so far around she thought it was going to fall off, and his eyes widened hugely.

"Holy smokes!" he declared in stupefaction, and, no longer taking his own sweet time, he had the car in gear and one foot on the gas and was steering out into the road even before he got his eyes facing front.

"Little lady," he said calmly, as his tires screeched around the first corner, "now, it ain't none o' my business, but what you done?"

Smith laughed, as much from the release of tension as from the thought of this stranger leaping to the aid of someone he imagined might be a criminal. The brotherhood of man, she supposed, but she saw that he was tucking his cash away in an inside pocket as though he had learned that prudence was the better part of brotherhood.

"Nothing," she said. "Just trying to visit my father. Will you pull up here?" There was another cab at the curb. Smith jumped out, dropping a one-hundred-dollar bill on the front seat beside him. "Always carry a hundred dollars" her father had told her, and she always had, though she had never before had such urgent need of it. She was gone before the man had finished thanking her.

OH, WHAT A LUXURY a bath was, after a few days on a boat. Smith lay back and let the perfumed heat soak away her worries, her aches, the memory of Johnny's body on hers....

She thought of her father and the reporters she had eluded. It wouldn't be long before they were at the house, she thought, and closed her ears against the muffled sound of a ringing telephone. She was going to have to do some thinking; she was going to have to get a story that would stick. She thought of Johnny Winterhawk with a vague sense of loss. If only she could discuss this problem with him. . . .

Stockholm Syndrome. "It's a mechanism that works to protect the victim," Johnny had said. But it hadn't protected her. It had exposed her to an emotional heat so scorching that at times it was difficult to believe she wouldn't carry the scars for life. And it had opened a caldron inside herself that she hadn't known existed.

Smith raised one leg and squeezed the cloth to let water trickle onto her brown thigh. It had seemed like paradise, that unbelievable closeness with Johnny Winterhawk. She had never experienced anything like it in all her life. It had really seemed like paradise.

"GOOD AFTERNOON, Miss St. John," said the man at the door, performing a sleight-of-hand with his wallet that was too fast for her to follow. "Sergeant Rice, RCMP."

Warning bells jangled along her nerves as though she was in the presence of her deadliest enemy. *Be careful! Be careful!* a voice shrieked in her head.

She glanced past him to the unmarked car parked by the steps. A week ago the van had been parked there, and Johnny Winterhawk had been her enemy. Now he was again—wasn't he? But somehow this man was, too. . . .

"I'm sorry, Sergeant Rice," she said pleasantly, "could I have a look at your identification again?" He held it out. "I don't know what tricks journalists are using these days, but I'm sure they've got plenty."

It was like talking to a mountain. Sergeant Rice's expression didn't alter by a hair. *Be friendly!* the voice shrieked. *Don't be frightened. Don't act hostile!*

She tried to school her expression to polite indifference. She had been on a holiday. What a lot of unnecessary anxiety and trouble there had been....

For the second time, Sergeant Rice put his wallet away in his inside breast pocket. "We'd like to talk to your for a moment," he said, and his voice was as expressionless as his face.

"Sure," said Smith, stepping back to give his huge bulk room. He was followed in by another man she hadn't noticed, performing a belated sleight-of-hand with his own wallet. Smith closed and double-locked the door behind them as they impassively watched her, then she led them into the lounge.

She thought it politic to fire the first volley. "What a lot of trouble you must have been put to," she smiled. "If I'd known that not listening to the radio would have such repercussions I'd never have—"

Sergeant Rice's silent partner flipped open a notebook. "Would you mind telling us just where you were?" Sergeant Rice asked.

"I can't tell you *exactly*, because I wasn't navigating." She smiled. "I was on a sailing holiday with friends. We sailed around in the Gulf Islands."

"You were on a friend's boat, your father tells me?"

"That's right."

"You were there voluntarily?"

She smiled. "Entirely voluntarily."

"What's the name of the boat, miss?" Sergeant Rice opened his own notebook.

She looked at him, "I'm sorry, Sergeant. I don't want to bring my friends into this."

"All right," said Sergeant Rice, nodding. "If you'd just like to tell me their names I'll make sure...."

"Sorry, no."

His expression hardened slightly. "Any particular reason?"

"I don't want them involved. It was a perfectly harmless trip. If it hadn't been for my father's heart attack nobody would ever...."

"There's also the little matter of the ransom demand," he said softly, and she had the feeling Sergeant Rice was suddenly watching her very closely. "Did you know about that?"

"I heard it on the radio this morning, and my father told me about it."

"How do you account for it, Miss St. John?"

Careful, said the voice. *Take a deep breath.* She shrugged.

"I'm afraid I can't account for it."

"Were you aware of your father's intention to start cutting trees in Cat Bite Valley?"

"What has that got to do with it?" She allowed annoyance to creep into her tone. "I didn't, as a matter of fact. I've been in Europe for a year studying the markets." *As if you didn't know,* she wanted to say, exactly as she had said to Johnny a week ago. *As if you haven't read your file on me....* She closed her eyes in sudden confusion. Was this how Stockholm Syndrome worked? A week ago the police had not been her enemy, had not filled her with suspicion and hostility. Was Johnny Winterhawk right about them, or was this a symptom of Stockholm Syndrome?

"So you didn't know about it before you were kidnapped." Sergeant Rice didn't seem to notice her confusion.

"No, I have nothing to do w—" She broke off, schooling her dismay as quickly as she could, turning it into faint irritation. "My father had not discussed it with me, nor was I aware of his plans regarding Cat Bite Valley before *I went on holiday*," she said levelly.

"What's your opinion on the dispute?" he asked calmly, nose in his notebook.

"My private business," she said.

He looked up. "You do believe in freedom of thought, don't you, Sergeant?" she asked brightly. *Steady,* the voice advised her jerkily, but Smith knew she was losing her calm.

They stayed for an hour. They were never hostile; they never attacked. But they were chipping away at her story with every question. "When we came to the house, your bed had been slept in. It looked as though...."

The housekeeper had quit a couple of weeks earlier. It must have been that way since the Friday night. She had left late Saturday. She wasn't used to keeping house, Smith told them grimly.

"You left your father to look after himself even though he was recovering from a heart attack?"

Unanswerable.

"Your watch and handbag were beside your bed."

She had taken another handbag, and she hadn't wanted her watch. It was a holiday.

"There were credit cards and money in the purse." All in a tone of Just Asking a Question, Ma'am, that was inarguable.

"Your father seemed fairly certain you were in the house the night of his heart attack."

He was mistaken. Perhaps the heart attack had made him forget.

"Who do you think the men in balaclava helmets were?"

She had no idea. Is it possible her father had had a sort of heart-attack-induced hallucination?

But then who had made the phone call summoning the ambulance? Did her friends own the old van that a neighbor had noticed parked on the street sometime that night, that was gone in the morning? Why hadn't she informed the office or her secretary of her forthcoming holiday?

On and on until she was dizzy with the effort of trying to keep her head. Sergeant Rice never triumphantly followed up a hit that had left her floundering. Never hammered a point home like a Crown prosecutor. He just asked and asked, and it never seemed to matter whether the question was obvious or unanswerable, his reaction was always the same—he asked another.

Johnny, she thought in despair, *look what you've abandoned me to. If we'd come back as husband and wife this wouldn't be happening, and you'd be here to make it all easy.... You and your Indian heritage,* she thought forlornly, temporarily forgetting Stockholm Syndrome and her own realization this morning that getting married had been madness. She felt bereft

When the policemen got up to go, she knew that what Johnny Winterhawk had tried to tell her was true: protecting him from the police was going to cost her.

"THEY TELL ME you're not cooperating," her father said later that evening when she visited him again. "What do you hope to gain by it, girl?"

Smith sighed angrily. After the police visit this afternoon, and reporters dogging her footsteps, she did not need this. "What do you want—blood?" she demanded. "I've told you and I've—"

"Yes, I want blood," returned Cordwainer St. John evenly. "I want the blood of every one of those bastards, and I intend to get it—one way or another."

She couldn't remember ever feeling so angry with her father. "I wish to hell you'd leave this alone, daddy!" she said.

"You know me better than that," her father said.

"That's right!" she said hotly. "I know better than to think concern for me could ever come before your honor or your money or whatever happens to be your buzzword of the moment!"

He looked thunderstruck. *"What?"* he demanded. She stared at him, surprised herself. She hadn't shouted at her father in all her life before. "My God, what do you think drives me, girl, if not concern for you? What else have I got?"

"You've got St. John's Wood, daddy," she returned dryly. "And you've got your memories of my mother, and you've got your—you name it, it comes before me on the totem pole."

"Is that what you think?" he asked slowly. "What you really think?"

Smith didn't answer. "Please leave it alone, daddy," was all she said.

THE NEXT DAY was Monday, but she simply could not face work. She had hardly settled in again since her return from Europe, but with her father ill she wondered if Rolly would feel he couldn't do without her. Not that she was interchangeable with her father yet, but Rolly liked someone around who wasn't afraid to make decisions.

"Don't worry about a thing," he said when she called him in the morning. "Whatever happened last week, Smith, you need a rest. Take the week off—take a month. Look, why don't you call Valerie? Go visit her—the twins are keeping her too busy to get out, and she needs some feminine company."

"I'll do that," she agreed, and got off the phone just as the tears started. Reaction, she thought. It was the concern in his voice.

Physically and emotionally she had been through an ordeal by fire last week, and the worst of it was she couldn't talk to anyone about it. She couldn't get it out of her system: she had to pretend that nothing had happened.

She thought longingly of Valerie. Although she was nearly ten years older than Smith the two had been close almost from the day Rolly had come to St. John's Wood. If there was anyone she wanted to talk to right now, it was Valerie Middleton.

If she told Valerie anything she would have to tell her

everything. Would that put Valerie in a difficult position? Did the law require that she report her information to the police? Kidnapping was a serious offense.

Maybe she had better find a lawyer and get some answers first, Smith thought, feeling the walls of self-imposed isolation thud into place all around her. She was on her own.

It was an old familiar feeling. *I let the walls down for Johnny,* she realized suddenly. *I let him inside.* No wonder she hadn't felt like herself. No one had ever got inside before. Her heart kicked against her breast in sudden fear. *What if I haven't pushed him out,* she wondered madly. *What if my need for him is locked up in here with me?*

SHE DIDN'T CALL VALERIE. She slept for three days, getting up only to eat and to go to the bathroom and sometimes to sit blankly in front of the television set while shrieking happy people won refrigerators and cars.

She visited her father once, but didn't remember what they said to each other. The police were not bothering her, so perhaps her father meant what he said, that he cared about her. It did not seem to matter. When friends came she greeted them sleepily in rumpled pajamas and sent them away. She took her phone off the hook and disconnected the doorbell, and when the news came on the television, she shut it off.

On Thursday she got up, showered and went out. Something else had replaced her in the headlines. She drove to the hospital to visit her father.

"What have you been doing?" he asked her.

"Sleeping," she replied, and he looked at her face and let it go.

"I'll be coming home soon," he said.

"Good," she replied. "I'll get a housekeeper."

On the way home she stopped in at a large bookstore and bought every book written by or about Indians in Canada. There were not many. Johnny's stock of books had seemed much larger. As she walked to the cash register she saw a large volume of poetry and on impulse added it to her small stack.

She seemed to be drained of energy. She went home and lazed around the lounge, her favorite room, bright and airy at the back of the house, overlooking the pool. She kept picking up the books she had bought and flipping through them, but often the style was discursive, and in any case it was an effort to concentrate.

The poems were easier. Most were short; they did not require a lot of concentration. There were several modern Canadians represented at the end of the volume, and she wondered what course her life might have taken if that summer at Paper Creek hadn't happened. Would her work have been included here?

She got some paper and began to doodle lines of poetry, as she had done in Johnny's study. She felt a vague sense of frustration that she couldn't define, that might have been anger at the passage of time, the waste of years when she ought to have been perfecting her craft.

But today she produced nothing that satisfied her, and after a while she wrote down from memory the poem she had written on the island, just to look at it. She had always had the facility of retaining in her memory what she had written—anything she considered close to final copy.

"Your kiss scorches my body...." Johnny Winterhawk had read the lines and been aroused by them to the point that.... Did that mean it was good poetry? She had written other lines, too, that day, some pretty erotic. Most of them had been rubbish; she couldn't remember them now.

But perhaps it had been a cumulative effect. Perhaps it had just been part of the spell that had enmeshed them both....

Smith let the pages of her writing drop to the floor beside her. It was an effect of Stockholm Syndrome that the hostage could become committed to the hostage-taker's cause. Smith had taken that to mean *against reason*. Because if a person became committed to a *just* cause—whatever the circumstances—surely that wasn't unnatural? Surely that wasn't a product of being taken hostage, but of logic?

Was Johnny's view of the world right or not?

With a new determination Smith eyed the stack of books beside her and put out a hand to the top one. *The Unjust Society* by Harold Cardinal. Smith straightened her back as though preparing for an ordeal.

"Chapter One. The Buckskin Curtain: the Indian-Problem Problem," she read. "The history of Canada's Indians is a shameful chronicle of the white man's disinterest, his deliberate trampling of Indian rights, and his repeated betrayal of our trust."

Smith took a deep breath. It was going to be hard, she knew. It was going to be a labor of love—not for Johnny Winterhawk, but for truth.

It was the most extraordinary week she had ever spent, bar none. Between long spells of reading she sat trying to write poetry, to express something of what she was feeling. Not much of what she wrote was good, and she would tear up the pages she had written and return to her reading, her anger not exorcised. Nor any other emotion.

By Saturday afternoon she was still at it, and now she could no longer sit still. Every few minutes she would throw down whatever she was reading and pace the house like a caged lion filled with an intensity of feeling that was almost frightening.

I've got to stop this, she warned herself. *I've got to get control of myself. The least little thing could send me over the top.*

Sometime in the latter part of the week she had put the phone back on the hook, and now it rang.

"Smith, is that you?" asked a woman's voice. Valerie. "It's Valerie. Listen, you'd better come over here. We've got to talk."

"What . . . ?" began Smith.

"The police have just been here. A man named Sergeant Rice. Asking questions. I've phoned a few people, and most of them say the same thing has happened to them. Sergeant Rice nosing around, asking questions."

Smith shook her head to try to clear it. "I thought they'd given up. What sort of questions?"

"Well, they haven't given up. You should come over here, Smith. We didn't tell him anything. We sent him away with a piece of our minds to chew on, but we heard enough to figure out what's going on in their fascist little minds.

"They think you did it, Smith. They think you wanted something from your father—they think you and some friends. . . ." Valerie's voice was high-pitched, and she took a deep breath and tried to calm herself. "Sergeant Rice had the goodness to inform me that if you had, it would be a criminal offense. Smith, for some reason they think you conspired in your own kidnapping!"

CHAPTER TWELVE

SHE HAD NEVER HEARD a voice as chilling as the one Sergeant Rice was using now, nor seen eyes as flatly inhuman. No amount of reason could reach him, it seemed. He had a theory, and he heard nothing that worked to disprove the theory, nothing that did not—however remotely—in some way support it.

He was like a dog worrying a bone, Smith thought, except that a dog could at least be reached. A mad dog, Smith thought wildly, a rabid dog, worrying a human bone. . . .

"I hear you hang around with Horse," he said, and his voice now had none of the ordinary respect he had shown her a week ago. It was as though she were already a criminal, already beneath contempt.

"I don't 'hang around' with anyone, Sergeant," she said clearly. Only the dreadful, sick fear of him that sat in the pit of her stomach allowed her to keep a grip on her anger. "And I am not acquainted with anyone with a name like Horse."

"Horse," he repeated. "The rock group Horse."

"Good God," she said, in contemptuous amazement. "I probably haven't said ten words to the rock group Horse in all my life. I hardly even know their names. Where do you get your information, Sergeant?"

Laboriously he consulted a note. "Richard Guardino of the rock group Horse," he said, "has served time in prison for a drug-related offense."

Richard Guardino, she thought—could he mean the one they had called Ricky-Ticky onstage? Mel had told her that in a few years he'd be the best lead guitar in North America. "Richard Guardino" Sergeant Rice had said, using his legal name, the one on his birth certificate and his police record. The sergeant's voice, like a mug shot, seemed to rob Guardino of all personality and human dignity.

"Since he is free now, I take it he has paid his debt to society?" she asked in a brittle voice.

"How well do you know him?" persisted Sergeant Rice.

"I don't *know* him at all. If I did, would I be guilty by association?" she countered.

His eyes were what she would have expected to see— blankly conscienceless. "You'd make things easier if you'd just answer the question," he said

"Easier for whom?" she wanted to ask, but suddenly she was afraid of hearing him say, "Easier on yourself." *Steady,* she told herself. *He hasn't said anything about thinking you did it. It's just the tone of his voice. Maybe Valerie was wrong.* "Sergeant," she said slowly, trying to remember that she had done nothing, trying not to let him make her feel guilty of something, "among my friends I happen to number a music producer by the name of Mel Ruff. He produces and manages several groups and individuals, among whom the most famous is the rock group Horse. I was introduced to them once, a year or so ago, after a recording session.

I'm not sure I even got all their names. In any case, what possible connection have they with all this?''

He waited till she had finished speaking, then went on as if she hadn't said a word.

"Were you in contact with Richard Guardino before your alleged kidnapping?"

Anger and fear sharpened her wits. "What alleged kidnapping?" she countered.

Sergeant Rice surveyed her from blank eyes, then flipped through his notebook. "On the tenth of this month, your father—"

"Sergeant Rice."

He stopped and looked up. She did not think she had met such an unimaginative human being in her life.

"For the tenth time," she said evenly. "I was not kidnapped. I was away with friends. Who they were and why I am keeping it a secret have no bearing on anything and are none of your business. But for your information I will tell you that Ricky-Ticky Guardino is not my friend and was not a member of the sailing party. In fact, what possible connection he could have with any of this is beyond me."

"How are your relations with your father?" asked Sergeant Rice. He had heard nothing.

SMITH PACED through the empty rooms, swamped by fear, rage and impotent self-loathing. She shouldn't have told them anything. She wasn't a criminal; she wasn't required to talk to the police about her friends and activities. Why had she answered their questions? Why had she been such a coward?

Because there was a chink in her armor. Because she

was trying to protect Johnny Winterhawk; and she had been afraid that if she stood on her citizen's rights she would make them angry enough that they might...they might what?

That's interesting, she thought mildly. *I live in a country where an innocent citizen is afraid of the police, as though they have some power they shouldn't have....*

When she had calmed down enough, she called Mel. Violet Ruff had been a college friend of Smith's, but it had been with her older brother that the real friendship had formed, and when Violet had gone east Mel and Smith had maintained the friendship.

"Have the police been talking to you?" she asked without preamble. Mel had been one friend she had been glad to hear from during her three days of almost constant sleep.

"Not that I know of," said Mel, in his deep pleasant voice. "These days, of course, one can never be sure."

"They were asking me about Ricky Guardino. Did you know he'd been in prison?"

"He makes no secret of it. Two years less a day for possession."

"They seem to think he had something to do with my 'kidnapping,' Mel. I haven't the least idea why. Can you think of anything?"

"Oh, *ho.*" He drew out the vowel as though something had clicked.

"What?" she shrieked. *"What?"*

"Is it merely coincidence, do you suppose, that Ricky-Ticky Guardino was arrested and sentenced with a wild but interesting young man who calls himself Chief Crowfoot, who also served time?"

"Good Lord," Smith said faintly. "What's that got to do with anything?"

"Maybe nothing. However, one does hear things about the police mentality. . . ."

She shuddered and wondered whether Sergeant Rice were questioning Chief Crowfoot today, and how. "Let's talk about something else, please."

"Certainly," responded Mel with alacrity. "I hear you've been cooping yourself up lately. What have you been doing?"

"Sleeping," she said. "Also reading a lot. And writing."

"Memoirs?"

"No," she said, although in a way she had been. "Poems, actually." She laughed self-deprecatingly. "And songs. At least I hope they're songs."

"Well, well," he said approvingly. "So you're finally doing something about it."

She blinked. "Doing something about what, Mel?"

Mel laughed. "You've been saying for years you wanted to write."

"I. . .*have* I?"

"Quote, I used to want to write poetry-songs once, end of quote. Note of wistful longing. Every time Bradshaw came up with a winner."

Bradshaw was the member of Horse who wrote most of the group's lyrics. Smith had never realized before that she was envious of him, though it seemed Mel had. Envious because he wrote and because what he wrote moved people. She had attended or watched videotapes of the group's concerts and had been too moved afterward to speak. It wasn't the music that got her—she had been too busy all her life to get caught up, as some of her friends had done, in rock music. And it wasn't the power the group exerted over their screaming, adoring audience. It was the way the audience would suddenly scream out the lyric of a favorite song along with the group, just one line or two, without any advance warning, as though the same frenzy had hit them all at once. And the lyric was always one that Bradshaw had written. "Take me home with *you*, babe, take me home with *yewwww*." The shout would shake the hall, and a chill of excitement would shiver up Smith's spine and prickle her scalp. Was that when she turned to Mel and said, "I used to want to write"?

"You keep it up," said Mel.

"The police will probably be calling you," Smith warned him.

"My lips are sealed."

"I THOUGHT you'd called off your dogs," she said to her father Sunday afternoon.

Her father frowned. "What dogs?"

"The police, daddy."

"Oh," he grunted. "What are they doing now?" Just the faintest expression of instantly repressed relief had flickered across his face, and she leaped on it.

"Damn it *all*, you haven't got private detectives on me, too?" she demanded.

If he was annoyed that she had guessed it, he didn't show it.

"If you want to try to fool the police, my girl, you go right ahead. But you won't fool me. I have better faith in my memory. I've lived with it for fifty-three years.

You were at home that night. You went to bed in your bed expecting to see me over breakfast in the morning. In the middle of the night five masked men got into my bedroom, and the next day you had disappeared. All of that is fact. None of it is imagination, and I intend to get to the bottom of it whether the police do or not.''

"The police intend to get to the bottom of it, too, daddy, or something they can *call* the bottom of it. Don't underestimate them. Thanks no doubt to your insistence on your version of things, they are now deciding that I conspired in my own kidnapping in order to make you pay somehow—to cause another heart attack.''

"What?'' thundered her father.

"Yes,'' she said in a cool light voice. "They may even decide I was trying to kill you. They've been questioning all my friends, daddy. And me, too. They don't call me Miss St. John anymore. Yesterday they wanted to know what our relationship was like—did I love you? Had I been aware that a deep shock would bring on another heart attack? Do I have connections with criminals and dope users? Et cetera.''

Her father's face was white with rage. "Why, those...'' he began. "You should have called me, girl! You should have told me!''

"I am telling you now, daddy. But having so insistently set this machine in motion, you shouldn't be surprised if I doubt that you can or want to stop it.''

He stared at her in silence. "I can stop that stupid line of inquiry!'' he bit out. "Hand me the phone! No—'' he looked at her "—I'll talk to them later.''

"Of course.''

"Why the hell won't you tell me what happened? I only—"

"All right, daddy, I'll tell you what happened: nothing happened. Nothing that is anyone's business but my own. But if you can stop this investigation, you'd better. And that goes for your private investigators, too."

"Shulamith," he said, "I'm your father. Why can't you tell me?"

And she looked at him across the yawning gulf of all her years of anger, hurt and rejection and saw that he knew nothing of it. To him she was no more than a hand's reach away. The anger in her urged her to tell him now of the decision she had come to during the long silent hours of the week just past, as though that way, better than any other, she could make him understand that he no longer held any power over her, that she no longer needed his love.

"When are you coming home?" she asked instead.

"Next week," her father said, a determination in his voice that told her he was arguing with his doctors over this. "Week after next at the latest."

"You'll miss testifying to the Cartier Commission?"

"They're coming here," said St. John.

"What?"

"They're convening a session here in my room next Thursday," he said. "To be sure of giving me the chance of testifying."

She said dryly, "You're going to explain to them how good timbering will be for the wildlife of Cat Bite Valley?"

He looked at her sharply. "I paid good money for those timber rights. I've got a right to exercise them."

She couldn't help herself. "A very latter-day right, father."

"What do you mean?" His voice was curt, as though he had not expected opposition from her and yet expected it from everyone.

"You think money gives you a right. What about the people who live on the land, have been living on it for centuries—maybe even millenia? What about their right?"

His eyes narrowed. He remained still, watching her. "What about them?"

"The land is their home, daddy. Sovereignty over it was taken from them by trickery and fraud. Why should you be able to destroy the life-style of thousands of people because you've got money?"

The arguments, the emotions were all confused in her brain. She couldn't construct a logical argument; it was all too new and devastating.

"Where the hell did you get all this?" her father demanded.

"What does it matter where I got it? It's true. We're going to destroy hunting and fishing in that whole valley. There are two reserves in that valley. The people depend on hunting and fishing for their livelihood. What will we get out of it, daddy? A little extra profit this year?"

He was looking at her as though she had transmogrified before his eyes, but what he said was, "More than a 'little profit,' girl. These are hard economic times. More than a few giants in the lumber business are tottering these days. Bill Campbell went under the week before you got back from Europe, and it looks as though Matt won't make it through the month.'' Bill Campbell and Matt Hurtubise were colleagues of her father's in the business; she had entertained them often at home. Bill was a small chip-barge operator who had held out against her father's buy-out attempt many years ago and thus gained his respect and friendship; she hadn't heard this news before and it saddened her. Matt ran Comox Paper Mills and was a big customer of St. John's Wood. If he were going under the industry was in a bad way indeed.

"Are you telling me Cat Bite River is going to save us from ruin, daddy?"

"I'm telling you that last year housing starts in this country were the lowest in ten years," her father told her grimly. "Don't ask me for a gesture, Shulamith. I can't afford one. I've got two thousand workers whose life-style depends on my staying solvent. How do their rights measure up against your new friends'?"

Smith was silent with shock. Since her return she had known things were bad, but she was taken by surprise by her father's grim acceptance of the fact that a bad economy could topple even him. And the concern in his voice for his workers was genuine.

"What's the name of the tribe on that land?" he asked her suddenly.

"The Chopa."

"You know a lot about it."

She was being a fool; she must recover. "I looked up the company file," she lied. "After all, *somebody* knew I was going to be away and took advantage of the fact—unless you invented the phone call."

He ignored the last part. "That's right," he said slowly. "That's right—somebody did."

SMITH SAT in her favorite chair a huge stuffed cream
leather armchair, in her favorite posture: back propped
in the niche between arm and wing, legs flung over the
other arm. The patio doors stood open onto a warm
evening and a small summer breeze.

She was reading the modern Canadians in the book of
poems she had bought.

> . . . my body leaves no scar
> On you. . .

she read. She was filled with a sudden harsh longing for
Johnny Winterhawk. *Yes,* she thought, *yes, you left
a scar on me. The scar of knowledge—of what your
body can do to me. . . .*

> So will we endure
> When one is gone. . .

Shulamith dropped her head back and shut her eyes.
She wondered how the poet meant that ''endure.'' To
last? Or to live through the ordeal?

Being without Johnny Winterhawk was an ordeal.
She might as well understand that the symptoms of
Stockholm Syndrome weren't going to wear off quickly. She had been without him a week now, and each day
had been harder, not easier, to get through. Now the
thought of him was a leaden weight on her thighs, an
empty ache in her mouth and breasts and hands.

Smith let her book drop to the floor, swung her feet
off the stuffed chair arm and stood. The memory of him
was an urgency in her, forcing her into motion like an
excess of energy. She began to pace the length of the

softly lighted room, her senses heightened, feeling the bunch and stretch of every muscle, the pull of the denim cloth of her jeans against each thigh.

Suddenly she could feel his presence like a physical thing, as though some sensory device in her brain had begun to glow.

You're going mad, she told herself. She was imagining things, she knew. Her need was trying to present her with a solution. But still she could not prevent herself from stopping at the open French doors to stare out into the early twilight.

Johnny Winterhawk emerged from the bushes at the other end of the pool. With a small silent gasp Shulamith froze where she stood, watching as he swiftly skirted the pool and moved toward her.

He was wearing black, as though to blend in with the night that hadn't yet arrived. His feet were silent on the smooth patio stones. A hawk on wings could not have approached more smoothly and silently.

"Johnny," she breathed soundlessly as he reached her; and he took her in his arms and bent to kiss her, slowly, carefully, the way a starving man forces himself to pick up a knife and fork at a banquet.

Smith evaded his lips. She was filled with a sense of danger, drawing him back into the softly lighted room with her. She closed and locked the door, pulled the drapes.

"My father has detectives everywhere. How did you get here?" she whispered urgently. She established a distance between them, because her heart was clamoring with need. If he kissed her, touched her now, her reason would take flight.

"I drove and walked," said Johnny aloud, and his

voice caressed her spine like a hand. "I parked at a country club about a mile down the mountain."

She sighed her relief. "That ought to do it," she said softly. She spoke in a lowered tone instinctively, as though she were surrounded by enemies. "Thank God you've come," she said, backing away as he approached, trying to maintain a distance so that she could stop wanting to fall into his arms. "Everything is absolutely crazy. Thank God you've come. We've got to talk."

Johnny took two quick steps to reach her side. "Talk be damned," he said hoarsely, and pulling her almost roughly into his arms he held her face and covered her mouth with his.

She was engulfed in a fog of need. At a stroke reason was blinded, while through the heady mist she felt her thighs against him, knew the comfort of her arms encircling his back and finding him flesh and blood against her. She was in a dreamworld, one she had inhabited every night for a week; but this was no dream. That, and desire, were all she knew.

Her hands clung and pressed and clung again. When his lips left hers to rest against her eyelids she kissed his cheek, his chin, his throat, wherever she could reach. His hand pulled aside her shirt and claimed her breast with a heat that melted her, and her voice caught in her throat with a sob of gratitude. But when she moved to pull him down onto the long leather sofa behind her, Johnny forestalled her, picking her up to carry her through the room, out into the hall and up the broad elegant staircase to the top.

"Which door?" he whispered, and briefly it seemed

strange that this man who knew her so well should not be sure where she slept. She lifted one clinging arm from his neck and pointed to the left around the broad gallery, then dropped her hand back to his shoulder and nuzzled her face against the column of his throat.

He set her down on the soft, misty green coverlet of her own bed, and she felt the weight of his body with a distant sense of the perfect rightness of things and an immediacy of hungry need that nearly choked her.

Her naked breast found his hand, his mouth; urgently her nipple met the caress of his lips and tongue. She whimpered her bewilderment as his longed-for touch did not satisfy but only fueled her need, body and spirit.

She sensed air and his hands on her thighs then, as Johnny stripped her hips and legs naked; then she was bereft for one long desperate moment as he stood over her and silently stripped off his own clothing, and then the blazing heat of him enveloped her.

It was a scorching heat; too much, she knew, and yet it was not too much for her. Her own heat rose to match his, fire for fire, flame for flame.

His mouth and his hands taught her again the torment she had learned on the beach, and her body remembered now, and rose to invite the caresses, the rough stroke of passion that destroyed and created her all at once.

Her abandoned response shook him, carried him to breaking point. He could wait no longer to possess her, and his body moved into the waiting cradle of her hips, and she lifted herself for the stroke of union that would make her complete.

She looked up into his face in the deepening twilight then and felt the force of his unleashed passion, felt it stir her to frenzy building on frenzy. She was no one; she was everyone; she was child, woman; mother, daughter; she was virgin and harlot. She was one with him, she was one with the universe; she was the universe.

The universe exploded in a myriad of bright bursting stars that skyrocketed through the dark infinity of her soul, and she heard her long high cry mingle with Johnny's, and then the deep shuddering of their breath.

He kissed her, though they were both starved for oxygen, and then tore his mouth away from hers. ''God,'' he breathed. ''God.''

He eased his weight off her and sank down beside her and drew her still-trembling body into the comfort of his hold.

WHEN SHE STIRRED she felt the weight of sheet and coverlet against her skin, though she did not remember having been asleep. She could feel the covers were on her, and she was not conscious of how they got there.

A hand in the darkness stroked her, and she felt as though the touch bathed her with light.

''Johnny,'' she said, smiling. For a moment she had been afraid it was a dream. He was curved protectively over her, as though he had been watching her while she slept.

''Have you had many lovers?'' he asked huskily, the memory of their lovemaking still thick in his voice.

''No,'' she answered with a drowsy smile. None at all, if this was what one meant by a lover. Nothing had ever come close to this. ''You?''

''A few,'' said Johnny. ''Nothing like this.''

"No," she agreed, turning to the warmth of his chest; and then, because he was waiting, she said, "I had a boyfriend in college for a while. He was nice, but... I had to work so hard, there wasn't any time. Daddy wanted me to learn everything all at once. So finally we... we broke it off." Johnny was silent, listening. The years-old hurt bewilderment was still there, inside, surprising her, and he stroked her hip comfortingly through the thin covering of sheet and coverlet.

"Were you in love with him?"

"Yes... no, I... he was sweet and very gentle. He was very different from my fa—" She broke off. "He couldn't understand why work meant so much to me."

Neither could she, now. Smith felt a deep regret for the missed opportunities of her university days. All the parties, the confiding friendships, the experimenting with philosophy and politics that she should have experienced then were lost to her, as though she had spent those years in a coma.

"I'll bet," she said softly, not knowing how the pain of the might-have-been glittered through her voice, "I just bet that *no one* I went to university with would have been surprised by what you told me about Indian rights and the way Indians are treated by the law! Not one. Just me. I was so damn buried in forestry—do you know I was studying so hard for my finals I didn't even know Trudeau had lost the election till I graduated that year?"

The indignation in her voice made Johnny laugh, and she was oddly comforted by the sound. "Don't you think that happens to a lot of students?"

"I don't know," Smith said. "Maybe. But I still feel

cheated.'' She pressed closer to him, loving his warmth and the sense of closeness. ''Anyway, I'm trying to catch up now. I've been reading a lot this week.''

''What have you been reading?''

''Aha. *The Unjust Society*, and *As Long As This Land Shall Last*, and *I Heard the Owl Call My Name* and her eyes dropped sleepily ''—and a whole lot of others. You know, when you told me you gave up your Indian status I didn't understand what you meant, or why you would want to do it. But you had to do it to be enfranchised, is that right?''

''That's what they call it,'' said Johnny.

''I can't believe Indians aren't allowed to vote in this country!'' she said. ''I still can't believe it. And you're not allowed to change your mind later! So to get the vote you're cut out of your tribe and out of your right to live on a reserve and inherit Indian land...and your children automatically lose those rights, too! Is that true? Because of a decision you made before they were born?''

''No,'' he said, and now it was his voice in the darkness that was bright with pain. ''I'm afraid the motive isn't as honorable as that. 'Enfranchise' doesn't mean getting the vote in this context—I had the right to vote as a status Indian. It just means assuming the rights and responsibilities of citizenship. Reserve Indians are more or less wards of the government—Indian Affairs runs a large part of their lives. I renounced my status for nothing more than a desire to prove I'd 'grown up,' that I was a responsible citizen.''

Smith was silent, understanding how that must torment him—to have sacrificed his history and gained nothing in return except a false sense of independence. After a moment she said quietly, "But, Johnny, one thing I don't understand. The books I read said that... that if an Indian man marries a non-Indian woman, she becomes an Indian and so do their children. But if an Indian woman marries a non-Indian man, she automatically loses her Indian status. Is that right?"

"That's right."

"But you...under that law, you...you're a non-Indian, aren't you?"

"Under that law."

"Then, Johnny, even if you married a status-Indian woman...."

"All I'd do is disinherit her, is that what you're trying to say? Even then my children would forfeit their birthright?"

"Isn't that right?" she asked.

Johnny rolled over on his back. By the distilled light from the three-quarter moon shining through the gauzy drapes she saw his hawklike profile, tense and still. In the silence she heard wind in the trees.

"Yes, that's right," he said harshly, but the anger in his voice was not directed at her.

"But then...Johnny...."

"But there is some reason to suppose that the federal government can be forced to change that section of the Indian Act in the near future."

"Why that one?" she asked.

"Because it's a way for the government to show they're listening to Indian demands without actually giving up anything. Also because it creates dissension among us—some people don't want this change because they feel that an influx of white men to the tribes and reserves would change the power structure in the bands. So the government can use it to prove that Indians don't know what they want. Fighting for treaty rights or land claims or equal education opportunities is probably a lost cause right now. But this is one change that just might go through.''

For some reason she was unbearably saddened by all of this. "But even if it does," she said miserably, "mightn't it take a long time—years, even?"

"It might," he answered. She leaned up over his chest, her long hair spreading out over them both.

"Change takes a long time," she said. "It might never be changed." He was silent. "I was reading in one of those books that the federal government might abolish the Indian Act altogether. Wouldn't that mean that nobody would be a status Indian anymore? That Indians would be forced to be assimilated into the mainstream of Canadian society?"

"It might," he said again.

She could tell by the tone of his voice that these thoughts weren't new to him. Johnny Winterhawk had been over this ground himself. And if he wanted to torture himself with an impossible dream it was not her business.

"Are your parents still on the reserve?" she asked gently. "Is it for them you want . . . ?"

"My mother died years ago, when I was a child. A couple of years after they took me off the reserve. She told me she didn't know for sure who my father was, that the tribe would take the place of my father."

"Oh," Smith breathed softly. "I . . . did they?"

He smiled and brushed back her hair with a gentle hand. "Oh, yes, I guess so. I had a grandfather, too, but he. . . he was harder to please."

"Like my father," smiled Smith, and that reminded her. "When are you testifying before the Cartier Commission?"

"Tuesday."

"Did you know they're convening a session around my father's bed at the hospital Thursday so he can testify?"

Johnny laughed as though it truly amused him. "I've underestimated them," he said dryly. "I wonder if they would have convened at Oakalla prison for me if it had been necessary?"

"You may still get a chance to find out, Johnny. I've been running into a lot of problems with the police and my father." As succinctly as she could she told him what had been happening.

Johnny lay in the darkness, swearing softly. "Damn," he said, putting up a hand to stroke her hair. "I'm sorry, Peaceable Woman, I had no idea this was going on. Why didn't you tell them the truth?"

She felt indescribably relieved for having shared her worries with him. She realized dimly that she had carried her troubles alone ever since the day she had asked her father about how to escape from quicksand. The relief was almost physical, as though Johnny had lifted half—more than half—of an actual burden. Shulamith smiled down on him in the faint moonlight.

"Because my father is a powerful man. I don't believe they'd convene at Oakalla prison for you," she joked lightly. She could hardly say, *because Stockholm Syn-*

drome hasn't worn off yet, and I still sometimes think I'm in love with you. "What can I do to keep them away?" she asked.

Johnny passed a hand over his eyes and forehead. "I'll have to think. Dammit!" he said impatiently. "Dammit! Whenever I try to think about this situation I feel as though I'm up against a brick wall. There doesn't seem to be any solution!"

"Well, I'll tell you one thing," said Shulamith calmly, "unless we admit we're married, we're never going to be able to get a divorce. And that's what we want, isn't it?"

"That's what we want," said Johnny Winterhawk.

IN THE MORNING he was gone. Smith awoke slowly, languorously, to a clear sunny day, and in every muscle of her body felt the imprint of their lovemaking. But his place in her bed was empty, his clothes were gone. Except for the shape of his head on a pillow, last night might have been a dream.

Smith felt relieved and lost at the same time. She wanted Johnny there with her; she wanted to talk to him, to curl up in his arms, to hear his voice as she had on those golden moments on the boat...but reason told her that the less she saw of him the faster she would get over the trauma of Stockholm Syndrome....

If only he had wakened her to say goodbye. She wouldn't feel so lost now, abandoned. She could have given him a cup of coffee and smiled when he walked out of her life again....

It was Monday again. She hadn't talked to Rolly much since last Monday. Did he expect her in the office today? She sighed. She was going to have to find the courage to tell them, her father and Rolly, what she had decided. She couldn't go on wasting her days in a kind of suspended animation. Then she glanced at her watch, which Johnny must have taken from her wrist and put on the bedside table. It was too early yet to phone. If her father were well he would have been in the office by this time, but neither Rolly nor Smith's secretary kept such early hours.

When she showered and dressed she walked down to the lounge that had become her workplace during the past week, where she read and wrote and thought. The table she had converted to a desk was littered with paper and pens and books, signs of her occupation during the long restless hours of trying to come to terms with her changed life.

The debris reminded her forcibly that she had to get another housekeeper before her father came home. She had put it off because she had wanted to be totally alone, but she wouldn't have minded finding coffee and breakfast waiting for her right now, she reflected.

Something about the sunny kitchen and the scent of coffee as she made it made her think of Johnny's kitchen and Wilfred Tall Tree. Had it all really only happened two weeks ago? It seemed almost impossible that all the changes she had gone through since that night could have been compassed in so short a time. She remembered her irritation that first morning with Wilf's illogicalities and thought with wonder what a very different person she was from that woman who had been so sure she was right about everything.

If Johnny and she had really been in love and she had

gone to live in his house, would Wilfred Tall Tree have stayed on the island? She would have wanted him to. She would have liked to get to know Wilf better.

Smith carried her breakfast tray of toast and coffee into the lounge and settled immediately to her writing. There was an urgency in her that she was learning to recognize again and take advantage of.

She wrote three short poems very quickly, straight from the pen, with almost no revising. They were neat, tight; they were good. Smith added them to the small but growing pile of her "finished" poems, which she would show to a publisher when she had enough of them, and then, at the top of a fresh sheet of paper she wrote, "Wake Me Up to Say Goodbye."

There was a kind of tuneless music playing somewhere just out of reach in her head, and as she bent to write she knew that this one would be a song, and it would be good.

"Wake me up to say goodbye, 'cause now it's over . . ." she wrote.

It would be very good.

CHAPTER THIRTEEN

"STAFF SERGEANT PODBORSKI, ma'am," said the tall, lanky man on her doorstep, leaning negligently against the doorframe as he flashed his wallet. He had a thin lined face and tired blue eyes, and he was chewing on a stalk of foxtail with all the savoir faire of a hayseed.

Smith sighed. "Staff sergeant, already?" she marveled. "My goodness, at this rate I'll soon be entertaining the commandant—I'm sorry, do I mean colonel?"

He gave her what might have passed for a grin and gnawed once on his bit of greenery. "No, ma'am," he said easily, "Colonel is a KGB term. We don't use it."

She affected amazement. "Really! How silly of me! Of course, this a *free* country, isn't it? I don't have to be afraid of police methods here! Do come in, Staff Sergeant Podborski!"

His eyes were not quite as hard as Sergeant Rice's, as though he had seen more and cared about less. He was a good deal older than Sergeant Rice.

He straightened and followed her into the house, where, deliberately keeping him away from her workroom, she led him to the large formal lounge at the front of the house. He was wearing casual trousers and a rolled-sleeve shirt, and with his bit of foxtail in his mouth he looked incongruous against the elegant grays of the room.

"Nice," he said appreciatively, looking around. "You do all this?"

"I'm a forester, not an interior designer," she said coldly. "Of course I didn't."

He nodded interestedly, as though you learned something every day, and eased his length into the designer armchair she indicated and began to ask questions.

They had obviously decided on a return to common politeness, but more than that she couldn't fathom. There seemed to be no trend to Staff Sergeant Podborski's questions, and he never once took a note. He seemed to be totally familiar with her case, if a little bored by it, until he said, "Do you suppose your father has any Nishga Indians working for him?"

Smith blinked. "Goodness, we might have. In fact, we must. In the logging camps up north, at the very least. Why?"

"Maybe one of the employees knew you'd be away and had a grudge against your father...."

"But why the Nishga?"

Staff Sergeant Podborski blinked. "Well, they want him to stop logging, don't they?"

"The Chopa," she said.

"Pardon me?"

"You're mixing up two cases. The Nishga are fighting Amax Corporation, the Chopa are fighting St. John's Wood, and the Haida are—"

"Oh, sorry. Now what exactly do they want?"

"They want to stop him exercising the timber rights the government sold him on their land claim area."

Staff Sergeant Podborski had recourse to his note-book at last. "Funny," he mused, "I've got it down here as Chopit."

"There are variant spellings and pronunciations of most Indian tribes, Staff Sergeant. The white man wasn't always accurate or consistent when transcribing Indian tongues. People pronounce it wrong, too. It's not Chop-it or Chop-ah, as you said, it's Choh-pit, and Choh-pah."

Podborski nodded. "How much of their land claim area does your father have timber rights on?"

She told him, detailing how the timber operation would interfere with wildlife in the area. He seemed truly interested, and Shulamith told him all she knew, what she had learned from Johnny and Wilfred and what she had learned from books.

"Do you know what Indians call the reserves?" she asked him at last. " 'The land we kept for ourselves,' or 'the land we didn't give the government.' But you see, they've never got what they were promised in exchange for their land. . . ."

"What do you think your father should do about his timber rights in Cat Bite Valley and the region?" he asked her softly when she had spoken a long time.

"I don't know," she said. "But something's got to be done, doesn't it? We haven't got the right just to cut that timber. Indians were guaranteed their traditional hunting and fishing long before my father paid his stump fee!"

She was flushed a little, with excitement and the sense of being right. Her smile at Staff Sergeant Podborski was nearly friendly.

And it was just at that moment that he leaned back in his chair, looked up from the notebook he was negligently flipping through and asked, "Have you ever heard of Stockholm Syndrome, Miss St. John?"

She blinked, blushed and swallowed air. "I...uh... uh..yes...no, what do you mean?" she stuttered in hopeless confusion. Her cheeks were as hot as a stove. "I've...I mean I...."

"Stockholm Syndrome," repeated Staff Sergeant Podborski in a bored tone, as though he hadn't noticed her discomfiture and didn't care. "One of the hallmarks is a sense of alienation from family and friends. The hostage feels that no one at home cares enough to work or pay for her release, that she has been abandoned to her fate with her kidnappers." He smiled a mild smile and looked round his notebook at her. "Did you feel that alienation, Miss St. John? Did you feel your father would not care enough to give in to their ransom demand?"

She stared at him wordlessly, feeling she had lost the power to think coherently.

"This sense of abandonment would be followed by a growing sense of identification with the hostage-takers' cause. A feeling that because of society's refusal to right the wrongs it has committed, the kidnappers have a right to the course of action they are pursuing."

He paused. She said nothing. The sound of a page flipping in his notebook punctuated the silence.

"Usually a female hostage becomes the sexual victim of one or more of her kidnappers. Sometimes willingly, as a result of her identification with their cause. Sometimes she is repeatedly raped first, and the sense of identification with her abductors may then arise as a form of self-defense. The woman shouldn't be blamed for this. Psychiatrists say a hostage shouldn't fight against the emotional attachment because it operates as a form of protection. Since the hostage-taker also feels an emotional attachment to his victim, he is reluctant to harm her or kill her.''

Smith sat in stony silence, marshaling her forces. The police officer was looking at her as though he expected her to burst into tears, as though this sudden appearance of an understanding friend would cause the scales to fall from her eyes. Yet she felt not the faintest sense of relief, nor any touch of a desire to weep against his understanding shoulder. What she felt was that she was looking at a deadlier enemy than any she had met so far.

"My father's been talking to you, right?" she asked coldly.

"Not to me, ma'am," he said apologetically.

"To your colonel," she said.

He looked at her. "Everybody hates the police," he observed mildly; but she thought that underneath he was angry, that whatever bored cynicism he felt for his work did not extend to his status. "But we're only trying to help you. This Stockholm Syndrome will wear off sometime," he pointed out reasonably, "and then you're going to be pretty angry at yourself if it's too late for us to complete an investigation." He paused, but she said nothing. He shook his head. "You should take us on faith," he said. "Your father, anyway. He's the one who knows you aren't acting normal. He's the one who knows about this sudden interest in Indian land claims."

She understood with a sudden exhilaration that he didn't know what he was talking about. He was quoting someone; he didn't know about Stockholm Syndrome from his own experience. Suddenly she was no longer afraid of him. It was knowledge that made people dangerous, and Staff Sergeant Podborski didn't have knowledge

"Look," she said casually, more in control than at any time since she had got home. "My father has a bee in his bonnet. I don't know what happened to him, and I don't know why. But I do know this: I was not kidnapped. I was on a holiday with a friend. You are wasting time, money and manpower." She stood up to end the interview, and Staff Sergeant Podborski followed suit.

'Would you be willing to be interviewed by a psychiatrist?" he asked.

She breathed in exasperation. "The one who fed you all that information?" she asked dryly. She saw that the staff sergeant was not as intelligent as his questioning had made him appear. He was more cynical, which made him seem more open, but he had the same lack of imagination as Sergeant Rice. She wondered if it was the training.

"No. I would not be willing to see a psychiatrist," she replied levelly. "Nor am I willing to be interviewed by any more police officers. In the future, if you want to talk to me, you will have to arrest me."

She showed him to the door and locked it after him. She felt calm and in control for the first time in days. What Staff Sergeant Podborski had said was wrong: even when Stockholm Syndrome wore off, and even though she didn't love him, she would never regret not having sent Johnny Winterhawk to prison.

That's that, she thought, wiping Staff Sergeant Podborski from her area of consciousness with characteristic efficiency.

She looked at her watch. Just after seven. Time for a couple of phone calls before she went to visit her father at the hospital. The courage that had failed her before was with her now.

"Rolly?" she said. "I'm sorry to bother you at home, but I wanted you to know that I'm quitting. I won't be in the office anymore, except to clear up a few things and clean out my office. Sorry to drop it on you like this." After a year abroad she had scarcely made herself indispensable in three weeks, and although Rolly was considerably taken aback he did not try to change her mind.

"You've been saying for years that he pushes her too hard," said Valerie when he had hung up. "It's about time she broke."

But Smith didn't know about that conversation. Her ears weren't even burning. She was too busy on the phone.

"Mel?" she said. "Smith. Listen, Mel, I've got a song, a good song. Would you have a look at it for me and see what you think?"

"WELL, AT LAST!" exclaimed Valerie the next day, enveloping her in an embrace that was a little too bony to be maternal. Valerie was long, thin and chic, and she had worn pregnancy rather like an unusual fashion that only she knew how to wear. "Let me look at you," she commanded now, stepping back to arm's length and giving Smith a searching look.

Valerie had been one of Canada's leading models at the age of nineteen. At twenty she had gone to New York. When she was twenty-one she and the famous photographer who was her lover produced a nude art calendar of her that left the world breathless. In the next ten years she made her name and her fortune, and after a failed attempt at movie-making she had retired in Vancouver, her hometown. She had met Rolly there.

Now the faint lines forming around the beautiful, pale green eyes that searched Smith's face only seemed to enhance their beauty. "The secret of Valerie's beauty," the photographer–lover had said on the calendar, "is that it is not attached to her ego. She offers you her beauty in the same way an art connoisseur might show you a great work of art he is lucky enough to have hanging in his home." And, "Valerie is the only beautiful woman I have known whose beauty has not impoverished her personality."

The subject of that essay drew in a breath through the small, perfect O her lips formed and let it out on an enlightened sigh.

"My God, where *were* you?" she demanded with a knowing smile, as though Smith might just have been in utopia.

"On a b—"

"Or should I have asked, *who with*?" she interrupted gaily.

"Why?" Smith was feeling the strangest urge to laugh, as though truly she did have a delightful secret to share.

"You know, I told Rolly it wasn't true. I was sure you hadn't been with friends. I thought you'd been kidnapped."

"No."

Valerie took her hand and led her to a seat in the comfortable sitting room. "All right, now, tell me all about it."

She did not like lying to Valerie. "Well, it was a nice holiday, we had good weather..." she began.

"I'll just bet you did—if you noticed it," Valerie put in dryly. "Come on, Smith, you can't fool me. You've fallen in love, and it's about time, and I want to know who he is!"

If her jaw fell any farther it would be in China. Smith goggled helplessly at her friend and groped for recovery. "I... what makes you think that?" she asked weakly.

"Isn't it true?"

"No...no...I...."

"Oh, my God, Smith, he's not *married*?" Valerie said with all the dismay of someone who has suddenly added two and two. "Oh, don't do it, honey, don't get involved." The sudden switch in her tone from gaiety to deep concern shook Smith deeply. She realized how desperately she wanted to confide in Valerie. She reached for her handbag and groped blindly in it.

"I've never given you the present I got you in Zurich," she said brightly. "I've been carrying it around with me all this time!" Her fingers closed gratefully around the little jeweler's box, and she passed it over. Valerie took it in a long elegant hand and did her best to forget what had just passed.

"I borrowed it last week," Smith smiled. "I needed it. I hope you don't mind."

"Of course I don't—oh, Smith, how lovely. Oh, it's so delicate! Look at the workmanship—it's gorgeous!"

If I'd ever wondered why you're my best friend, Smith thought gratefully, *I'd have my answer now.*

Valerie fastened the bracelet on her wrist as if the previous minute hadn't happened and lifted it for inspection. Valerie collected bracelets, ancient and modern, from all over the world. She had begun the collection during her days as a model, when she had traveled literally all over the world, and now she had over a hundred. Each one had its own story and memories, and Valerie sometimes wore as many as a dozen, in combinations only she could have carried off.

This one had memories and a story, too, one Valerie would never know. It was the first time Smith had seen the gold bracelet since her wedding day, and her throat constricted unbearably. She had been so happy that day. It had been the most serenely happy day of her life. What had possessed her? What was Stockholm Syndrome, that it could have made her believe she was so deeply in love with Johnny Winterhawk?

MEL RUFF thought her song was good. "I like it," he said that afternoon as she relaxed in his office with a cup of coffee. She had stopped off to see him on her way to the hospital. " 'Wake Me Up to Say Goodbye.' It's got something. Do you want me to show it to Bradshaw?"

That was quite an offer. A song recorded by Horse would certainly put her squarely in the ranks of the songwriters. It was very tempting, but Smith shook her head.

"It's not a rock number, Mel. It's a ballad. I want it to be a ballad."

"Uh-huh. Have you got any ideas for the music?"

"I thought you might know someone," she suggested.

"Sure I do. Do you want to send it off—I've got someone in L.A. who can do it—or do you want to work with the musician, collaborate?"

"Is there someone in town who wouldn't mind collaborating with a beginner?"

"Sure," he said. He picked up the phone. "You free tonight?"

When she nodded he dialed a number and arranged a time with a man named Lew. He scribbled an address on the back of his own business card and slid it across the desk to her. "Lew's good," he said, and named two currently popular songs he had written the music for. "He's not going to pawn you off with schmaltz. You have to be careful with ballads not to get syrupy."

"Yes," Smith whispered, suddenly nervous. She was trying to carve out a whole new career for herself, and Mel was treating her as though she knew all the ropes, had been doing this all her life.

"Don't give me that wide-eyed stare," he laughed when she tried to express this. "You've been hanging around this office every spare moment you had for years. You know all about it. I've missed you this past year, but if it took a year in Europe to wake you up, I'm glad you went."

It wasn't the year in Europe, but she certainly had

finally wakened up. Smith clutched the card with the musician's address on it as though it were a lifeline and stood to go.

"Thanks, Mel."

"I think you'll like Lew. Call me. Let me know how it goes," he said.

It was raining when she came out. Smith slid Mel's business card into the back pocket of her jeans and settled herself behind the wheel of her little car. "Can I buy a red sports car, with my hair?" she had laughingly asked Valerie, and Valerie had said, "Black would be better, but you can do anything as long as you can carry it off, you know." Whether she could carry it off or not, Smith had wanted red, a bright, fire-engine red, and that was what she had bought. Sometimes she wished—as now, trying to negotiate the heavy rush-hour traffic near the hospital—that she had bought an automatic transmission, but she never regretted her choice of color.

She was nervous about telling her father of her decision to quit. It had been hard enough telling Rolly, and he hadn't spent his life grooming her to take over. Her father had. And she had something else to tell her father, too—she was going to look for a place of her own. She had meant to tell him last night, right after talking to Rolly, but she hadn't been able to find the right moment. If she waited any longer there was a chance her father would hear about it from someone else. Today she would *make* the right moment.

Smith walked along the hall to her father's room, screwing up her courage. The worst of it was, her reasons were a confused jumble in her mind, and incoherence would look to her father like weakness and indecision. He hated both.

She squared her shoulders and opened the door to her father's room. He was sitting upright in the bed, holding a few sheets of typed paper in his left hand. His right, on the white sheet, was clenched till the knuckles were nearly as white.

There was a bald man with a mustache standing beside him, a stranger whose face was somehow familiar.

Her father looked toward her with a hard steady gaze as she entered. He lifted the papers fractionally. "All right," he said. "Maybe you'll tell me now. Who the hell is John Winterhawk?"

She could not have said how long she stood there, staring at her father, her mind numbed by shock. Then her gaze moved to the familiar stranger. Was he a policeman? Had someone talked? Had they arrested Johnny?

She gave a strange little laugh. Today was the day he had been due to testify before the Cartier Commission. What an awful irony it would be if, in spite of everything, he had missed it.

"Suppose you tell me," she said finally. "Who is he?"

Her eyes moved to the papers her father held, and then to the bald man. He did not look like a police officer, or not like any she had met. There was something missing—the hard arrogance, the sense of being above the law.

Suddenly she knew why he had looked so faintly familiar. Outrage flooded her, and she crossed the room.

"Who are you?" she asked him coldly. "Snoop, Incorporated?" She strode across to the bed and lifted the papers from her father's hand. She eyed the bald man again before letting her eyes drop to the paper.

"At 5:00 A.M. left the premises by the rear door and went on foot to the parking lot of Mountainview Country Club. He entered a black, late-model. . . ."

Her hand shook as she dropped the private investigator's report contemptuously onto the bed. Her heart was pounding its response to danger in her temples and stomach so strongly she felt she might have to throw up.

"Well, daddy—" her voice was coming out tight and high, but there was nothing she could do about that except inject as much sarcasm as she could into it "—surely you weren't entertaining hopes of my being a virgin at my age?"

Her tone somehow made it seem cheap, even in her own ears. She could not have blamed the detective or her father if they had assumed from that that she was used to letting in a different man every night by the back door.

"He's an Indian!" her father was nearly shouting. "The man's a Chopa Indian!"

"And what are you, daddy?" she asked sweetly. "A racist?"

Her father spat his exasperation. "Race has nothing to do with it, girl, and you know it!" He picked up the report again and pointed to it. "He's a Chopa! He testified before the goddamned Cartier Commission this afternoon! Don't tell me you didn't know that!"

She had known. The thought had been with her all

day, even if she only knew it now. She had been wishing him luck all day in the back of her mind.

"And how did he do?" she asked the bald detective, who looked as though he sat in on embarrassing family scenes every day and had learned the fine art of being deaf and invisible.

"Sorry?" he asked. He had an English accent.

"Was his submission effective?"

"I couldn't—"

"What I want to know," said her father, in a cold deadly voice, "is what kind of hold he's got over you."

Sexual. Purely sexual, a voice said inside her head. Shulamith closed her eyes and took a deep calming breath. It was impossible, she thought. She was standing in a brightly lighted hospital room surrounded by danger and the smell of antiseptic, yet the longing for Johnny was suddenly tearing at her, ripping her stomach hollow, making her breasts ache.

"He has no hold over me, father!" Smith exploded, letting desire fuel her wrath. "Certainly not Stockholm Syndrome, and why you set the Mounties on me with that half-baked theory I'll never know!"

"I—"

"Now you listen to me, daddy! I want you to call off your detectives and call off the cops and get the hell out of my life! All right? And I'm telling you if you don't leave this alone *now* you are going to end up looking like a fool in front of *everybody*!

"I have some other things to tell you, too, but I'd hate to put your friend here to the trouble of writing them up in a report, so I'll tell you when we can be private. Good night." Smith turned on her heel and strode to the door.

"I am going to give this man's name to the police." Her father's voice was harsh behind her.

She stopped, her hand on the door. "Be sure to tell them you think we're lovers," she said without turning. "Staff Sergeant Podborski is very big on the sexual exploitation aspects of Stockholm Syndrome."

She went out.

WITH HER HAIR HIDDEN under a denim cap, and her eyes behind sunglasses, Smith sat on the hard cockpit seat of the *Outcast II* and watched as Johnny Winterhawk, unaware, approached her along the dock.

He was wearing a gray suit and tie, and he was pulling at the tie as he walked. And though his stride was long and swift she had never seen such fatigue in him. Even when he had been telling her, "I've been up fifty hours straight and I'm seeing double," he hadn't looked like this. It wrenched at her heart, and she thought of all the times his presence had comforted her and suddenly, desperately, she wanted the power to comfort him.

Johnny Winterhawk checked his stride momentarily and looked around; and then his black gaze swept down the length of the dock to where she sat—hidden almost completely from his view by the boats between them. But he knew she was there as surely as she had known his presence in her garden.

She saw from his change of stride how much he needed her, and she knew then that she had the power to comfort him. When he stood at the dock beside her, gazing down, and she looked up, there were tears in her eyes.

He dropped his briefcase on a seat and threw his tie after it and crossed to her as she stood.

"Thank you," said Johnny hoarsely, and wrapped her in his arms.

He held her for a long time without speaking, and she felt him take comfort from her with something like joy. Then, after they went below, talking quietly, Johnny changed his loafers for canvas deck shoes and Shulamith moved around making coffee.

"A string of bureaucratic minds propped up by their business suits looking at you in blank incomprehension has got to be one of the world's most depressing sights," he was saying. He shook his head and laughed. "I wouldn't have wanted to be selling that bunch a building design, Peaceable Woman. One of them actually wanted to know if we were sure Cat Bite River was a salmon *spawning ground*, and not just a place where there were a lot of salmon."

You had to laugh, and Smith did. "What did you say to that?"

"I told him we'd been sure of that for several centuries. He wondered if a scientific study had ever been done."

A grim note crept into his voice. "And?" she prompted curiously.

"I told him the kind of science he was talking about was white man's science, and we had better deal in Indian science because white man's science was destroying the world."

"Oh, boy," said Smith faintly, handing him a cup

of coffee. "Have you had time to regret that yet?"

"Not yet." He took an appreciative sip. "It's a lost battle, Peaceable Woman. We might as well get our licks in where we can." He stretched out on the sofa as though the cares of the world were slowly falling off his shoulders. He took a long drink of coffee and sighed. "That's a good cup of coffee." He smiled at her so companionably that for a moment she wished their marriage was real, and she could look forward to a lifetime of this. "Thanks for coming."

That reminded her. "Johnny," she said urgently. "My father...my father's detectives tailed you to your car on Monday morning. He's got your name now. He told me this afternoon. I...he said he's going to pass it on to the police."

Johnny swore softly and sat up. "What did you tell him?"

"I...I insinuated that we were casual lovers and called him a racist."

"Did it work?"

"I don't know. My father doesn't bluster much. He seems convinced you have some kind of hold over me."

Johnny grunted. "Women really aren't much better off than Indians when it comes to being considered intelligent enough to run their own destinies, are they?"

She laughed. "Not much, I guess."

"Well, Peaceable Woman, what are we going to do?"

"I thought...could we announce that we're married? Surely that would put them off?"

A grimace of something like pain flashed across his face. "No," he said. "No, I...anyway, what good would it do?"

She felt a quick anguish and wondered fleetingly what it would be like to be the woman who meant more to him than the hold his tortured history had over him.

"And no room for regret...." The words of her own song came into her head, and suddenly she sat bolt upright and put her cup down.

"Lew!" she exclaimed, looking at her watch. "I've got to go—I'll be late!"

The grim lines around his mouth were suddenly more pronounced.

"Do you have to go?" he asked, but she was suddenly excited with what was ahead of her, and she did not notice. She pulled Mel's business card out of her back pocket and looked at the address he had scrawled on the back.

"My God, I'll never make it!" she exclaimed. "We have to talk," she said to Johnny. "Sometime soon. We've got to decide what to do. Goodbye!"

She went lightly up the companionway and over the ropes without looking back; and it wasn't till she was nearly at her car that she heard his question in her head. "Do you have to go?" Smith stopped and put a hand up to her mouth in dismay. What had he meant by that? Did he want her to...?

Smith whirled. She *didn't* have to go, and if Johnny wanted her to stay, she didn't want to go.

But as she started back toward the dock, she saw that she was too late. The *Outcast II* had already cast off. Out in the bay its mainsail was sliding up the mast that glinted in the setting sun.

She told herself she had been mistaken in the tone of his question, that he had meant nothing by it but common politeness. Then she resolutely turned her mind to business.

She would not be very late. The address wasn't more than fifteen minutes away in the light traffic she was encountering now. Smith thought of the song that was in her glove compartment, and a shiver of anticipation ran down her spine.

She had never collaborated with a musician before, unless you counted the boy up at Paper Creek. She had no idea what to expect. Would Mel have chosen well? Would they get on? Would he want her to change a lot of her lyrics?

It was the sort of excitement she could not recall ever having felt for the lumber industry. The sense of challenge was heady—she was going to make something out of nothing.

The apartment building where Lew had his studio was a small four-story yellow stucco box near English Bay that had a pleasant airy atmosphere in spite of its barren exterior. The inside door was open, so Smith walked through without pushing the buzzer. She was ten minutes late—Lew would be expecting her.

He was on the fourth floor, and as she walked down the hall she heard the faint sound of a piano that got louder as she neared the door.

There was no pause in the music when she knocked. "It's open," called a male voice, and she pushed open the door with the sense that *this* now was the Rubicon. She was really and truly changing her life from this point on.

The first thing she saw was the black baby grand across a wide, businesslike working studio. The second thing she saw was the face of the man playing it. She gasped in astonishment.

"Luther!" she exclaimed blankly, as the name came to her from the other side of eight long years.

Lew was the boy up at Paper Creek.

CHAPTER FOURTEEN

"HI THERE, SHEELAH." Luther grinned at her, his eyes kind but much more worldly-wise than when she had seen him last. "Long time no see." His hands, which were hidden from her, brought a delicate trill from the piano and then stopped.

She crossed the room to him, smiling. "Did you know it was me?"

"I was talking to Mel again this afternoon. I asked him what kind of a woman had a name like Smith, and so I wouldn't be inalterably prejudiced before I saw you he told me it was a contraction of Shulamith. I figured there could only be one Shulamith in Vancouver, if not in Canada."

"Well, I didn't know it was you. What a shock!" It wasn't embarrassing, though it might have been. Lew had obviously long since forgotten the episode with her father.

"A shock for me, too," said Lew, leading her to a sofa. "Smith? Where did you get a name like that?"

"I've always used Smith!" she protested.

"The hell you have. We used to call you Sheelah, or just Shee."

"Oh, that's right—it started later, in Dog's Ear, maybe, or my first year of university...."

"Where you went on to study forestry, if what they've been saying about you in the papers lately is true."

"So you remember that you were there that summer I was deciding...."

"Bad choice, girl. You should have chosen poetry." He smiled, taking the sting out of it. "You'd have done better."

"*You've* obviously never looked back."

Lew laughed. "I've looked back quite a few times, but not lately."

"Mel told me a few of your song titles. I'm surprised I never heard your name."

"That's the way it is with musicians," he said, as though he welcomed anonymity. "Some of the people I admire most, the giants of the industry, the public has probably never heard their names."

Suddenly it was as comfortable and easy as it had been eight years ago. Lew Brady offered her a drink, and they chatted, and after a while he took the pages of the song from her and moved to the piano, and she leaned on it as he tinkled out a melody or two, and they talked some more.

"A ballad, mmm?" Lew said.

"I had a sort of tuneless tune in the back of my head while I was writing it, Lew," Smith said. "I can't quite...." She tried to hum a sense of the tuneless tune. "Do doo doo doom dah doo doo dah," she sang, giving him rhythm without much melody and looking hopefully at him.

His brown straight hair was parted at the side and flopped untidily over his forehead, and though his face was not handsome his deep blue eyes twinkled with humor. He was laughing. "Stop looking at me as if I were a doctor going to save your son's life!" he protested. He ran his hands up the keys in a preparatory trill. "All right," he said, "you obviously are after something with a few teeth in it—not total schmaltz. How about...."

He began to tinkle out a tune with one hand, then picked out a few chords as his left hand joined in. "Bridge," he announced. "So wake me up to say goodbye...up to say good...so wake me up to say goodbye...'cause now it's o-ver...."

Smith's heart was thudding with excitement. She stood breathlessly watching him, listening to him turn her poem into music.

He stopped playing suddenly and slapped his ear. Smith stared at him. "Got a pencil?" he demanded, patting his other ear futilely. "Over there on the coffee table." He took it from her and began to make squiggles on the paper. "Okay, now, Smith—do I have to call you Smith—I hear a great line in here, if we could just... listen to this...." He began to sing, "I feel it...see the rhythm here...dum dum dee...can you give me one less syllable here, a stress syllable...listen. I feel it dum dum *dum* da dee..." he played for her. Entranced, her mind whirling with the rightness of the music, she moved around to sit beside him on the piano bench.

"Yes," she said, "I see that. Can you give me your pencil a sec? How about... 'I feel it in my heart and in your eyes...'?"

He was nodding his head in time to the music. "Right... right..." he said, playing and singing the lyric, "and now what do you think of this...?"

"LET'S CALL MEL!" Smith said excitedly. The song was finished, and it was good, and she was feeling intoxicated, as if the creative process were a potent wine. "I want him to hear it!"

Lew looked at his watch and said dryly, "If Mel is awake at this hour, it's usually because he's entertaining a lady. If he's not awake...."

"Two o'clock!" Smith looked at her watch in amazement. She shook her arm and held the watch to her ear. "Two o'clock in the *morning*? But we can't have been working so long!"

"Come on," said Lew, leading the way to the kitchen. "I'll make you another coffee."

She must have had a dozen cups already tonight—at this rate she wouldn't fall asleep till dawn. But she felt too excited and energized to go home yet.

"Just like old times," Lew said as they sank onto the sofa, coffee cups in hand. "That was quite a summer."

"Oh—Paper Creek," Smith said ruefully. "That was traumatic. You know I hardly even went out on a date for two or three years after that. And I forgot your name completely. I called you 'the boy up at Paper Creek.' And I never told anyone about it." Except for Johnny, of course.

"Except one person?" suggested Lew.

She laughed. "Yes—just recently. How did you know?"

"You said you'd called me the boy up at Paper Creek. You must have been telling someone."

"Yes," she said, remembering how telling Johnny about that long-ago humiliation had taken the sting out of the memories. She looked at Lew and wondered how she would have reacted to meeting him tonight if she had still been carrying the full weight of the memory. Would she have been able to work so easily with him?

He said, "I couldn't believe that summer that you were actually considering a career in your father's business. You seemed really unsuited to it."

"Did I?" No one had ever told her that.

"Well, you had a tendency to be tough and defensive, and I thought how much tougher and more defensive you'd have to get just to survive in that industry, and what a pity it would be." He touched a lock of hair back from her forehead. "But you didn't get tougher. You got softer."

"I did, though," she said quietly, sadly. "I got a lot tougher. I had to have a skin so thick I—" she grimaced "—I hated every minute of it. It was like being in solitary confinement. I didn't even know how tough I was."

Lew stroked another lock of hair and moved closer. "Well, you don't look tough anymore. You look very soft and very feminine." He bent his head, and it was obvious he meant to kiss her. "What changed you?" he whispered.

She couldn't let him kiss her. She didn't know why, because Lew was sensitive and intelligent, and she trusted him instinctively. But his lips on hers, his hands on her body, would be a betrayal of something deep and important.

"I . . . I fell in love, Lew," she said.

He went still. "Hmmm," he said, absorbing it. "Recently?"

"Very recently." She didn't know why she was saying

it, except that she had to stop him from kissing her—but certainly not for Johnny's sake.

"And are you still smitten?"

"Yes, very much," she said. It wasn't that she didn't like Lew, she *did* like him—so why couldn't she let him kiss her? Why was she lying to keep him away, as though even a simple kiss would be sacrilege?

Lew sat back with a rueful smile and picked up his coffee cup again.

"There's always someone coming between us, Sheelah. Do you think I'll ever get my chance with you?"

Of course he would. Lew was a gorgeous sensitive man any woman would count herself lucky to know. As soon as she got over this thing with Johnny, she'd be....

"I'm sorry," she heard herself say softly. "I'm married, Lew. We got married secretly last week."

Lew's head snapped back with surprise. "Is *that* where you were?" he demanded curiously. "Why—don't tell me you had to elope to escape daddy's vigilant eye?"

With belated caution she said, "No, well—it was sort of sudden. We hadn't planned on getting married. My father didn't know anything about it."

"And where's your husband now? You're not living with him, or the papers would have said so."

"No...we...because of daddy's heart...."

Lew got up with his coffee cup and strolled over to the piano, where he bent to read from the papers still lying there.

"We didn't wait to fall in love. We loved and then we met..." he read. "So wake me up to say goodbye, 'cause now it's over. I feel it in my heart and in your eyes. We'll have coffee and for just a single moment, we'll whisper 'maybe' to ourselves, then say goodbye.''

His eyes found hers across the room. ''Daddy's heart be damned,'' he commented softly. ''What went wrong?'' And it was as though he was an old friend and really wanted to know.

''Nothing. I can't explain it. It was just....'' She closed her eyes tightly as hot tears burned her. Her heart was suddenly hurting in her breast, as though...as though it really had been broken the morning after her wedding, when Johnny Winterhawk looked at her as though she were a stranger and said ''My God, what have I done?''

''It was just one of those things,'' she told him.

''Daddy, I'm quitting,'' she told her father the next day. ''I don't want to be in the business anymore.''

''What?''

''I have a new career, daddy. I'm going to write. I'm going to be a poet and songwriter.''

He was looking at her as though she might have taken leave of her senses.

''Hell,'' he muttered blankly. ''What did they do to you, girl? You love your work. You love St. John Forest Products as much as I do.''

''No,'' she corrected gently. ''I love *you*, daddy. And you love St. John Forest Products. So to please you, I did, too. But poetry was always my real love, you must remember that.''

''I remember you've wanted to follow in my footsteps ever since you were sixteen. I never forced you. I told you at the time it would be a tough occupation for a girl.''

"Did you?" she smiled. "I guess I thought you wanted me to be tough, different from other girls."

Her father's eyes kindled. "Well, you *were* different. You were as smart as a whip. You still are." His voice held pride, and she had to fight the old response to it, the need to make him proud of her.

"Do you remember my first summer up at Paper Creek?" she asked.

"You insisted on going," he said, and she wondered how the past could be so confused in memory.

"You wanted me to go, daddy." But feeling that, had she insisted on going, hoping to please him? "Do you remember the day you flew up in a helicopter and took Luther Brady back with you?"

Her father shook his head. "Was he the camp superintendant?"

"He was a student—a boy I was friends with."

He wrinkled his brow at a faint memory. "He was bothering you—somebody called down and told me he was bothering you."

"And you never bothered to ask me for the facts. You humiliated me, and then you left me there alone for the rest of the summer to face all the men who'd seen it happen. I was afraid to look at a boy after that."

Her father was watching her as though he knew his world was going to crumble, but he said nothing. "You used to tell me not to date any of your employees because they'd only be looking for a promotion by marrying me," she accused him. "I thought there was something wrong with me. I thought no one could ever love me for myself. Is that true?"

"No," said her father. He looked shaken.

She asked levelly, "Do you love me?"

"My God, don't you know it?" He was whiter than he had been after his heart attack, if that was possible.

For an answer, she looked at him steadily.

"You and your mother are the only two people in the world I've ever loved," he said hoarsely. "Of course I love you."

"I thought you stopped loving me when mother died," she said. "I thought you hated me, daddy. I've always thought you hated me."

"My God," he whispered.

"You never spoke to me, daddy. When we left Paris and came to Vancouver you never spoke to me. I thought you blamed me because mother died and I was still alive. You never even told me she was dead. It was Madame Stubelski, from downstairs, who told me."

"Pauvre enfant, pauvre enfant!" She could hear the stream of French as though Tante Marie were behind her now. *"Ta mère est morte. Elle est morte en Israël! Ah! Ah!"* And she could have cried now the tears she had not known how to cry then.

"You never said anything to me about it, daddy. You sat in your corner in front of your easel for days and days and never moved, never said a word.

"And then one day you painted thick red smears over the canvas and stood up and went out. And the next day we were flying here.

"I looked at the canvas after you left, daddy. It was a painting of mother and me. I could still see bits of mother's face under the red, but my face was completely blotted out. You couldn't see me at all."

She was crying now. A flood of tears was pouring unchecked from her eyes and bathed her face.

"I didn't know," her father said. "I didn't know."

She turned her face away. "I loved mother, too," she said. "But you never said one kind word to me. We could have comforted each other, shared the pain, daddy. When you chose to bear it alone, I had to do the same. I was too young, daddy, I was too young to bear it alone."

"Yes, I see."

"I told Rolly Monday I wasn't going back to work. I'm telling you that I want to sell off my shares as soon as possible. And I'm moving out, too. I'm going to find an apartment in town. So when you do come home from the hospital, you'd better make arrangements for a nurse."

"I won't need a nurse."

"All right. I've hired you a housekeeper. She can start anytime. I'll make arrangements for her to move in a couple of days before you're released."

"Do you intend to sever all relations with me?" her father asked gruffly.

"No, daddy," she said tiredly. "I just intend to start living my own life."

"I love you," he said. "I thought you knew it. I thought I showed you. I'm sorry, Shulamith."

"That's the first time you've apologized to me since I was eight years old," was all she could say.

"WHAT DO YOU WANT?" Smith demanded irritably. "I told you I wasn't going to answer any more questions!"

Staff Sergeant Podborski looked at her coldly. "I am a police officer investigating a crime," he said.

"What crime?" she wanted to know. "There hasn't been any crime."

"Extortion," Podborski said doggedly.

"Staff Sergeant Podborski," she said in measured tones, as though she were having to communicate with a rather dim child, "I don't know if you've looked lately, but nothing has been extorted from anyone in this business."

"Attempted extortion and conspiracy to extort are criminal activities even though the plot does not succeed," he said softly.

"What?"

"For example, if I could show that you ran off with some of your Injun friends to try to make your father surrender his lawful rights to some timber, that might be conspiracy to extort even if your father didn't cave in. See?"

She stared at him speechlessly. "Why, we wouldn't even bother charging your friends with kidnapping in that case, see?" He had not moved from his negligent posture, leaning in the doorway. "But of course, if you had been forced to go with them against your will, why, that would be a different thing altogether. See, that would be kidnapping and conspiracy. And if you were raped, too, why the jury would sympathize with your reasons for not telling us the truth right away. And the judge would put those boys away for ten years with no parole."

Smith was shaking. "I have made my statement. Please—"

"If you don't testify, you won't pull down anything like ten years, of course. Maybe only five, or two. You might even get a suspended sentence. Mind you, some people don't like the idea of having a criminal record—"

"Please leave," she said coldly.

But Staff Sergeant Podborski made an agile move that prevented her from closing the door, and said, "Would you have a look at this and tell me if you recognize it?" and rippling out in front of her eyes was the brilliant dragon robe.

"What have you done to it?" she shrieked before she could stop herself, for the beautiful blue silk was creased and torn, and a great smear of black grease defaced the dragon.

"I'm afraid someone dropped it in the bottom of the boat, and we stepped on it a bit before we noticed," he said apologetically, and she knew the defacing had been deliberate.

"This is priceless. This is a work of art," she said, touching the robe with helpless, loving fingers. "Can't you see the workmanship? What you've done is *criminal*!" she choked.

"Is it yours?"

"No, it's not mine. If it were, I'd sue you."

"Where have you seen it before?"

She froze, her hand on the robe. "I haven't seen it before," she said stupidly, not thinking of the consequences, thinking only that they must not connect her to Johnny.

"But the last time you saw it it was in good condition," Staff Sergeant Podborski suggested softly.

"Pardon me?"

He winked at her, but not kindly. "Think it over," he said. "A woman can always change her mind."

And then he was gone.

I‌T WAS THE HEIGHT OF STUPIDITY to go to the island. The police might be watching it or her or both. But she couldn't stop herself. She had to see Johnny, to warn him. . . .

There was no point in taking *Sweet Cherry Yacht*, though. A motorboat would be faster and more efficient. Smith rented one from a marina. They might be able to trace her actions by checking the rental slip later, but at least they would not recognize her on sight, as they would if she took her father's boat.

The boat was small and fast, the journey over in less than half the time it took under sail. She had been afraid she might not find the island easily but discovered she knew the way exactly.

Outcast II was moored at the dock, and she slipped around the other side and swiftly docked. She smiled at the sight of the navy-and-gold-trimmed sailboat, its white finish gleaming pink in the sunset. There were more happy memories than ugly ones connected with the sight of it. Even if it had been a fool's paradise, she had passed the happiest moments of her life on board the *Outcast II*.

She ran up the pathway through the trees and stopped when she came to the rock staircase. The house was beautiful and peaceful, and she came on it with the same sense of surprised discovery as the first time. Soft light spilled out a few of the windows, and the waterfall made its soft hushing noises.

She waited what seemed a very long time for Johnny to answer her ring, long enough for her to become impatient and then worried. And then at last the door opened and light streamed out around his dark figure.

She had been so full of speech, but suddenly she was tongue-tied, standing and gazing at him in helpless need.

Johnny Winterhawk made a startled noise and drew her inside, wordlessly shutting the door. Even this small touch comforted her, and when he took her in his arms she clung to him and knew for the first time why she had come here. She had not come to warn him. She had come so that he would take her in his arms and kiss her as deeply and tormentedly as he was kissing her now.

"Johnny," she whispered urgently, when he let her go. "Johnny, they know—"

"Yes," he said. "What did they tell you?" He turned and led her up through the house to his study.

"They've got the robe—the dragon robe!" she said harshly.

"Have they?" he said as though the information was of only distant interest. "They've—"

Her shocked scream cut him off. At the door of his study she stood frozen in shock, while Johnny picked through the debris and made his way to the phone.

His study was destroyed. Every drawer of the four filing cabinets had been smashed or pried open and every one emptied. All around them were piles of papers, books, newspaper clippings, file folders, all in a mess that looked like a garbage heap. The drawers of Johnny's desk had been taken out and thrown helter-skelter. The bookshelves were empty. A lamp was on its side on the floor, smashed. The Indian carpet that had lain in the center of the room had been hurled against the window wall, where it lay over two broken plants. Other plants had been uprooted, as though someone had been looking for something hidden in the soil, and lay dying on the floor. Three framed prints had been taken off the walls and set on the floor, one of them so violently that an ugly crack ran from corner to corner of the glass. A ritual mask lay facedown in a mound of plant soil.

Johnny stood across the room, the telephone in his hands, trying to raise the operator. Smith hadn't moved, couldn't move, after her first shocked scream.

"Who did it?" she whispered through dry lips. She would forever afterward be ashamed that her first thought was not of vandals, but of his friends among the Chopit, who had wanted to hold her for ransom.

Johnny Winterhawk held the phone to his ear and laughed mirthlessly. "Who did it?" he repeated. "Who do you think did it? The same ones who took the dragon robe. The same ones who've arrested Wilfred Tall Tree and are holding him I don't know where."

She couldn't take it in, not all at once. She had to reject some of it, to pretend, just for a few saving minutes, that she did not know what she knew. She thought instead of Wilf. A strong sense of disquiet cloaked her at Johnny's last words, and before she was even fully aware of it she heard herself say "We've got to get him back!"

"Hal?" Johnny said into the phone. "Sorry to get you at home, but I'm going to need some help. . . ."

Smith began to pick her way around the destruction, wanting helplessly to do something to put it to rights.

"Writ of habeas corpus," Johnny said on the phone, and she guessed that Hal was a lawyer. Gingerly she bent to pick one of the drawers out of the rubble, then became aware that Johnny was shaking his head at her. He covered the mouthpiece and said quietly, "Photographs," and gestured to her to come to him.

She went gratefully to his side, as though he was the only light to guide her in a hostile universe. She felt stunned and shaken and very threatened. It was too much to accept, too much to believe that this should be happening in her country. Johnny was luckier than she, she thought: he had started out with no illusions.

"Hang on a sec," said Johnny into the phone. "What's the name of the one who came to see you?" he asked her, and she knew what he meant.

"Staff Sergeant Podborski," she said. Johnny repeated the name into the phone.

"Oh, and Sergeant Rice! He was first."

"The preliminary investigation was handled by a Sergeant Rice," said Johnny, and after a few more words he hung up.

"What's happening?" she asked.

"I've been calling the local lockups," he told her, "but no one is willing to admit to any knowledge of his whereabouts. Hal can't get a writ of habeas corpus till the courts open in the morning."

"We've got to leave him in there all night?" she gasped, and a black dread crept into her mind. "We can't, Johnny, we can't!"

He looked bleak. "We haven't much choice. We could add prison break to the list of our crimes if we could find out which lockup, Peaceable Woman." He tried to smile. "But unless Hal can find that staff sergeant—and we don't know for sure that he was the arresting officer—we won't know till morning."

"Why didn't Wilf phone?" Smith demanded suddenly. "He's allowed a phone call—who would he have called?"

When he looked at her now the look in his eyes was pity. "He may not have been allowed one phone call," he said softly. "That's a right under United States' law, which Canadians only think they have."

"What?" she whispered. *"What?"*

"Canada has it by tradition, not by right. The police are not bound by tradition. Wilf would have called me—either here or at the office—and at the very least left a message with the answering service. So we're assuming that they want to interrogate him first. He'll probably be allowed a call later tonight."

She repeated helplessly, "But we can't leave him there."

"We can't do anything till Hal calls back," Johnny pointed out. "I'm going to take some pictures of this stuff. Can you make a pot of coffee? I could use some."

"All right," she said, but as soon as she stepped away from him she felt the sense of menace multiply a thousand fold and stepped back to his side. "I'm sorry," she said, "I don't know what it is, but I don't want to be alone."

"All right," he said, and together they went to the kitchen to make coffee, and together to his bedroom to find his camera, and back to the study. There were signs of search everywhere in the house, but nowhere was the damage so extensive as in the study, almost as though whoever had searched the study had been venting a personal hostility.

Involuntarily Smith thought of the ruined dragon robe, but she did not tell Johnny about it. He had had enough for one day, she thought. She had never found out who had originally owned the robe. Suppose he had loved the woman as dearly as he had once thought he loved Smith? Suppose it was his only remembrance of her? She would tell him later; she would warn him before he saw it—but not tonight.

With a detached efficiency, he took the pictures of the destruction in his study and they had begun to put it back together again when the phone rang.

She stared intently at Johnny as he listened to the voice at the other end. "Hal," he mouthed at her, and then he said yes a few times, and then, "Okay, Hal, thanks," and then he hung up.

"Neither Podborski nor Rice is available. He's left messages for them to call him. He suggests we sit tight until we hear."

"Can't we *do* something? Can't we go looking for him?" Smith asked. The nameless horror was still there in the back of her mind, filling her with disquiet.

"If they're keeping him under wraps till they've interrogated him we won't find him, according to Hal."

"They can't do this!" she exploded. "They can't do it! This isn't a police state!"

"Isn't it?" asked Johnny softly, and she couldn't answer.

Until this moment her sense of disquiet had been all on Wilf's account. Now, for the first time she thought of what it would mean for Johnny and herself. "Johnny," she said slowly. "What will Wilf say to them?"

Johnny shrugged, as though he had long ago considered the question and tossed it aside. "That depends on what the interrogation is like."

They worked in the study together for an hour, exchanging only the odd comment or question and answer. There was never a suggestion that Smith should go home; it seemed right that she should be there.

Yet her sense of disquiet continued to grow till it was almost intolerable, flooding her brain till it drowned out every other thought.

When she couldn't stand it any longer she set down the scissors she had been using on one of the broken plants and turned to Johnny.

"I can't wait anymore!" she said huskily. "He's in trouble. He needs us. We've got to find him, Johnny!"

Johnny nodded and without comment stood up from the pile of papers he had been sorting through; and she knew that he felt the same disquiet.

She crossed to his side. "I came in a powerboat," she said. "It'll be faster."

The phone rang, and Johnny reached out and snatched the receiver off the hook, "Hal?" he said into the mouthpiece, and then held it away from his ear so Smith could hear, too.

"Okay, Johnny, I just got the word. Apparently he *was* arrested, and he was put in one of the local lockups for the night, but now he's been taken to the Royal Columbia Hospital. They're saying he collapsed in his cell, but just between you and me it sounds as though the interrogation got a bit rigorous, and the old man wasn't up to it. Just between you and me, mind. Lawyers aren't supposed to slander the police."

CHAPTER FIFTEEN

THEY WENT TO BED, in Johnny's big bed high above the ocean, but they did not make love. She lay in his arms, and they held each other and comforted each other and spoke and thought of Wilf.

It was too late to visit, the hospital had said, and in any case Wilfred Tall Tree was unconscious. He had suffered a sudden large drop in blood pressure and might have a ruptured spleen. He should not be disturbed now, and *of course* he would live through the night....

Shulamith slept and woke in the comfort of his hold and smiled lazily at the rightness of things. "Do you remember that first morning," she asked him, "when we were sleeping down in the other room?"

"And you moved over and snuggled up against me," Johnny said.

"You were asleep!"

"With you snuggling against me?" he laughed. "Not likely."

"You looked as though you were asleep—you pretended you were!"

"I was trying to convince myself that it was not my urgent desire to make love to you," he said.

"Oh! Was it?"

He chuckled and kissed her, and her response tingled along her nerves.

"We do have that, don't we?" she said. "We do have a strong physical attraction to each other. I mean, you don't feel this with everybody?"

"No," said Johnny levelly, "I don't feel it with everybody."

"It is special between us?"

He looked at her without speaking, but she knew. She said hesitantly, "Johnny, do you ever think that. . .that it might be love after all?"

His jaw tightened and his eyes went black. "No, Peaceable Woman, I never do."

"HELLO, JOHNNY," said the old man drowsily. "Hey— it's Nalohga'am Kah! How you been, eh?"

"Fine." Smith swallowed over a lump in her throat. Wilfred Tall Tree looked sick and pale and old. Two weeks ago she might have guessed his age at sixty or sixty-five. Now he looked eighty. "How about you?"

"Not so good," he replied matter-of-factly. "Hey, Johnny," he said, "those guys are gangsters, eh? They called me a drunken old Indian, and they beat me up." He tried to waggle his eyebrows. He laughed feebly and instantly winced. "I told them I don't drink that white man's poison, Johnny. I said that even though I didn't have any more land to lose to the white man I figured it was better not to give them any more advantage than they already had." He laughed again, a dry throaty chuckle.

Johnny shook his head. "You got your licks in, then."

"Yeah, but so did they, Johnny."

"So I see. Do they know what's wrong with you yet?"

"Oh, a little of this, a little of that—haven't you ever been laid into, Johnny? You got no imagination?"

"Uh-huh," Johnny returned dryly. He was calm, but she could sense the angry tension in him. "How long were they working you over?"

"No time at all, Johnny." Wilf grinned. "Not much pleasure in kicking an old dog," he said, as though he were quoting a proverb. "They must have hit something interesting right off, 'cause I just fainted on them right away."

"Yeah," said Johnny dryly. "I can see that."

They spoke to a doctor, who gave them a clearer account of his health but was unwilling to speculate about what might have caused Wilf's injuries.

"Johnny," Smith said as they stood in the lobby about to part, "if we told them we were married, wouldn't they give up?"

"They might."

"Well, then. . . ."

He looked at her. "You've never thought of telling them the truth?"

"If you mean, that you kidnapped me, no," she said.

"If it gets too rough for you, Peaceable Woman, tell them the truth," he said.

She was suddenly angry, as though he did not appreciate what she had gone through to protect him. "Do you realize what you're saying?" she demanded. "You'd rather go to jail for kidnapping and extortion than let your people know you fell so much in love with a white woman—or thought you did—that you married her! Don't you see how ridiculous that is? Really, don't you see?''

He was looking at her impassively. "Oh, to hell with it!'' she burst out. "Do what you damned well want! Go to prison—and take me with you! I just don't care anymore!'' And she strode away from him through the hospital doors.

The phone was ringing when she got home. "Yes?'' she answered abruptly.

The voice at the other end introduced himself as a television newsman. "I'm wondering if you can tell us more about your father's condition?'' he asked.

"More about my...! Why, what's wrong with him?'' And she had just been at the hospital and hadn't gone to see him!

"Oh, you don't know? We've been trying to get a statement all morning. According to the hospital, your father is too ill to testify to the Cartier Commission this afternoon. The special convening at the Royal Columbia Hospital has been canceled, and they've asked us to cancel our planned news coverage.''

She could hear him rattling paper on his desk. "I... uh, look, I haven't been home. I haven't seen my father yet this morning. I'll have to phone the hospital...."

Somehow she got him off the line and then with shaking fingers dialed her father's number at the hospital. A woman answered.

"Are you a nurse?'' Smith babbled. "Is my father— how is my father?''

"Just a moment, please. All right, will you say something, please?''

"Daddy?" she asked. "Daddy, are you all right?"

"It's okay," her father said to someone. "Hello, Shulamith. Yes, I'm fine."

"But they say you've canceled your appearance before...."

"That's right," her father agreed.

"But what's happened? How sick are you?" She was feeling guilty, wondering if the things she had said to her father had brought on some sort of relapse.

"Nothing to worry about," said her father, and he certainly sounded healthy. "The doctor and I decided I might be better off without the excitement. And I'm sure the Cartier Commission won't flounder from lack of my testimony."

"You mean, you're not going to testify at *all*?"

"I don't think the public hearing is going beyond next week."

She was confused. This wasn't like her father. He never let anything—including his health—stop him from doing what he wanted to do.

"You're sure you're all right?" she asked again, and he had reassured her there was nothing for her to do but hang up.

The phone rang immediately. "Yes?" she answered guardedly, expecting another journalist, but it was Mel.

"Lew tells me you've got quite a song," he said. "He wants me to listen to it this afternoon. Care to be here?"

Smith laughed weakly. "Bring on hysteria!" she muttered to an uncomprehending Mel. Was this really her life that was going off like a skyrocket in all directions? Or had she somehow shifted into someone else's more tempestuous lifestream?

"Of course I want to be there," she told Mel. "What time?"

We didn't wait to fall in love
We loved and then we met
No promises
No thought of time
And no room for regret
I feel you watch me in my sleep
It's time for you to go
Already you're a memory
No one will ever know

So wake me up to say goodbye
'cause now it's over
I feel it in my heart and in your eyes
We'll have coffee
And for just a single moment
We'll whisper "maybe" to ourselves
Then say goodbye

We both know it doesn't happen very often
There'd be fewer lonely people if it did
We shared a moment out of time
But now it's over
Now all that's left is how to end
How to begin

So wake me up to say goodbye
'Cause now it's over
I feel it in my heart and in your eyes
Another place, another time, a better season

But now it's over, all that's left is just
Goodbye

It's kind of funny how it happens
In the first place
There seems to be so much to give
All through the night
But in the morning when you wake
And know deep down it's a mistake
You have to wonder if it ever works
And hope it's not too late

So wake me up to say goodbye
'Cause now it's over
I feel it in my heart and in your eyes
I know it's all been done before
And I won't ask for any more
Please wake me up to say goodbye
'Cause now it's over

Smith and Lew looked at each other with a wide con-
spiratorial grin as the tousle-haired, black-eyed woman
looked up from the music and sang the last note in her
smoky sexy voice. Before anyone spoke the singer took
a deep breath and smiled with excitement.

"Dynamite!" she announced. "Too much!"

That was pretty exactly what Smith thought about
this intense, pale, black-haired woman who had just
sung her song as though she owned it. Who would have
thought the words she had written could sound so significant, so real?

They smiled at each other, and then, with one accord, Lew, Smith and the singer—whose name was Cimarron King—turned their eyes on Mel.

"Like to do a single of it?" he asked Cimarron.

Smith merely blinked. Things were moving so fast around her that sometimes she had to remind herself to breathe. Two hours ago she and Lew had been sitting side by side at the piano, singing the song to Mel. "Okay," he had said, "we've got a song." And then he had told Smith about the singer he was grooming. "She doesn't write enough of her own stuff," he'd said. "We're putting an album together. I'd like Cimarron to hear this. I'd like to use it on the album."

She had never dreamed it would happen like this. If she had had time to think about the possible fate of her song she might have imagined they would send it off to an established singer and wait months or years to hear anything....

"Look," Mel had said, "established singers use established writers. If you go with an unknown, when she makes it, you make it. Anyway, this is right up Cimarron's street. Not quite ballad, not quite rock."

Smith had looked at Lew. "Do you know Cimarron?" she had asked curiously.

"I know Mel's looking for material for her. And I know her style." Which meant he had written the music with her style in mind. Smith had grinned, suddenly caught up in their suppressed excitement. "Okay," she had said, "I'll go along with the experts."

And Cimarron King had been summoned and had listened to the song; and now she had sung it and electrified them all.

Cimarron was looking intently at Mel. "Yes, can I?" she asked, nodding. "A single now, and then if it goes, the title song on the album?" She and Mel exchanged a grin. "It's perfect," she said. "Thanks." She looked at Smith and Lew. "It's dynamite."

The song had changed dramatically, Smith felt, from that first morning she had written it. Although she had heard that formless music in her head as she wrote, Lew's music, very different from it, had seemed to suit the words perfectly. It was as though he had looked at the song from an entirely different angle. She had changed her lyrics to suit the angle of his vision, feeling that odd perfection that collaboration sometimes gives—as though his music, his angle of vision, were giving her a clearer view of what the song was meant to be.

And now Cimarron King was throwing the light of her interpretation on it, making the vision even clearer. Shulamith was surprised at how much a singer could change a song. "Do you want me to change anything?" Smith asked now. "If there's a lyric you're not comfortable with...."

Cimarron King laughed her smoky laugh. "Look," she said, "don't worry about this song. It's great. Just write me another, okay? Write two more—write ten!"

"AND A STRANGE FOLLOW-UP," said the news announcer over her car radio as she drove toward the hospital, "to the St. John heiress no-kidnapping kidnap case. Last night police searched the island home of Vancouver architect John Winterhawk and arrested Wilfred Tall Tree, a member of the Chopa Indian band, on suspicion, apparently in connection with the alleged kidnapping three weeks ago of Shulamith St. John. Miss St. John, who was thought by her father, lumber baron Cordwainer St. John, to be missing, turned up nearly two weeks ago after a sailing holiday, categorically denying that she had been kidnapped.

"Mr. Winterhawk, whose home was extensively searched last night, and who says some belongings were seized, is the controversial architect who designed the new West Coast Cultural Center. Photographs of the aftermath of the search of his home in the Gulf Islands are appearing in each of the city's newspapers this afternoon.

"Wilfred Tall Tree, who lives on the same island, was admitted to the Royal Columbia Hospital last night approximately five hours after his arrest. A police spokesman said that Mr. Tall Tree, age 76, had fainted in his cell. The spokesman said that the kidnapping case was still 'very much under investigation.' The only article seized from Mr. Winterhawk's home, the spokesman said, was a woman's bathrobe, which was thought to belong to Shulamith St. John.

"Mr. Winterhawk says he is looking into the possibility of pressing charges against police under the new Charter of Rights and Freedoms. Police apparently searched his home under the power of a writ of assistance, a type of arbitrary search warrant, which is rarely used nowadays and which has been under fire from civil liberties groups."

Smith nearly went off the road. As soon as she could she got out of the stream of traffic and pulled into a no-stopping zone. She sat quietly, trying to think, until a traffic warden pulled up behind her, and then she moved back into traffic, changed her course and drove home. But her ideas were no clearer than before. What did Johnny expect her to do now. What could she do?

The phone, of course, was ringing when she got home—the first of many journalists who wanted her version of events. She answered two questions only, even for the more persistent of the questioners: she had not been kidnapped, and the robe was not hers.

Was there some reason she might have publicly denied being kidnapped, while secretly telling police otherwise, one wanted to know.

"No reason at all," said Smith. "I have consistently and repeatedly told the police that I was not kidnapped."

"Do you know Johnny Winterhawk?"

"Sorry, no comment."

"Do you know why the police are connecting him with your disappearance?"

"I did not disappear. . . ."

When she could hang up the phone without its instantly ringing again, she called her father.

"Are you snowed under with reporters?" she asked him icily.

"Not anymore," he said.

"You mean, not yet," she told him, the fact that her father had been left in peace making her even angrier.

"What's happened?"

"You'll see," she said. "Or maybe you won't. You probably qualify for the Blind Man of the Year Award. If my homicidal rage cools down you may see me."

"Good," said her father. "I've been—"

"But don't hold your breath."

She hung up without slamming the receiver down, though her hand had itched to do it, and fought against the guilt that rose in her. Then she took the receiver off the hook and flung herself down in her favorite chair and rubbed her forehead.

What were the earmarks of Stockholm Syndrome? "Stockholm Syndrome," she said aloud, as though that might help clarify her thoughts. One: an emotional bond with the kidnapper. Well, she had that, all right, and it was getting worse, not better, with time. Two: a sense of alienation from the family. She had that, too, but she had always had that. Had her feeling that her father didn't love her grown significantly while she was with Johnny? No. The first thing she had thought was that her father wouldn't pay a ransom for her. She had started out without hope, not grown into it. Three: an irrational conversion to the kidnapper's cause.

There was the crunch. She had accepted and continued to believe what Johnny had told her about Stockholm Syndrome, mostly because of this point, because of what she had suddenly learned about Indian rights and the operation of the Canadian justice system and how she had felt about them.

But *did* her reaction qualify as "conversion"—or "irrational conversion"? Not "irrational," surely. Johnny and Wilf were not fanatics. They had not given her rhetoric. What they, and the books she had read, and, more recently, what her own experience had told her were *facts*. Accepting facts was not irrational. Now she questioned the country's system of justice whereas before she had not. A questioning mind did not qualify as "converted."

She sat thinking for a long time. At the end of it she had one hard bright fact: whatever temporary insanity had assailed her with regard to Johnny Winterhawk, it hadn't sidetracked her reasoning capacities, and *that* was the hallmark of Stockholm Syndrome.

If she still ran to Johnny in times of trouble, if she wanted to protect him, if she needed his company, his comfort, his love, it wasn't because of Stockholm Syndrome.

ON FRIDAY she cleared out her office at the St. John's Wood head office. Her goodbyes were anticlimactical: she had only been back a few weeks and hadn't found her niche yet. But her secretary stood at the door and watched her pack up sadly.

"I'm sorry you're going," Maia said wistfully, "I really enjoyed working for you."

"I enjoyed working with you, too," said Smith.

Maia had been upgraded from the typing pool, and Smith realized guiltily that now she would be going back. "I'm sorry. Does this mean you'll take a drop in salary?"

"I don't know about that," answered the young woman, who was shy, but a very hard worker Smith had discovered early on, "but I liked working for you. People say it's horrible working for a woman, but it's not. I really liked working for you."

Smith smiled, remembering her first week back, when she had handed Maia a cluster of tapes and notes she had made abroad—a complex collection of field reports

and market evaluations that required cross-referencing
and indexing and a great deal of concentration. She had
come back from lunch to find her bent over her type-
writer in tears. "And it's too complicated, and I'm too
stupid." Maia's distress had been mostly incoherent,
but at last she had lifted her head out of her Kleenex.
"And besides," she had wailed, "I've got my period!"

Not the sort of thing you could confess to a male boss
without having him use it against you in the future,
Smith reflected now. She wondered mildly if it was that
incident that had convinced Maia of the advantages of
having a female boss and gained her loyalty.

Three copies of the completed report, spiral bound,
color-tabulated and impressive looking, were on her
desk now, mute testimony to Maia's competence. She
had finished it during Smith's absence, and Smith's last
act as executive in her father's company would be to
deliver the report to Rolly.

"Good grief," said Rolly, when he saw the three-
inch-thick report. "Didn't you take any time off to
enjoy the sights over there?"

"Not as much as I wish now," Smith said. All her
experience of overseas markets would be wasted in
her new job, but a little more attention to Europe's
art and history would certainly have enriched her creativity.

"Is this your last day?"

"My last hour. Minute."

"What are you going into, or do you know yet?"

"Song writing." She smiled. "And poetry. I intend to
be a major addition to modern music, if not to Can-
Lit."

"Well, we won't lose touch, will we? You'll be dropping in on Valerie?"

"Of course," she said. "Give her my love—and the twins, too. Tell her I'll call her if she doesn't call me."

At the door she stopped, struck by a sudden thought. "Rolly—I never asked you. Why didn't you ever tell the police about that phone call?" She turned, and his face was blank with surprise.

"What phone call?"

"When I was away on that trip I called you one afternoon, and then I changed my mind and hung up. Just as you answered. The police never mentioned it to me afterward."

Rolly shook his head. "Sure you had the right number? I don't remember—or wait! Was that *you*? I thought that was Valerie. I phoned her and asked her if she'd called and been cut off—one night just as I was about to leave."

Smith clicked her tongue. "Tsk, Rolly," she laughed. "What if I'd really been kidnapped and was trying to get help? You didn't even recognize my voice."

He boggled at her. "My God," he said softly. "Is that what happened? I didn't even think of you that day! I—"

Great. Nothing like starting up another hare herself. "No, no," she said hastily. "Rolly, I was joking. I was just calling to ask how Valerie was, because I'd forgotten to tell her I was going to be away, and it took an age to get through, and by the time I did, everyone was ready to leave. That's all." She was babbling, and she wondered if it sounded like a lie.

"Tell Valerie I'll be around to see her soon, okay?"

She smiled and opened the door. "Oh, and listen—it's been great working with you!"

And that was it. The company around which her life had revolved for eight years moved out of her consciousness as easily as that: she closed her office door and, carrying a heavy briefcase, walked down the hall, into the elevator and then out the front door without once looking back. It had been a chapter in her life. She was starting another.

"YOU'RE IN THE NEWS AGAIN," Lew observed as he followed her blue-jeaned, barefoot figure into the lounge. After the formality of years of office wear, going to work dressed like this was a luxury that was almost sinful.

"Tell me about it," she responded dryly. She paused in the doorway to the lounge. "There, what do you think?"

Her father had a gardening service one day a week—Friday. This morning Smith had asked the man to help her shift the grand piano from the conservatory into the lounge, which she was rapidly turning into a professional-looking workroom. The sofa had gone out, a desk moved in. There were papers and books and sheet music everywhere.

Lew whistled softly and approached the impressive-looking black piano that now dominated the room. "Who plays this?" he asked.

"No one," said Smith dryly. "It's my father's idea of style."

Lew ran his fingers down the keys and winced at the tinkling sound. "It needs tuning." He bonged middle C and played a few chords. "He paid something for this, though. It's a beauty."

"My father always gets the best," she said. "Want to look at what I've done?"

"Of course."

She brought him two songs she had been working on and one of the poems from the growing pile she was making. "I thought this could be worked up if you liked it," she said of the poem. "But I haven't had time yet."

Lew moved back to the piano, reading. "Are you thinking of these for Cimarron?"

Smith shrugged. "Why not? At least we get published that way."

With that understanding they began to work. The excitement of working as a team was with both of them, and Smith might never get over the joy of doing this for a living; and so they worked well, if not with the marvelous inspiration that had gripped them on Tuesday night.

Lew had brought along some music he had written before, and when they had worked with some of his musical ideas for her lyrics, he played it for her. Smith flung herself down in her armchair and listened, trying to imagine what words would affect Lew's music as his music affected her lyrics.

The music was softer and sweeter than what he had written for "Wake Me Up to Say Goodbye," and Smith thought suddenly that it needed contradiction, it needed a lyric that would make the music a bitter comment rather than a syrupy statement.

"This music makes me feel contrary," she said. Lew stopped playing.

"It what?" he asked with a grin.

"Well, it makes me think of lines like 'don't ask me to say I love you, there's no such thing as love,'" she explained.

Lew laughed. "That's good," he said. "I was hoping you'd get that from it." He went back to playing. "Dah da dum da dum," he hummed and sang at intervals, "Dum there's no such thing...as love.... Yeah," he said over the music. "That's good. Let's work around that...dum dum, 'cause there's no such thing as love."

It was true, she was thinking suddenly. There was no such thing as love—if what she and Johnny had felt for each other wasn't love, then it must all be an illusion.

She was scribbling odd notes and bits of lyric on a pad as she lounged in the chair. "Have you got a cassette of this?" she asked Lew.

He kept playing. "I can make you one."

"Yes, please." She flung down her notebook as the telephone rang. "What time is it?" she wondered aloud, stretching and looking at her watch. Ten o'clock was late for a call. "News that comes at night is always bad news," she observed to Lew, as she crossed to the phone, but she wasn't thinking of her father. She was thinking of Johnny.

"Turn on the news!" shrieked Valerie in her ear. "You're on the news! CBC! They're saying you got married! It was in the headlines!"

Smith slammed the receiver down on the table and dashed across the room, where, much to Lew's amazement, she began pushing and pulling at the knobs of an oak sideboard. Finally the doors opened to reveal a television screen, and Smith snatched up the remote control and snapped it on.

When she found CBC, a reporter talking from Jerusalem was just finishing, and the anchorman's face appeared on the screen. "In Vancouver tonight," he said, "a secret marriage makes a happier-than-usual ending to a mysterious kidnapping drama and has caused red faces among the RCMP. From Vancouver, here's Susan Kalman."

"Three weeks ago," said a pale young woman, "on the night of the tenth or early morning of the eleventh, Shulamith St. John left this exclusive home on Hollyburn Mountain where she lives with her father and disappeared." Smith sucked in a startled breath: the house behind the woman's head was this house. They must have been here tonight; she must have just missed them. "That night, her father suffered a heart attack. An ambulance was summoned by someone in the house and took him to the Royal Columbia Hospital—" Smith closed her eyes and let the voice flow over her "—received a ransom demand from a spokesman...suddenly turned up at her father's bedside. She denied the kidnapping story. She had been on a sailing holiday with friends, Miss St. John told reporters—and police.

"For reasons that were undisclosed at the time, and will probably remain forever locked in the breasts of the RCMP investigators, her statement was not believed. On Wednesday of this week, following a lead from an unknown source, police apparently connected...with Vancouver architect Johnny Winterhawk, whose home was violently searched on Wednesday night under the power of a writ of assistance...so far as to arrest another inhabitant of the island, a Chopa Indian named William Tall Tree...an RCMP spokesman says, may be finally closed. At Robson Square today, this reporter received a copy of the marriage registration of...took place the day before her return...."

Smith moved numbly to the phone and picked up the receiver. "Are you still there?" she asked Valerie.

"Is it true, Smith? My God, is it true?" demanded Valerie's appalled voice.

"Yes, it's true," she said.

"Everything?"

"Yes—except his name is Wilfred, not William." She spoke distantly, because she couldn't concentrate on the conversation. She kept wondering if Johnny was watching this and what his reaction would be. And then she knew. Johnny's dark face was suddenly filling the screen. "No comment," he was saying as if it was the fifth time he had said it, and if no one else knew, Smith knew by the black glitter in his eyes how angry he was. *Outcast II* was in the background: they had caught him at the dock.

"Do you have any comment about the police handling of his case?" the woman asked.

Johnny looked bored, but he wasn't, he wasn't. "Sure I have a comment," he said lazily. "It's been said before: 'the law is an ass.'"

"IT WASN'T ME!" Shulamith said urgently as Johnny Winterhawk opened the door and stood impassively staring down at her. It was late. He was in a bathrobe, and his hair was tousled. She must have got him out of bed.

"Fine," he said. "Is that what you came to say?" and he was moving to close the door.

Panicking, Smith flung herself against him and pushed her way inside. "Don't you judge me without a hearing!" she stormed. "I have a right to be heard and I—"

"Not by me," he said coldly.

"Oh, yes, by you! I'm caught in this as much as you are, you know! I'm married to you as—"

"Be careful about claiming any conjugal rights," he said softly, closing the door behind her. "I have conjugal rights of my own." And his arms came around her from behind, and he turned her head and bent to kiss her mouth.

If the savage pressure of his lips could be called a kiss. How dared he kiss her in such an ugly mood, as though he were using it to punish her? Smith fought her way out of his embrace.

"Look, Johnny," she said. "I was not the one who tipped off the CBC, but even if I were I wouldn't put up with rape as some kind of punishment!"

Johnny showed his teeth. "Not rape," he said briefly.

"Well, I'm—"

"It's hard to prove rape between husband and wife," he continued and pulled her body against him.

"Leave me alone! Leave me alone!" she shouted, fighting and pushing to get away. He let her go, and her breast heaved for breath. Her nipples showed through the thin cloth of her navy T-shirt, hard and aroused. He aroused her; there was no denying that. Even in this cruel angry mood he aroused her.

Smith put a hand out to keep him away. "So help me

God,'' she whispered hoarsely, then cleared her throat, ''so help me God, if you lay another finger on me in this mood, Johnny, I'll call the police and I *will* charge you with kidnapping!''

He looked at her and laughed. ''Too late,'' he said. ''Didn't they tell you it would be too late?''

''Why?'' she demanded. ''What do you mean?''

''A wife can't always testify against her husband in this country, didn't you know that?'' Johnny asked, and his voice was deep and angry. ''You wouldn't be a competent witness for the prosecution.''

And that was when she knew she loved him. When she was standing there, learning for the first time what she had never suspected: Johnny's love for her had been fake right from the beginning. He had been plotting a way out, that was all. Marriage had been his way out. She looked at him then, and knew that she loved him with all her heart and would love him all her life. And what she had gone through with her father was nothing compared to the agony life had chosen for her now.

CHAPTER SIXTEEN

SMITH STEPPED UP against him and looked up into his face. His arms closed around her convulsively, and she smiled. He might not love her, but he still wanted her.

"All right," she said. She closed her eyes. His closeness was making her faint, and she knew why.

Johnny's hands gripped her shoulders, and he looked down into her face. "All right?" he asked.

She said, "It'll be the last time, won't it? We won't need to see each other after this. Let's say goodbye the way we said hello."

Before she had finished speaking his hands were burning on her waist and denimed thighs. He turned and carried her up through the house all the way to his bedroom at the top. There was a fury in him that was almost frightening, and the fury grew as he walked.

He set her on her feet inside the bedroom door and pressed her against it with a sudden kiss. Her hands were on his arms, caressing the firmness of muscle under the rough terry-cloth; his hands encircled her cheeks and throat, while his thumbs stroked her willing lips and he lifted her face to his.

As quickly as that, erotic need had her in its grip. When his tongue moved between her open lips she trembled with the knowledge that it was his tongue, her mouth, that it was his body and no other that was giving her this pleasure; that it was from her body that he needed his own pleasure.

He felt the trembling in her and thrust with his tongue again and again in the cruel necessity to feel his power over her.

When at last he raised his head she was enflamed. Her hair had long ago fallen loose under his fierce caress, and the belt of his robe had let go. Underneath it, he was naked.

She was assailed by a need she could not name, then, and her eyes darkening, she sank slowly to her knees in front of him and pressed a kiss against his thigh.

"Shulamith!" he hissed in sensuous surprise, and then, looking up, she saw his eyelids droop and heard the tortured intake of his breath. His hands clenched in her hair, and he wrapped it around his body, ensnaring both of them in its net. When he let it fall, she shivered as its weight brushed her naked arms.

He picked her bodily off the floor, then, while she moaned her needy dismay, and carried her to the bed. There, he stripped off her jeans and the navy T-shirt, and looked at the curve of her breasts through the wild disorder of her hair with a face that was tortured. "You destroy me," he whispered. "You take my soul."

The black wings of his hair fell forward over the high bones of his cheeks, and behind his eyes leaped the dark flame. She saw every separate hair of his head, as familiar to her as time, and every glistening black brow and lash. She put her hands up to his face. *Yes, this is the curve of your lips, which I have always loved,* she thought, *and this is the texture of skin that only you*

have, and only I know. And this is the last time and the
first time—this is all the times I would ever have known
you, in one.

He moved; and she felt the pleasure as deep as pain,
and her heart twisted in her breast. "You could have
loved me," she whispered, not knowing that tears stood
in her eyes. "If the world had been different, you could
have loved me."

The pleasure as he moved in her was too great: it
disturbed her soul and left her vulnerable to his guarded
need, to her knowledge that in him there was no love,
only desire.

She began to resist, to build barriers against the
mounting pleasure. After a moment he sensed it.

"Shulamith!" he whispered urgently, commandingly.

She smiled her refusal with a small defiant smile, and
answered, "No."

"Yes," he growled. "Yes, by God, I want it!"
A rough hand stroked her hair and breast and arm, with
a pressure that made her gasp. He called her name
again, and she saw in his eyes a need so deep it drowned
her.

She felt that need enclose her, and closed her eyes and
gritted her teeth against her ow sudden need to give
him the response that was necessity to him.

But she could not close her ears. His deep voice was
hoarse and shaken, but it stroked her nerves with a
warmth like honey. "I need it, Shulamith," he said.
"Let me hear it, let me see it in your face. Moan for me,
Shulamith, need it, need what I can give you. I need it,
Shulamith, give it to me, please, please...."

Her body was moving of its own volition now, seeking, pushing against the rhythm he created; and she was shuddering and shaking and crying.

"That's it," he whispered, the triumph of need in his voice. "That's it...give me it all, Shulamith, I need it all...."

Her cry tore loose from the roots of her soul as her body heaved its final, deep response. It was a cry of surrender and discovery, a cry of acceptance of the deep, shuddering pleasure that coursed through her body, pleasure he had given her. His power over her was all-consuming, and he saw it and lost himself in it. Suddenly it was she who had the power; and Johnny trembled then and shook and cried out his surprised surrender.

THE COFFEE was hot and strong and Smith stirred sugar into hers to give her the strength for what was to come. She wasn't whispering "maybe" to herself this morning, she thought. She knew there were no more maybes. She made a little noise of self-mockery, and Johnny's eyes met hers over the breakfast table.

"I wrote a song about us," she said brightly, as though her heart wasn't breaking. "Would you like to hear it?"

There was a momentary pause. "All right," he said.

She sang it with a smile, and her scratchy voice was somehow right in that bright sunny kitchen overlooking the gorge on a summer day.

"There seems to be so much to give all through the night...I won't ask for any more, please wake me up to say goodbye 'cause now it's over."

His eyes were unreadable, but he smiled. "You seem to have hit expert status pretty quickly," he said, and then as though he did not want to ask but couldn't stop himself, "When did you write that?"

"Last Monday," she said. "I didn't do the music, that's by.... Do you remember what I told you about the boy up at Paper Creek? Well, I met him again. He's a musician now. He did the music."

Johnny nodded, but his eyes were on the coffeepot as he poured himself more coffee. "Are you taking it seriously?"

"Oh, you don't know! I quit my job, now I'm writing full time! 'Wake Me Up to Say Goodbye' is going to be recorded, maybe as early as next week. And Lew and I are a team. We're collaborating."

"Congratulations," said Johnny.

"I have to go," she said. She stood up.

"Thanks for waking me up to say goodbye."

Smith laughed, to ease the terrible grip of tears on her throat. "Oh, well, I had to, didn't I? When the song gets famous—did I tell you it's being recorded by a woman named Cimarron King? We're going to make each other famous—I'll probably have to wake up every lover to say goodbye in the future, or they'll complain!"

He didn't laugh with her. He didn't frown, either. He didn't do anything except look at her. "You foresee a lot of lovers in your future?"

"Oh, well," she responded lightly, "I'm going to be rich and famous. Rich famous people in the arts always have lots of lovers, don't they?"

"I guess they do."

She didn't know what she was saying. Anything that would keep the tears at bay and the terrible knowledge that this was the end. It must be the end.

"I guess we can split the cost of the divorce," she babbled as they walked down through the trees and onto the dock in the bright sunshine. "I haven't talked to a lawyer yet, but I think it's either one or three years of living apart, isn't it? I should find out about annulment, too...."

The little motorboat she had rented was bobbing on the gentle swell. Smith turned. "Well, goodbye, Johnny," she said, and for all her determination her voice caught in her throat.

He put his hands on her shoulders. He was going to kiss her. "Please," she said, "please don't kiss m—"

But his mouth had already covered hers. She could taste tears in the back of her throat, feel the upsurge of emotional need in her, and then he lifted his mouth from hers.

"You have to kiss lovers goodbye," he said with a smile. "Husbands and lovers—it's one of the rules. You'd better write a song called 'Kiss Me Goodbye.'"

She turned away and jumped into the boat. "All right!" she cried, smiling through the tears she hoped he didn't see. She kept her head bent as she turned the key and started the motor, and didn't look at Johnny Winterhawk again until she was far enough out to sea that she could wave cheerfully while the tears at last forced their way down her cheeks.

"I TOLD YOU, DADDY!" Smith cried in a high voice. "I told you to leave it alone!"

Her father had been released from hospital that afternoon. Smith had forgotten all about the housekeeper, who was now unable to come until the evening, and the house was a mess. The furniture she had evicted from the lounge to make way for the piano and desk was still awaiting a new location, and except for her workroom, nothing had been dusted for weeks.

Smith had cleaned up her father's bedroom after the call from the hospital, but her father had no intention of going to bed. They sat instead in the gray sitting room, which still had bad memories of interrogations with Sergeant Rice and Staff Sergeant Podborski.

And now another one, with her father. "That bloody cop," said her father, "came around this morning insinuating I'd known about it all along."

"I told you you'd be sorry," was all Smith would say.

"All right," said her father. He was thinner; his clothes were a little too big for him now, but the heart attack had been very minor; he was still powerful. "All right, I saw what I saw on the news last night, and I still don't believe it. I want to hear it from you. You're married, Shulamith?"

"That's right, daddy."

"Why?"

"Because I love him, daddy. Why else?"

"Then why isn't your husband here with you? Or why aren't you with your husband? And why don't you wear a ring?"

"Because we've agreed to split up."

It took him a moment to get over that one. "What?" he asked disbelievingly. "Why?"

"Because my husband doesn't love me, daddy. He never did." She was trying to remain matter-of-fact, but the pain kept seeping back. "If you hadn't made such a bloody noise about everything, we could have divorced quietly, and no one would ever have had to know. But then you've never listened to what I wanted, have you, daddy? So why should I be surprised that just to satisfy yourself you had me harassed by the police, the papers and your private detectives? How could I expect my happiness and peace of mind to be important to my father?''

Her anger was a flood, a raging sea, pushing and pounding against the reserve that had held it back for so many years. The force of it was frightening. If she let it loose, its power seemed enough to kill her father with words. But she looked at her father and told herself she didn't care. Let her father look out for himself. She always had—ever since she was eight years old she had been alone and unprotected.

"I don't understand," said her father. "If you were eloping, then who were those men? Who made the call?" He looked shaken, and she realized triumphantly that for perhaps the first time in his life her father was actually doubting himself. He was actually entertaining the possibility that his view of reality might be wrong.

She wished she could have proved him wrong. She wished she could tell him he had hallucinated the men. She looked at her father for a long moment, then got up and left the room. When she returned she held a Bible.

"Do you believe in God, daddy?" she demanded, and she was trembling now with the need to tell him the truth.

If he was surprised by her intensity he did not show it. "No," he said.

"Well, I do. I don't know who, and I don't know what, but there is a God. There is a God somewhere."

She held out the Bible to him. "I want you to put your hands on this and swear before my God that you won't tell anybody one word of what I'm going to tell you. If you don't swear, I won't tell you. But if you do swear, daddy, if you swear and break your oath, then God will kill you for it. And if God doesn't, then I will."

He was looking at her as though she was breaking his heart. He put out one and then the other hand to touch the book she held out to him. "I swear," said her father, looking into her eyes, "not to tell anyone what you tell me."

"Do you believe you'll die if you break your oath?" she demanded.

He blinked sadly. "Yes," he said, in the gentlest voice she had ever heard him use. "I believe it, Shulamith."

Then she told him.

"THERE'S ONE THING I don't understand," said her father when she had finished. "You say you love him very much but all he feels for you is a sexual attraction. And you're going to give him up, you're never going to see him again."

"Yes," she said.

"If there's one thing I know about you, Shulamith, it's that you're not a coward. You made a lot of mistakes working for me, but never by backing away from something. You were always my daughter that way." He sighed and shook his head. "But you're backing away from this. Marriages have been built—and built successfully—on less than what you and your husband have. Why don't you fight this thing of his heritage? Make him love you."

She laughed—a high bitter laugh that was more of a punishment to him than anything that had gone before. "You don't understand that, daddy?" she asked. "You really don't understand? Well, I'll explain: I've had sixteen years of chasing around after a man, trying to make him love me! I've spent my life up to now trying to make you love me, daddy, make you proud of me! And I've had a bellyful of it. I've had enough to last me a lifetime! From now on, men are going to chase *me*, daddy! Because now I know I've at least got something to offer! You used to make me think any man who showed an interest in me was only after your money. At least Johnny did me that favor. At least he showed me I'm a woman—a desirable woman!"

Her father looked away. "Yes, you are," he said. His voice was hoarse and he cleared his throat. "If you want my opinion the man's in love with you. Either that or he's a complete bastard."

She snorted. "Those are the only two choices?"

"A man's a man," said her father, ignoring her sarcasm. "Race doesn't change that, Shulamith. If he put you through all that only to save his own neck, he's a blackguard and doesn't deserve your loyalty or your silence." He raised his hand. "I'm not going to break my word. It will have to be up to you. If he is not a blackguard he has some feeling for you, Shulamith. Something you could make a marriage out of. Don't forget you're *married* to him. There's *your* solemn oath. How will your God feel about you abandoning your oath after a few days without even trying to make it work?"

"What do you know about it, daddy?" she asked dryly.

"I know marriage is the greatest happiness there is," he said softly.

"Then you know it doesn't last, too!" she said cruelly. "Nothing lasts forever, daddy! You should know that!" She jumped up to leave, because she knew that had hurt him, and she felt suddenly guilty. When she got to the door his voice spoke behind her.

"Two things last forever," he told her quietly. "Love, and regret."

ON THE NEWS that night an RCMP spokesman conceded that the kidnapping case was closed. "As far as the extortion is concerned," he said, "we have to assume that someone was aware of Miss St. John's planned absence and used the information for their own ends. But all our avenues of investigation are exhausted, and in view of a lack of cooperation from the principals the file is now no longer active."

"Thank God!" said Smith. "I'm last week's news!" She was one of the uncooperative principals. She had made a very brief statement to the reporters who had come around today, but to Staff Sergeant Podborski she had been less forthcoming.

"I told you you were wasting your time," she had told him coldly. "Don't expect me to save your bacon now. I don't know who knew, and I don't care. As far as I'm concerned, good luck to them. They should stop all the industrial despoilers and polluters the same way. I am free to say that without being charged with conspiracy, I hope? And free to think it?" Then she had closed the door on him.

"Not wise to get the police angry at you," her father had observed.

"No, it isn't, is it?" she agreed. "That's why I do it. Because everyone else out there is going to be so wise we're going to end up a police state!"

"Oh, now," began her father.

"You should be grateful," she said ironically, "that they haven't thought of charging you with laying false information!"

"They have thought of it," he said.

"What?" she laughed. *"What?"*

"Your staff sergeant there was wondering if I objected so strongly to my daughter marrying an Indian that I invented the whole thing to put them on your trail and prevent the wedding."

She laughed again. "What did you say to that?"

Her father looked ashamed. "I told him that if he used that kind of ingenuity sussing out child killers British Columbia might be a safer place to live."

Smith sucked in her breath. "Oh, daddy," she chided him. If anything would make the police angry, it would be that sort of reference to a case that had brought the police such terrible negative publicity. "What would you do if he did lay a charge against you?"

"I'd sue him for malicious prosecution," her father had said instantly.

The two of them had laughed together for the first time in days. "We'll both end up in jail," Smith had said.

"They're not always so unreasonable," her father had said suddenly, as though struck with a sudden guilt. "Don't condemn every cop on the actions of Podborski. We had some bad luck with these guys, Shulamith, but there've been times in my life when I was damned glad to see a man with yellow stripes on his trousers. Hell, you know what lawlessness is like, girl. You've been in a lumber camp."

He was right, of course. There were good and bad sides to everything. Before, she had tended to see the police as ideally good. Now she had had one consistently bad experience of them—and she must use that to balance her opinion, not change it completely.

"We make mistakes," said her father. "But we've lived abroad and we've lived here—you don't need me to make comparisons between countries for you, Shulamith."

"Okay," she smiled. Still, it was a relief to be old news, an old case; not to have to worry any more about police—or reporters or private detectives.

Soon after, when the housekeeper arrived and had begun to settle in, Smith drove down to the hospital to visit Wilf.

He had three visitors already in his room, dark-haired men standing around the bed. She was reminded suddenly of the men who had stood around her father's bed with Johnny. As she opened the door they looked up at her and then exchanged rapid glances among themselves. They were younger than Johnny, and except for their bronze skins they didn't resemble him at all: their faces and noses were broader than his. Yet a chill of something like recognition shivered along her spine as she advanced into the room.

"Hello, Wilf," she said, passing him the packages of fruit and reading matter she had brought him. She waited till he smiled and called her by her Indian name, waited till she saw the cautious blank behind his eyes, and then turned and said deliberately, "We meet again."

The three men started and then stared. Smith smiled, as if this were a cocktail party and she the hostess. "Of course, we didn't have much chance to get acquainted, did we? Shall we make up for it now?" She lifted her hands to her head, pulling her hair back above her ears. "These are my ears," she said. "You probably haven't seen them closely, but you wanted to mail one to my father." She turned her head to let them see, as though she were showing off earrings. "And these are my hands," she said, dropping her hair to hold them up. The three men, about her own age, were beginning to look sheepish. "Note the little finger on each one." She displayed them. "You've probably never noticed my little fingers before, but you wanted to cut them off." She looked at her hands. "Of course, I don't play the piano, so it wouldn't have mattered. What's a finger, after all?" She stopped smiling and faced them squarely. "Now look at me!" she said. "Take a good look! I'm human, you know! I'm a real live human being! And you didn't care! You wanted...you wanted—" She couldn't go on; she had no more words.

"I'm sorry, Wilf," she whispered, pulling a tissue from her pocket as she began to cry. He nodded at the three men, and they disappeared out the door. "My God," she said, blowing her nose. "I've been shrieking at people all day. I think I'm going crazy."

"Good," said Wilf approvingly. "In this world you have to go crazy to stay sane!"

In the long hot summer that followed she thought of Wilf's words many times. When she woke in the night crying from a nightmare of loss, when she had written a poem that reflected a despair blacker than she had known before, when the world lost its color before her eyes and she felt in the deepest reaches of her soul that for her it would be gray forever, she would cling to what Wilf had said like a lifeline, and repeat the words over and over until she believed them. She was going crazy, but it was necessary in order to stay sane.

There were other words that she repeated just as often. When the anguish was on her, when her body and her heart screamed that she could not last another minute without Johnny Winterhawk, she would clench her fists and her jaw and repeat the other talisman: "I am not going to beg for a man's love ever again!"

CHAPTER SEVENTEEN

IN THE MIDDLE OF JULY, Cimarron King, with some of the members of Horse backing her up, recorded "Wake Me Up to Say Goodbye." Shulamith sat in on the rehearsals and the recording, and it was more satisfying than anything she had achieved in the previous eight years.

"How long before it's released?" she demanded of Mel, because everything about the song seemed to work—the backup Horse provided bringing one more coloration to the enterprise to change it yet again.

"Three months minimum," he told her. "If I really bust my ass we're looking at, say, the beginning of October."

In July and August her poetry appeared in several nonpaying but prestigious literary publications in both Canada and the States, and in late August two were accepted for a publisher's anthology of modern Canadian poetry. She was to be included in a section that would be called the Poetic Future, or something similar, but still, she would be in the same company as the poets she had read in her high-school days, the poets she had revered and whose work she had cut her eyeteeth on.

"CanLit, here I come!" she laughed, showing the publisher's letter to Valerie. The publisher had chosen two poems that had appeared in an American literary publication.

"CanLit with the American seal of approval," Valerie said dryly.

"Oh, well, what's a little inferiority complex among friends?" laughed Smith.

She continued to collaborate with Lew Brady, not always with the inspired perfection of their first few efforts. They rarely fought, but there were times when neither could see virtue in the other's work, and times when they couldn't "get the song off the page," as Lew called it. By late August they had learned to stop expecting so much of themselves and each other, learned that sometimes they were better off working alone, each on his or her own contribution. Smith had always been a hard worker, but this was a different kind of hard work, and she had to learn, like so many amateurs moving toward a professional status, that sometimes she had to work whether the muse was with her or not.

In spite of this period of adjustment, the collaboration was fruitful and worthwhile and quite often as exciting and inspired as the night they had worked on "Wake Me Up to Say Goodbye." They had decided to concentrate on producing a few numbers for Cimarron King's projected album, a decision Mel encouraged and Cimarron was delighted with. By the end of August she was rehearsing "There's No Such Thing as Love" and "Dark Night of My Soul," and Mel had begun to talk about her needing numbers with more "upbeat" lyrics.

But the upbeat lyrics wouldn't come. "Think of this as my blue period," Smith told Mel, because by this time she and Lew had learned that their big blocks occurred while she was trying to write lighthearted or happy lyrics.

That summer she discovered Gerard Manley Hopkins and spent the dark hours of many a sleepless night with his "terrible sonnets."

No worst, there is none. Pitched past pitch of grief. . .
Comforter, where, where is your comforting?

She would read aloud, but the face of God she had touched the day she had married Johnny was no longer within her reach.

O the mind, mind has mountains; cliffs of fall
Frightful, sheer, no-man-fathomed. Hold them cheap
May who ne'er hung there.

The poet's agony did not comfort her. But sometimes, as she hung above her own mind's black abyss, it was Gerard Manley Hopkins who saved her from falling in.

At other times, it was her work. Smith had always known what hard work was, and she had an enviable energy. Once she learned the lesson of creative work—of being able to compose without the blessing of the muse—she applied it constantly.

Early in September she moved into an apartment of her own in a building very close to Lew's. It made their collaboration simpler, and even though she and her father had scarcely seen each other, living in the same house, she wanted to be in her own place. In fact, she saw her father more often after her move, because when she visited him once or twice a week she was sure of seeing him.

Her father was deeply involved in some new aspect of the business, but she did not ask him what it was that kept him so absorbed, and he didn't tell her. They talked instead of the past, of her mother and his artistic life in Paris. Her father was trying hard to get to know his daughter, to see the person she was rather than what he had wished her to be. They came to a troubled reconciliation: after all her outbursts it was difficult for him to feel that he could ever know her or be the father she needed, and once she had let the lid off her years of hurt anger it was difficult to get it back on again.

But she loved him still and wanted him to love her—it would be hard to change that. And she no longer felt the deep revulsion toward her past and St. John's Wood. So when her father suggested that she hang on to her shares in the company for a while, she let the matter slide: it was no longer of urgent importance to cease to have any connection with the place where she had spent eight unnecessary years.

She had a remarkably busy and absorbing summer. She did everything she had intended to do and then some. Of all the things she had promised herself she would do, there was only one she had not had the energy for: she had not gone to a lawyer to file for divorce.

"I'M SELLING OUT," her father said to her one evening in September. They were sitting by the pool drinking cocktails, enjoying the last of summer. Smith was lounging in a deck chair with her feet up on another, but at this she sat up with such a jerk she spilled her drink.

"Selling out of what?" she demanded, then, thinking she might have misunderstood, "The stock market?"

"I'm selling St. John Forest Products," Cordwainer St. John said. "Lock, stock and chain saws."

He had a half smile on his face, but Shulamith was aghast. "Daddy, *why*?"

"Why?" He smiled more broadly and shook his head. He had expected her to understand without being told, expected, perhaps, that she had known what he would do. "Well, I had three reasons for coming to the decision. First, my health. I've been told that I was very lucky to have had not one, but two minor heart attacks: either one could have been much worse. So unless I want to die, I can't work the way I have done in the past. If I can't work hard, St. John Forest Products will never be as valuable as it is right now. It needs a younger person at the helm to keep it growing.

"Then, there's this damned problem with the Indians up in Cat Bite. Your husband's people: I have to keep that in mind, Shulamith. If the commission decides in our favor—as it almost certainly will—the decision of what to do with those damned trees will be on my plate. I don't usually back away from a decision. But I can't decide between something that might drive a permanent wedge between you and your husband, and something that, if economic conditions continue as they are for another two or three years, might mean the difference between the company's scraping through and disaster.

"But most importantly—now that you're not interested in stepping into my shoes when I retire, what am I working for? A man doesn't kill himself to build a company when there's no one to pass it on to."

He said it matter-of-factly, without reproach, but she felt a reproach anyway. She wondered how many times in their lives she had read things into his voice that were not there.

"You should have had a son, daddy," she said nonsensically.

"I didn't want a son," he returned emphatically. "You are exactly what I wanted—you are tough and smart, smart as a whip, and you have just enough of your mother in you to—" He broke off. "You're my child. Why should you have to be a son before I would want to pass the business on to you? You blame me for that now, because you've found out it wasn't what you wanted after all. But suppose I'd been different? Suppose I'd ignored your talent and your brain and wanted you to *marry* someone I could pass it on to? You'd have been telling me this summer I'd destroyed your confidence, your resourcefulness—whatever it is these women's libbers are saying. You expressed an interest in forestry—as I'd hoped you would, I admit—and I gave you every opportunity to prove yourself. If I pushed you, it was no more than I would have pushed anyone who was going to be president some day."

It seemed it was her father's turn to respond to the charges she had leveled at him during the summer. He was right—his treatment of her, his expectations had always increased her sense of ability, her self-confidence. Perhaps the eight years under his tutelage had not, after all, been entirely wasted.

"I guess there aren't many blacks and whites in

human experience, are there?'' She suddenly wanted to try to express to him her confusion over her view of the past. ''I'm sorry, daddy,'' she said softly. ''I'm trying to understand.'' She looked into his eyes in the fading light and knew that though she had hurt him, he had somehow accepted it without anger. They smiled ruefully at each other.

''Have you worked out a deal yet?'' she asked him then. ''For the sale, I mean?''

''The only part that isn't finalized yet is whether you want to sell out your shares along with mine or whether you'd like to keep an interest. Jake will give you back shares in the new company if you like, or you can take cash. I don't guarantee you'll have any control over what he decides about Cat Bite Valley, but at least you'll have the right to say your piece.''

''Who are you selling to?''

''Conrad Corporation,'' said her father. ''I wanted to get a—''

''*Conrad* Corporation?'' she nearly shrieked. It was almost dark now, and she bent to stare more closely at her father's face, as though she might discover that he was joking. ''Daddy you're not selling St. John's Wood to *Jake Conrad*?'' She had never met Jake Conrad, but she had heard of him. He had started out in trucking, but he had not stayed there. Nor had he, like her father, been content to stay in one industry. His conglomerate was a mixed bag. Shulamith had heard his name every time his reach extended into the forestry industry. He was a bastard, she had learned. He was lucky, and he was a bastard.

"He's an excellent, hard-working young man. He's exactly—"

"He's a *bastard*! Daddy, he's a ruthless *bastard*. Everybody knows it—and you know it, too! He'll be cutting in Cat Bite before the ink is dry on the contract!"

Her father stood up to flick on the patio lights and the bug light. There were cricket noises and soft night smells. It was pleasant here, Smith reflected. This was something she missed down in the city—the sense of privacy. Even having the ocean and park so near didn't make up for this.

"I don't think so," said her father, pouring himself another drink. "Jake Conrad has mellowed a lot since his marriage. I don't think he'll do what you think. He's very shrewd and intelligent, and I expect him to give a lot of thought to whatever he does in Cat Bite Valley."

"He's married? When did he get married?"

"Last year. I suppose you were abroad. A very beautiful young widow. I've met her."

"Well, if she can mellow Jake Conrad, I wish her luck! I still think—oh, never mind." What did it matter to her anyway? Indians' rights were being ignored and abused all across the country. What difference did it make to her whether it was the Chopa? "So what will you be doing, daddy?" she asked. "Are you retiring completely?"

"No, I'm going to be chairman of the board, as befits my age," her father said with a twinkle.

"Of Conrad Corporation?"

"The new company will be called Concord Corporation. It will be a very big conglomerate," he said with satisfaction. "Probably one of the top one hundred, in terms of sales, in Canada."

"The 'Cord' comes from Cordwainer?"

"Your grandmother's maiden name. She was the last of her line. I think she'd be pleased that the name isn't quite going to die."

Shulamith's middle name was Dayan, her mother's maiden name. Her mother had been related, though not closely, to Moshe Dayan. "You get your courage from the Dayans," Shulamith had been told over and over. "Also your strong chin."

"Mother did the same thing," she said now. "If I ever have a child, look at all the family names it's going to be saddled with, to keep up the tradition. It'll be the last of the Cordwainers, the last of the St. Johns—"

"You've got St. John cousins," her father said. The branch of the family he had not spoken to since going to Europe to study art. "Second cousins."

"That's good," she said, the blackness coming on her, as it did at unexpected moments. "There are lots of Dayans, too. It's a good thing the Cordwainer name is on the business, because I won't be having children."

"You never see your husband?" asked her father after a moment.

"He's not my husband, daddy.' She shook her head and looked into her empty glass. "He's just...." She stood up. "It's getting late, I should go."

"I haven't talked to you about the house yet," her father said. "We'll have to discuss it another time. I thought I'd sell it."

Smith looked around at the pool, the house, the landscaped lawn. She had thought she didn't like this house, and yet it had its own peace.

"It's funny," she said. "Do you remember who I wanted you to get when we were building—when you got Hughie to design this?"

"Some young fellow who was barely starting out," her father said. "A little too innovative, I remember thinking at the time. Why?"

"He wasn't exactly *starting out*—he was already designing a big office building that year," Smith told him. "Right now—" she had read it in the paper "—he's doing a hotel in Amsterdam. It was Johnny Winterhawk."

ON OCTOBER 7, a local radio station aired "Wake Me Up to Say Goodbye" for the first time. Smith had been warned by Mel, so she was tuned in to the station while she worked that day, waiting to hear it, but still it was a shock.

I wrote this, was her first thought, and a flower of surprised pride unfolded inside her. *This is my song!*

Suddenly she was remembering the day she wrote it. The morning she had wakened up, full of contentment, to find the bed empty beside her and gone downstairs to write it straight from the pen. She laughed lightly. She hadn't known how lucky she was that day. She had thought then—if she had thought about it at all—that all her writing would be as easy and inspired.

Oh, Johnny. The morning when she had sung the song to him, knowing that she loved him and that it was goodbye.

"But now it's over, all that's left is just goodbye."

Cimarron King's voice had a quality in it that said everything the song did not say. She had found the truth of the song, which Smith had not understood while she was writing it, had not known herself until the morning at the island. "But in the morning when you wake and you know deep down—" her voice caught then, giving the lie to the next three words "—it's a mistake...." Smith wondered how it was she had never noticed before that Cimarron King had added a whole new dimension to the song: that the singer was a woman who was afraid to ask for love.

By MID-NOVEMBER Smith was being driven crazy by her own song. Wherever she turned, whatever she did, "Wake Me Up to Say Goodbye" would sooner or later assail her ears. It was being played on every station in Vancouver, perhaps every station in Canada—except the classical stations, and of course, the CBC.

It kept Johnny constantly in her mind. She couldn't divorce the song from her memories of Johnny, and her memories of Johnny were going to drive her mad.

In late November there was something else that kept him in the forefront of her mind: the Cartier Commission brought down its preliminary report, and it recommended against the Chopa. "In the light of various background papers and policy papers it had considered, as well as the 1974 Pierce Commission paper on forest tenure...in light of the fact that the new Charter of Rights had not seen fit to entrench native rights in such matters...the economic situation and the practical results...but also considering the very real concerns of the native people who enjoyed the use of the land...the

commission recommended that the timber rights granted to St. John Forest Products on the land bounded by
Salmontail Lake, Hackle Ridge, Feather Mountain and
Cat Bite River, including Cat Bite Valley, be honored.
But it further recommended that care be taken to ensure
'that the damage inflicted on the environment be no
more than is held to be necessary' and, as far as possible
ensure 'the least damage to the wildlife habitat consistent with the cutting of the timber.'

The full report would not be published until after
Christmas, but everyone knew all it was necessary to
know. Only fools would imagine that the concern for
native claims and wildlife preservation was anything
more than lip service.

Smith was in a fury over it. A helpless fury. She could
fire off a letter to the editor, which she did; she could
buttonhole her friends at parties and over lunch and de-
nounce the system, which she did; she could write to
Victoria and Ottawa. She did that, too. What she could
not do was convince herself that citizens had any voice
in the running of the country.

Her friends listened to her, of course. They all knew
she was married to Johnny Winterhawk, who was a
Chopa Indian, and they all knew it had gone wrong.
Nobody knew how or why. T· some, like Valerie and
Lew and Mel, who knew how she was suffering from
what they thought of as "the breakup," this fury on his
behalf came as no surprise. They listened because they
knew she needed to vent her rage. Others, who knew
nothing except the bare facts, were surprised at this
revolutionary zeal toward her estranged husband's
cause and listened because they hoped to find some clue

to the still fascinating mystery of Shulamith St. John and Johnny Winterhawk.

What she wanted to be doing, of course, was not blowing off steam to everyone who would listen, but comforting Johnny. She knew that comfort was impossible, yet she had learned from Johnny that sharing pain meant halving it, and she wanted to share the ugliness of the commission decision with him.

Well, at least there could be no immediate cutting, she knew: lumbering operations had been packed up for the winter. She would have time to talk to Jake Conrad, try to convince him.... When the deal had gone through she had taken shares in the new Concord Corporation rather than selling out. She could make a nuisance of herself if she had to.

Perhaps if she could tell Johnny that there was still hope it might be a way of sharing the pain. She could do that without asking for anything. She could just phone and say "I've still got some influence...."

On the third day after the decision was released, Smith picked up the phone and called his office.

"I'm sorry," said the receptionist, "Mr. Winterhawk isn't in town. He's still over in Amsterdam. But he should be back next week. Would you like to leave a message?"

"No," said Smith. She hung up. She had been saved from her own stupidity once. She must be careful not to tempt fate again.

"ALL RIGHT," said Mel, rubbing his hands and smiling. "We've got a hit, and we've got a star. I got nibbles—bites, in fact—from two American companies this week, and one of them is CBS. They are very excited about Cimarron and literally bowled over to know that we are only a few numbers short for an album and even have half of it laid down already.''

"*Have* we got half of it laid down?" asked Smith in surprise.

"We will have by Christmas. We'll work flat out after this. They were suggesting Cimarron might do a promotional tour of the States in the spring." He stopped and looked around at their three amazed, incredulous faces. "Ladies and gentlemen," he said, "what I am trying to tell you is—our ship has come in."

Cimarron was swearing with a kind of religious awe, something Smith had long ago got used to. She herself swore when she was angry, but Cimarron swore to express any emotion, from excitement through minor annoyance. Smith had once threatened to write a song called "I Love You, Goddammit" for her, but the others had laughingly convinced her it would sound too "country" for Cimarron's image.

When she had sat a moment taking it in, Smith jumped up and ran to embrace Cimarron. "Congratulations," she said. "You're going to make us all rich. Isn't she, everybody?"

"You're rich already," Cimarron protested stupidly, tears starting in her glistening dark eyes. She hugged Smith tightly then and smiled at them all through her tears. "Oh, God!" she choked on a half giggle, half sob. "Goddammit, you guys, what if after all this, I don't make it?" She meant in the States. She might have a very popular record in Canada, but she still would not "make it" till she had made it in the States. That was the way Canada dealt with its stars: it did not package and export its own talent, it waited for other countries— mostly the United States—to buy the raw material. This "discovery" now by the American recording studios was more than just a chance to be seen by the American public. It was Cimarron's chance to become an international star and then be exported back to Canada and be accepted as "legitimate."

"A 'profit' is without honor in his own country," a famous actor had quipped, after going this route and returning a star to shoot a movie in Canada, and being, predictably, lionized by the media and the populace. But everybody knew it. It wasn't news to Canadians. It was a fact of life.

"If you don't make it," Mel said easily now, "just remember, 'Lizzie—you bin ast.'"

On an evening at the end of November Smith sat sprawled in her favorite armchair—a piece of furniture she had begged from her father when she'd moved—her feet over one arm, a cup of coffee balanced on her stomach as she listened to a tape of Lew playing his latest composition. Actually, it was not new—it was an old composition that he had resurrected and revamped in the hope that she could do something with it. And while it was certainly not Lew at his most inspired, there was something about the music that she liked.

What it needed was a light-hearted lyric that demanded no more of the listener than did the music. "You won't be happy till I come up with something with boop-boop-a-doo in it, will you?" she had laughed to Mel, who would have liked nothing better than to cut an album of Cimarron with all original songs, composed only by Cimarron or by Lew and Smith.

For that, he needed some upbeat songs. "Listen, ladies and gentlemen," Mel had said during one of their frequent conferences, "the music business is very fragmented these days. Nobody knows what is going to be selling next week, let alone next year. I want Cimarron to cover as broad a base as possible—to get as wide a public as she can. That means somebody has got to move out of Depression City here and cough up a pretty little song that will go right down the middle...."

That was when Smith had said, "You won't be happy till I come up with something with boop-boop-a-doo in it...."

"Boop-boop-a-doo," she said tentatively now during what she considered a particularly cloying phrase of Lew's music. Lew was scraping the bottom of the barrel now. None of his light music had so far inspired her.

"This is the chirpiest thing I've ever put my hand to," he said. "If you come up with a maudlin lyric for this, I'm throwing in the towel."

"Boop-boop-a-doo," Smith sang again, then reached out a hand to flick off the cassette and swung her feet to the floor.

The buzzer sounded from downstairs, and she walked to the intercom with her coffee cup, glancing at her watch. Not late. It could be almost anybody.

"Yes?" she pushed the button for Talk, and then Listen.

"Shulamith?" said a voice, and even over the distortion caused by the cheap intercom speakers the tone was unmistakable. Smith clutched the cup and felt her heart set up a pounding that would deafen her.

"What do you want?" she demanded hoarsely, then laughed helplessly, moved her finger onto the Talk button and asked the question again.

"Just you," said Johnny's deep voice. "To see you."

More than anything in the world at that moment she wished she had the power to say no. But her finger had already moved over to the button marked Door.

She unlocked the apartment door and, still holding the cold coffee cup, moved over to sit in a chair facing the entrance. By the time the knock sounded she was stiff, trapped between hope and fear. "Come in," she called, when she could make her mouth move, and then he was in the doorway, as dark and beloved as ever. He stared across the room at her, but she could not read the message in his eyes.

"How did you find me?" she asked in a voice that seemed rusty with disuse.

"Your father," said Johnny. "I called and he gave me your new address."

"When did you get back?"

"An hour ago." He closed the door and leaned on it wearily. "I've just come from the airport."

Suddenly she understood. She could read the message in his eyes. It was his first time home since the Cartier recommendations, and after all this time, he had come to her for comfort.

CHAPTER EIGHTEEN

"WHAT DO YOU WANT?" she asked, still in the same level voice, still sitting there with her coffee cup held against her like a shield.

A faint amusement glimmered for a moment behind his eyes. "Did you know that damned song of yours is even playing on the inflight music channel?"

She laughed as well as she could over the lump in her throat. "Is it? Oh, well, it's all money in the till. We're making a deal with CBS now."

"You're doing well, then." He moved away from the door and she got up to sit in the white leather chair. "Congratulations."

"Thank you." She waved at a chair, and Johnny sat down as she found her usual pose in her own. "How's the hotel going?"

Just so might a divorced couple have met, after long years, to talk over the children's futures. Polite and wary and afraid of the past. She wondered suddenly if she was wrong, if he had come to talk about divorce proceedings.

"They seem to like it so far," Johnny said. "We had a bit of a problem with the contractors—we had to develop a new method for laying—" He broke off, as though surprised to hear himself talking. "Old dogs don't like new tricks," he finished briefly.

Silence fell. "I heard about the Cartier decision," Smith said. "I'm sorry."

Johnny rubbed a hand over his forehead. He was wearing a three-piece suit, and he had unbuttoned his shirt collar, and his tie was missing. He looked as though he would rather be wearing jeans. "It was a foregone conclusion. Depressing, but predictable." He didn't sound as angry as she expected him to be. She wondered if he had vented most of his anger already, at a distance.

Smith jumped up. "Like a drink?"

He was rubbing his head as though his scalp were too tight. "Got any coffee?" he asked gratefully. "My body thinks it's three in the morning."

She moved into the kitchen, and after a moment she could hear the sounds of Lew's music coming from the tape recorder.

"What's this?" called Johnny.

The coffee she had made earlier was still hot; she had left it on the burner. Smith laid a tray quickly and returned to the living room.

"I have to compose a lyric for it," she told him. "It's not coming easily."

"It sounds like Muzak," Johnny said, without judgment. She passed him a cup.

"Yeah—well, that's what's needed," she said shortly, and reached out to switch the machine from tape to radio where music was playing. "It's supposed to put me in a more upbeat mood."

"You're kidding," said Johnny faintly.

She laughed. "Once the band gets hold of it, it'll change. And with Cimarron's voice...but I can't seem to come up with anything.'' She let one beat go by and then said hesitantly, ''Is it...how's the divorce thing coming? I'm afraid I haven't—''

''Neither have I,'' said Johnny. ''I'm sorry. I've been too busy.''

Smith leaned her head back against the upholstery. ''Funny how it happened, isn't it?'' she said softly. ''We've never talked about it since, but you...I don't believe it *was* Stockholm Syndrome, you know.''

The music from the radio played softly for a moment. ''No?'' asked Johnny.

''You know what I think it was? I think I wanted a man to love me so badly—after my father, I mean—that I just fell for you because it seemed as though you loved me. I'd probably have fallen for anyone who acted as though he was crazy about me.''

His dark eyes were hooded. ''You mean I'm the first man who's ever acted as though he was crazy about you?'' he asked in disbelief.

''No....'' She thought suddenly, *I am trying to keep you at bay. I am lying to save myself the hurt that tonight will inflict on me if you stay and love me the way you want to, the way I want you to....* ''But there was a man in Paris last year. He seemed to be really smitten...I let him—'' She broke off. It was a horrible memory, but Johnny had taken the pain away long ago. He had shown her how womanly she was, and the memory of Roger had lost its power over her. A pity Johnny had substituted a far greater pain. ''I realized afterward that he wasn't a nice man at all—but somehow I couldn't see that as long as he was telling me he was crazy about me.''

"There are men who don't show their true colors until they've been rejected," Johnny observed dispassionately.

"I didn't reject him," Smith said with wry humor. "That's what I mean. I haven't any judgment. Other women my age know all about the Rogers in the world."

His face looked bleak. "And all about the Johnny Winterhawks?"

Oh, God, as quickly as that he could tear her heart out. As quickly as that she had to bite back the words that had been so safely locked away, the loving words, the begging words....

"Johnny," she began helplessly, "I...I...."

"We didn't wait to fall in love." Cimarron King's voice was suddenly rising from the radio on the floor between them. Smith swung her feet off the chair arm with such clumsy haste she kicked the radio and set it flying. "And then we met...."

She shot out of her chair to her knees beside the machine, scrabbling with nervous hands to turn it off. "And no room for regret...."

She managed to shut it off, and then Johnny was bending over her, helping her up, close to her, so close her throat closed and her breathing stopped.

She stood motionless in his embrace, feeling the warmth of his hands on her, feeling his tender mouth bend closer and closer.

Oh, it had been long, so long. Her pulse thudded in her temples and body, her blood flooding out from her heart to meet his touch; and her throat ached with unshed tears and the need to tell him....

"Shulamith," he whispered. "Shulamith." There was no fury in him now, only need.

"I can't, Johnny," she whispered brokenly. "Please don't, please don't ask me. I can't anymore. I can't, Johnny. Oh, God—" the tears were starting out of her eyes "—please go away, Johnny! Please let go of me and go away!"

His hands dropped instantly away from her. "Sorry." He swallowed. "I'm sorry, I...uh...." His eyes were hooded. He did not look at her as he let her go and moved away from her.

At the door he paused. "I'll file for divorce," he said. "My lawyer will let you know."

Her heart was being ripped apart. Oh, God, just one more word before he closed the door! She stepped forward. "Isn't it funny?" she said brightly. "We were so concerned about the world tearing us apart, taking us away from each other. That's why we got married so quickly, remember?" She laughed a little. "Well, that's what you said. Oh, well, I only meant...the world didn't have to do anything—we did it ourselves."

In the open doorway Johnny paused. "Yes," he said quietly. "We did it ourselves."

ON DECEMBER 1, Concord Corporation sold all the timber rights in the Cat Bite Valley area to the Chopa Indian band for one dollar. The province nearly dropped into the Pacific in shock. For a week Jake Conrad was on every talk and news show going on radio and television.

"Well," he was quoted as saying, "I admit to curiosity. It's always seemed to me that the people protecting the environment are the ones who don't stand to profit directly from the polluting or despoiling. For example, the Chopa band stood to benefit only if the trees were *not* chopped in Cat Bite Valley. Now, they can benefit either way—if they choose to despoil their own environment and destroy the hunting and fishing grounds, they stand to make a hefty profit. There are a few dreams the Chopit nation could realize with sufficient cash. If I want to see how honorable our environmental moralists are, well, in this case I can afford to indulge my curiosity. Besides, I needed a tax write-off.''

There might be some question about that, it transpired. Although Concord Corporation lawyers had managed the sale in a way that ought to have guaranteed tax-write-off status, the federal government was making noises about disallowing the deduction.

"Can he afford to indulge his curiosity if that happens?'' Smith asked her father.

Cord St. John shrugged. "Well, it would be expensive, but not as expensive as it would have been for St. John Forest Products alone.''

Her father had at first been merely resigned to his relative inactivity since the merger of the two companies, but now he seemed to be positively enjoying it. He had taken up art again and set up his easel in the same bright lounge Smith had used for a workroom.

"There must be something about this room,'' said Smith, breathing in the atmosphere of oil paint and turpentine with a sweet nostalgia.

"Lots of light,'' said her father succinctly. Shulamith laughed. After sixteen years it still seemed strange to see her father as anything but a hard-driving businessman.

"And no broadloom." This room, unlike most of the others in the house, had a hardwood floor that until recently had been covered with a Persian carpet. Her father had had it taken up, and now oil paint spattered the floor's bright gloss. "It reminds me of the flat in Paris a little."

Her father looked around. "Does it? Yes, I suppose it does—on a somewhat grander scale. I had a skylight in Paris—that gave a better light."

She had learned more about her father and his early life in the past few months than she had done in all her previous life. At the age of twenty-two, he had told her, he had left a disapproving family to follow an artist's life. He had traveled Europe and ended up in Paris, where he had met and married her Israeli mother, who had been studying at the Sorbonne.

Smith had not imagined the happiness in that little flat. Those years had been the happiest in her father's life, too. And then her mother had gone—against all his pleading, and his presentiments of disaster—back to Israel to be at her brother's funeral.

He had heard the noise of the bomb blast in a dream, and then silence. The silence of perpetual loneliness. He had given up the flat and his artistic life and returned home to Vancouver, where his parents had already died, and a small inheritance awaited him.

He had thought he loved his small daughter as much as ever, but his grief had made him silent and unreachable, and he forgot how much he had given her in the golden time. It had never occurred to him that he had stopped holding her—and that therefore no one held her; that he had stopped listening to her dreams, had stopped praising her. He had been as proud of his bright little daughter as ever; he had not noticed that he did not tell her so.

"So, what sort of man is your husband?" he asked her that evening as they sat and looked out at a soft sunset. "Is he proud of you? What does he say about your new work—this song of yours?"

She took a deep breath. "Daddy, I don't see him."

"What about the other week there? Wasn't that Johnny who called me?"

"Yes. And I think you should have asked me be-fore—"

"He's your husband, Shulamith."

"Father, don't tell—"

"Is he proud of you?"

"*Yes*, damn you! Yes, he's proud of me! He congratulates me, and he comes all the way from Amsterdam just to tell me he's heard them playing my song! All right?"

Her father was nodding. "That's good, that's good. A woman like you doesn't want a man who's competi-tive. You need a man whose manhood won't be threat-ened by your talent. You're too bright to bury it all for such a reason."

The idea of Johnny's manhood being threatened by anything she did was so ridiculous it nearly made her laugh. He had always expected the best from her—right from the beginning when he had expected her to know all about St. John's involvement in Cat Bite.

"I have no intention of burying my talents for love or anything else," she said dryly, but her father was im-mune to sarcasm.

"Good!" he said. "You'll go a long way, whatever you do. I've always thought so."

STRANGELY ENOUGH, there began to be a kind of angry sentiment against Jake Conrad, especially in the lumber trade. Old friends of Cord St. John's called on him to try to enlist his aid in an effort to halt the assignment of the timber rights to the Chopa band. There was a sort of grass-roots feeling against it, as though Jake Conrad had given the Indians a major victory in an undeclared war.

If one group of natives had the control of their land returned to them, surely that would inspire other groups to greater efforts against government and industry? Besides—and this feeling was very strong—what did Indians know about running their own affairs? The Department of Indian Affairs controlled every day of their lives. They might use the advantage Jake Conrad had given them to cause boundless harm to themselves and the forestry industry and even, if some were to be believed, the whole Western way of life.

Jake Conrad laughed and went on more television shows. He sat on a panel and accused his opponents of being "backward, blind and balky." He said those who had to be forced into the future usually did not survive there and invited them to check the direction of the winds of change and put their sails up accordingly.

Johnny Winterhawk went on television, too. He was suddenly highly visible, being both successfully assimilated *and* a militant Indian. He was also an expert, it was shortly discovered, on the Indian Act, the Department of Indian Affairs and all its leaked memos and such things as the differences between treaty and status Indians, as well as their similarities—"the policy of suppress and destroy is being applied indiscriminately to all." He kept a studio audience breathless one day while he listed all the minor decisions of a reserve Indian's daily life that had to be submitted to Indian Affairs for approval.

"Are you allowed to suck your thumbs on your own?" had asked the shocked television host faintly.

"If we can find them under all the paperwork," Johnny said, and the studio audience had broken into laughing applause.

In the meantime, the provincial attorney general stayed the charges Johnny had brought against the police for wrongful search, which meant his hands were tied; and the Crown declined to prosecute the officers involved in Wilfred Tall Tree's arrest and "alleged" beating. Wilfred, Smith learned through the press, was back at home on the island, but after six months had still not fully recovered from the beating. But old men take a long time to recover, his doctor had said, and Wilf's prognosis was good.

No more canoeing trips over to Oyster Island, I bet, Smith thought when she read that, remembering Wilf's cabin and the afternoon she had spent watching him carve a ritual mask.

Meanwhile, amid great jubilation among her collaborators and friends, Smith wrote "No Time Like the First Time"—upbeat and sweet, with only the faintest hint of nostalgia.

"I've been wanting to meet you for ages," said Vanessa Conrad with a smile. "This is a lovely party."

"I've had a staff Christmas party every year," Smith's father had said. "This year I don't have any staff anymore. But I'd like to have a few people here at the house. And I'd like you to be hostess again."

Her father had not had many parties—one or two a year—but Smith had begun to attend them at fourteen and had become his hostess at sixteen.

"I'd like it very much if you'd invite some of your new friends along," St. John had said. Smith laughed at a private vision of Cimarron King mixing with her father's establishment cronies.

"I think I'd better throw my own party," she had said.

"Now look," returned her father. "All my friends have known you since you were a child. They're all very interested in your new career. They'd like to meet these people, Shulamith. They probably aren't quite as shockable as you imagine. And I'd like to meet them, too."

"It's your funeral, daddy," Smith had said.

But it wasn't a funeral at all. Smith looked around the room where Cimarron King, smashing in red velvet with holly in her hair, was holding court for several of her father's vintage business friends; and to Lew, holding his own in a political discussion; and Mel, fascinating several wives with talk of the music industry. Several other of her friends were there, too, including, of course, Valerie and Rolly, but the gathering did not include the wild profane young men of Horse. They were playing a Christmas concert in Toronto, a fact for which Shulamith had been grateful, however much her father might think she underestimated his friends.

"I'm glad you could come," Smith said now.

It was the first time she had ever met Jake and Vanessa Conrad, though she had seen Jake on television. Vanessa was another redhead, although her hair was a deep russet shade quite unlike Shulamith's mane of foxfire. She was tall and elegant, with smooth hair and an enormous emerald-and-diamond ring.

And on the waistband of her long black silk dress— the most elegant Smith had seen in years—there was a small, curved U-shape picked out in rhinestones.

Smith bent closer. Diamonds.

"A horseshoe!" she exclaimed. "A diamond horseshoe! I bought a dress awhile ago with a horseshoe on the cuff. In gold thread. Where did you get yours?"

"I designed it," smiled Vanessa Conrad. "The dress you bought must be one of mine—the horseshoe is my trademark."

"Your trademark?" Smith opened her eyes wide. "You have your own company then?"

"Number Twenty-four Fashions," Vanessa told her with a smile. "I went into evening wear for the first time with the summer line. I hope you like the dress."

"Oh, I do," Smith eyes softened as she smiled at the other woman. "I wore it as my wedding dress."

Maybe it was stupid to bring it up, but everybody knew she had had a runaway marriage, and there was lots of speculation that she and her husband were living apart. She hadn't discussed it much, even with Valerie. It felt good to talk about her wedding like this, as though it had been a normal occurrence, like other women's weddings.

"Well, I'm honored!" said Vanessa Conrad sincerely. "Darling?" She mouthed the word across the room, and Jake Conrad detached himself from the group around her father and came over.

It was obvious that *this* marriage was working. Although Jake and Vanessa had been separated much of the time at this party, Smith had seen them connect across the room time and time again with a smile or a glance. Their obvious love for each other brought a lump to her throat.

"Jake, Mrs. Winterhawk wore one of my dresses at her wedding. Isn't that something?"

The name ripped through her like a bullet. "Oh, please!" she smiled and recovered. "Call me Shulamith—or Smith, everybody does. Anyway, I—I kept my own name. I don't use Winterhawk."

"I'm sorry, Shulamith," Vanessa smiled. "I never thought... but tell me which dress it was."

She was desperately grateful to be given something to do. "Cream-colored—it wasn't silk, but it looked very good...a jacket and dress...." She put her hands up to indicate the neckline.

"I know the one." Vanessa came to her rescue again, pretending nothing was amiss. "You remember that one, don't you, Jake? You said you liked it very much when I showed you the prototype."

Jake grinned helplessly at her. It was obvious he did not remember. "Have a heart!" he said. "If it was a prototype I saw it had to have been at least six months ago."

"Philistine!" murmured his wife in a loving tone. She turned back to Smith. "You're certainly not wearing one of my off-the-rack numbers tonight. That is really beautiful."

Smith in fact looked stunning. In the cloth-of-gold tunic she wore, and her hair rolled into a wide chignon at the back of her neck, she was beautiful and almost as smoothly elegant as Vanessa Conrad.

One of those small silences fell over the room just then, a universal momentary pause, into which the single rather shocking profanity uttered in a smoky feminine voice dropped with perfect timing.

Every eye was involuntarily drawn toward the diverting picture of Cimarron King, who, totally oblivious, was discoursing good-humoredly on the trials of life on the road.

The pause held for a tiny moment, and then everyone stepped delicately back into their own conversations.

Across the room Smith met her father's eye and twinkled her "I told you so" at him. Her father was not in the least discomposed. He grinned back and deliberately winked at her.

But Smith was not looking at him any longer. She was looking past his head, to the large dark figure that had just entered the room behind him and stood surveying the crowd. It was a moment before his eyes found her, but when he did Johnny Winterhawk smiled at her as though his presence in her father's home was the most natural thing in the world.

The people who a minute ago had been blasé enough to ignore Cimarron King's irrepressible profanities weren't up to this one. There wasn't a soul in the room

who wasn't agog to know the true story of what was going on between Smith and Johnny, and no one even
pretended to look the other way as Johnny Winterhawk
made his way across the room to Shulamith St. John in
a silence that, except for the Christmas music playing in
the background, was total.

Johnny ignored the stares and the silence and bent
and kissed his wife lightly. "Hello, darling," he said.
"Sorry I didn't get back in time."

What was that supposed to mean? Involuntarily
Smith returned his kiss and played along because she
had to: it was beyond her to make a scene here.
"Johnny, you know Jake...."

"Of course." The two men shook hands, obviously
pleased with one another. They had appeared on a discussion panel together and had taken on all comers.

"But I don't know if you've met Vanessa."

She performed the introduction as calmly as she could
and then slipped into silence as Johnny and Jake and
Vanessa chatted together. A waiter passed by and took
orders for drinks, and a moment later someone
squeezed her hand and said brightly, "Aren't you going
to introduce me?" and there was Valerie smiling
fascinatedly up at Johnny Winterhawk.

In the end she had to introduce him to most of the
people in the room. Almost everyone recognized his
face, of course, and they knew all about him and were
much more thrilled to meet him than they had been to
meet Cimarron—another fascinating representative
from an alien life-style.

It was the sort of thing that must be happening to him
a lot lately, and during a lull in conversation she asked

with a smile, "How does it feel to be lionized by the enemy?"

"These people aren't the enemy," he grinned back, totally at ease in this house. "They're potential clients!"

A hoot of delighted laughter escaped her, and around the room meaningful glances were exchanged, several of the wives deciding there and then that it wouldn't be the first time the rumor mills had been completely mistaken.

One couple in the room were old clients of Johnny's and met him again with delight.

"Do you know," bellowed the man with rough good humor, "that that danged floorboard *still* creaks?"

Everyone except Smith laughed, and the man's little wife smiled kindly at her. "Hasn't he told you?" she asked. "There's a floorboard that creaks in every house he's built. You can't get rid of it, no matter what. It's sort of a trademark nowadays, isn't it Mr. Winterhawk?"

"Is *that* what that is!" Smith grinned up at Johnny, then told the couple, "There's a creak in front of his study door. I thought it was a Distant Early Warning System."

The man winked at Johnny. "I'm sure you're your own Distant Early Warning, isn't she, John?"

He looked down at her the way a loving husband of a few months would. "That's right," he said, with a grin.

It was an evening in hell. After a while the smile became fixed on Smith's face, till the muscles ached, and she was sure it looked like a mask. They were constantly surrounded by guests. There was no chance to speak to him alone, to ask why he was here or demand that he leave.

Nor could she leave herself. She couldn't bear to be in the limelight again, the subject of comment and curiosity. So she stayed till nearly everyone had gone home and the caterers were clearing up. Her father sat by the dying fire with Rolly and Valerie and Matt Hurtubise and his wife, old friends who might not leave for another hour.

Drooping with exhaustion, Smith made her farewells, and Johnny Winterhawk did the same. Then he helped her into her wrap, and they went out together into an unseasonably mild night.

"The charade ends here," Smith said, as her shoes crunched on the drive, and he followed her to her car. She bent to unlock the car door and then stood to face Johnny. "What the hell possessed you to come here tonight?" she demanded.

"Your father invited me," he returned quietly.

"He's got his nerve! Men! And you just came? You didn't think to check with me?"

"I thought perhaps the invitation came, indirectly, from you."

"Well, it—"

"It didn't. Yes, I could see that, but would you have been happier if I'd turned and walked out again and left you alone with all those curious people?" he asked mildly.

"Oh, Lord!" she exclaimed weakly. "Can you just imagine?"

"Graphically."

"Why on earth did my father invite you?" she asked, climbing into her car lest he should imagine she was making excuses to keep him near her, talking. "I mean, what excuse did he give you?"

Johnny slipped his hands into the trouser pockets of his black dinner suit, and the wings of his hair fell forward as he looked down at her in the little sports car. His face was carved in shadow. She had never seen a man look handsomer in formal wear.

"Your father is my client," he said at last. "I'm building him a house. Didn't he tell you?"

"ARE YOU OUT OF YOUR MIND?" Smith shrieked. "What do you think you're *doing*?"

Her father gazed at her placidly. "What do you think gives you the right to object?"

"He's *my* husband!" she shouted. "And it's my life, and will you please keep—"

"That's interesting," said her father. "Not so long ago you told me that he wasn't your husband at all."

"Daddy," she said grimly, "what the hell do you want with another house?"

He shook his head. "Not another—I'm selling this one."

"You know perfectly well what I mean!"

St. John ignored that. "He's pretty steep, your husband," he said conversationally. "I should have taken your advice a few years ago and got a Winterhawk house before it was such an expensive proposition."

"You should keep out of my business, you mean. He's probably charging you twice his going rate," she said with relish.

He looked at her. "I don't think so."

"Have you signed a contract yet?" she asked. "Or whatever it is you do with architects?"

"Not yet." Her father leaned back and scratched his beard. She had arrived early this morning, and her father was still in pajamas and robe and unshaven. In sixteen years she hadn't seen him unshaven, though before that, in Paris, she was reminded suddenly that she used to like sitting on the tub talking to him as she watched him shave. "He'll do some preliminary sketches for me first. He's hardly had time to see the site."

"All right." Smith picked up her jacket and stood. "You'd better talk to Hugh again, daddy. Because Johnny is not going to design a house or anything else for you!"

Her father laughed. "He may even design the new Concord head office," he told her amiably.

CHAPTER NINETEEN

"WHY NOT?" Johnny Winterhawk sprawled at his ease across two kitchen chairs, his back against the window and the raging northern storm that howled outside the house. He sank his teeth into the white flesh of the apple in his hand and grinned at her.

Shulamith was dripping wet. Her hair had been in a ponytail, but the harsh wind had whipped the elastic away, and it now hung in sodden tendrils all around her back and in her face. Her jeans and jacket and shoes were soaked through, but she didn't care. "Because I say so!" she stormed.

She had crossed the choppy strait in her father's boat, because the waves were too rough for anything smaller, and on the water the storm had been even harsher than she had expected. But she had been in too much of a hurry to stop to adjust the canopy or to put on a mac.

And after half an hour in the cold driving rain it was almost an insult to come in and find Johnny so warm and lazy in his kitchen. She hadn't even waited to greet him. She had simply shouted that he was not to build a house for her father.

Johnny chewed for a moment. "What's the matter?" he asked. "You don't have to live in it, do you?" His voice sounded casual, but there was a bleakness around his eyes, as though something she had said had hurt him.

She glared at him. "I don't—" She broke off, shivering violently, and her teeth began to chatter. Watching her, Johnny shook his head.

"You look like a drowned hen," he observed. "Hadn't you better take off those clothes and get into the bathtub?"

"I'm not cold!" It wasn't a lie. Inside she was burning up. "And I want to have this out r—"

He slung his sneakered feet off the chair, stood and walked to the stove, and Smith fell silent. He turned the oven on full blast behind her, then reached to draw her closer to its warmth. And to him. Smith clenched her jaw and shivered as Johnny's hands touched the neck of her jacket. "Will you stop that and listen to me?" she demanded, pushing away his hands; but he merely brought them back again, and this time she let him unzip her soaked clammy bomber jacket and slide it off her shoulders.

"Thank you," she said. "Now—"

Underneath she was wearing a navy cardigan and a blue shirt, and without a pause Johnny's hands moved to the buttons of her sweater.

"You're soaked through," he said. "Why didn't you put on a mac?"

"I was in a hurry," Smith muttered. The oven was fast; its warmth was already reaching her.

He chuckled in his throat. "In a hurry to see me? Oh, Peaceable Woman, I'm honored!"

It had been a long time since she had heard that endearment on his lips. Her breathing checked and then resumed.

Johnny slid the cardigan from her shoulders and dropped it, too, on the floor. His hands moved to the top button of her shirt, just above her breasts. He looked into her eyes.

"Johnny," she whispered, half longingly, half afraid. His hands slid down between her breasts and found another button, but his eyes never left her face.

Her breathing altered. She opened her mouth, and her breath came audibly through her parted lips, and then the flame was there between them, and they were caught in its heady heat. She could not move; she could only gaze into his eyes and wait for him to undress her and pray with all her being that he would love her then.

He pulled the blue shirt from the waistband of her jeans and dropped it on the floor, and then his dark warm hands found the catch of her lacy blue bra between her breasts and opened it.

Johnny closed his eyes and dragged in a shaking breath, and the warmth of his hands cupped her breasts and the heat of his mouth was a caress; and she had waited so long for this. A long sob of need came from her throat, and Johnny looked into her eyes and smiled as though he were on the rack.

"You, too," she whispered in discovery, although she should have known.

He smiled more gently and brushed her cheek with his large, strong fingers. "Every day," he said quietly. "Every hour. Every minute."

It had been like that for her, too, though she had tried her best to conquer it. She realized with a dim foreboding that after today she would have to start all over again battling her need of him. She wondered where she would get the strength to bear it again.

He dropped her bra on the floor, and as though this were some kind of torture test, he let go of her and bent to pull off her soaking shoes and socks. Over his head she gazed out at the increasing fury of the storm that smashed in angry gusts against the trees and clawed vainly at the house. The icy rain drove against the broad expanse of glass in bursts of a frenzy that she found almost frightening, as though she were out in the storm, as though she were in danger from it.

The cold clammy fabric of her jeans slid down her thighs then, and she was naked. In spite of the warmth from the stove, she shivered. Her hair was cold on her scalp and skin, and droplets of icy water still dripped from it.

Johnny's warmth enveloped her, and he lifted her up in his arms and bent to kiss her.

Neither of them spoke. There was no need for speech. This had been foreordained from the moment Smith walked in the door. Johnny turned to carry her to his room. knowing that she had no protest to make.

SHE LAY AGAINST HIS CHEST and gave herself up to the feeling of rightness. For a long moment she listened to the rain. She would have to pay for this, she knew, but not now. She would pay tomorrow.

Johnny stroked a tendril of hair from her forehead, and she lifted her head to smile at him. Their lovemaking had been burningly tender, a fierce giving and taking that had made her lose herself, made her deaf to the voice that warned her not to give too much. She had given him everything, except the words. She had not said "I love you"; but he must have felt her love, he must have heard it in her loving cries.

"Why don't you want me to build a house for your father?" he asked her softly. Her heart contracted.

"Oh, God, do I have to tell you? Don't you know?"

He shook his head, and for the first time since she had known him his eyes were afraid of what she could do to him.

"Oh, Johnny," she said helplessly. "Can't you understand? You'd be there all the time, you'd be a business associate, at his parties. He'd talk about you...and the house—Johnny, I'd never be able to visit him without remembering."

It would kill her. She could live without Johnny if she could create her own little world around her, a world in which no one said his name. How could she survive a life where her father lived in a house Johnny's hands had shaped?

"It would kill me," she whispered.

She could feel his heart beating in the silence. "You told me once you wanted a house of my design," he said conversationally, but there was a sound of pain in his throat that she did not understand. "When your father approached me I thought it was...I thought you were behind it."

"No," she said softly.

"I nearly refused. I nearly told your father that if that was the kind of house you wanted you would have to come and live in mine."

His hand stroking her naked back pressed her briefly. Smith started and then froze into stillness.

"What did you say?" she asked hoarsely. *Oh, no,* she thought. *Oh, please, no.*

"But for all I knew, your father.... I decided instead that I'd make a deal with you. You'd have to come and be my wife till the house was built, you'd have to give me the chance to make you love me."

Smith's throat closed up, and her breathing stopped. Johnny's hand was clenching her arm as if he could not let her go.

"Well," he said, in a voice so filled with pain it hurt her, "you have to take the chances fate gives. I'll promise not to build your father's house, Shulamith, if you'll come and live with me for six months. After that, if you want me to, I'll let you go. I'll keep away from you. But I want the chance. I want the chance to make you love me."

He rolled her onto her back and bent over her, and his black eyes met hers, and there was no gentleness in them. "That's my best offer," he said. "If you turn it down I'll build your father's house, and I'll build the Concord building, and I'll get every commission I can from your friends and your father's friends, and you'll never be free of me. I'll refuse to divorce you. I'll hang on like death till I've made you love me or hate me."

Her heartbeat was loud in her ears, and wherever he touched her her flesh ached with need. He had not known after all. Thank God, he still did not know.

She swallowed. "Do you love me?" she asked.

His lips stretched into a line. "I love you," he said hoarsely. "You're my life."

She closed her eyes. "What would it mean, if I

learned to love you? Would it mean you could stop loving me?''

He looked shaken. "No," he whispered.

She said, "I couldn't go through it again. I loved you. I let myself love you, and you—you looked at me as though you hated me. You said...you said, 'Oh my God, what have I done?'"

She remembered the horror of that morning with a sudden clarity that brought a lump to her throat. "I was nervous that morning," she said. "But if you hadn't looked at me like that, if you'd loved me then.... It was never Stockholm Syndrome!" she cried accusingly. "I loved you! You asked me to love you, and when I did, you stopped loving me!"

There were tears on her cheeks. "And now you want me to love you again, but you don't say why." She sobbed once. "You want me for six months. What will happen to me then? What if I loved you for longer? What if I didn't stop loving you on time?" *What if I loved you forever,* her heart cried, but she didn't say it. She couldn't ever say that. She would never beg for love again.

He kissed her. He kissed the tears from her cheeks, and then he kissed her mouth, and he looked at her and she knew suddenly that he did know, that he had read what she had tried to hide.

"Love me forever," he begged her softly. "Please love me forever."

"No!" she wailed on a high, pleading cry. "Please, don't, please, Johnny, it will kill me! I'll love you for six months, I'll do whatever you want, but please don't laugh at me, please don't make me—"

She began to sob in earnest, and he held her and let her cry. "You don't understand," she sobbed brokenly. "You don't know what it's like, Johnny. It would kill me. I spent so long trying to make my father love me, and I couldn't do it, it's impossible, I can't make anyone love me. It wouldn't be fair to pretend I could, Johnny, don't make me think I could. He says he always loved me, but why didn't he tell me? Why did he act as if he hated me? And I kept trying to please him, Johnny, but nothing ever pleased him!

"I said I'd never beg you for your love, but if you made me live with you, I'd start trying. It would be the same thing all over again, Johnny, I'd be trying to make you love me! Don't!" she begged desperately, covering her face and knowing that she had told him everything he wanted to know, everything she had meant to keep hidden. Nowhere was safe now; she would never be safe from him again. "Please don't."

He kissed her and let her cry out her despair against his chest until at last there were no tears left. She lay still in his arms then, while her shuddering breath calmed, and all the pain of a lifetime was in her eyes.

In the silence the sound of wind and rain was loud. Johnny lay back and drew her onto his chest and stroked her hair with a tenderness that shook her.

"I love you," he said quietly. She moved, but he held her fast. "Just listen," he said. "Just let me say it. Afterward, if I have to, I'll let you go. I love you, Shulamith. I loved you the first moment I saw you, when you burst into your father's room and started to give us all a piece of your mind." He laughed a little. "I felt as though some...it was as though my spirit and yours were suddenly bound together—I could almost see it. Looking back now I know I didn't take you with me because I thought you'd recognized my face. That was the excuse I gave myself. I took you because you were mine, because we belonged together.

"There was that legend in my family. Do you believe in race memory? Sometimes I thought it was happening again, that you had come to me to fulfill that legend. And somehow I knew that something would try to separate us, too. I thought if I could get you to marry me I could prevent it from happening. I didn't know—I never imagined that the danger was from myself.

"What I told you about myself that morning was right. I have always felt the need to get my heritage back, to be accepted by my people. When I fell in love with you, it seemed to me that it was no longer important, that I had to accept what I had done with my life and go on.

"But in the morning—you know what happened in the morning. Everything I had thought unimportant came back to haunt me. I told myself that what I had done was irrational, that I had been possessed...perhaps if I hadn't been so eager to marry you so quickly, I might have got over it with less...but it was done, it was as though there was no going back, and I panicked...."

"But you married me so I wouldn't be able to testify against you, didn't you?" Shulamith asked.

He seemed shaken. "No," he said. His voice trembled. "*No*. My God, is that what you thought?"

"Yes," she whispered. "Afterward, when you told me—"

"You thought it was all a lie? You thought I was lying to you?"

She nodded wordlessly, and he shut his eyes. "The first lie I told you was the morning I said I didn't love you," Johnny said. "I lied to myself, too. Afterward I needed you so desperately I had to go to you—even though the police were as thick as flies around you—but I was still lying to myself. I was lying to you, too. I don't know why. It's not true that a wife couldn't testify in a situation like that. I knew that when I married you. It never crossed my mind that marriage would be a way out."

"When did you stop lying to yourself?"

He breathed. "That morning you sat at my table and sang your song to me and told me how many men you'd be waking up to say goodbye to in the future wasn't the first time I knew, but it was the hardest. There was a knife in my gut and you were twisting it, and you didn't even know. I told myself if I'd killed your love it was my own fault, and I told myself I'd have my heritage to keep me warm. I thought I could let you go."

Slowly, tentatively, a ripple of happiness nudged against her heart. "You still think it," she said. "You said you would let me go."

He grasped her arms and pulled her over and held her tightly to him, more tightly than she had ever been held—safe and secure. "Did I?" he rasped. "It's a lie. I can't live without you. I can't let you go. Be sure it's what you want, Shulamith, because if you ask me to love you now, I will. And there'll be no going back. You're mine, and you'll be mine till we're in our graves. And I will never let you go."

He stroked her hair with a passion just barely held in check. "Tell me you want me to love you," he whispered. "Tell me it's what you want."

He didn't know what he was asking. A fear as cold as death reached out and clamped her heart, and the rippling happiness shrank back.

"Why?" she whispered. "Can't you love me unless I beg for it?"

He looked at her. "Unless you beg?" he asked amazed. "God, what have I done to you? In the summer you didn't care what you asked, what you begged for!" The passionate fury in him broke its rein, and he began to stroke her and kiss her. "You used to beg for everything I could give you," he said. He kissed her eyelids, her cheeks, her throat. "I want to kiss you," he said hoarsely. "Do you want me to kiss you?"

"Yes," she said.

"Tell me," he demanded. "Tell me it's what you want. That's all it is."

But her lips would not open on the sound.

"You trusted me!" he said. "Did you remember that? I was your kidnapper—I abducted you, but you trusted yourself to me. You gave me your love as if...." He flung the blankets from her naked body and ran his hand down her side from shoulder to knee. She shivered with need. "Do you like that? Shall I touch you again?"

She needed him so desperately it was an ache. Why was he tormenting her? Why couldn't he give her the love she needed freely? Why did she have to ask for it?

"Tell me."

"Why?" Smith demanded. "Why do I have to ask?

Why can't you just love me, if that's what you want to do?"

"Because I don't want just to love you. I want you to want my love as much as you want this...." His hand cupped her breast, and he watched the goose bumps trace across her skin at the unexpectedness of the caress, and then raised his eyes to hers. "I want you to want everything I have to give. If you don't—you've closed a door on me. I don't want any doors between us. But I can't break this one down. Only you can do that. Unless you're willing to trust me and trust love again, we'll never have what we had. And I want that."

She remembered the feeling she had had after that terrible morning, when she felt gates fall into place in her mind, protecting her from the world's hurt. Suddenly she felt frightened, because either way was impossible: she could not remain in her lonely prison, nor could she ask for love.

"Say it," said Johnny softly, watching the fear in her eyes. "Just say it." His voice was so gently demanding. "Please, tell me." It was too much. It almost made her hate him.

"All right!" she cried harshly. "All *right*, dammit! Please love me, okay? Yes, I want you to love me!" she said coldly. But there was something pushing at her heart, and she was suddenly gripped with pain. What she had said in mockery became the truth. "Oh, God, Johnny, I want you to love me, I want it so much!" Tears started in her eyes, and for a moment she despised her own weakness. But distantly she knew that this weakness was strength, that the fear and pride that kept her from needing his love were not strengths. "I love you, Johnny," she cried, "I need you to love me. Oh, God, if you leave me now it will kill me, Johnny, Johnny...."

He gathered her up against him, and her tear-wet cheek met the perfect curve of his shoulder. "I won't leave you," Johnny Winterhawk promised. "I'll never leave you again." He kissed her hungrily, and his body found hers with an urgency that raised her need to fever pitch, and her giving was free and open, and she would never be afraid again.

"THEY GAVE IT BACK TO YOU!" Shulamith exclaimed in delight. "Is it all right?" She rushed over to take the robe from him and flung it out over the bed. The brilliantly colored dragon glittered and postured as before. Only a faint discoloration—a kind of dulling—showed where the long smear of grease had been. Shulamith bent to examine it more closely. The tears in the delicate silk had been invisibly mended and the signs hardly showed. The robe had been cleaned and pressed.

"It must have been a painstaking job to mend it," she said. "It really is beautiful."

"It took an art restorer two months to do." Johnny was looking at her oddly as she knelt on the bed and examined every inch of fabric and embroidery. "You knew it had been damaged?" he asked.

"Mmm," she nodded absentmindedly. "Staff Sergeant Podborski showed it to me. He wanted to know if it was mine. Did they pay for the repair?"

"The police don't pay for anything. My insurance paid. You never told me, you know," Johnny added curiously. "You told me they had it, but you didn't say they'd mutilated it."

She looked guiltily at him. "I was afraid it would be too much for you to take all at once. Besides—"

"Besides?"

"I didn't know who it had belonged to, who you'd bought it for. I'd always thought you must have loved her very much. And I was afraid—well, you'd had enough that day."

Johnny tied the belt of his robe with a snap and walked over to her. "You were protecting me from the pain of losing a memento of another woman?" he asked gently.

"Yes, why not?"

He bent and kissed her. "No reason, Peaceable Woman," he said. "But for your information the last woman to wear this robe died probably two hundred years ago."

"What?"

"It's a robe from Imperial China, from the Ching dynasty," he told her. "The dragon is a symbol of power. The flowers and birds are prayers for happiness or long life." His hand traced the shape of a flower. "Only the emperor or his courtiers were allowed to wear the dragon. This is a woman's robe, with a five-clawed dragon. Only a very favored powerful woman close to the emperor would have been allowed to wear it. Perhaps a very beloved wife." He kissed her and smiled. "Like you.

"I bought the robe in Japan. It reminded me of the decorated cloaks that were used among the Chopa for religious rituals. I intended to have it framed and hung."

Shulamith looked at him boggle-eyed. "It's a museum piece?" she demanded in astonishment. "It's an antique? I knew it was a work of art but—Johnny, I could have spilled coffee on it, or—" She began to fold it up in delicate haste. "Why on earth did you let me wear it?"

"Because when I saw you I knew that its proper place was on a beautiful woman. I wanted to see you wear it. Did you know that when you move the dragon seems alive? You bring it to life."

"I'm not wearing it anymore!" Shulamith declared firmly. "You must be crazy!"

"It was made to be worn," he said, "not hung behind glass. It belongs in life. There are other dragon robes preserved in museums around the world. I want to see this one on you." He held it up for her, and she stood up and slipped her naked arms into its cool, silky folds. His arms encircled her and held her enwrapped.

"Perhaps there is something about a dragon...." She rested her head against his shoulder. "I feel like an empress. It makes me feel powerful."

She felt the lightest of kisses on top of her head. "Do you feel happiness, too?"

She turned in his arms. "All the happiness in the world."

"There's something else I want to see you wear." He let her go, crossing to the closet again and pulling open one of the drawers that ran up one wall inside it. He took out a small golden circle and brought it back to her.

His slow smile made her weak at the knees as she held out her left hand. Johnny slid the wedding band back where it belonged and bent and kissed her hand. "Wife," he said, as though the thought gave him satisfaction. "Don't take it off anymore," he commanded softly, and she shook her head, and then he kissed her mouth to seal the renewal of their promise.

"Did you save my wedding dress, too?" she asked as they walked to the kitchen. The floorboard creaked as they passed the study, and she grinned at him. "I used to think that was a deliberate booby trap!" she told him. "And now I hear it's a fatal flaw!"

"Fatal? I hope not," he grinned. "Of course I saved your dress. It's hanging up in a closet on the boat."

Neither of them was hungry, but they made coffee and sat looking out over the gorge. The storm had died down; the rain was much gentler, but the wind still bent the trees.

"How's Wilf?" she asked as she got up to pick up her damp clothing from the floor and threw it into the passage to take to the laundry. "You know, you need that washer and dryer down here in the kitchen."

"Do we? Whatever you want. Wilf's getting around okay, but he's not as active as he used to be."

"Can he still paddle over to Oyster Island?"

"Yes, but not so often. He's down at his cabin. Would you like to visit him this afternoon?"

"Yes," she said. "When my clothes are dry."

Johnny said, "You know, if I hadn't been such a fool Wilf would never have been hurt. If we'd announced our marriage the police would have lost interest."

"Yes," she said sadly.

"That was one thing that woke me up—by yearning after something I couldn't have I risked losing what I did have. Wilf could have died that night. And you might be next: they'd already threatened to arrest you...."

"Was it *you* who tipped off the CBC, then?" Smith inquired in amazement. "I always wondered who...." It hadn't been Lew. She had asked him point-blank.

He shook his head. "No. I checked around—it was one of the witnesses at our wedding. He apparently didn't put two and two together until he saw our names connected in the news."

"That'll teach you to bring charges against the police," she laughed. "But none of your people ever talked, did they?"

"No," he agreed. "The whole thing put a scare into the new provos. They knew that any of them could have been in Wilf's place."

Shulamith glanced involuntarily at her hands. "I hope they've learned something. Everyone's been lucky." She looked at him. "My father could have died, too."

"Yes," he said. "I'm sorry. Did I ever say that? It was a stupid venture from the start."

She leaned across the table to kiss him. "It worked, though," she told him. "If you hadn't been in my father's room that night Jake wouldn't have sold the band the timber rights three weeks ago." She grinned. "And we would never have met."

"Yes, we would," said Johnny. "It was only a matter of time. I'd been looking for you too long not to find you."

Their eyes met. Shulamith took a breath and looked away. "But under other circumstances you wouldn't have let yourself fall in love with me," she pointed out. You'd have been thinking about your Indian heritage and your children's...."

"Maybe," he admitted. "I almost lost my chance with you as it is. But I'd like to think—" he reached out to touch her cheek "—that I'd have learned the lesson I had to learn in time."

She looked steadily at him. "You won't regret it if...if they do change that law?" If marrying a native woman would give him back his heritage....

"I won't regret it," he said. "I've stopped regretting that part of my life. In these past few weeks I've proved I can help my people as much from the outside as I could have from the inside. *They* accept that—they always have. Only I could never see that. Because they didn't count me as one of them, I saw it as rejection. But I'm not one of them. Legally and every other way. *They* take me for that and always have. I was taken from the reserve when I was eight. I could never go back there to live, and they know it. I've always known it, too. I just wouldn't admit it to myself."

There was still a note in his voice that sounded to her like strain. She asked, "Why couldn't you? Why did you see it as rejection, Johnny?"

He bent his head and rubbed his hand over his scalp. "The year I graduated from college," he said, "I went back to Eagle's Nest to visit my grandfather. He was very old then, one of the elders of the tribe. I had only seen him once or twice since they took me off the reserve, but I'd always remembered him." Johnny paused to breathe, and she knew it was an unfamiliar thing, to be telling someone this story. How much had it hurt him, kept inside all these years?

"I was proud of myself. I'd made it, and he was the only member of my family left. I went to tell him.

"He invited me in. He had a little two-room hut on the reserve, no plumbing, no amenities. And I sat there telling him about my successes.... He heard me out, he listened to all my—" He broke off and looked into the dregs in his cup. "He didn't say anything till I finished. He just looked at me, and then he asked me if I had done it all as an Indian or as a white man." The pain was nearly a shriek threading his words, a counterpoint of strident anguish under the deep quiet voice. "Then he told me what I'd done, from his point of view. I had sold my birthright, traded away my heritage for acceptance into the society that was destroying my people."

"I'm sorry," she whispered, because there was nothing else to say.

"My Indian name is Hawk Who Hunts in Winter. That name was given to me by my grandfather and the elders when I went to Eagle's Nest after my mother died. Everyone knew I wouldn't be allowed to come back to the reserve. They told me I would be like the hawk who hunts in winter, that I would need to be tougher and harder than other children, that like the hawk I would live by my wits in a hostile landscape.

"The Chopa people have a tradition of changing their names as they make transitions.... That day—the day after I graduated—my grandfather told me that the Indian part of me had made no growth, that I was still the Hawk Who Hunts in Winter; that the path of clawing out acceptance in white society was now my heritage. I had never realized before how I had always thought of the reserve as my one fixed point of reference in a changing world. I had imagined it always there, unchanging. Not that I had visualized myself as going back there to live, but they had always been there, the people who would always accept me for all that I was, with whom I could be truly myself.''

She had heard Jews speak like that of Israel. She protested, "But he wasn't right, your grandfather. You were accepted by white society long ago."

"Yes," he agreed. "It's among my own people I've been trying to claw out acceptance."

"None of it was your fault, anyway, Johnny. My God, a child of eight—what choice did you have? Who took you away from Eagle's Nest in the first place?"

"Oh, the social workers. They said my mother wasn't looking after me. I was at residential school for a while, but when my mother died I was put in a foster home. They were good to me; I stayed there till college. They thought the best they could do for me was help me assimilate into white society. They weren't wrong, but later I regretted that last choice—renouncing my status."

"Did you tell them that?"

"No." He shook his head. "I never blamed them. They couldn't know my past would rise up and claim me. Anyway, they died a couple of years after I graduated. They were pretty old when they took me in. They left me enough money to start my own business years before I'd have been able to otherwise."

The coffee in the pot was cold, and Smith got up to make more. "You've never told me so much about yourself before."

"No? I wanted to. But we've always had a lot to talk about. I've never talked to anyone the way I've talked to you."

She had felt the same. "There are things I've told you," she said softly, "that I've never told anyone. And it always comforted me to tell you. I used to wish I could give you comfort, too."

He looked at her. "You have always had the power to comfort me," he said. "Don't you know that?"

He had been comforted the day he had testified to the Cartier Commission. She knew that. "But when you came back from Amsterdam. . . ."

"I came back from Amsterdam," he told her, "to tell you I loved you. To ask you if you'd be willing to try to make our marriage a real one."

"Oh," she breathed. "But you didn't ask—you didn't even hint."

He said dryly, "You were very sure that night that you didn't love me, you know. You informed me you'd only thought you loved me because I thought I loved you."

"But you never *asked*. . . ."

"I asked," he said, as though the memory still held pain. "I took you in my arms, and I asked for you. You said, 'I can't,' and you cried, and you asked me to go away."

"Oh, Johnny," she said sadly. If only she'd known, what a lot of pain they would have been saved. "I thought you. . .at first I thought you came to me for comfort—because of the Cartier Commission report."

"I did."

"And I thought the comfort you wanted was. . .was to take me to bed, to make love to me."

"That, too."

"But I thought that was all you wanted. I thought...
you'd told me it was only physical, the special thing we
had. You said you never wondered if it might be love.
So I thought.... It would have killed me to have you
love me like that and then just...just...."

"Wake you up to say goodbye?"

She laughed, then, and Johnny shook his head.
"That song!" he said. "I couldn't get away from it. Do
you know I even heard it in Amsterdam once or twice?
And I kept hearing you telling me about all the lovers
you'd have to wake up to say goodbye.... In Amsterdam I had a long time to think. You'd written that song
to me, and there was a yearning in it that must have
been meant for me, once.... I didn't want to accept
that I'd lost that, destroyed it for the sake of giving a
heritage to children that I wouldn't want to have anyway unless they were yours.

"That's when I came to terms with it—in Amsterdam. Up until then I'd convinced myself that even
though I loved you I had to give you up."

She smiled. "So it was all the fault of my song?" she
teased.

Johnny pulled her into his lap. "You're a poetic
genius," he agreed. "What happened to the song you
were working on the night I got back from Amsterdam?
Did you write it?"

"Ah!" she said, kissing his cheek. "That was 'No
Time Like the First Time'—another of my great successes! The band was rehearsing behind Cimarron with
that—it's going on her album—and suddenly Bradshaw
said, 'Hey, I hear a harmony here! Let's have her

double-track a harmony.' Then he came up to show us what he meant—he sang it with her, and Johnny, we all just went crazy! I mean, it was perfect with the two of them. So Bradshaw did the harmony, and that's going to be Cimarron's second single release! And we've got CBS so excited they want to do a video of Cimarron!''

"What does that mean?"

"They shoot a video of her singing—oh, Johnny, she's going to be so popular down there—and they show it on the Top Ten on television and shows like that. And they want to do it in New York. They want to bring in a producer who's—well, Mel isn't so happy about that, but Cimarron really wants to do it.''

The coffee was ready, and she got up to pour. The beautiful square sleeves of the dragon robe were a liability, and she was terrified now of damaging it.

"And what about your poetry?" asked Johnny. "Have you kept that up, or is it all songs nowadays?"

She told him about the literary quarterlies and about the Canadian anthology. "The same publisher is looking at a possible book of poems all by me. I was going to call it *Songs of Love and Loss*." She looked into his dark eyes and saw how proud of her he was and wrapped her arms around his neck. "I'll have to call the next one *Winning*."

He pulled her down to kiss her. "It's lucky we get second chances, isn't it, Peaceable Woman?"

She kissed him on his forehead between the two black wings of hair and then on his sensuous mouth.

"It's a good thing my father interfered, though I hate to say it," she said. "Or we'd never have had our second chance."

"Your father be damned. I'd have been around a lot sooner if he hadn't approached me about the house he wanted built." He touched her lips. "I thought that was your signal to me that you needed time, that you wanted to use your father as a go-between. So I waited. It wasn't till I saw your face at that damned party that I realized what he'd done."

"What would you have done if he hadn't interfered?" she asked in surprise.

"I was going to get you out here to visit Wilf. If necessary I would have had Wilf fake a relapse just to keep you here a day or two." He smiled lazily and stroked her arm. "And I would have made the best damn love to you I know how."

Shulamith looked into his smiling eyes and took a deep breath. "And you do know how," she said softly.

He clenched his jaw and swore softly. "Peaceable Woman, we're going to have to get you a new name more suited to you. Something like Fire Woman, for example." He stroked her hair from scalp to ends, and she shivered appreciatively.

"To describe your hair and your body," he whispered, and pulled her face down to meet his mouth, "and your nature."

When he let her lift her lips at last she was trembling with need.

"Wilf," she whispered. "We were going to—"

"Tomorrow," said Johnny softly. "There's always tomorrow."

ABOUT THE AUTHOR

Alexandra Sellers, the highly acclaimed author of two previous Superromances, *Captive of Desire* and *Fire in the Wind*, grew up in more than a dozen small towns across Canada, but the one she remembers most fondly is Yorkton, Saskatchewan. All that early movement must have put travel into her blood, because she has spent much of her adult life, too, as a wanderer, trying to absorb as many other languages and cultures as her brain and budget would allow.

Alexandra has a fellow feeling for anyone who has nowhere to call home, but that didn't make the character of Johnny Winterhawk in *Season of Storm* an easy man to deal with. He originally entered her life in 1975, she says, and "immediately began dragging his heels. It took me years to sort him out—or is that vice versa?"

Aside from travel, Alexandra's abiding passion, obviously, is escape fiction, notably romance. "Once you have discovered the world of books," she says, "you're as free as your own imagination."

Begin a long love affair with
SUPERROMANCE.
Accept LOVE BEYOND DESIRE **FREE.**

Complete and mail the coupon below today!

- -

FREE! Mail to: SUPERROMANCE

In the U.S.
2504 West Southern Avenue
Tempe, AZ 85282

In Canada
649 Ontario St.
Stratford, Ontario N5A 6W2

YES, please send me FREE and without any obligation, my
SUPERROMANCE novel, LOVE BEYOND DESIRE. If you do not hear
from me after I have examined my FREE book, please send me the
4 new **SUPERROMANCE** books every month as soon as they come
off the press. I understand that I will be billed only $2.50 for each book
(total $10.00). There are no shipping and handling or any other hidden
charges. There is no minimum number of books that I have to
purchase. In fact, I may cancel this arrangement at any time.
LOVE BEYOND DESIRE is mine to keep as a FREE gift, even if
I do not buy any additional books.

NAME _____ (Please Print)

ADDRESS _____ APT. NO. _____

CITY _____

STATE/PROV. _____ ZIP/POSTAL CODE _____

SIGNATURE (If under 18, parent or guardian must sign.)   **134-BPS-KAJT**

SUP-SUB-3